BENE

BLA...
WATER
RIVER

CW00508275

BOOKS BY LESLIE WOLFE

BENEATH BLACK WATER RIVER

LESLIE WOLFE

Bookouture

Published by Bookouture in 2021

An imprint of Storyfire Ltd.
Carmelite House
50 Victoria Embankment
London EC4Y 0DZ

www.bookouture.com

Copyright © Leslie Wolfe, 2021

Leslie Wolfe has asserted her right to be identified
as the author of this work.

All rights reserved.
No part of this publication may be reproduced,
stored in any retrieval system, or transmitted, in any form or by
any means, electronic, mechanical, photocopying, recording or
otherwise, without the prior written permission of the publishers.

ISBN: 978-1-80019-500-4
eBook ISBN: 978-1-80019-499-1

This book is a work of fiction. Names, characters, businesses,
organizations, places and events other than those clearly in the
public domain, are either the product of the author's imagination
or are used fictitiously. Any resemblance to actual persons, living or
dead, events or locales is entirely coincidental.

ACKNOWLEDGMENT

A special thank you to my New York City legal eagle and friend, Mark Freyberg, who expertly guided this author through the intricacies of the judicial system.

CHAPTER ONE

Falls

Malia wore a flower in her hair.

Not just any kind of flower; she'd gone through online shopping hell to get the plumeria blossom delivered to the hotel that morning, just in time for her planned trip to Blackwater River Falls. She'd paid a fortune for it, worth every cent.

She wore the scented bloom over her left ear, a Hawaiian custom that told the entire world her heart was taken. By a twenty-seven-year-old, good-looking, and slightly awkward computer nerd from San Francisco named Tobias Grabowsky, who'd probably miss the symbolic meaning of the plumeria, and that was if he even noticed it in the first place.

She didn't care. She still wanted the flower to be just right, her hair perfectly shiny, the scent of the petals surrounding her like a mist from heaven, bringer of love and good fortune. But she wished she could've worn something else for that special occasion. She cringed at the thought of being proposed to in cream-colored stretch shorts and a red tank top instead of a breezy, white, ruffled gown that bared her shoulders. But if Toby wanted to take her to Blackwater River Falls that morning, she had to pretend she didn't know why and wear the appropriate attire for hiking.

But she knew, and the excitement had overwhelmed her since she'd first found the diamond ring in his jacket pocket.

She'd been worried about his strange behavior the night they'd arrived in Mount Chester. Soon after dinner, expertly served by a blond with cleavage so deep it should've been restricted to adult audiences only, she'd noticed that Toby kept touching his right pocket as if to make sure something precious was still in there, tucked safely. That pocket was where he'd shoved the change and check from dinner, and Malia feared that Miss Cleavage might've sneaked in her phone number. Anxious for the rest of the evening, Malia could barely wait to get back to their hotel room. There, she lingered with the patience of a hungry spider for Toby to get into the shower, then plunged her hand into the pocket and found it.

That 1-carat beauty was definitely not for Miss Boobs.

Before Toby had come out of the shower, she had her plan in place. She'd make sure it was one to remember, and even if she had to wear shorts, at least everything else would be perfect.

Blackwater River Falls was a one-hour hike from their hotel, climbing at a gentle rate on the western versant of Mount Chester through a stunningly beautiful, fall-tinged forest. As they gained elevation, oaks and maples gave way to a variety of pines and firs, their cones littering the paths. They held hands and hiked with enthusiasm, her impatience causing Toby to ask, "Why the rush?" a couple of times. She'd just smiled in response and slowed down a little, even stopped to press her lips against his for a quick moment, before rushing uphill again.

They were a good ten minutes away when the whooshing sound of the falls started to be heard, faint and distant, yet precise, melodious, echoing against the rocky slopes of the mountain.

"I can see it," Malia announced cheerfully, letting go of Toby's hand and sprinting ahead. "We're there."

"All right," Toby replied, panting heavily. "It will still be there in a few minutes, you know," he quipped, stopping for a moment and looking around.

She rushed back to him and grabbed his hand, then pulled him ahead on the trail.

"Come on, you'll rest when we get there," she said, and he followed her with a resigned sigh. "You need to work out more," she added. She was barely out of breath, the fresh air filling her lungs with pure energy. "All day long you sit in front of a screen," she started, then bit her lip. Maybe she should wait until after the wedding to start criticizing him. She burst into laughter instead, imagining herself as a nagging wife, hands propped on her hips, tapping the tip of her slipper against the gleaming hardwood floors in their future home.

"What?" he asked.

"Ah, nothing, I'm just happy," she replied, lifting her arms in the air and turning in place like a dervish. "Whoo-hoo," she cried, and the mountain promptly echoed back. "Did you hear it?"

"Yeah, and so did half the state of California."

A punch to his side was quick to follow, and she burst into crystalline laughter as he feigned injury and collapsed to the ground, holding his side and groaning as if he were about to die a wretched death. Now he would have dirt and pine needles on the white T-shirt he was going to propose in, but she didn't care as much as she thought she would. She just loved hearing him laugh.

When he stood, he touched his pocket briefly, and then brushed some dirt off his shoulders. She ran her hands over his back, wiping away whatever stuck to the cotton fabric, then they joined hands again and sprinted ahead.

In a few minutes, they cleared the forest and stopped, hand in hand, to admire the tall, narrow falls against the blue sky, flanked by rocks tinged rusty red. Still panting, Toby gave her a long, loving look, as if trying to figure out what to do next, and then crouched to undo his laces and remove his shoes.

"What are you doing?" Malia asked, her voice filled with disappointment, after her heart had promptly stopped thinking he was going to take a knee and propose in front of the majestic falls, only to see him preoccupied with the entangled shoelaces on his left sneaker.

He kicked off both his shoes, then invited her to do the same. "Let's go in there," he pointed at the waterfall, "behind that water curtain. I read there's a cave, not too big, and the water's only a few inches deep."

She hesitated as she imagined dipping her bare feet into the freezing water. She forced a smile and took off her shoes and socks, then tiptoed, faltering on the sharp-edged gravel that littered the path to the fall's basin.

He jumped in first, without hesitation. "Yup, it's freezing, but you won't feel it," he reassured her, once he had caught his breath. "Come on." He tugged gently at her hand. "Take the leap with me."

Her face lit up in a beaming smile. She was ready to take a leap with him, the biggest leap of all, for the rest of her life. She put one hesitant foot into the icy water, then the next. He was right. After a few moments, she stopped feeling the cold as badly.

They splashed toward the water curtain, and she winced at the thought of wading through a shower of freezing water to get to the cave, but that wasn't the case. There was a narrow opening to the side, enough to allow them to sneak in. Inside the almost dark space, the loud sound of the waterfall was dimmed and seemed distant, as if the silence of the cave absorbed the screams of the crashing cascade. Filtered and powerless, the light that came through the torrent barely touched the glistening walls.

She studied her surroundings for a quick moment. The walls were stained in hues of green and rusty red, with off-white blotches here and there, where calcareous stone interlaced with the granite. She dipped her hand in the freezing water, and cupped her palm to collect some. She wanted to taste it, but Toby stopped her hand before it reached her lips.

"I wouldn't do that," he said. "You never know what's in it."

She looked at the water still pooled in the cup of her hand. "It looks like it has a pink hue, or is that just the light?"

"Could be what stained these walls." He looked around briefly, then smiled widely, visibly nervous. "But I'm not here for spelunking." He lowered himself on a bent knee, dipping it in the freezing water, while his hand revealed the ring nestled in its black velvet box. "I wanted it to be just you and me, my lovely Malia, when I ask you, will you marry me?"

Her eyes widened in feigned surprise and sincere delight, while her smile broadened. She clasped her hands together in excitement, then extended her left hand toward Toby. He took out the ring from its box and slid it onto her finger. She looked at him grinning, sealing every detail of the image in her memory, to always remember, till death did them part.

Then she screamed, a long, searing shriek of pure terror.

A pale hand with long, narrow fingers grazed Toby's calf, shifting slowly into the rippling water.

Toby jumped to his feet and rushed to her, grabbing her shoulders. "What? What is it?"

Speechless, she pointed at the body moving slowly back and forth under the water surface, barely visible in the dim light.

In the flashlight coming from Toby's phone, she saw a large boulder held the girl's body in place, pinning it to the bottom of the cave. Her long black hair and her right arm had surfaced, the water only a foot deep, brought forward by the constant pounding of the cascade.

She looked alive, her hair drifting freely in the water as if flowing in the wind, her beautiful face pristine, her red lips gently parted, as if to let her final breath escape. Her eyes seemed to stare at them, surprised, aghast, the terror of her last moments still alive in her irises. A small red locket floated right by her face, still attached to her neck with a silver chain.

She couldn't've been more than seventeen years old.

CHAPTER TWO
Home

Detective Kay Sharp was still getting used to living with her brother again, in the childhood home she'd left in her rearview mirror eight years ago. It was a broad and sometimes unsettling mix of emotions. She loved Jacob and had missed him over the years. On the flip side, after having lived by herself for all that time, she'd developed a low tolerance for clutter, mess, dirty dishes in the sink, and any other form of disorganized living, especially when her baby brother had also grown used to being the typical slovenly bachelor. The house itself held memories, some sweet, of her mother baking cookies or birthday cakes or singing to them. Others were bitter and angering, of her father's alcohol-fueled rages and their painful consequences.

After having returned to Mount Chester for less than a month, she was getting antsy about moving out of her family home. But the last time a house had been listed for sale in Mount Chester had been over a year ago; it was a posh ski lodge up the mountain, and some Silicon Valley stockholder had rushed to put a truckload of money on it. Nothing else had hit the market since. Even their local Realtor held a day job.

Mount Chester was a small place, ski resort included. Most of the town's dwellers worked seasonal jobs on the mountain, in restaurants or hotels, operating or maintaining the ski lifts or catering to tourists. A great place to visit and spend some time on the slopes, or, during summer, on the endlessly meandering beaches of Silent Lake, Mount Chester was home to only 3,823 people, as it stated on the city limit sign. Although, very recently, when driving by at high speed, Kay had noticed the number had been adjusted to 3,824, making her wonder for a brief moment if the additional dweller someone had censused was actually her. After all, she'd updated the address on her driver's license, and that made her, officially, a Mount Chester resident. But she didn't have to wonder for too long. Soon after, something scribbled under the sign's population count had made her put her car in reverse and take a closer look. In white chalk, someone had written, WELCOME HOME, DR. SHARP, in block letters on the green sign.

That was small-town living, something she was still trying to adapt to, after all the time she'd been away, taking it one day at a time.

Kay had been up since dawn, although her shift didn't start until later. It wasn't the traditional shift per se; Mount Chester Sheriff's Office was barely large enough to qualify for two detectives on the payroll, and she still wondered why Sheriff Logan had chosen to extend her the job offer only a week ago. One of the benefits of the small team size was she had a bit more flexibility in her start time, given she'd put in long hours whenever she worked a case. Same rule applied to her partner, largely the man whose blue eyes and handsome looks had persuaded her to stay, Detective Elliot Young from Austin, Texas. She'd assisted him with a serial killer case in an unofficial/somewhat official capacity as a consultant. Then, she was surprised to be offered the permanent position with the local sheriff's office. Finally, she surprised herself by accepting it, and one particular detective carried some of the blame, albeit unknowingly.

Because life was like that: weird, convoluted, more loaded with twists than a bestselling novel. She'd lived in the San Francisco Bay Area for years, a city of over seven million people, and never met anyone even remotely interesting. Yet she came back for one visit to Mount Chester, the place she'd sworn she'd never return to, and there he was, cowboy hat and Texas drawl and all, smiling when he saw her, ever so briefly, before lowering his head and covering his eyes underneath the wide felt brim.

And she'd stayed. She still wasn't sure she hadn't made a mistake, given how much she missed her old job as profiler for the San Francisco regional FBI office, but she just couldn't bring herself to leave Mount Chester again.

The coffeemaker beeped twice with its urgent, high-pitched sound, and she flared her nostrils, welcoming the bitter aroma with hints of hazelnut. Grabbing a mug from the cabinet above her head, she stepped sideways and poured herself a hefty helping.

"Fix me up, sis," Jacob said, then yawned heartily, scratching the back of his head. He was still in pajamas, although it was almost nine.

She took another mug and filled it, then handed it to him with a smile. "You working today?"

"Uh-huh," he replied as he took a sip of the hot liquid. "We're replacing a roof over by the hotel."

"So late?"

"That's what the customer wanted. I'll be happy if we finish before sundown." He set the mug on the table and opened the fridge, then took a cold croissant and bit half of it, chewing it hastily.

"I can warm that up for you," she offered.

"You're not Mom," he pushed back. "I lived on my own and managed to survive, you know."

Frustrated, she raised her arm in the air. "I don't want to go there, Jacob. The house was—"

"Thank you for the new vacuum, and the new washer and dryer, and for everything, but I was fine."

No, he wasn't fine. He hadn't been fine in years, but he refused to acknowledge it, no matter how hard she tried. "I'll, um, find somewhere I can move."

He took two steps and stopped squarely in front of her, then grasped her shoulders. "You don't have to leave, sis. I know why you'd want to," he said, while his gaze veered off to the side, turning dark for a brief moment. "But you're welcome here just as much as I am. It's your home too."

She smiled, warmed by her brother's love. It was pointless to try to make him understand. "What if you want to have a girl over?"

"Ha, ha, I haven't had a girl over since forever. But now that the house is clean and all, I can try to get hooked up. Maybe I'll get lucky." He tucked a rebel strand of her blond hair behind her ear. "Don't worry about me, Kay. If it comes to that, we'll do it like we used to when we were in school. Hang something from the door, like a sock or whatever."

She laughed, her reaction surprising him. "We're adults, Jake, for crying out loud. Adult people get their own homes and—"

A chime interrupted her train of thought. Picking up her phone, she read the message.

She had a case.

CHAPTER THREE

Scene

When Kay reached the crime scene, Dr. Whitmore had already started working, and Elliot's car was pulling over next to hers. The drive up to Blackwater River Falls had been challenging. She'd hiked there many times, but never thought it could be reached by SUV or, in Dr. Whitmore's case, by county coroner's van. She'd made it after a long, nerve-racking journey going 10 miles an hour and scaling boulders, afraid her car would fall apart.

Climbing out of the white Ford Explorer, she took in the scene. The small clearing was swarming with people, some wearing the sheriff's colors, others the medical examiner's insignia. A few were wearing tall rubber boots and were working in the waterfall's basin, taking photos, samples, and measurements.

"Howdy," Elliot greeted her. "Interesting setting to kill someone, huh?"

"Yup," Kay replied, wondering why the killer chose it. Did it carry a meaning to him or her? How was the unusual setting relevant? "Let's take a look."

Sitting on a large boulder to the side, a couple of tourists huddled together, the man's arm wrapped around the woman's shoulders. She was crying bitterly, trembling under a blanket borrowed from the coroner's van.

"Morning, Detectives," Deputy Hobbs greeted them. He was chubby and jovial, and he'd managed to break a sweat in the cool

November breeze, most likely exerting himself on the slopes surrounding the crime scene, setting a perimeter, and searching for evidence. "I got some boots for you over there." He pointed at one of the vehicles. "Dr. Whitmore said to bring you in as soon as you got here."

Kay's eyebrows instantly rose, lines crinkling on her forehead. "In?"

"Um, yeah, there's a cave behind the falls," Hobbs said, "but don't worry, you won't get wet."

She wasn't worried. She stared at the couple who sat on the boulder and wondered why the woman sobbed. Of course, finding a dead body on your vacation hike was disturbing, but those sobs seemed personal, as if her heart was breaking. Was the victim someone they knew?

"They found the vic?" she asked, gesturing toward the couple.

"Yeah," Hobbs replied, surprisingly grinning. "Can you imagine? Dude came over here to propose. That'll be an engagement they'll never forget." He leaned forward, going through several pairs of rubber boots until he chose one. "What are you, a seven?"

"Eight." She sat on the edge of the SUV's bumper and removed her shoes, then slid the ugly, smelly boots on and tucked her jeans inside the calves to keep them dry.

"Eleven," Elliot said, taking her place as soon as she stood up.

"Doc's in there?" she asked, pointing at the cave entrance.

"Yeah," Hobbs replied. "He's been in there a while."

The closer they got to the falls, the louder they had to shout to make themselves heard, their voices muffled by the roar of the falling water. She entered the dark cave and stopped almost immediately, taking a moment to adjust her vision to the darkness slit open by powerful light beams coming from field LED lights installed on portable tripods.

Three of the beams converged on the body, still submerged under the cold, restless water. The ripples pushed in by the falls ebbed and flowed with her hair, undulating it rhythmically around her face, covering it almost entirely. The body shifted slightly, a ripple washing the hair off her face, and Kay gasped. It was as if the victim was still alive, staring at her with an unspoken question in her eyes. Shimmering water made her pupils seem as if they were moving, following Kay's motions, while the gaping laceration across her throat contradicted that impression. Kay willed herself to look away from those haunting eyes, and turned to speak with the medical examiner.

Dr. Whitmore was hunched over the body, his hands immersed to the elbows, looking for something.

"Finally," he said when he heard them approach. He stood and shook the water droplets off his gloved hands. "It's not that warm in here, and these boots don't do anything for the damn cold. It gets to my bones." He shifted sideways to make room for them to draw closer. "Here," he pointed at the girl's body. "I wanted you to see how she was found, weighed down like that, with a large boulder. I'd say, about a hundred pounds heavy, that rock." He beckoned the technicians waiting by the cave entrance, and the two men carefully removed the boulder and set it aside.

The girl's body remained submerged, but started drifting away, carried toward the back of the cave by the movement of the water. Then the technicians brought a foldable stretcher and set it up, unzipping a body bag and laying it on top.

Dr. Whitmore grabbed the girl's wrist and bent her arm, checking the flexibility of her elbow joint. "No rigor whatsoever," he said. "Environmental conditions are a factor. We won't be able to use that for time-of-death estimation." He opened his kit and extracted a small device fitted with a long, sharp probe at the end of a blue tether. "Let's see liver temp instead. Please put her on the stretcher," he said to the two technicians.

They lifted the body carefully, and Dr. Whitmore had to step in to support the girl's head. Her throat had been slashed open from side to side, a death that must've been almost instantaneous.

A locket hung around her neck, and the medical examiner carefully removed it and placed it inside an evidence pouch. Kay took it from him and scrutinized it through the clear plastic. The wooden locket was unusual, an elongated hexagon with rounded corners, and appeared to have been hand carved. The shape was imperfect, the red dye and lacquer of the finish uneven, like handcrafted jewelry found at county fairs and rural craft shows. The chain was also cheap, the type a child would wear, bought from a dollar store.

When she raised her gaze from the locket, she found Dr. Whitmore by her side, staring at the strange design. He took the pouch from her and studied it closely.

"I've seen this before," he said, turning the locket on both sides. "I know I have." He chuckled lightly, then turned to Kay and Elliot. "I might be old and semiretired, but my mind still works. It was a missing person case from years ago. I don't believe there are two of these lockets alike. This is handmade, unique."

"A missing person?" Kay asked. "Do you remember her name? Or when she went missing?"

He almost scratched his scalp with his gloved hand, but stopped just in time, before his wet fingers touched his white hair. "Oh, it was at least ten years ago. Her age would be a match, I believe; this girl is sixteen, seventeen tops. The girl I'm talking about was three years old when she vanished from her bedroom in the middle of the night." He paused, his eyes darting to the left as he recalled details about that case. "That girl wore a locket just like this one when she was taken. Her mother had made it for her." His voice, loaded with emotion, faltered a little as he spoke. He sighed, then turned his attention back to the liver temp probe. "One thing at a time. I'll run her DNA against the case file once I reach the office, and we'll know soon enough if it's her."

Dr. Whitmore lifted the girl's blouse to expose her abdomen and inserted the probe into her liver. The digital device beeped almost immediately. "I have to compensate for environmental, but she hasn't been dead more than two to four hours. I'm calling preliminary time of death," he checked his watch, "between eight and ten a.m. today. Her corneas are almost perfectly clear."

Approaching the body, Kay looked at the victim. With hesitant fingers, she gently removed the strands of hair clinging to the pale face, holding her breath, as if afraid the girl could come to life, startled by her touch. Her lips were red, probably tinted with one of those expensive lip stains that guaranteed twenty-four-hour color with one application. Her skin was alabaster pale, contrasting with her dark hair. Her eyes were still open, almost lifelike. Maybe it was the dim light in the cave where the worklights didn't reach, but her eyes still seemed fearful, terrified, as if her assailant was still there, blade in hand.

"This looks execution style to me," Elliot said. "Did she bleed to death?"

"There was still blood in the water when I got here," Dr. Whitmore replied. "I took a sample and tested it. The water had a red hue and that was unusual." He shrugged, then gestured to the cave behind him with a gloved hand. "Like everything else about this murder."

"Was she killed here, Doc?" Kay asked. She wondered how the girl was lured there, to the place of her demise. Tourists hiked there all the time; maybe she'd been a hiker too, accompanied by a man she trusted.

Because only a man would've been able to lift that boulder and place it over her body, to pin her down. A man with significant upper body strength.

"Yes, she was killed here," Dr. Whitmore replied. "The water we're standing in holds enough of her blood to support that theory."

The sound of the zipper being pulled shut signaled they were ready to leave the cave at Blackwater River Falls. Kay smiled sadly, thinking how appropriate the name was. Maybe the river had been named Blackwater, or Katseka in the old language of the Native Pomoan tribe, because of the iron oxide staining the rocks, or maybe the torrent had been tinted by blood before.

Leaving the cave, she blinked into the sunlight a few times, until she could bear to keep her eyes open. She was anxious to head out to the sheriff's office, eager to pull up old missing person reports involving a locket.

She was about to climb out of the fall's basin when Dr. Whitmore caught up with her and touched her forearm with frozen, ungloved fingers.

"Preliminary cause of death is exsanguination due to severed carotids," he said, his tone firm, professional, but seeping sadness. "She bled to beath. No hesitation marks, significant strength in the assailant, and expertise in taking lives. You're looking for a man, Detectives, a strong man who's killed before. Many times before."

CHAPTER FOUR

Runaway

Six Days Ago

My life sucks.

Kirsten stared at the stained ceiling for a good, long moment, then cursed loudly. If her mother would've heard her, she would've slapped her silly. But even if she were home, she wouldn't've been able to hear a thing with the ruckus in the living room.

She hated when her mom worked second shift at the hospital. She hated it even worse when she worked graveyard. That's when her stepdad's friends would gather in the living room, holler and drink and snort all night, forgetting to leave. Hostage in her room, Kirsten spent her evenings trying to ignore the roars, hoots, and screams mixed with profanities sprinkled generously at every other word, while trying to postpone the moment she'd have to leave to eat or use the bathroom. While wishing they'd be gone already.

Another chorus of hollers preceded a hearty round of cackles. She slammed her science book shut and took out her phone. She texted her best friend, Marci, who didn't need too many words to figure out what was going on.

Hey, it's happening again. Need your science homework tomorrow. Come early, please?

She waited a little, then her phone chimed and shut down. It was out of power. She plugged it in on her nightstand, then tiptoed to the bathroom, hoping the men were too much into it and wouldn't notice.

When she came out of the bathroom, three of them were waiting for her, standing on the narrow, dark hallway with excited grins on their faces.

"Hump said you'll let us snort some blow off your belly," one of the men said, the one whose potbelly overflowed his belt buckle. Hump was short for her stepfather's last name, Humphrey. She hated that name, and the day she'd become legally obligated to wear it.

The other, a bald and heavily tattooed thug who worked with her stepfather, let out a loaded groan and grabbed her arm, dragging her into the living room. There, the third man, a thin guy with mean eyes who'd just got out of jail, cleared the table with one quick swipe, then grabbed her and set her on it, forcing her flat on her back. She kicked and screamed, clawed at their faces, but her resistance only fueled their frenzy. She soon settled. Unfortunately, she'd done that before; she knew her chances. Her slender body was no match for three intoxicated men.

Really, really sucks, she thought, as eager hands pulled her top up and set powder lines on her abdomen. She closed her eyes, eagerly waiting for it to be over.

One of the men tugged at her jeans, and she opened her eyes wide, in a panic. *Hell, no.*

"Dad?" she called, using the appellative her stepfather had demanded her to use. Yet he remained silent, watching from the sofa, smoking a stogie and scratching his privates. "Dad!" she called again, squirming to get free of the hands holding her down.

She didn't stand a chance; they were too strong for her.

"Dad!" she called again, raising her voice over the sound of the TV.

This time, he responded. "Huh?"

"Dad, I'll tell Mom. Tell them to stop—"

"Uh-huh, okay," he replied, sounding absentminded. "When you're done there, get me a beer, willya?"

Potbelly and Ink Skin were snorting the white powder lines off her belly, their stubble scratching her skin, their heated, stinking breaths burning a trace against her flesh that made her sick to her stomach. She propped her heels against the table surface then pushed her abdomen up, without notice, as hard as she could, her sudden move shoving the straw Potbelly was using up his nose. He screamed and stepped back, holding his nose with both his hands. The other, in a stupor, stood and watched as she kicked the third man hard below the belt and made for the door.

She only stopped briefly to grab her sneakers and her jacket, then bolted, not bothering to slam the door shut behind her.

She didn't stop running for a couple of blocks, not feeling the raindrops against her face, not even to put on her shoes, until she was out of breath and at a safe distance from those pervs. Then she sat on a curb, panting. After tying her shoelaces, she put on her jacket and zipped it all the way up.

It was cold.

The street was almost deserted, rain keeping everyone indoors. The small shops that lined both sides had been closed for hours, barricaded behind folding security gates locked shut with large padlocks. A few yards away from where she'd stopped, loud snoring came from a large cardboard box pushed against the recessed entrance of a two-story office building, where the wind couldn't do much harm. The occasional car sped by, but no one cared about the hunched silhouette sitting on the curb, probably dismissing her as yet another homeless person.

She felt a chill.

She reached into her jeans pocket for her phone, but it wasn't there.

Oh, crap. The image of her phone charging on the nightstand taunted her. She would've rung Marci and maybe spent the night at her place, like she'd done a few times before. But it was late; she couldn't just land on her doorstep without calling first.

The hospital where her mom worked was a solid thirty minutes away on foot, but she started walking in that direction, hands shoved deep into her pockets, her jacket's collar raised to hide her blond hair and as much of her face as possible. She kept close to the walls, distancing herself from the sparse traffic, hoping she wouldn't draw anyone's attention.

Her anonymity didn't last long; within minutes, a patrol car bearing the insignia of Lane County Sheriff's Office drove by and spotted her. The cop lit up the flashers and pulled to the curb, lowering the passenger window.

"You shouldn't be on the streets so late," the deputy said, smiling.

She stared at him, panicked for a brief moment until she recognized him. Her mother's second cousin, technically her uncle, Deputy Rutledge, a chubby and lighthearted fellow, oftentimes mocked at family events for being too nice to be a cop.

She knew better than to speak the truth to adults. If she whispered one word about what was going on in her home, the cops would lock everyone up and put her in foster care. She'd learned that from a school buddy of hers. Even if her mom wasn't home, she could be charged with child endangerment, or neglect, or whatever these people thought of throwing her way, when all she was doing was earning a living for her family. Kirsten would never see her mother again.

"Just getting some snacks," she said, forcing a smile and pointing at the 7-Eleven across the street. "My folks have people over."

Uncle Rutledge stared at her for a few, endless seconds, then said, "Make it quick and then go straight home, all right?"

She nodded and he left, turning off the flashers as soon as he set the patrol car in motion. She stood there, watching his taillights disappear around the corner, wondering what to do, where to go. She needed to get out of there, out of the small town of Creswell, Oregon, where everyone knew everyone, and no one ever minded their own business.

Kirsten came to a crossroads and paused, although the light was green, and she could've crossed ahead. If she continued on, for another twenty minutes or so, she would reach the hospital where her mother worked. She would have to explain what happened, and fight with her mom who refused to accept things were so bad in her absence. The cowardly parasite she'd married was a con artist with a record, and good at tricking her into believing whatever lies he told. Every time she'd tried to tell her mom what was going on, Kirsten had ended up grounded and crying, even slapped across the face one time.

But if she turned right, within a few yards she'd reach the highway, where maybe she'd be able to hitch a ride to... Where?

To out of there, anywhere.

She'd find a way to survive. She'd just turned fourteen, but looked older, more mature. With her long, silky blond hair and her full lips, she'd be able to land a job somewhere, waiting on tables for cash at the end of the day, or cleaning motel rooms. Her athletic build and the endurance she'd built running 10-mile races told her she'd be fine, as long as she could get the heck out of there.

Turning the corner, she entered the highway, then started walking south along the almost deserted lanes. Whenever she saw headlights approaching, she held her hand out, but no one stopped, whooshing by at frightening speeds, the whistle of air rushing against metal a stern warning to stay away. The interstate wasn't like some big city road, where she could take a bus or something. Hundreds of miles of asphalt stretched across farms, forests, and tumbleweed-roamed fields, with no other option to get away than hitch a ride.

After a while, shivering in a cold drizzle that had started falling out of the leaded sky, she realized she'd left the lights of the town way behind. Darkness surrounded her, engulfing her completely. Panic made the bile in her throat rise as she fought the urge to throw up.

A strong pair of bluish headlights appeared in the distance, blinding her as they approached. She squinted and held her breath. Maybe this one would stop. She held her hand out, waving it, even stepped out into the lane, hoping she'd be seen.

And she was.

The eighteen-wheeler came to a screeching stop after passing her by about 100 yards, but she ran quickly and climbed onto the chrome step eager to get some shelter from the freezing rain. She opened the massive door and looked inside. The driver could've been Potbelly's twin. The same stubble, the same stink of sweat and stale booze, the same stained, crooked teeth behind a lascivious grin.

"Welcome aboard, sweetheart," he said, inviting her with an excited chuckle. "Where to?"

She hesitated, still standing on the step, not sure if she should climb into the toasty cabin.

"Um, San Francisco," she replied, throwing the only city name that came to her mind. It was south of there, and south was where she wanted to go.

The man slapped his hands excitedly against his knees. "Papa Bear can take you there," he replied, his voice coarse, loaded. "How you gonna pay for the ride? Gas, grass, or ass?"

It took her a long moment to process what he'd just said. Stunned, she let go of the door handle and stepped down.

"Your loss, sweetheart," he replied. "Now be a doll and close that door, willya?"

She slammed it shut as hard as she could, wishing she had the strength to break it into a million pieces. Then she ran away toward the side of the road, jumped over the railing and dashed into the woods, as if the truck driver hadn't already peeled off, honking his horn three times, having the last laugh.

Feeling a warm liquid on her frozen face, she realized it was her own tears, flowing in steady streams. She leaned against a tree trunk and crouched to the ground, the highway barely visible from where she was, and hugged her knees tightly, trying to stop her shivering. The barren tree crowns shifted in the wind, menacing and dark above her head, like monsters waiting to pounce.

Teeth clattering, she wondered how much longer until daylight. Once the sun came up, things would be different, she told herself. She wouldn't feel so alone.

So terrified.

CHAPTER FIVE

Identity

"Found it," Kay announced, clapping her hands together excitedly, leaning closer to the screen.

Her voice resounded loudly in the bullpen, where most of the desks were empty as their usual tenants were out working the beats of Franklin County. A couple of deputies were catching up on paperwork, and Sheriff Logan was on the phone, his baritone carrying over the bullpen effortlessly. One of those present must've been responsible for the strong smell of microwaved burrito that filled the space, although it wasn't lunchtime yet. Her stomach gave her a growling nudge, reminding her she'd skipped breakfast that morning, settling for black coffee instead.

Passing by her desk, a deputy gave her a long look, measuring her in a way she found insulting.

"Detective," the man greeted her in passing, sarcasm heavy in his voice.

She pasted a forced smile and nodded, then looked at Elliot. "Who was that?" She hated to ask, but she was still new. She remembered everyone's faces, but not everyone's names had stuck. Their paths rarely crossed.

"Deputy Daugherty, one of the veterans here," Elliot replied in a low voice. From his flat tone, she deduced that her partner wasn't a fan either. There was something off about that deputy, about how he looked at her, as if she didn't belong, as if women were not worthy to wear a badge. But she shrugged it off and trained her eyes on the screen, where old records were displayed in a list organized by victim name.

Elliot leaned over, their shoulders almost touching, and looked at the records on the monitor.

"I believe this is it," she said, displaying the first screen in an older police report. "I'm surprised this case is digitized, being it's fourteen years old." She pressed a couple of keys, and the image shifted, showing a grainy photo of a locket. Despite the low-quality shot, it was clear the locket was red and shiny. The shape was similar to the one they'd found on their victim, the design matched, and the links of the chain also seemed alike, at least as far as she could remember. The actual locket was now with Dr. Whitmore, who was going to swab it for evidence and run forensics.

"Yeah, could be," Elliot replied, not sounding convinced. He straightened his back and leaned sideways against the desk, facing her. "The color is way off, and I'm not sure about the markings. I wouldn't throw my hat over the windmill yet."

Kay concealed a smile, imagining Elliot standing next to a spinning windmill, balancing his hat in his hand, aiming to throw it over the revolving blades, for whatever reason Texans do that.

"Just add fourteen years of wear and tear, and you'll see it's a match. The one we found is weathered, that's all. I'm willing to bet it was red and shiny, originally, exactly like this one."

He tugged at the brim of his hat with two fingers, arranging it better, although it didn't seem out of place. It never did.

"Rose Harrelson," he read slowly the girl's name off the screen. "Doesn't ring a bell, but this was way before my time."

"Mine too," she replied quietly, her gaze riveted on the three-year-old girl's photo. She had a sweet smile, dimples in her cheeks and chin, long, brown hair in wavy curls, and hazelnut eyes that would melt a heart of stone.

The case of Rose's disappearance was cold, unsolved, fueling a pile of disappointing statistics that marked one of the most difficult types of cases to solve in law enforcement, regardless of state or county. Once the first twenty-four hours passed and no ransom call was received, the chances of ever finding a kidnapped child, dead or alive, plummeted to nearly zero. In Rose's case, the chances had been in line with the national statistic, at least for the past fourteen years.

If the girl behind the waterfall was indeed Rose, where had she been all this time?

The detective who had investigated the child's kidnapping had done an amazingly poor job, or maybe the digitizing of the case files had missed a few critical pages. He'd conducted some interviews, talked to some people, and gathered some evidence, but there was no follow-through, no conclusions drawn, and the sparse evidence had yielded no answers.

"Amazing that Dr. Whitmore remembered this case," Elliot said, whistling quietly between his teeth. "One heck of a hooty owl. Didn't he used to be a medical examiner in San Francisco when you were a fed?"

"Correct," she replied, while her mind wandered. There were thousands of missing children, teenagers, and young adults. Why had Dr. Whitmore remembered this one in particular? Kay wondered if it was because he'd bought his cabin about that time; she still recalled when the doc had shared his retirement plans with her, which included the plan to buy that piece of real estate. Many law enforcement people researched local crime records before investing in property.

Running a quick search to sate her relentless curiosity, she confirmed that Dr. Whitmore had acquired his cabin a few months after Rose had vanished. She let out a frustrated sigh; sometimes she went down dozens of rabbit holes. Those rabbit holes had the gift of offering fresh perspectives and interesting points of view, but not this time, and not where Dr. Whitmore was concerned. The man was an absolute saint, dedicated to his profession, passionate about crime solving, about giving victims a voice from beyond the grave.

A chime broke her chain of thought, followed immediately by another, coming from Elliot's phone. The message, from none other than the subject of her thoughts, was simple.

DNA confirms victim identity as Rose Harrelson.

"Yeah, we got that," she mumbled, starting to review the case notes in detail.

Elliot pulled up a nearby chair and sat by her side. "Want to do next of kin?"

She was dreading that part. She'd done it often as a federal agent, and it didn't get any easier, no matter how many times she'd banged on people's doors to tell them a loved one was never coming home again. As a psychologist, she was able to say the right things under the circumstances, and keep herself shielded emotionally as much as possible, but it still took a toll. Because she'd failed. The FBI, the sheriff's office, law enforcement as a whole had failed when people lost their lives, leaving their families heartbroken and unsettled, some never to find closure or the answer to the haunting question, *why*?

"One moment," she whispered, quickly reading the sparse notes on the file, scribbled by hand in a barely legible chicken scratch. "I don't believe I've ever seen such a badly worked kidnapping case. Why weren't the feds called? The girl was three years old," she added, frustration taking the pitch of her voice higher. "They should've been called in. They never were. They have resources, specialized teams, you know? They could've found her before she ended—"

Elliot touched her elbow gently. "Just a cop doing a bad job, that's all. You've seen it before." His voice was calm and supportive, understanding yet pacifying. She looked toward him for a beat, her gaze meeting Sheriff Logan's in passing. She hadn't realized how badly she'd raised her voice, and that everyone in the bullpen was staring at her.

Lips pressed firmly together, she redirected her attention back to the screen. She needed her mind to be clear and focused, factual, analytical, rid of all feeling, of all resentment. Still somewhat choked, she cleared her throat before starting to read what little information the case file held. "Rose Harrelson, age three, was taken from the house of her parents, Shelley and Elroy Harrelson, fourteen years ago." She flipped to the next screen and started scrolling though handwritten logs from what seemed to be the detective's notebook, scanned into the system. "Forensics found no fingerprints, and the kidnapper had gained access to the house without breaking in, seemingly familiar with the property, the family and their routine. Therefore, the investigator was quick to determine the father, Elroy Harrelson, was somehow responsible for her abduction, although the parents were not separated. It goes on," Kay added, skipping forward over endless yet unsubstantial notes documenting the interviews with both parents. "Oh…" she whispered, not realizing her hand had left the keyboard and had covered her mouth. "Rose's father killed himself a few months later."

"Does it say why?" Elliot asked, squinting at the screen and drawing closer.

"He was exonerated in Rose's kidnapping, says here," Kay added, speaking slowly, as she perused the almost illegible notes in the endless pages. "The same detective was assigned to the suicide case, and some of the notes were crossed over. Seems Elroy's life was destroyed by the suspicion, although he was cleared. He lost his job, couldn't find another." She looked briefly at Elliot, then back at the screen. "He hung himself in the garage, seven months after Rose was taken."

"Who was that detective?"

"I have his initials here, H.S." Scrolling back up to the top of the notes, she added, "We're the only detectives here, so we know he's no longer on the payroll. He might be retired. We should pay him a visit. But first, I have a last known address for the Harrelsons. Let's go talk to Rose's mother."

Grabbing her keys from the desk, she led the way to the parking lot, noticing how unusually quiet Elliot had been since the crime scene, and wondering why exactly that was.

CHAPTER SIX
Searching

He'd been driving through the rain for hours, aimlessly roaming on dark, almost barren streets. It was after midnight, and the wet asphalt shone in shades of streetlight orange and brake-light red, on occasions sparking with headlight bluish-white. He hadn't stopped for a while, not since he'd gassed up north of San Francisco, his restlessness keeping him motivated to go on, mile after mile, delaying the inevitable.

Soon he'd have to go back to the empty, dark, unwelcoming house he'd been dreading returning to again. Without her, without his Mira, the house was just a cold and damp dwelling, not a home. Without her warm body wrapped around his like a vine, the bed couldn't be slept in, condemning him to wander aimlessly looking for what he'd lost and never finding it.

He had to call it quits and head home.

Like he'd done the night before, at about three in the morning, exhausted, hungry, and cold, frustrated he'd failed again.

She wasn't out there, not in that rain that promised to turn into snow before morning, layering a dangerously slick coat of black ice on wind-washed sections of the road.

No one was out there.

Just him, driving, still clinging to the idea that maybe, just as he turned the next corner, he'd see her.

Because the night before had been unbearable. The old house had creaked back to life as soon as he'd turned the power back on, and the heater had kicked in. In the cold darkness, he could still feel Mira's presence, expecting her to fall into his arms any moment, while he wandered through the empty house calling her name, feeling for her in the dark with open arms, listening for her breath while holding his.

She wasn't there.

Desolate, he'd turned on the lights, flooding the house with the harshness of reality. It was empty, a soulless carcass he'd held on to against all odds and all reason, the last, enduring memory he could preserve of her.

It was her shrine.

And he hated the house he'd preserved intact since the day she'd left it behind, dreading its emptiness, its silence, the absence of her more painful there than anywhere else. Unbearable, yet the last enduring memento of their searing love. Of the life she'd torn apart when she'd left.

He couldn't go back, not again, not for another night of torture.

Resigned to what he needed to do, he turned the car around and headed back south, toward San Francisco, speeding the entire time, even though the rain had grown heavier as soon as he'd left the mountains.

By the time the Golden Gate started to gild the sky in the distance, the rain had turned into a light drizzle, almost indiscernible from the thick fog that engulfed the city. His wipers still ran, their rhythmic thump almost organic, the heartbeat of his car as it sped through the night.

A few blocks east from the highway, slowing down as he entered the heart of the city, he looked for her. Even at that late hour, San Francisco wasn't asleep, not like Mount Chester was, its less-than-fortunate dwellers still huddled in small groups on the cold, humid streets, trying to survive yet another night without a roof over their heads.

He didn't see her on any of the streets he'd driven thus far. He halted at a stoplight, the bright red coloring his pale hands, as they gripped the steering wheel, a weird shade of ghostly crimson. The light changed, and he turned left, his breath caught in his chest as he decided to turn back to the highway. Forcing the air out of his lungs, he waited a moment before inhaling deeply, feeling the burn of oxygen deep inside his chest. Then he screamed, rage rushing out of his lungs in a loud and loaded roar, rattling his windows as he sped through the almost-deserted streets, no one to hear him, no one to soothe his excruciating pain.

That's when he saw her.

A mere shadow in the corner of his eye as he sped by, a pale and shivering figure hiding in the dark near the entrance of a five-story office building. Her long, blond hair escaped the black hoodie she wore pulled over her head almost to her eyes, her hands hid from the cold shoved deeply in the kangaroo pocket.

Mira?

He slammed the brakes so forcefully the tires screamed, and the car swerved as it came to a stop. Then he put it in reverse and drove back to where he'd seen her. Fog seeping through the lowered passenger window, he waited, endless minutes flying by while he looked at her, mesmerized, and she stared at him with fear building in her round eyes.

Hesitantly, she approached the car, after looking left and right a few times, as if afraid she'd be spotted talking with him. She stopped in front of the passenger door and bent forward a little, probably to see him better.

He smiled, but didn't say a word.

She was shorter than Mira, and her eyes were brown, not blue. She wasn't Mira... not even close. But she could help scatter the cold emptiness of that house, at least for a night or two.

She wasn't a prostitute, not one of those skanks who trolled the Tenderloin neighborhood day and night, clad in trashy, stretchy outfits that hugged their curves and showcased their availability. No, this girl was different, a runaway maybe, someone hopefully no one would miss. She wore dirty, torn jeans and a pair of worn-out sneakers that had seen better days.

"I have a room," she eventually said, her inexperienced smile revealing stained teeth. She'd probably been living on the streets for a while, although she didn't seem too competent at turning tricks. Life on the streets wasn't for everyone.

He shook his head gently. "That's not going to work. My house isn't that far," he said, still smiling invitingly, his hand gesturing at the empty seat next to him. "I have good food, and you can take a hot shower." His smile widened. "I'll bring you back, I promise."

She held on to the door with both hands as she leaned forward, her eyes on the same level as his, enough for him to notice the doubt nestled in there. Her hands were swollen and red from the cold, and her dirty fingernails had been chewed on. A few details that told an entire story of loneliness and destitution.

"How old are you?" he asked gently, reaching inside his pocket for his wallet.

"Eighteen," she replied much too quickly, veering her eyes sideways, then looking at him again for a brief moment before lowering her lying gaze.

He opened his wallet and slowly took out several hundred-dollar bills, one by one, the rustling of paper the only sound between them for a few loaded seconds. The girl stared at the cash without a word, then grabbed the door handle and squeezed it gently. She opened the door and put one foot inside, ready to slide onto the heated leather seat, as he shifted into gear impatiently.

She changed her mind lightning fast, her eyes riveted on the finger he'd used to press the D button. She pulled away and closed the door behind her, throwing the cash in his hand a regretful look.

"Sorry," she said, stuttering a little, "I can't."

"Get in here already," he fumed, raising his voice as the distance between them increased with each rushed step she took. "Get back here!"

She didn't turn to look at him; just shoved her hands in the center pocket of her hoodie and dashed away, her brisk walk becoming a light jog, then rapid running as she turned the corner into an alley.

He was alone again.

CHAPTER SEVEN

Mother

The Harrelson residence was an old ranch on the south side of town, tucked between the state route and a ravine, Mount Chester's snowy peak rising to touch the sky a few miles behind it. The clear blue sky and bright fall colors were at odds with the state of the property. It had fallen into disrepair, the siding showing scars from the storms that had passed through town, and the patchy roof must have been responsible for water puddles inside the home whenever it rained. The withered lawn had not been mowed in years, and the state of the weeds pushing their way stubbornly through the cracks of the narrow driveway stood as testimony that no car had pulled into the old garage in a while. The far corner of the shed had been damaged by a fallen tree trunk and had since been claimed by raccoons.

Most of all, the Harrelson residence was boarded and posted.

Panels of fiberboard covered all the windows and doors, and had clearly been nailed in place for a while, the nails rusted or broken by raging winter storms and summer showers. Only the four corners of what used to be a posted sign still clung to their nails, the rest blown away by the wind.

At a loss for words, Kay stared at what was left of the property, a shudder running through her body as she circled it slowly. That's all it took, one fateful night, one taken child, one cop who didn't care enough to do his job or call others who could do it for him, and an entire family's existence was wiped, reduced to a pile of rubble.

"Excuse me." Kay heard a frail, slightly trembling voice behind her, and turned to face a chubby woman dressed in a fuzzy turquoise housecoat and slippers to match. She must've been at least seventy-five, her white hair tinged with yellow and unkempt, and her parchment skin stained with liver spots.

"What can we do for you?" Elliot asked.

The woman's tentative smile widened. "Oh, nothing, dearie. I might be able to do something for *you*. I've seen you looking at Shelley's house." She pointed toward the house next door with arthritis-knotted, trembling fingers. "I live over there, behind those maples."

Her eyesight was impressive, if she'd seen them circling the property from at least 100 yards away and through low-hanging maple branches loaded with rusty leaves. Kay smiled and approached the woman who waited patiently, their presence probably a rare spell of excitement in her life.

"Do you live alone, Ms.—"

"Ms. Duncan," she replied quickly, with a slight nod of her head. "You can call me Martha. Everyone does."

"Thank you, Martha," Kay replied, shaking the woman's warm, dry hand. Her handshake was still strong, although her fingers seemed unable to stop trembling. Most likely Parkinson's. "I'm Detective Sharp, and that's my partner, Detective Young." Noticing a slight frown on Martha's brow, she quickly added, "Kay and Elliot." The frown vanished. "What happened here?"

"Strange that you should ask, being you're cops and all," she replied, her eyes darting for a moment toward Kay's badge, bearing the seven-point gold star of the Franklin County Sheriff's Office. "You know, poor Rose was taken, um, must be almost fifteen years ago, when she was just a little girl. They never found her," she added, wiping a tear with the knotty side of her index finger. "That poor child… Who knows what happened to her?"

"Were you living here when it happened?" Elliot asked.

"Dearie, I've always lived here," she chuckled, "and I'm pushing seventy-nine." She turned serious again. "Funny you should come calling after all these years. Have you found Rose?"

Kay and Elliot exchanged a brief look. There were strict rules—no victim's name was to be released to anyone else before the next of kin. Not to the media, not to friends or family. And Rose's next of kin was her mother.

"We have a few questions for Mrs. Harrelson," she replied instead, wishing she could bend that rule just once.

"Oh, dearie," Martha replied, quickly wiping another tear from the corner of her eye with her fingers. "Poor Shelley, she never recovered after losing Rose, and then Elroy. She had a stroke a few months after Elroy passed. I'm not sure she's going to be much help, that poor lamb."

"Do you know where she is?" Elliot asked.

"Yes, and I try to visit every chance I have, but it's far, you know. I can't drive like I used to." She must have noticed the look on Elliot's face, because she quickly added. "It's called the, um, Glen Valley Commons or something like that, over in Redding. It's one of those nursing homes run by the state. Terrible place if you were to ask me."

All leads had seemed to disintegrate in Rose's disappearance case, yet Kay knew she had to find out what had happened fourteen years ago before she could catch Rose's killer. With Shelley in assisted living, she couldn't hope for much, but any hint, any piece of information might prove valuable. The detective who'd investigated the kidnapping had been sloppy, but the mother might still remember something useful.

She thanked Martha for her help and turned to leave, but the woman seemed to have something else to say, because she grabbed Kay's sleeve.

"You know," she said, lowering her voice as if afraid of being overheard, "I never understood how something like that could happen. Shelley and Elroy were both at home when their daughter was taken, yet the police accused them, instead of looking at other people who came to the house and knew their way around." She smiled, her watery eyes sparkling. "I watch crime shows on TV, all day really. Nothing else better to do." Kay nodded with a smile, but Martha still held on. "There were other people who came here. Me, of course, but I didn't take her," she clarified with a quick scoff. "Elroy's work buddies. Rose's nanny is dead now—

ovarian cancer, I heard—but she vanished right around the time the girl was taken. Her mother said she'd moved to South America somewhere around that time. There were others, though. Have you spoken with any of them? Has anyone?"

CHAPTER EIGHT

Preliminary

"Redding is about an hour away," Elliot said, but Kay was quick to interrupt.

"Not if I drive." She flashed a quick glance his way, amusement gleaming in her hazel eyes.

I bet, he thought, because the woman holding the wheel drove the speed of a prairie fire with a tail wind. Whatever distance they needed to go, she'd take it as a personal challenge and get there in half the time.

He hid the smile tugging at the corner of his mouth, afraid she might see right through it. Perceptive, bright as a new penny, and beautiful too. One heck of a cop, instincts rock solid, doubled by all that science she wielded around like loaded six shooters, reading people's emotions, anticipating what they'd say and do, and never being wrong.

His smile widened, but he kept his face turned away from her, pretending to look at the edge of the thick woods lining the road, patches of it still green in needles of pine and fir, while others were bare, where oaks and maples had shed their foliage, littering the moist ground in fire colors. He deliberately avoided her two-second scrutiny, because that's how long it would take her to read his thoughts like an open book.

He welcomed the possibility to learn from one of the best profilers in the FBI. Through some sudden and favorable twist of fate, one of the country's top-notch criminalists had returned to her hometown and had decided to stay, becoming his partner. As far as career fortune went, he couldn't've asked for more.

What a load of sundried manure.

Who was he kidding? Learning how to profile a perp or study victimology wasn't the only reason he lingered after shift end, building the nerve to ask her out to dinner. But the last time he'd mixed business with pleasure and had fallen for his partner, it ended so badly he had to leave Texas. Now every time winter drew closer, he remembered the oath he'd taken that day. Never again.

His smile waned.

She caught the shift in his thoughts uncannily, like she seemed to do everything, without even taking her eyes off the road.

"What's wrong?" she asked casually, and he had to swallow a curse.

"Even with your driving, Redding's a three-hour trip, with the time we'll spend there. Let's drop by Dr. Whitmore's first."

"Yup," she acknowledged, glancing at him again just as briefly. Then, without a word, she took the next exit and turned left.

He hadn't fooled her for one moment.

Busying himself with the water bottle nestled in the door panel, he unscrewed the cap and drank thirstily about half of it. By the time he slid the bottle back, Kay was pulling in front of the county morgue. At the far end of the parking lot, a news van waited with its engine running.

They rushed inside, unwilling to answer any questions from the media. He held the door for Kay, and she walked in without any hesitation or any indication she wasn't one hundred percent comfortable visiting Doc Whitmore's turf. The place was kept chilly, for obvious reasons, and the air was loaded with the heavy stench of death and chemicals, their mixed odors more bothersome than usual.

"Hey, Doc," Kay greeted the medical examiner.

Dressed in a long white lab coat and wearing a headband with LED lights and magnifying lenses, he was standing next to one of the autopsy tables, where Rose's body lay, the slash across her throat gaping and discolored in the absence of blood. When he heard Kay's voice, he turned and smiled widely, visibly pleased to see her, then greeted Elliot with a polite nod. He pushed up his headband, exposing his thin-rimmed glasses and tired eyes.

"We're keeping you busy, it seems," Kay added, her voice tinged with sadness. "We're disrupting your retirement way too often."

"The problem is not the disruption," Dr. Whitmore replied. "The problem is this young life wasted." He sighed, leaning against the table with gloved hands as if to ease the weight off his feet. "Only seventeen years old, can you believe it?"

There was silence in the cold room for a moment, then Kay drew closer to the doctor.

"I see you haven't started the Y incision yet," she said. "Any preliminary information you can give us? I'm dying to get my hands on the bastard who did this."

Yeah… no kidding, thought Elliot. He wanted to snatch the son of a bitch bald-headed and leave him flat for the buzzards to feast on.

Elliot drew closer, but chose to remain several feet away from the autopsy table. He was still uncomfortable looking at the girl's partially covered body. Somehow, staring at a vulnerable, young woman exposed like that contradicted everything he'd been taught by his modest, church-going mother. That was a part of the job he was happy to cede in favor of his partner, the psychologist who could handle any autopsy without flinching. Kay was a natural, whatever life threw her way, while he was the awkward cop trained on the streets of Austin, Texas, who'd made Mount Chester his home five years ago but still felt he didn't belong.

"We established a positive ID," the doctor said, sounding a little pedantic, as if he were teaching a class, "so I can confirm she is a couple of months short of turning seventeen." He cleared his throat silently and mumbled an apology after coughing a couple of times. "Cause of death is exsanguination due to laceration of both carotid arteries." He pried open the neck wound by removing the foam block that supported the girl's head, and pointed his gloved finger at the discolored, fibrous tissue. "As you can see, the attack was forceful, one slice cutting through both carotids, all four jugular veins, the esophagus and trachea, the blade leaving marks in the cervical vertebrae here."

Kay leaned closer and examined the open wound, then nodded, and Doc replaced the block supporting her head.

"Was he left-handed?" she asked.

"Excellent observation," Dr. Whitmore replied. "Yes, he was. The cut originated here," he pointed at the right side of the girl's throat, taking a position behind the head of the table and wielding an imaginary knife with his left hand. "The man you're looking for is strong and tall. The cut started at a slightly lower position on her throat than it ended, the upward angle an indication of his height." He frowned for a moment, as if trying to remember something else he was going to say. "He held her by the chin and mouth, like this," he demonstrated again, pretending to cover Rose's mouth from behind, pulling her head backward. "You can see that at the terminal edge of the laceration, where the skin is torn for a few millimeters after the cut ends. That means he continued to force her head backward even after he finished slicing."

"What kind of weapon are we looking for?" Elliot asked.

"I'd say a twelve- to fourteen-inch blade, probably serrated, but I can't be sure."

Elliot kept his eyes riveted on the doc's face, silently insisting that he give them something they could use.

"If I had to guess," Dr. Whitmore added with a sigh, "I'd be looking for a military knife, but that's inference, and medical examiners are bound to stick to facts and evidence."

"So, army knife—" Elliot started to say, but the doctor interrupted.

"*Possibly* an army knife."

"Got it. Tall, strong man, possibly an army knife, experienced killer." Elliot frowned, wondering if he should state the obvious. To him, the conclusion was evident. "Are we looking for former military?"

"Former or active," Kay intervened. "Someone who spent years in the forces, and most likely has seen action and learned how to take lives quickly and silently. Slicing her trachea left her completely silent for the few moments she lived after that point. I've seen this MO in special forces, Army Rangers, Navy SEALS."

"Got it," he replied.

Kay squinted under the sharp lights, then asked, "Was she sexually assaulted?"

"I don't see any evidence of assault," Dr. Whitmore replied. "She was sexually active, but not recently." He moved to the side of the autopsy table and removed his gloves, threw them in the bin, and plunged his hands into his pockets. "She was in excellent health." His tone changed as he added, "This is preliminary, of course." Kay nodded, and he continued. "Perfectly aligned white teeth, no cavities, recent cleaning. Recent manicure and pedicure, all professionally done." He turned, then walked over to the evidence table, where he sifted through a few large evidence pouches containing Rose's clothing. "Her slacks were labeled Anne Klein. Her blouse was from Neiman Marcus, one of its exclusive brands." He looked at a couple of pouches, but didn't say anything else. Putting his hands back into his lab coat pockets, he returned to the side of the autopsy table.

"How does a kidnap victim from fourteen years ago end up wearing high-end fashion and having her throat slashed in a cave behind a waterfall?" Kay asked, starting to pace the floor slowly.

"That's for you two to find out," Dr. Whitmore replied, putting on a fresh pair of blue nitrile gloves.

"Do you think she stayed local since she was taken?" Elliot asked, wondering how that could've been possible. Any kidnapper in his right mind would've put some serious distance between the scene of his crime and the twenty-five-to-life sentence carried by the offense.

"It's possible," Kay replied, speaking slowly, the way she did when she seemed to be thinking things through. "Where did she go to school? How come no one had recognized her? We're not exactly a big city." She turned to Dr. Whitmore and said, "Doc, you recalled this case from back then. That was impressive, by the way, remembering that locket after fourteen years."

He smiled and lowered his gaze for a moment, visibly flattered.

"I collect certain cases that pose interesting forensic challenges," he explained. "There are a couple of hundred cases in my filing cabinet, mostly child abductions. When I was younger and more ambitious, I thought I could figure out a way to improve the rapid response procedure in preteen abduction cases." His gaze veered sideways. "Nothing much came out of that effort other than a collection of cold case files I've been moving along with me wherever I go. Sometimes I reopen one of them, unofficially, of course, and start digging."

"Should we ask the sheriff to give you a badge, Doc?" Kay asked, smiling.

"Nah, I'm just an old and bored retiree criminalist who can't let go." Pulling a four-legged stool closer to the autopsy table, he picked a scalpel from the instrument tray. He rested his arm on the side of the table, the scalpel frozen midair. "Science has delivered so many new forensic tools we can use in crime investigations. DNA is the single most important one of them, and some of my cold cases precede the wide-scale use of DNA in forensics. When I have time to spare, I run a test or two," he said with a shrug.

"Do you remember hearing anything about Rose Harrelson in the year or years after her kidnapping?"

He ran his sleeve across his forehead, where white hair strands touched the ridged skin of his brow. "Unfortunately, I don't recall that much. I remember hearing of her father's suicide; that was disheartening. But nothing else, I'm afraid." He tilted his head and frowned. "There was one thing. For as long as he lived after Rose's disappearance, Elroy Harrelson papered every tree in Mount Chester with posters of his missing daughter. I recall those clearly. If she stayed local, it's amazing no one recognized that sweet child. My wife and I had just bought our cabin here, and everywhere we went, we saw those posters."

Kay touched the doctor's arm gently, just as he was lowering the scalpel to the girl's chest.

"Thanks," she said with a heavy sigh Elliot rarely heard coming from her. "Seems to me we have to solve the fourteen-year-old kidnapping case before we can learn anything about this girl's life."

"You two have your work cut out for you," Dr. Whitmore said, and Kay turned to leave. "By the way," he added, "have you noticed that KYBC news crew parked outside my shop? They won't leave until I give them the girl's ID."

"We're going to see Mrs. Harrelson next," Elliot explained. "We'll confirm when next-of-kin notification has been delivered and you can throw them a bone."

When they exited the building, the news crew rushed toward them and a young, slender brunette planted a mic in front of Elliot's face, irritating him worse than a dry burr under a stallion's saddle.

"Is it true that Blackwater River Falls girl is connected to Rose Harrelson? Rumor has it you're looking into that case."

Thank you, Martha, Elliot thought bitterly, *thank you very much.*

"Who is the waterfall girl?" the brunette insisted. "Is she Rose Harrelson? Where has she been all this time?"

Kay wriggled her way between the three newspeople and climbed behind the wheel, Elliot quick to take the passenger seat.

From there, through the open window, she said, "I only have one comment at this time: I'd get out of the way if I were you."

She revved the engine enough to get their attention, then shifted into gear and peeled off in a cloud of dust and fallen leaves.

He couldn't help but smile. There was no slack in Kay's rope. Not a single, skinny inch.

CHAPTER NINE

On the Road

FIVE DAYS AGO

A large drop of water rolled on a withered maple leaf then fell, hitting her forehead with a splat. She woke, instantly hypervigilant, pulse throbbing in her throat. With her senses revived, Kirsten started to feel the wet cold that had seeped through her clothing and numbed her limbs, the sore muscles stiff from so much trembling, and the dull ache in the pit of her stomach.

Unsure her legs would be able to sustain her weight, she remained crouched to the ground, hugging her knees tightly, breathing into the collar of her soaked jacket. She looked around, wary of every sound and every movement, thankful for the break of dawn putting an end to darkness, at least for a while.

The grayish light of early dawn revealed a thick layer of moist, fallen leaves at her feet, their once bright colors already fading to brown. Wet tree trunks loomed around her like dark, ominous giants, but she'd found shelter against an oak's wide girth, the few remaining leaves up in the majestic crown shielding her from the rain, at least in part.

When she could see clearly ahead of her, she stood, faltering, unsure on her numb legs. As blood started to rush to her extremities, pins and needles reminded her she was still alive. She stomped her feet a couple of times, welcoming the warmth brought by movement. Then, as traffic picked up on the highway, she dared leave the cover of the woods and headed to the road. She crossed over the guardrail and put her hand out with her thumb raised, hailing passing cars in the hope someone would stop. Who would take a soaking wet hitchhiker in their car, only to soil their seats and mess up their carpeting with the thick mud on her sneakers?

The threat of tears burned her eyes, but she willed it away. She needed to survive, to get as far from that place as possible, before her uncle and all his coworkers hunted her like a posse hunts a wanted fugitive.

The rain had stopped, making room for the scent of wet earth and soaked, fallen leaves, and a fine mist lifted from the ground under the sun's filtered rays. Heavy clouds lingered, threatening more rain, but Kirsten's heart swelled when a delivery truck slowed its speed and pulled to the side of the road, passing her by a few yards.

She hurried to catch up, hoping she wasn't going to run into another freak like the one she'd met the night before, the pervert in the eighteen-wheeler. When she reached the truck, she peered through the window and breathed, the relief almost suffocating.

The driver was a middle-aged woman with a kind look in her eyes.

Kirsten opened the door, hesitating a little before climbing inside.

"Come on up, hon," the woman said. Her voice was raspy and dry, giving away years of smoking, the stink of the habit still prevalent despite the two pine-shaped fresheners hanging from the air-conditioning knob.

Kirsten paused, seeing how water was dripping from her jacket and pants. The woman, as if reading her mind, waved her concern away.

"Never mind, it will dry up. Here, take this," she said, reaching into a duffel bag behind the seat and extracting a colorful towel with a musty, soapy smell. "Dry yourself with it, take that jacket off, and put this under your butt."

Kirsten followed her instructions silently, struggling to find words to say. Kindness had been a rare occurrence in her life. Fighting back tears, she strapped herself into the seat, then put her hands closer to the heating vents, warming them up.

The woman set the truck in motion with a gear-grinding noise, the engine roaring as it struggled to pick up some speed.

"This old jalopy can't handle its loads anymore," she said, shooting a quick stained-teeth smile her way. "I'm Hazel. What's your name?"

Kirsten faltered, panic rising to her throat.

Hazel laughed, but there was sadness and understanding in her voice, not an ounce of derision. "Make something up, hon. I gotta call you something, right? No shame in telling a little white lie."

"Um, Kirsten," she muttered, stuttering on her own name, but deciding the woman's kindness deserved her honesty.

"And where are you off to, Kirsten?"

"California," she replied, a little more confident. "San Francisco, if you can take me all the way there."

Hazel laughed again. "With looks like yours, I thought you were going to Hollywood." Her smile waned into a sigh, her big chest heaving with it. "I can take you all the way to the California border, but that's where I have to stop. That's where this is going," she added, patting the center of the steering wheel twice, right where the Ford logo was affixed, scratched and discolored by the long years of use. "To Caldwell Farms."

"Thank you," Kirsten replied.

Her stomach grumbled, and Kirsten leaned forward, trying to hide the sounds it made. Hazel shot her a quick look, but didn't say another word. When the next exit came, she put the blinker on and took the off ramp.

Panicked, Kirsten shifted in her seat. "Where are we going?"

"To get some gas," Hazel replied. "Darn piece of junk won't run without it." She winked, and, after a brief moment, chuckled heartily at her own joke.

Kirsten waited by the truck while Hazel refueled, watching the numbers shifting quickly on the pump and warily looking at the passing cars, afraid she'd soon see her uncle's patrol car approaching fast, flashers and sirens, ready to drag her back into her own hell.

After Hazel finished gassing up, she invited Kirsten inside to use the restroom. She happily accepted, and took as little time as she could in there, washing her face and hands thoroughly, the smell of rainwater and dirt still strong on her.

When she came out, she found Hazel seated at a small table in front of the burger joint. Two plates loaded with cheeseburgers and fries awaited, the smell of sizzling bacon and molten cheddar driving a dagger through her empty stomach.

"For me?" she asked, eyes rounded in surprise, pointing at the plate in front of the empty seat.

Taking a bite from her burger, Hazel invited her to sit with a hand gesture. She chewed loudly, then said, "I don't see anyone else here."

It must've been the tastiest meal she'd ever had. Every bite she took filled her mouth with juices of grilled beef and melted cheese. The fries were just right, crispy on the outside and a little raspy with grains of salt, and soft on the inside, the smell filling her nostrils as she bit into them.

When she was almost done wolfing it down, she regretted not having taken more time to savor its taste. She picked the fallen sesame seeds off the plate with the tip of her finger, and even the tiniest speck of leftover French fry found its way into her mouth.

"Thank you," she said, looking at Hazel briefly then glancing away, afraid the woman would see her eyes welling up.

"You're welcome, hon," Hazel replied quietly. "It ain't much, but I figured you'd love a bite." She wiped her hands on a paper napkin, then ran her fingers through her thinning, bleached hair and stood. "Ready to hit the road?"

"Yes," Kirsten replied enthusiastically.

They drove in silence for a few miles, Kirsten fighting to stay awake, torn between the comfort of the heated cabin and the thought of what she was going to do once she reached San Francisco. She'd never been there. Where would she go? She almost asked Hazel, but it would've sounded as if she was pressuring the woman. Her life wasn't Hazel's problem.

"What made you leave home, hon? And what will you do when you get to San Fran? Know someone there?" the lady asked, as if reading her mind.

Kirsten shuffled in her seat, and shot Hazel a quick, panicked look.

"Listen, I'm pretty sure I'm breaking the law by taking you on instead of reporting you to the cops," Hazel said, her voice kind and understanding as it had always been. "You can't be more than fifteen years old. Wanna know why I do it?"

Kirsten didn't reply. She just stared at the woman, waiting for her to continue, anxiety gripping her chest in a vise.

"I used to be you," she eventually said. "A runaway from a torn family, thinking I could do better on my own than live on with my boozing mother and my absent father." She lowered the window and lit up a cigarette, inhaling sharply and holding it in for a moment. "And I did just fine for myself." She patted Kirsten's knee. "You'll do just fine yourself; you'll see. Don't let anyone push you around, and don't sell your body for cheap."

Kirsten's cheeks caught fire. She lowered her gaze, staring at the mud on her shoes for a while. She hadn't run from home to sell her body to some freak. The thought of a stranger touching her was so horrifying she shook her head as if to dislodge the nightmare. She squeezed her eyes shut, pushing away the images that rushed into her mind, bits and pieces of recent memories,

Potbelly's hands on her, Ink Skin holding her down on her back on the dining room table, the burning touch of the man's stubble, his slimy tongue leaving trails on her abdomen, lower and lower.

She willed all those images away, reminding herself that was why she'd run. It would never happen to her, not again. When she opened her eyes, letting the sunshine dissipate the memories, she met Hazel's concerned glance.

The woman quickly turned her head, looking straight ahead at the road.

"Did I tell you where I'm going, hon?" she asked, drawing another lungful of smoke from the cigarette, then flicking the butt through the open window. "I haul farm equipment for Caldwell. Have you heard of them?"

"Um, no," Kirsten replied.

She waved the lingering smoke in the truck's cabin with a swat of her hand. "They're a big farm," she continued, rolling up the window. "As soon as we cross into California, you'll see their land. It stretches on and on for miles, on both sides of the highway."

Kirsten looked out the window, passively listening to Hazel's stories about the farm, the Caldwells, and the farming equipment she hauled, for sale or lease. Before long, she'd be dropped off on the side of the road, and she'd be alone again.

She almost missed the WELCOME TO CALIFORNIA sign, yellow, cursive letters on blue, adorned with what seemed to be three flowers. She couldn't be sure; Hazel was going 70 miles per hour, and Kirsten didn't dare ask; it wasn't important. But soon Hazel started to slow down, pulling to the side of the road.

"This is where you get off, hon," Hazel said, sending a lurch of dread throughout her body. She pointed at a side road to a large gate, off the next ramp. "Your chances are better here, on the highway, than on the service road." She squeezed Kirsten's hand with both of hers. "I wish you the best of luck."

She thanked the woman and got out, watching the truck grinding its gears back into its lane, then disappear on the off ramp, and through the farm's gate.

Putting on her jacket, she zipped it all the way up. The air was crisp, and the wind blew from the north, catching speed along the highway. She shoved her hands into the pockets and felt something unfamiliar in her left one. When she removed her hand, there were five crumpled, twenty-dollar bills in her palm and a note. It had a phone number under Hazel's name, and a few words: *For when you need to stop running*.

Blinking away tears, she started walking with her hand in the air, hoping someone would stop. A flatbed honked loudly as it passed her by at high speed, covering her in dust and small pebbles. Startled, she took a few rushed steps sideways without looking. Her foot slipped on loose gravel and her ankle twisted. She shrieked and tumbled into a deep ditch, rolling underneath the guardrail into the tall grasses, where she slammed straight into a boulder.

CHAPTER TEN

Next of Kin

It was mid-afternoon by the time Kay pulled in front of the nursing home. One look was enough to see what kind of facility they were about to enter. The front sign, spelling "Glen Valley Commons" in rusty cursive letters above a rain-stained stone block was only the first hint of the property's condition. The building's windows were foggy, probably the place's budget for window cleaning a big fat zero, the paint was cracked, and pieces of siding were barely clinging to the walls.

She braced herself before going in, hesitating in front of the door Elliot held open for her. A whiff of the smells awaiting inside gave her chills, bringing back painful memories of her mother's final battle with cancer. Disinfectant struggled to cover the pervasive stink of defeated human bodies, of urine and feces and acrid burned food.

Stepping inside, Elliot followed, hat in hand. Approaching the front desk, Kay presented her identification. A large woman in a tight lab coat met them with an unwelcoming gaze from under bushy eyebrows and a narrow forehead.

"Detectives Sharp and Young, here to speak with Mrs. Harrelson," Kay said.

The woman stared at the ID, then, pressing her lips together in a crooked lip curl, picked up the phone and dialed an internal extension.

Several minutes later, a tall and bony nurse rolled in Mrs. Harrelson, who was seated in a wheelchair that had seen better days. The nurse beckoned them to follow her into a room, then closed the door.

The woman in the wheelchair looked absentminded, staring into nothingness, seemingly unaware of their presence. Her skin was pale and wrinkled, as if the time spent in that horrible place had run at a different rate than outside, where the air was fresh, and the sun still shone in the sky. Her knees and shoulders poked through her gown like sticks; she couldn't've weighed more than 80 pounds.

"Mrs. Harrelson had a stroke twelve or thirteen years ago," the nurse explained, not at all concerned whether her patient heard. "She retains some cognitive abilities, but don't expect much. She's paralyzed on her left side and can't handle the most basic tasks without help."

Kay noticed Elliot's justifiable frown as he glared at the nurse. The woman in her care had lost every ounce of will to live when she'd lost her family, and deserved some consideration. It seemed like the yellow hallways of Glen Valley Commons hadn't seen an empathic, sensitive nurse in a very long time.

"Thank you," Kay replied, trying not to grind her teeth as she spoke, her curt voice betraying her anger. "We'll take it from here." She waited for the nurse to leave the room. For sure, the woman would've loved to listen in and get some juicy gossip on her patient; it wasn't every day that a nursing home tenant received visits from the police.

"I'm sorry," the nurse replied coldly. "I can't leave her alone with you. She could have medical needs—"

"And I'm a medical doctor," Kay replied. "We'll call you when we need you."

Her lips pursed and her chin thrust forward, the nurse left the room, closing the door behind her a little louder than she needed to.

As soon as the door slammed shut, Kay crouched by Shelley Harrelson's chair and touched her right hand. "Mrs. Harrelson?"

The woman's lost gaze focused on her for a brief moment, then her attention floated away.

"Mrs. Harrelson, I'm Detective Kay Sharp, and this is my colleague, Detective Elliot Young. We're here to talk to you about Rose."

As soon as she heard her daughter's name, Shelley's eyelids fluttered quickly, blinking a few times, then focused on Kay, meeting her gaze.

"What... about my daughter?" she asked. "Have you found her?" The woman grabbed Kay's hand with thin, trembling fingers in an unexpectedly strong grip.

Kay closed her eyes for a moment and filled her lungs with air, getting ready to deliver what could very well be a fatal blow to the woman. Should she just walk away instead? But it would be immensely worse if Shelley heard the news of her daughter's demise in the dimly lit hallways of that dreadful place, from people like that awful nurse.

When she looked at the lady again, a tear was rolling down the woman's prematurely aged face. Before Kay could reply, Shelley started speaking, her words faltering at first, choked by the sorrow that was to come.

"I know why you're here," Shelley said. As she spoke, she kept her eyes riveted on Kay's. "I dreamed of the day the cops would come to my door." She paused for a moment, lowering her gaze. "But not like that... not like you, afraid to say what you came here to say." She swallowed hard, struggling to speak. Her words were barely intelligible, her paralysis making it difficult for her to articulate.

"I'm so sorry," Kay whispered. "I can't begin to understand how it must feel. I just wish there was something I could—"

"This was the nightmare that kept me awake at night, every night after she was taken," Shelley whispered. "This, cops like you, telling me my baby's gone." Tears stained her gown, falling one after another from her closed eyes. "I'll join her soon, and we'll be together again."

"Mrs. Harrelson," Kay asked gently, "can you tell us what happened that night?"

The right side of the woman's mouth flickered into the beginning of a smile. "She used to have nightmares, my sweet little Rose. She kept saying monsters were banging on her window, trying to get in. She said she'd seen their faces, but she was only three years old—" Her voice trailed off, swallowed by sorrow. "We didn't believe her."

Kay and Elliot exchanged a quick glance. She wondered if that piece of information had any relevance. Had the little girl noticed anything out of the ordinary going on outside her window? Or had she been sleeping soundly, unaware her life was about to take a wrong turn?

"Maybe she was right. I should've listened to my baby. Now I'll never know," Shelley continued. Her voice was breaking up, her words spoken out slowly, loaded with pain. "Elroy thought it was just branches from the maples, hitting the windowpanes when it was windy. He took a chainsaw to them, I hung drapes, but we still checked on her at least twice during the night, to make sure she was all right." She stopped talking, and took her hand off Kay's and raised it to her throat, as if to loosen the knot tightening in there. "That night, when I went to check on her, she was gone. The window was open just an inch, like I'd left it; it was summer. The bug screen was in place, there were no holes in it, the wind moving the sheers a little." She paused for a beat, her head hung low. "That was everything I saw. It was as if she'd just vanished. Then… that cop accused Elroy and stopped looking for my baby."

Shelley raised her head, but her eyes were staring into emptiness again, through a vale of tears.

Kay stood, gently touching her shoulder. "Thank you, Mrs. Harrelson. If there's anything—"

"How did my baby die?" she asked, her voice barely a whisper.

Kay hesitated for a moment. "Quickly and painlessly, I promise you that." She crouched in front of Shelley's wheelchair, looking her straight in the eye. "And I promise you we'll catch your daughter's killer. We'll make him pay."

CHAPTER ELEVEN

Mistake

The drive back from Redding started with a prolonged, heavy silence in the car. Kay's knuckles were white, as she was gripping the steering wheel tightly and flooring it all the way. She kept her eyes on the road, but her mind was on Rose Harrelson's case file, and the notes she'd read in there. How was she taken? How did the kidnapper gain access to the child? Most of all, why didn't the original detective on the case answer that question first? Or was it that he couldn't come up with any answers, and took the easy way out and accused the girl's father?

She glanced at Elliot for a split second, registering the frown on his face, the tension in his jaws. Seemed like a whirl of thoughts kept his mind busy, but he wasn't willing to share.

Why was he so quiet as of late? Was he worried about his job? Had she said or done something to upset him? Sometimes she took over crime scenes, interactions, or interrogations, leaving her partners behind as she followed her own ideas, racing and forging ahead at the speed of her expertise as an FBI profiler. She was a loner, by all means, not much of a team player; she knew that. It was a turnoff to some people, especially young and ambitious detectives from Texas with seniority in the sheriff's office.

As if responding to her thoughts, a chime from Elliot's phone broke the silence.

"Huh," Elliot said, reading the message. "I'm being put on a new case." His voice was laced with undertones of surprise.

"What case?" she asked, processing the cues in Elliot's voice and body language. The regret she'd noticed was an unexpected note she needed time to understand. Why was he regretting the reassignment?

"A missing girl from Lane County, Oregon." His phone chimed again. "And Doc Whitmore released Rose Harrelson's identity." He scrolled through the message, before typing a reply. "Doc said the news crew was interviewing the sheriff next."

She barely contained a smile. "Ooh, and the boss really hates those," she commented, sarcasm heavy in her voice. "I'll swing by the office, for your car."

"Sure," he replied, seemingly absentminded, withdrawn.

"Tell me about the new case. Any connection with our murder investigation?"

"Not even a gnat's whisker." He looked briefly at the phone's screen, then slid it in his pocket. "It's the niece of one of Lane County's deputies, who ran away from home after some words with her stepdad. They found a witness who puts the girl on the highway getting into a truck with California tags."

"Ah, okay," she replied, before the gnawing thoughts about Rose Harrelson's abduction took hold of her mind and she fell silent. After a short while, she figured she might as well pick Elliot's brain, while she still had him handy. "How do you think she was taken?"

"Who? The girl from Lane County?"

For a moment, the question confused her. Wasn't the girl from Lane County a runaway? She shrugged it off. "No, Rose. The window was open just an inch, Shelley said, and the screen was in place, intact. How do you think the unsub took her?" She still used the FBI terminology; she found it simpler, easier, a mere five letters to replace the lengthy definition of an unknown subject, the unidentified perpetrator of a crime.

"There were no fingerprints, right?"

"N—no," she replied, hesitating a little as she wondered about the thoroughness of evidence collection. There was no report on file, just a note in the detective's handwriting, stating all the fingerprints lifted at the scene were accounted for. "I wonder—" she started to say, then stopped in her tracks. "It's been fourteen years, no way we could reopen the crime scene now. You've seen the state of the property."

"It must've been someone close to the family, someone who knew their way around the house." He checked the time on his phone, then frowned ever so slightly.

"What's wrong?"

He looked away for a moment. "I can't come to terms with the way the case was worked, that's all."

She chuckled. "No kidding."

"We'll have to go back and interview all those people Martha Duncan was telling us about. Elroy's work friends, the nanny Martha said had died, let's verify that." His frown returned, more visible this time. "*You'll* have to interview them, that is, while I chase down a fourteen-year-old runaway from Lane County, Oregon."

"Yeah," she replied, turning left and then pulling over in front of the sheriff's office. "I'll start over from square one, and I'll reopen the crime scene after all. Who knows what *we'll* find?"

He looked at her with an unspoken question in his glance.

"Something tells me you'll track your runaway in no time. Until then, I'll get started on the legwork. We have to figure out who took Rose Harrelson, and why. And where she was all this time."

They climbed the concrete steps that led to the main entrance. Heading into the building, they were about to go their separate ways. Elliot was looking to check in with the sheriff about the new case, and Kay to run another search in the system for the people who were identified at the time as being close to the Harrelson family. More than anything, she wanted to get the home address for the detective who had conducted the original investigation; it was time to pay him a visit. She couldn't wait to start pounding on him with questions, his appalling incompetence the reason why she'd been grinding her teeth all day. His inability to find Rose, and the mystery as to why he hadn't asked for help from the feds were the reasons why an entire family had been destroyed. He could've just as well hung Elroy with his own hands, and put Shelley where she was.

But none of that happened as planned. Sheriff Logan rushed to meet them in the bullpen the moment he saw them coming in.

"The phone's been ringing off the hook," he said, without any introduction. His voice was tinged with frustration, and his hands were clenched tightly together, not a familiar posture for the bold sheriff.

Several deputies were tending the phones, and the moment one set the receiver down, another call would come through.

"What's going on?" Kay asked.

"We got the girl's ID wrong, that's what's going on," he replied, huffing while running his hands through the gray hairs on his temples. "The moment we released the vic's identity as Rose Harrelson, the media picked it up and published it with her photos, one from back when she was taken, and the more recent one the ME had provided. Then everyone started calling in to laugh in our face and say we got it all wrong. That the vic is Alyssa Caldwell, none other than Bill Caldwell's daughter. With a profile like theirs, everyone's seen that kid's photo in the media or online. Some of them actually remembered what they saw in the tabloids, unlike any of us. Sheesh."

"Bill Caldwell, as in Caldwell Farms?" Kay asked, letting his bitter words go unanswered.

"Yeah, him," Logan replied. "How the heck did it happen? How did the ME screw it up so badly? Get over there and figure it out," he ordered, looking at her.

"That can't be possible," Elliot said. "The doc had DNA, he matched it from the original kidnapping file."

"You're working the missing girl for now," Logan said to Elliot, then turned to Kay. "Have you ever seen a situation like this? We look like idiots, and people are laughing at us. Just what we needed."

Kay didn't rush to answer. In her mind, she went quickly over the facts. There was DNA on file for Rose Harrelson. Doc Whitmore had taken a sample from the victim and run it against the sample in the file, and it was a match. A hundred-percent, no-room-for-error match, admissible in court, and considered forensically solid beyond any reasonable doubt.

Then, what could've been the explanation?

"I'm wondering… the DNA Dr. Whitmore had on file," she eventually said, "was it an actual tissue sample stored somewhere at medico-legal? Or was the result of the DNA test attached to the case file?"

Sheriff Logan stared at her as if wondering why she was asking him questions, instead of bringing him some answers.

"I'm thinking," Kay carried on, "maybe the DNA attached to Rose Harrelson's case file was from a different case, one involving Alyssa. Maybe the reports got mixed up somehow. Had Alyssa Caldwell ever been reported missing?"

The sheriff pressed his lips into a thin line, his patience visibly running dry. "You figure it out. You find out what the heck happened, and what we're going to tell the press when they stop laughing long enough to ask us what excuse we have for such ineptitude."

"You got it," she replied, then exchanged a quick glance with Elliot before turning to leave.

Until a few moments ago, she believed she knew who the victim was, and that single piece of knowledge was all she had in a kidnapping cold case. Fourteen years cold. Now, even that piece of evidence, Rose Harrelson's DNA, her identity, was disputed.

As she walked toward her desk, a troublesome thought took shape in her mind. What was it about Rose Harrelson's kidnapping that made all leads, all evidence, disappear like wisps of fog in the morning sun?

CHAPTER TWELVE
Undoing

Unlike Rose Harrelson, seventeen-year-old Alyssa Caldwell had a solid social media footprint, going back many years, since she was a preteen. Kay had no problem locating her accounts and sifting through years of photographic evidence of her identity. Alyssa, the only child of William Earnest Caldwell II, was featured prominently in local print news archives, going back to her birth date, a day celebrated by the Caldwell family with the usual flurry of messages, statements, interviews, and articles in the media.

After all, Caldwell Farms was the largest farming business in Franklin County.

Kay stared at a photo of baby Alyssa, held by her mother and with Bill Caldwell smiling by her side, their faces touching. She wasn't sure what she thought. Maybe, for one split second, she'd clung to the hope that the girl in the morgue was Rose Harrelson. Not because she wanted Rose to be dead, but because she needed a starting point in uncovering what had happened to the little girl all those years ago. That starting point, the thread that could've led Kay to her abductor, had vanished.

Because the girl lying on Doc Whitmore's morgue slab was Alyssa Caldwell. There was no doubt about it. Seventeen years of documented history, in print and online, stood as testimony to that fact.

That meant Rose Harrelson was still missing, absent since the day she'd been taken fourteen years ago, and she could still be alive.

The biggest question was how did Rose's DNA get mixed up with Alyssa's? What scenario could possibly account for that? Dr. Whitmore would probably be able to come up with some explanation; she was sure, even without speaking to him, that he was diligently investigating the DNA screwup by now, eager to uncover the truth and restore his unblemished professional reputation. Fourteen years ago, when Rose Harrelson was taken, Dr. Whitmore was the medical examiner for a different county, in San Francisco. Hence, he hadn't been the one to handle or attach Rose Harrelson's original DNA to her kidnapping case file. The Franklin County ME at the time had since passed away. Regardless, it was Dr. Whitmore's reputation at stake now, an undeserved blow to the dedicated professional who came out of retirement whenever his services were needed, helping the cash-stranded county make ends meet without keeping a full-time medical examiner on staff. The stigma of the DNA blunder would end his distinguished career under a cloud of shame so thick it would probably kill him.

But before she could visit with Dr. Whitmore, she had something else to do. She'd just delivered a next-of-kin notification to Shelley Harrelson, informing her that her daughter had been killed. That was no longer true, and that poor woman was mourning a death that could've not yet happened. Because, for all Kay knew, Rose could still be alive, out there somewhere.

Mumbling a long oath, she grabbed her keys and rushed out of the office, then drove off the parking lot raising swirls of dust.

The road to Redding seemed to fly by, mile after mile, while Kay's thoughts whirled, constructing scenario after scenario that could've accounted for Alyssa's DNA to have been filed in the system as Rose Harrelson's. When was Alyssa's DNA collected by the county medical examiner, and under which case number?

Had it been found at a crime scene, unidentified, and filed erroneously under Rose's name? A search into the database had not revealed any current or older cases involving the Caldwell daughter.

She'd tried ringing Dr. Whitmore, but it had gone straight to voicemail. She'd left him an encouraging message, pledging her support in unraveling what had happened to account for the mix-up, but he hadn't since returned her call.

It was almost completely dark by the time she arrived at Glen Valley Commons. The stench of the facility repulsed her just the same as that morning. Another déjà vu moment was the encounter with the receptionist, whose politeness had decreased another notch with the demise of the day.

"It's after five," she said coldly, barely looking at the badge she presented. "If you weren't a cop, you'd be asked to come back tomorrow, during visiting hours." She dialed a number, then spoke into the receiver, "It's that cop again, for Shelley. Uh-huh, I told her no one pays for overtime here." Then she hung up, and invited Kay to take a seat while she waited, with a stern gesture of her hand and a frown on her brow.

Kay didn't obey. The chairs aligned along the off-yellow walls were stained and worn to the thread.

"Detective," Kay heard the nurse's voice call. She turned and walked briskly in her direction. "Or should I call you doctor?" The woman's crooked grin was filled with disdain.

"Detective is fine," Kay replied, following her into the same room where they'd spoken with Shelley before. "Dr. Sharp, if you prefer." Then she stared her off until the woman left the room and closed the door behind her.

Shelley looked at Kay with inquisitive eyes, still red from the tears she had wept. Kay crouched in front of her wheelchair, like she'd done before, and took the woman's hand in hers.

"Mrs. Harrelson, I don't know how to tell you this—"

"Whatever it is, it must be serious, since you drove all the way back here," she whispered, her voice filled with tears. "I'm not afraid anymore, so go ahead, say it. I have nothing left to lose."

Filling her lungs with air and bracing herself, Kay chose her words carefully before letting them leave her lips. "I'm afraid we've made a terrible mistake, and I can only hope you can forgive me." She hesitated still, not sure how to best say what she was about to. "You see, the girl whose body we found at Blackwater River Falls was not your daughter."

"It wasn't my Rose?" she asked, her thinning eyebrows shooting up.

"No, it wasn't. For some reason, the DNA we had on file was wrong—"

"That means, my baby could still be alive?"

"Yes," Kay said, still holding Shelley's right hand. "Yes, that's exactly what it means. We have no new information regarding Rose; this has all been an unfortunate case of mistaken identity, for which I'm asking you to accept our most sincere apologies—"

The woman squeezed Kay's hand so tightly it seemed unbelievable, considering how frail she was. "Find her," she pleaded, her voice filled with tears and a shred of hope. "Find my baby, please. If anyone can find her, you can."

"I promise you I'll leave no stone unturned until I find out what happened to your daughter that night fourteen years ago, and maybe, if we're lucky to find her alive, we'll bring her back to you." She choked a little, seeing the woman's intense emotion and wondering if she wasn't giving Shelley false hope. But Rose could, in fact, still be alive out there somewhere, and she would find her. She would bring her home.

"Thank you, my dear," Shelley replied, tears streaming down her face while a timid smile stretched her lips. "Tell me, who was the girl you found murdered?"

Kay hesitated, wondering if she could disclose the information, being she hadn't notified Alyssa's next of kin yet. In that particular case, it seemed warranted she break the rule. "It's not yet been made public, but the girl was Alyssa Caldwell."

Blood drained from Shelley's cheeks, leaving them a cadaveric shade of gray. "Bill Caldwell's daughter?" she asked, her voice barely a whisper, her hands trembling.

"Yes, Alyssa was Bill Caldwell's daughter. Did you know him?"

Shelley pulled her hand from Kay's and took it to her chest. With frail, trembling fingers she grabbed the fabric of her gown and pulled hard, as if she was suffocating. She struggled to fill her lungs with air, then she let out a heart-wrenching sob.

"Oh, God… oh, God… all this time… my baby… no, please, no…"

Kay frowned, seeing the woman's mouth, previously agape in agony, turn crooked, while her left pupil dilated. "Did you know Bill Caldwell? Have you ever met him?" Kay asked, while taking out her flashlight and checking the reactivity of Shelley's pupils.

"No… no… my baby…" she cried, her voice fainter and fainter, her words less and less intelligible.

The flashlight lit her left eye, but her pupil didn't contract. Shelley Harrelson was having another stroke.

Rushing to the door and opening it wide, Kay called for the nurse, then ran back to Shelley's side and dialed emergency services for an ambulance. She stripped a blanket off the nearby bed and covered the woman in it, before rolling her to the main entrance.

"What's your ETA?" she asked into the phone, with the 911 operator on the other end of the line. "I need that ambulance stat, or this woman will die."

CHAPTER THIRTEEN

Touched

FIVE DAYS AGO

Sharp pain shot through her ankle. Kirsten lay still on her side, her right leg flexed at the knee so she could keep a cool, soothing hand on the swollen joint. She didn't count the minutes, nor did she worry about what was to come. She lay there, patiently waiting for the sharp pain to turn into dull throbs, slowly subsiding, while she kept her eyes on the crystal blue sky of the California morning.

There was nothing like the azure of the Golden State's clear sky, especially after rain had washed through. She'd only seen it on TV until that day, and had yearned to witness it with her own eyes one day. That day had finally come, and found her lying in a ditch with a swollen ankle and nowhere to go but straight ahead.

She wasn't going to stop now or turn back to serve as a naked blow platter for her stepdad and his homies. Even if it killed her, she'd move forward. She'd get herself to San Francisco somehow, then find a job, doing anything, no matter how menial, as long as it was honest work. She'd live with little and get herself on her own two feet before long.

Moving slowly, she brought herself up to her knees at first. Grabbing the side of the guardrail for support, she stood on her left foot, then tested putting some weight on the right. She clenched her teeth, a tense breath of air escaping with a loud hissing sound when she felt the pain traveling up her bones.

It felt better if she put most of the weight on her heel, and that sounded like a plan, at least for a while. Then, she'd catch another ride and she'd be able to rest her leg a little longer. Hazel's money had made sure she'd get to where she wanted to. Maybe one day she'd look her up and repay her kindness somehow.

She climbed over the guardrail slowly, careful not to fall again, the loose gravel at the side of the road treacherous and slippery. Then she leaned against the railing, holding her hand up in the air whenever a vehicle approached.

It was mid-afternoon when a car finally slowed down, stopped, then reversed toward her, probably when the driver had noticed her limping and realized it was going to take forever to wait. The car was luxurious, not a make she was familiar with, in a stunning gray-blue color that sparkled under the sun's dimming rays.

A twenty-dollar bill clenched in her sweaty palm, she peered inside the car through the open passenger side window. She was prepared to pay for her fare. Behind the wheel, a man dressed in a suit smiled kindly at her.

"Where are you headed?" he asked, his smile revealing two strings of perfectly white teeth.

"Um, San Francisco," she replied. "I can pay—"

"Nonsense. Hop in, let's get the weight off that foot."

Her suspicion flared. He was used to giving orders, and to people obeying; that was clear in the way he spoke. Could he have been a cop?

The thought sent shivers down her spine, as she saw herself arrested, then dragged back home, where nothing good awaited her. But no, that man wasn't a cop. No cop she knew of could afford that car, those clothes, or the fine scent that filled the space around him.

With a timid smile, she grabbed the door handle and opened it. "Thank you," she whispered, feeling choked for some reason. Not with fear, but with something close, intense, something between excitement and the instinct to run. But that was ridiculous. This man wasn't the eighteen-wheeler driver from the night before.

"What happened to that foot?" he asked, genuine interest and concern coloring his voice.

She smiled, glancing briefly at him then looking away. He was over forty, maybe even fifty, but that didn't seem to matter, not when she looked at him, not when he smiled at her. He was appealing, his elegant charm a powerful, numbing force, despite his age. She'd never felt that in a man, not ever. "I slipped on some loose gravel. I'll be fine."

"Okay." His smile widened. "If you say so."

"Are you, um, going to San Francisco?" she asked, unfamiliar with the kind of emotion that strangled her throat dry with an iron-gloved fist.

"Yes, I am." He kept his eyes on the road, barely looking at her, but she could hear the smile in his voice. "Thanks for keeping me company. These trips can get boring really fast."

She couldn't think of a single thing to say, so she stayed silent, hating herself for appearing dumb and mute at the same time. She kept her eyes riveted to the pristine carpeting lining the car's floor, and the contact it made with her mud-soiled sneakers. She feared he would be mad when he saw the mess... But maybe it didn't matter. What mattered was she'd soon get to San Francisco, where she could start her new life.

When she dared look around, she started noticing details about the man. His charcoal suit, appearing brand new. The shine on his shirt's collar and cuffs, just like satin. The monogrammed cufflinks. The polish of his black leather shoes, impeccable as if it never ever rained in his world.

"Listen," he said, shooting her a brief glance. "I was going to stop by the house anyway, to drop something off. Would you mind if we made a quick detour?"

Her heart skipped a beat. Terrified, she clasped her hands together, kneading them without realizing. Could she say no, and risk infuriating the man and losing her ride? It was soon going to be sundown, and that meant another night spent in the woods, in complete darkness, soaked to the bone by mist clinging to her clothes and chilling her to the core. But to go to this stranger's house? Every instinct in her body screamed against it, despite a streak of excitement prodding her to take the leap. She'd probably never meet anyone like him again.

Looking at her and clearly reading her like an open book, he added, "We could grab a quick bite to eat, and I'm sure you could borrow some dry clothes from my wife's closet. She won't mind, I promise."

She released a breath when she heard him mentioning his wife, but she still wasn't sure she could trust him. Being around her con-artist stepdad and his buddies had taught her never to believe a word anyone was saying. An angel from the heavens could stop by to help her, and she'd treat her with suspicion. That's what life had taught her so far, and she wasn't even fifteen yet.

"Um, I'm not sure," she mumbled, an apologetic whisper the best she could do.

He took the next exit, slowing down. Kirsten stiffened in her seat, her blood suddenly chilled. Was he taking her home with him anyway?

He stopped on the side of the road and turned the four-way flashers on.

"This is the road to my house, but if you say no, we'll head straight to San Francisco. I promised I'd take you there, and I'm a man of my word."

He looked straight at her, the kindness on his face seemingly genuine, his charm powerful, irresistible.

"Okay," she said, feeling unexpectedly relieved as the word was spoken.

"All right," he acknowledged, then drove off. "It's not far, only a few minutes."

With each mile they drove closer to his house, her tension grew, her instincts screamed. What would his wife think, when she saw him bringing a teenage girl home with him? She'd probably want to kill her where she stood. If she were the man's wife, she wouldn't take kindly to him bringing strays home—definitely not young, slender, teenage blonds.

When he finally pulled onto the driveway of a farmhouse, her heart was in her throat, its loud thump in her ears. He cut the engine, then came around the car and extended a hand to help her climb out without putting too much weight on her leg.

The touch of the man's skin was electric, sending shivers down her spine, swelling her chest at the same time it froze her blood. Speechless again, she followed him to the house.

Everything was dark; not a single window was lit. The porch light was off, and the security lights by the garage failed to engage as they approached. The house number, 1301, hung crookedly by the door, its brushed metal digits now rusted just as badly as the nails holding the wooden plaque in place.

He unlocked the door and turned on the lights without touching the wall switch, using something that made an almost inaudible beep.

The house was older and furnished with weathered pieces that looked as if they were pricey and posh at least thirty years ago. It was as if she'd entered a time capsule, not a shred of anything modern in sight. Even the TV was an antique, an old tube TV set covered in a fine layer of dust.

The kitchen was all white, and the dining set simple, in varnished oak. The entire space was decorated with country accents, plaids, ruffles, and hammered copper roosters, giving the house a homey feel despite the smell of stale air, a little musty and too chilly.

His wife was nowhere in sight. She would've probably adjusted the thermostat higher, bringing heat and drier air into the house. She would've probably dusted the old TV set or, most probably, told her man to get a new flat panel 60-inch TV instead.

But she wasn't there.

Unsure if she should be worried or relieved, Kirsten entered the house hesitantly and took a seat at the dining room table, on the chair the man held for her.

He took off his jacket, then proceeded to open the fridge and lay out food in front of her. He brought plates and cutlery, offering her deli meats and cheeses, while he warmed up a few dinner rolls he took out of the freezer in the vintage microwave.

"If you'd like a hot meal, I can—"

"Oh, no, thank you," she replied, feeling her cheeks kindle and turn red. "This is perfect."

She gobbled a few slices of cheese, taking advantage of his turned back to swallow quickly and take some more, before he could notice how hungry she really was. The warm rolls smelled amazing when he took them out of the microwave, and her mouth watered promptly.

He cut a dinner roll in half, then buttered both sides, depositing them on her plate. He smiled, the look of tenderness in his eyes intense and unsettling. She wasn't this man's kid, lover, sister, or wife. He was a complete stranger to her, but seemed to have forgotten that fact.

He layered a sliver of ham on one of the halved dinner rolls, then added a couple of slices of Swiss cheese and a squirt of mayo. It was delicious. She willed herself to behave like an educated adult, and chewed patiently with her mouth closed.

When she was finished, he cleared away everything, leaving the dishes in the sink. Then he went into one of the bedrooms and returned with a woman's shirt and some slacks.

"I believe these will fit," he said, offering them to her.

She took them from his hands and placed them against her body. Yes, they would fit well. His wife must've really known how to keep her slim figure. But there was something deeply unnerving about him, the clothes, the stale air in that house, everything at odds with his charm.

"Thank you," she said, fear coming across in her trembling voice more than she wanted it to. "When do we leave?"

"In a few minutes," he replied, without bothering to look at his watch. "It's only about three hours to San Francisco; we have time." He stood, gazing at her with a strange look in his eyes. "How would you like to take a shower before we leave? I can wait," he offered. "I can make us some coffee for the road."

Clothes in her clasped hands, she hesitated. The promise of a hot shower after last night's ordeal was inviting. She didn't know when she would get a chance to wash again, probably not for a while.

He took a seat at the table, turned sideways to watch her, as if telling her he had time and he would give her the space to take a shower in peace.

She opened the bathroom door. The light was already on inside. The same musty smell filled the chilly air. She rubbed her hands against her arms, to warm herself up.

"Oh, I'm so sorry," he reacted, then sprung to his feet and turned on the thermostat. Within seconds, the smell of burned dust filled her nostrils, carried on jets of warm air coming from the vents in the floor. "I didn't realize."

She smiled, embarrassed. "It's okay." She entered the bathroom, less and less inviting as she noticed its cracked tiles and green-stained, copper faucets, but knowing it would soon become appealing once the air warmed up and the musty smell went. When hot water poured down, washing away the cold in her bones.

She turned to close the door and froze when she found him standing there, an intense look in his eyes.

He caressed her long, blond hair with gentle fingers, running his fingertips along the length of a strand, feeling its texture. It sent shivers down her spine, icing her blood and unsettling her skin.

"Tell me, my dear," he asked, his voice a husky whisper. "Have you ever been touched?"

CHAPTER FOURTEEN
New Case

Mile after mile the road back to Mount Chester was a straight stretch of asphalt, the markings brightly reflecting her headlights, but Kay's mind was still back in the Glen Valley Commons room with Shelley when she had her stroke.

She went over the exchange in her mind again and again, the woman's reactions not making an ounce of sense. Nothing in Rose's disappearance made any sense, and now her mother's reaction to the fact that her daughter could still be alive had been overtaken completely by the news of Alyssa Caldwell's death.

Why did that matter to Shelley so much it triggered another stroke, this time a potentially fatal one? Who was Alyssa Caldwell to Shelley?

Kay recalled asking her if she knew Bill Caldwell; she'd actually asked her twice, and the answer had been *no* both times. Or had it? Perhaps Shelley hadn't answered *no* to her question; maybe her words had been a desperate plea that wasn't addressed to Kay; maybe to God, or to life itself. Whatever the truth was, Shelley had locked it deep inside her mind, and it would probably never be spoken of again.

When the emergency medical technicians had loaded her frail body into the ambulance, her vitals were so poor they didn't anticipate she could survive the drive to the hospital. Kay drove ahead of them with her flashers on, opening the way, and when they took Shelley into surgery, her heart was still beating. Barely.

Kay entrusted Shelley into the hands of the emergency team and took the attending's name and contact information to follow up later, despite the grim prognosis.

Then she headed back to Mount Chester, planning to pay Bill Caldwell a visit and officially notify him his daughter was dead, in the off-chance he wasn't already aware, considering the media blunder with Rose Harrelson's identity. The local media and TV stations had already released the victim's photo, albeit with Rose's name, and then the whirlwind of comments and questions triggered by the wrongful identification couldn't be stopped, despite an intervention from the sheriff and the local judge.

Impatient, she checked her GPS for an estimated time of arrival at the Caldwell residence, and swallowed her frustration. Then her thoughts went back to Shelley, and her weird reaction. She'd been genuinely thrilled to hear it wasn't her daughter who'd been killed. But it seemed as if there was something else going on, and Kay couldn't put her finger on what that was, regardless of how many times she played back their conversation in her head.

A phone call interrupted her thoughts. Recognizing the name on the display, her eyes widened but she smiled as she took the call.

"Greg, what an unexpected pleasure." Her smile lingered, wondering why her former supervisory agent at the FBI would call her a couple of months after she'd left.

"Likewise," he replied, sounding relaxed. "I should've called sooner. How are things in Mount Chester?"

"Um, rural," she replied laughing, "but there's no place like home. I miss the office, the team, but I'm happy to spend some time with my brother."

"That's good," he replied.

"And I'm working as a cop, if you can believe it," she added, a wide smile coloring her voice. "I'm a detective, and I'm about to take the lieutenant's exam."

"So, you're staying?" he asked, the cheerfulness in his voice gone.

She paused a beat and breathed. "For now," she eventually said. "Won't be forever, I promise. I'll come back."

"Okay, I'll hold you to that, so you know."

"It's a deal," she replied. "How's everyone? Tell them I miss them all."

"Stop by one day, Kay, don't be a stranger."

"Copy that, boss," she replied, calling him what she used to, knowing it would make him curl his lip before laughing again.

"Until then, I was wondering if you could do me a favor."

"Sure, just name it."

"We landed a case, something from your jurisdiction, Detective." He paused, and she heard the shuffling of papers on his desk. She could visualize him, speaking with her on hands-free while reviewing the case file nested in a manila folder. "It's a domestic abuse case."

"And why is it federal?" she asked. That almost never happened. In fact, she couldn't think of a time when they'd been involved in domestic violence cases, no matter how serious.

"It's because of who the allegedly abusive spouse is. A cop on your new team."

"What? Really? I can't think of anyone who—" She stopped mid-phrase, remembering that you never really know anyone, and even perceptive profilers as herself could be deceived into believing a lie, a carefully constructed façade. Especially if they weren't paying much attention.

"Yeah, exactly," SSA Strickland replied. He'd worked with her since the day she'd joined the regional bureau as a rookie, and had taught her how to think, how to keep herself from jumping to conclusions. "The wife claims she reported the abuse several times, only to have the report buried and her actions leaked back to her husband."

"That's terrible," Kay reacted, imagining how awful that must've been. "Is she—"

"She's still there, local, and she begged us to not go through the regular channels, because he would find out. Last time, he put her in the hospital with a broken cheekbone and four cracked ribs."

"I'll look into it," she said. "I'll need temporary reinstatement on the FBI systems. I won't be able to do my work on the office laptop, if that's the case."

"Consider it done. Her name is Nicole Scott, and she's married to a Deputy Herbert Scott."

"I know him." Everyone called him Herb. He had a streak of cruelty about him, something she'd seen manifested in rougher-than-necessary arrests and brutal interrogations, but nothing so extreme to justify action on her part. She'd assumed the sheriff might've spoken with him about the issue, but now she found herself doubting that assumption. Herb loved to hang out and drink with the other cops at the local bar, and pushed iron obsessively when he had a chance, his almost cartoonish biceps a testimony to that fact. "Yeah, he fits the part."

"Report to me only, and don't talk to anyone on your new team. Let's keep this as quiet as possible. I don't believe Nicole can survive another one of her husband's rage fits."

She didn't say anything, while sketching a plan of attack. "These things can get dicey," she eventually said. "I'll let you know if I need anything."

He wished her good luck and then hung up, leaving silence to reign over her space, to bring back the unwanted ghosts of her past. Her late father, drunk and out of his mind, pounding on her mother. Screams of pain tearing through the tension-filled air in their home. Her own powerlessness watching that happen day after day. Her heart breaking when she cleaned her mom's wounds, wondering why no one was helping them. Someone must've heard her mother's cries, her father's bellowing, the blows and the oaths and the sobs.

She wiped a tear off her cheek with the back of her hand. Maybe no one had helped her mother, but Nicole Scott wasn't alone anymore. History would not repeat itself, and Herb Scott would soon pay dearly for every bruise and every cracked rib.

She wished she could've had Elliot with her, to share as much of what she was feeling as she dared, but he wasn't there, and she suddenly realized she'd been missing him. She frowned as the thought passed through her mind; he was her partner, nothing else. Emotions didn't belong. But still, she would've appreciated his input on the new case, feeling tempted to bend a little of Greg's order of absolute confidentiality. That's how much she trusted Elliot; she'd bet her career on the honest kindness of his big, Texan heart.

Exiting the highway, Kay headed toward Caldwell Farms. The property gates were near the highway, right off the service road, but she kept her eyes on the GPS, making sure she didn't take the wrong turn and further delay her arrival. She wanted the death notification to be over and done with, so she could ask Caldwell the question that remained at the forefront of her mind. Why did Shelley have a stroke when she heard about Alyssa's death? When she believed her own daughter, Rose, was the victim, she was heartbroken, but she didn't have that extreme reaction. Maybe it was nothing... Maybe the cumulative effect of the recent stress and devastating news had built up and caused the attack.

She turned onto Caldwell's wide, well-lit driveway, still immersed in thoughts, completely unaware that an SUV that had been on her tail since she'd left Redding Hospital had pulled over to the side of the road, behind some bushes, killing the lights.

The SUV's window lowered silently, and the man behind the wheel lit up a cigarette, cupping the lighter's flame in his hand. He inhaled deeply and held it in for a moment. Then he exhaled, muttering in a cloud of smoke, "Not good. Not fucking good at all."

CHAPTER FIFTEEN
Father

The Caldwell residence was larger than she'd anticipated. A new wing had been added to the original house, at a 90-degree angle and in a matching style and design, the resulting structure harmonious yet visibly serving two different purposes. The Craftsman house welcomed her with yellowish porch lighting and sconces, and second-level, warm-colored siding that contrasted nicely with the dark shingled roof. On the wide front porch, chandeliers cast a glow above the patio table and the lounge area. The right section had fewer accoutrements, appearing colder, less hospitable.

The Caldwells owned the largest farm in the county, one of the largest in the entire state. She'd read a brief history of their business before leaving her vehicle; it had been in the family for three generations, but only the last generation had grown the business to its current size. The first William Caldwell, Bill's father, had acquired more and more land as his business grew, having the ambition to build the farm he had inherited into what it was when he passed, last April.

Kay chose to walk to the nearest entrance and rang the bell. Within seconds, a middle-aged woman dressed in a crisply starched uniform opened the door, giving Kay's badge a disapproving and suspicious glower.

"All business calls have to use that entrance," she said coldly, pointing a stern finger at the other section of the house.

"This is not a business call," she replied. "I need to speak with Mr. Caldwell immediately." She paused, expecting the woman to comply, but she was measuring her insolently from head to toe, as if to prove her worthiness before announcing the unwelcome cop to her employers. "That is, if it's all right with you," Kay added, her voice dipped in sarcasm.

"Do you have an appointment?" she asked, without batting an eyelash.

Kay started to raise her hands in exasperation, then let them drop. "This is an urgent police matter. Would you prefer I return in about ten minutes with a dozen deputies and warrants to cover everyone and everything in this house?"

The woman hesitated, her arrogance tickled the wrong way. Then she stepped out of the doorway, inviting Kay in without a word or any other gesture but a stiff upper lip. She closed the door behind her, before inviting Kay, in an ice-cold tone of voice, to follow her.

The housekeeper led the way upstairs, their footsteps swallowed by the thick, wall-to-wall, burgundy carpeting. Kay noticed the fixtures, speaking of the family's generational achievements. Faded portraits hung on the walls in the main living room, some as old as a hundred years, judging by hairstyles and attire.

Once upstairs, the woman knocked twice on a door, opening it and announcing Kay.

"I have a detective here, demanding to see you. She says it's urgent."

Caldwell must've nodded or silently expressed his approval, because the housekeeper allowed Kay to step inside and then closed the door quietly as soon as she did.

Kay found herself in a large office, lushly decorated in classic furniture, with a massive desk by the window, and bookcases lining the walls. Bill Caldwell was seated behind the mahogany table, his white shirt unbuttoned, his tie loosened, and his sleeves rolled up. He held a few sheets of paper covered in a fine print in one hand, fanned out as if he were looking for something in those pages. When she approached, he set them on the desk's shiny surface and stood, a gesture of courtesy.

An elderly woman sat on a chair in front of the desk, her thin legs crossed at the ankles, her expression one of annoyance with the interruption. Yet she was classy enough to display a faint smile, half-turned toward Kay. She wore a black turtleneck with three strings of pearls, and pearl earrings to match. Black slacks completed her attire, and black, kitten-heeled shoes, one tapping nervously against the oriental rug.

"Yes, Detective," Bill said, standing with his hands propped on his hips. "What can I do for you? As you can see, I'm in the middle of something."

"Is your wife available to join us for this conversation, Mr. Caldwell?" she asked.

Caldwell frowned and put his palms on the desk, leaning forward into them. "My wife hasn't been available in years. She's got MS." He paused for a moment, locking eyes with the woman on the other side of the desk. "Terminal."

"Oh, I'm sorry to hear that—"

"On with it already," the elderly woman invited her with an impatient hand gesture.

"And who are you, if I may ask?"

The woman scoffed and shook her head in disbelief.

"This is my mother, Carole Burgess Caldwell," Bill specified. "Whatever you have to say can be said in her presence."

Kay took a deep breath, settling her nerves before broaching the emotional subject. She'd expected to find the family grieving Alyssa's loss, she'd expected to hear from the mayor, the governor, or someone else in a position of power about her blunder in delivering the next-of-kin notification before the identity of the victim had been released to the media. She'd expected anything else but this, to be interrupting a routine business meeting between mother and son.

"It's about your daughter, Alyssa," Kay said, watching their reactions. The two Caldwells showed no emotion. "When's the last time you saw her?"

The two Caldwells looked briefly at each other. "Yesterday morning," Bill replied, the uncertainty in his voice unmistakable. "Last night I came home late," he added, quickly running his hand against the tip of his nose, as if it was itching, a dead giveaway of a lie. "I didn't want to wake her."

"And this morning?"

"I was traveling last night, and I slept in; I just woke up an hour ago. I didn't think much when she didn't join me for lunch." This time, there were no other signs of deception that she could notice. But what was he regretting? That he didn't check on Alyssa when he came in? His demeanor was open, relaxed, not what she'd expect to see from a man concealing any kind of involvement in the death of his daughter.

She inhaled, steeling herself for what was to come, ready to notice any unusual behavior. "I'm afraid I have bad news. Your daughter was killed yesterday."

The blood left Bill Caldwell's face a sickening gray as he let himself drop into his chair. No one could fake that. Whatever he was hiding, it had nothing to do with Alyssa. Maybe it had something to do with his mother being in the room.

"Oh, God, no," Carole Caldwell whispered, sobbing, hiding her face in her hands. Her shoulders heaved, but she controlled herself, weeping silently.

"How certain are you?" Bill asked, standing so forcefully he pushed the chair back. It rolled until it hit the wall and bounced back a few inches. "I want to see her." He clenched his fists. "I want to see my daughter."

"We're fairly certain," Kay replied cautiously, ignoring his demand. "There has been an issue with the identification, as you might have seen on TV."

"We haven't seen anything," Bill replied, grinding his teeth. It seemed that controlling his grief was taxing for the devastated parent. "What are you talking about?"

Kay hesitated, knowing she was about to make things worse for the Caldwells. "The victim was originally identified based on DNA found on a missing person case file dating fourteen years ago. Seems there has been some confusion. Maybe the DNA sample had been filed in error under a different name." She paused for a beat, seeing Bill slack-jawed, his brow furrowed, and his eyes focused somewhere behind her, as he was trying to comprehend what she'd said. "Has Alyssa ever been reported missing?"

"No," he whispered.

"Was there any reason why the police would have her DNA on file?" she asked, realizing she'd been holding her breath. His answers might hold the key to Rose Harrelson's disappearance.

"Um, no," he replied, seemingly lost in his grief-ridden thoughts. "My sister did one of those ancestry profiles for her, and sent her DNA out, but I'm not sure how—"

"What name had she been identified as before?" Mrs. Caldwell asked, pressing her eyes and nose gently with a tissue. Outside of those red, swollen eyes still glistening, there was no trace of the earlier breakdown. She tapped her hair carefully with her hands, to make sure every strand was in place, then arranged her clothing as if she was getting ready for a photoshoot in some magazine. The woman was made of steel, but the heartbreak Kay had witnessed before was real.

"Rose Harrelson," Kay replied, then held back her questioning, seeing how Carole shot Bill a strange glance, lingering and inquisitive.

Bill avoided his mother's scrutiny and touched the blinking voicemail light on his desk phone. "The housekeeper told me the phones were ringing all morning," he whispered, "That's why. The house staff must've known… All these people knew… *Everyone* knew my daughter was dead, except me." He closed his eyes and breathed, visibly struggling to keep his composure. "Can I see a photo?"

Kay's eyebrows shot up. "Of Alyssa? Of, um, her body?"

"Yes," he replied angrily. "After you people fucked up so badly, don't you think I have the right to see for myself?"

Her lips, pressed into a tight line, kept her reaction in check, because the Caldwells weren't to blame for the mix-up. Law enforcement was responsible; she was the face of law enforcement in the Caldwell residence at the moment, and she was going to own the mistake and take whatever they decided to dish out. After all, they were grief-stricken parent and grandparent, with every right to be angry and ask questions.

She took out her phone and flipped through some of the crime scene photos until she found one that didn't show the gaping slash across Alyssa's throat. "Mr. Caldwell, is this your daughter?" she asked, as she showed Bill the phone.

He broke down in tears, his face flushed a dark red. "Oh, no, my beautiful little girl," he whimpered, then covered his mouth with his hands as if to hold the sobs in.

Without a word, his mother pushed the box of tissues his way across the lacquered surface of the desk.

"How did she die?" Mrs. Caldwell asked. Her eyes had dried, and a brief glance at her revealed nothing of her agony.

"Quickly and painlessly, I can assure you," Kay replied in a gentle voice.

The woman patted dry a rebel tear welling at the corner of her eyes. "You must think me a sissy, Detective, but I was asking for specifics. Was she shot? Stabbed?"

Kay couldn't believe the woman's callousness. While her son struggled to contain his grief, she showed no trace of empathy. She hadn't hugged him, like people usually do when devastating news is delivered to family members; it's human instinct to cling to others when hard times strike.

Mrs. Caldwell didn't share that instinct, and neither did her son. Both had remained on their respective sides of the massive mahogany desk, worlds apart instead of united by the grief they shared.

"The official cause of death was exsanguination due to severed carotids," she replied, looking at Bill, wondering how he was taking his mother's cold and factual approach to his daughter's demise.

Mrs. Caldwell still kept her eyes riveted on her, expecting more.

"Her throat was slashed," she added, then exhaled, turning her attention to Bill. "If you can, Mr. Caldwell, we need you to come by the coroner's office tomorrow morning, to formally identify the body."

Bill opened his eyes and nodded. "Do you have any suspects?" His low, contained voice was menacing, loaded with anger like a barrel of gunpowder ready to blow up at the tiniest spark.

Kay shifted her weight from one leg to the other, uncomfortable with the answer she was about to offer. "We're investigating," she replied, her tone calm and professional, reassuring. "Her body was found yesterday, and we haven't had much time—"

"Because you screwed up her identity, didn't you?" he snapped. "You wasted time, while Alyssa's killer is walking free. Do you at least have any leads?"

"N—no, none at this time," she replied, instantly regretting she hadn't informed him that the police aren't at liberty to discuss the details of an ongoing investigation.

He circled the desk, stopping a couple of feet in front of her. It took all her willpower to not take a step back, knowing people like the Caldwells read meaning in every gesture, and all their interpretations were about power and weakness, status and confidence, and opportunity to apply pressure and get their way. "Then let me point you in the right direction," he said, dark, menacing undertones coloring his voice.

His mother sprung to her feet and grabbed his arm. "William Earnest Caldwell, you are out of line."

Bill ignored his mother, keeping his eyes riveted on Kay. "Why don't you start with my sister?" he asked nonchalantly, the shift in his voice as unexpected as his words. "Then continue with Mother here, who can explain my sister's and her no-good, bastard son's motive. They'll keep you entertained until I return."

CHAPTER SIXTEEN

Trapped

Five Days Ago

Kirsten's breath caught, but she somehow managed to smile and close the bathroom door. Perhaps she'd read him wrong. She didn't get the creep vibe in his presence; well, maybe just a little, because he seemed so genuinely interested in her well-being.

But had the man really done anything wrong? His words still resounded in her mind. *Have you ever been touched?* His weird question might've been about something else, his concern whether she'd been assaulted, maybe? She closed her eyes, replaying the moment again in her mind, while her instinct told her to run out of there screaming.

She wanted him to be a kind, charismatic man who'd taken a real interest in her, someone she could trust. She really wanted that to be the case, but, if living with her stepfather and his buddies had taught her anything, it was that the world was full of creeps, and that her instincts never lied.

She held her breath and pasted her ear against the door, listening intently. She didn't hear a sound, not even the slightest murmur, as if she were alone in the entire house. Somewhat relieved, she started looking around for a way out.

There was a side-sliding frosted window above the tub, large enough to fit her slim body through it. The farmhouse wasn't far from the highway. In ten, fifteen minutes of running straight across the fields, she'd be safe.

She turned the sink faucet to let the water run. The sound of that would put the man's mind at ease and cover any noises she might make. Then, thinking the running water wasn't loud enough, she flushed the toilet, and climbed into the tub. Stretching a little, she was able to reach the window's lock and push it open. Then, grabbing the edges, she pulled the sash to the left, opening it as wide as it would go.

She didn't see the security bars at first. It was almost totally dark outside, and the half-inch wrought iron was camouflaged against the night sky. Ignoring the burn of tears, she grabbed the bars with both hands, pushing outward as hard as she could, whimpering from the effort.

They didn't budge.

There was no way out.

Out of breath, she slid the sash shut and locked it, leaving it just the way she found it. Then she sat on the side of the tub for a while, lost in a nightmare she couldn't awaken from.

She weighed her options, trying to figure out what to do. Was that man really going to harm her? Or was he going to do what he'd said, take her to San Francisco? Still shivering, she decided a shower was the best option, although she felt vulnerable taking her clothes off, even with the locked door between them. Who was to say he wouldn't break down that door any moment?

She let her clothes fall to the floor, then climbed into the tub and turned on the shower, adjusting the water to the hottest temperature she could bear. Even so, she couldn't stop shaking, as if fear had struck an alliance with the cold rain from the night before, conquering her body, and deciding never to leave.

She shampooed her hair, taking extra care to keep the foam from getting into her eyes so she could keep them wide open. What if he was a little weird, a little creepy, but a nice guy?

Someone who was turned on by her youth and wanted to spend some time with her? Maybe cheat on his wife with her? Even that, she'd understand. A tiny smile tugged at the corner of her mouth, then quickly withered, turning into a grimace of fear. He was good-looking, rich, powerful, and behaved impeccably well, like she'd only seen in movies, but things rarely worked out that way, and she'd learned appearances could be deceiving. She'd be better off miles away from the man; despite his reassuring appearance, her gut was sending her all sort of signals, seeding panic into her weary mind.

Good-looking or not, he was a creep.

Regretting she had to leave the relative comfort of the shower, she turned off the water and stepped out of the tub. She dried herself thoroughly with a clean towel she'd found arranged in a tight roll in the open cabinet under the sink, then looked around and found a dryer at the bottom of a drawer. Plugging it in, she dried her hair thoroughly. A furtive thought of the man's wife made her put everything back just the way it was, the herb-infused shampoo that smelled of lilac, the dryer, the towel, even if it was damp.

She put on the clean clothes the man had offered, noticing again how well they fit, and wondered what kind of woman was able to maintain such a thin figure despite her years. She could've been in her forties, considering his age.

That's when everything went dark.

She froze in place for a while, a silent scream stuck in her constricted throat, and listened. She backed carefully from the door until she reached the wall, feeling her way with her hands, afraid she might trip and fall. Then she waited until her eyes adjusted to the darkness enough to fuel her courage to explore the deathly silent house.

She felt her way to the bathroom door and found the knob, then turned it slowly, afraid it would squeak and give her away. Opening the door as gently as she could, she forced her eyes to see in the pitch darkness. She couldn't distinguish anything, the only exception being the living room window that let the faintest of shadows in, whatever moonlight made it through the foliage of the trees behind the house.

She moved toward the window, feeling her way along the walls, wherever she could. Every few steps she stopped, leaning against the wall, listening, forcing herself to see. Where was he? She took one more step, feeling the edge of an area rug under her toes, and remembering she'd seen that rug, she'd felt it under her feet before, while she was seated at the table, eating.

She reached forward with both her hands, feeling the air for the edge of a chair, something she could grab. She found it, turned away from the table, just as he'd left it when he'd sat there, watching her getting ready to enter the bathroom. The chair was empty.

Where was he?

Feeling her throat parched, she swallowed hard, and whispered, "Are you here?" She listened, but no one replied. "Where are you?" she asked again, a little louder this time. "Are you here?"

Silence raged in her mind, the sound of it louder and louder, fueled by the frantic beats of her heart. She moved away from the dining room chair, toward the picture window facing the woods, dimly lit by the setting moon. Soon, even that tiny shred of light would be gone, once the thin crescent disappeared behind the horizon. Not knowing if he was still in the house with her made the hairs on the back of her neck rise, playing tricks with her fear-tinged imagination.

She needed to get out of there.

Moving a little faster, she felt her way to the main door. She remembered seeing a light switch on that wall. She found it and flipped it on, but nothing happened. Whimpering, she recalled how he'd seemed to turn all the lights on without touching the wall.

Then she felt the door on both sides, looking for a handle, a knob, or something she could use to get it to open, and found nothing. Under her frantic fingertips, all she could feel was the spot where the handle had been, a barely detectable indentation where the lock's tumbler had fitted, now covered with some sort of putty and painted over. Whatever held that door closed wasn't in her power to control.

But there was a window she could break.

Feeling her way across the room, she reached the window and felt along the edges of the large glass pane, looking for fixtures to get it open. There were none. Quick on her feet, she grabbed the dining room chair and, after balancing it in the air for momentum, she threw it against the window with all her strength. It bounced right back, landing on the floor with a rattling noise.

The window was intact, not even a scratch on it.

Feeling renewed fear tickling the roots of her hair, she put her face against the pane and looked outside, hoping she could see someone, anyone who could help. There was no one. Only darkness-engulfed forest, as far as she could see, stretching on both sides, barely lit by the setting moon, its crescent touching the upper branches of the oaks and maples and poplars.

A coyote appeared from the woods, sniffing around, looking for some grub. It stopped a few yards away from the window, scratched behind the ear, then started howling, its neck extended toward the sky, its mouth open, its eyes almost entirely closed.

Panic made the bile in her throat rise when she realized she couldn't hear a sound. Frantic, she banged against the windowpane as loudly as she could, but the coyote continued its midnight concert unperturbed.

No one could hear her.

She was trapped.

CHAPTER SEVENTEEN
Grandmother

"William Earnest Caldwell," his mother shouted, "come back here this instant!" The woman stood and stomped her foot against the floor, visibly frustrated with her inability to control her son. The thick oriental rug swallowed the noise almost entirely.

Carole Caldwell's composure was completely gone for a few moments, the classy smile and relaxed forehead replaced by a bitter expression that revealed her true nature, a woman used to having her orders obeyed without delay.

The door slamming behind Bill as he left the room was the only answer she received. She stared intently at it with fiery eyes, as if she could somehow reach her son with her mind and hold him in place.

Kay had no idea what Bill Caldwell was planning to do. She waited patiently, watching the events unfold, knowing that Carole would be thrilled if her son changed his mind and came back. To Kay's surprise, when Carole turned her attention away from the door and looked at her, she was smiling politely, not a line on her forehead, not a trace of the exasperation she'd just exhibited.

"Come, Detective, please take a seat," she gestured to the seat across from hers.

Kay obliged with a smile and a quick nod.

"Has anyone bothered to offer you something to drink? Water, coffee?"

A flicker of a frown touched Kay's forehead, the change in Carole's attitude toward her a red flag waving high up in the air. "No, thank you, I'm good."

Carole looked past her for a moment, as if her thoughts escaped her control. A cloud of sadness touched her face, at odds with the detailed makeup and perfect hairdo.

"Such a terrible tragedy," she said, her voice low, subdued by grief. "I can't begin to understand how someone so young, so innocent, could end up killed." She put her hand on her chest. "My son is out of his mind with sorrow; please forgive him. I'm sure you understand."

Kay waited to see if she was going to add anything else, but Carole had finished what she wanted to say. "I completely understand," she replied. "Please accept my condolences."

The woman nodded with a perfectly appropriate smile; the right amount of sadness conveyed in her demeanor. Kay found herself wondering if she was going to sob her eyes out later, in the privacy of her own room, or if she was going to go about her business, planning the funeral, making arrangements, pushing everyone around.

Checking the time discreetly, Kay wondered how much longer Bill was going to take, and if what he had gone to collect was really that relevant to the case. He'd urged her to wait, and she wasn't going anywhere until he returned. Her eyes veered to the walls, where several framed photos of buildings and people adorned the satin wallpaper in silver with fine gold accents.

Carole followed her gaze and was quick to provide some insight.

"That photo was taken almost a hundred years ago, when my father established the mill," she said. "Oh, he was so proud that day… You can imagine." She leaned forward, as if to share a precious secret with Kay. "Our family had always been strategic about marriages. When I married my husband, I brought the farm, and my dear husband, may God rest his soul, brought the forest business." Pride lit her eyes. "Then we had children, four of them."

Kay leaned back into her seat, eager to hear more.

"Bill, whom you just met, is my oldest. He runs the working forest, the timber business, and the paper mill. His sister, Blanche, runs the actual farms." Her smile widened; talking about Bill and Blanche had lifted the cloud of sadness off her features. She was in her element talking about the family business, her lifelong achievement. "Then Madelyn, my younger daughter—"

"Oh, my goodness, I just realized," Kay interrupted. "Madelyn Caldwell, the movie star, is that your daughter?"

Carole nodded with a forced smile. "Yes, she chose Hollywood over the family business," she replied, her voice touched by disappointment. "Well, as long as she's happy with her life as an actress, what else can a mother ask for? We rarely see her… All the time she's filming some place or another." She picked up the cut crystal glass of water from the silver tray on the desk, barely dampened her lips, then set it carefully back. "Finally, Kendall, the youngest, he's another failure. I should've stopped having children after Blanche." This time, bitterness colored her voice, unchecked, acute.

"What does Kendall do?" Kay asked, treading carefully.

"As close to nothing as possible," Carole replied with a long sigh. "He took what little money was left to him by his father after his death, and put it in some hedge funds, deciding to live off capital gains instead of building something with his own hands, instead of making a difference." She clenched her fists in her lap. "A meaningless existence, parasitical and hedonistic." She paused for a beat, but Kay didn't interrupt, curious where all that was going. "Although he's smart, in his own way," she added, unclenching her hands and folding them in her lap. "He's brilliant."

Kay continued to listen, encouraging the woman to keep going. "Interesting. What makes you say that?"

"He spends as little as possible, because his one true passion is his own laziness. This boy has made an art out of doing as little as possible. But he loves luxury, my youngest son, and to get that without spending, he preys on unsuspecting rich women who let their guard down, knowing he's also well off. Brilliant." Her bitter voice trailed away, as if bearing the load of disappointment had taken the breath out of her chest.

"I see," Kay said, wondering if Carole had finished sharing the story of her family. She had dozens of questions she wanted to ask, about Alyssa's social life, her friends, her daily routine. About Shelley, and if she had known Bill Caldwell.

"These two, Madelyn and Kendall, had absolutely no reason to get rid of the heiress," Carole said, her voice stern and purposeful. "Bill will tell you that Blanche and her son, Dylan, had all the reasons, but don't believe a word a grief-stricken father will say. He's wrong." She'd raised her voice somewhat, pleading with Kay to believe her, the entire story she'd shared about the family nothing more than a calculated preamble. "My Blanche wouldn't hurt a fly," she continued, the shine of tears in her eyes. "She wouldn't do anything to harm Bill or his family. She... loves her brother very much."

CHAPTER EIGHTEEN
Aunt

Heiress? What heiress? Kay wondered, looking at Carole's display, her perfectly calculated cocktail of grief and persuasion. The Caldwells owned a farm, the biggest one in the county all right, but still, just a farm. Not a megacorporation or a billion-dollar venture. Heiress, to a farm? Huh. She wondered what Elliot would think about that.

And still, Carole behaved with the sophisticated elegance of someone who had been born rich and had been rich all her life. She had been educated to contain her emotions and not say a single word that didn't have a purpose. The change in her attitude toward Kay showed she had something to fear, something she was desperately trying to manage. A threat of sorts, perhaps a secret she was trying to protect. Carole was clearly hiding something of crucial importance, enough to keep her riveted across from Kay, her legs crossed at the ankles and her hands folded neatly in her lap, the only sign of the tension she was feeling showing in the tightness of her jaw and the steely fire in her eyes.

Yet she'd been caught off guard by the news of Alyssa's death; she'd had no prior knowledge of it. As soon as she'd managed to contain her initial emotional response to that, her interest in catching her granddaughter's killer had dropped to zero. Maybe she was afraid that the killer was someone close to her, someone she was trying to protect, even if that meant protecting a murderer.

It was time to find out how much the Caldwell farming business was really worth. Typical farmers don't refer to their offspring as heirs or heiresses. Was Carole living a delusion of grandeur, in her mind being the queen of the land, or was her arrogance founded on financial reality? Had the generational farming enterprise been extremely lucrative? Even so, what was Carole hiding, and why did she seem terrified of what her son had set out to do?

"Tell me about Alyssa," Kay asked, deciding not to probe into her apparent fear of her son's actions. She leaned forward, her elbows on the chair armrests, and kept her voice soothing and calm, determined to pace herself through the dozens of questions she had.

Carole patted the corner of her eye with the crumpled tissue she held in her hand. "She was a sweet child, even as a teenager," she said, her voice tinged with genuine sadness. "She grew up with a sick mother, as you already know, and we all tried to compensate for that. I, my oldest daughter Blanche, even the house staff spoiled her rotten, but she didn't grow up entitled or with the nasty attitude some of the kids these days have."

She stood and started pacing the room slowly, studying the walls as if she'd never seen them before, keeping her face effectively hidden from Kay's scrutiny. The old woman was smart.

"I honestly don't know why Bill didn't divorce and remarry," she added, keeping her back turned to the detective. Her voice had hardened, disappointment seeping with every word. She turned and looked at Kay for a brief moment, then gazed away. "You must think me callous, but Alyssa's mother, well, she's been sick all her life. What kind of marriage is that, for my poor Bill? He would've been better off divorcing her and finding a woman who could make him happy. A strong, healthy woman who could've given him sons."

Slack-jawed, Kay was speechless, grateful Carole was looking away, unable to see the consternation on her face. She shook it off quickly. "I believe it's admirable, his loyalty to his sick wife, to his child's mother."

"Yes, you'd believe that, wouldn't you," she replied coldly. Then she must've realized she was pushing it too far, because she smiled and apologized. "I'm just thinking about my son, that's all. He lost his daughter, and soon he'll lose his wife too. Any mother would be concerned."

"Who was Alyssa closest to in the family?" Kay asked. "Who was her best friend here?"

Carole walked to the window and looked outside, at the rolling fields in gold and light brown, stubbly and coarse where the harvesters had passed. "I'd have to say Blanche, Bill's sister, although many times I caught Alyssa chatting with the help. Our domestics are not here to be anyone's friends; I'm sure you must agree."

"Of course," Kay replied, unable to hide the sarcasm in her voice, but that flew undetected by Carole, lost in her aloofness and whatever anxious thoughts that kept her on her feet, pacing restlessly. "Oh, I meant to ask, do you know a Shelley Harrelson?"

A beat of taut silence, while Kay stared intently at Carole's back. Tension brought her shoulders up just a hint. "Who?"

The door swung open, and Bill stormed inside, dragging a slender, middle-aged, blond woman by her arm. She wasn't resisting him; she was letting herself be hauled around, her expression resigned, exuding sadness. Her hair had partially escaped the bun at the back of her head, and loose strands covered her face. When she noticed Kay, she froze in place, flush with embarrassment.

Kay had seen Bill only a few moments earlier, but now she barely recognized him. He was disheveled, his hair tousled as if he'd been trying to pull it out, his shirt covered in sweat and missing a couple of buttons. His eyes were maniacal, his rage all-consuming, filling the air inside the room with a kind of static charge.

Springing to her feet, Kay took two steps toward Bill, concerned for the safety of all those present. She'd seen it happen, when people destroyed by the grief of losing a loved one took to violence, giving into moments of insanity fueled by unbearable pain.

"Here, meet my *beloved* sister, Blanche," Bill shouted, letting go of the woman's arm and looking straight at Kay. Blanche faltered a little, but then stood tall, holding her head up high, although her eyes were filled with an unspeakable sorrow. She wrapped her red cardigan around her body, then crossed her arms at her chest. "Tell her what you told us," Bill commanded.

Kay stared at him for a brief moment, surprised.

"Come on," Bill insisted, raising his voice, "tell her she's a murderer."

The woman's pupils dilated as she looked straight into Kay's eyes. "What…"

Kay cleared her throat silently, then said, "I'm afraid I brought some bad news to the family today. Alyssa Caldwell has been murdered."

She gasped, her hands quick to cover her open mouth. "What happened?" she managed to articulate, her voice strangled, the knot in her throat seemingly painful enough to make her swallow hard a couple of times.

"You should have the nerve to ask," Bill snapped, his eyes shooting fiery arrows at his sister. "You killed her, Blanche." He grabbed her shoulders and shook her, but Kay stepped between them and gently removed the man's hands.

"I hope there's no need for violence here," Kay said, the unspoken threat in her voice abundantly clear. "If you'd rather continue this conversation down at the precinct, I'd be more than happy to drive you there myself."

Bill took one step sideways, glaring furiously at his sister, then turned to Kay and lifted his palms in the air, shaking them ostentatiously. "There, happy? I'm not touching your precious killer."

Carole approached Bill and touched his arm. "Son, you're heartbroken, and we understand," she said. "Blanche will forgive you—"

He yanked away from her touch as if it burned his skin. "Forgive me? *She* will forgive *me*?" He was turning livid, crimson coloring his face and neck in unhealthy blotches. The man was about to have a heart attack. He stuttered, trying to say something, his inability to articulate fueling his anger. "She needs to confess," he eventually said, pointing a trembling index at his sister.

Blanche cried silently, looking at him through a web of tears. She wasn't angry, nor was she insulted by his accusations; she was heartbroken. There wasn't anything in the woman's reaction to the news of Alyssa's death and to her brother's accusations to indicate she'd been involved in her murder, or she'd known anything about it. From what Kay could see, Blanche Caldwell wasn't a viable suspect, although Kay still wanted to know why Bill had thought about her the moment he'd learned his daughter had been killed, and what all that *heiress* business was about.

There was something slightly off about Blanche's demeanor, though. She had just been physically and emotionally abused by her brother, and yet she showed nothing but empathy for his sorrow, understanding for his grief, and forgiveness for his bitter words and rash gestures. Carole had been right; Blanche loved her brother very much.

"Yeah, go ahead," Bill bellowed, "cry me a river."

"Bill," Carole interjected, raising her voice and sharpening the tone. "That's enough. Blanche didn't do anything."

"I don't believe it!" he shouted, turning to his mother and taking a couple of menacing steps toward her. Kay grabbed his shoulder firmly, stopping him in place.

"Mr. Caldwell, please, this ends now."

Bill froze. "How would you know she didn't kill my baby? Huh? Just 'cause she's crying?" He ran his hands through his hair in a gesture of pure despair. "It's your damn system, Mother, it's what you always wanted, to see us fighting for your precious estate." He paused for a moment, panting, out of breath, while Carole's jaw dropped. "Yes, Mother, that's what you've always wanted, for us and our children to kill one another over your *money*." He spat the word, as if it was poisonous. "Well, now we've done it. One of us has killed at your whim," he added, his voice loaded with tears. "Damned be the day I agreed to stay here and be your puppet, Mother. Madelyn and Kendall were the smart ones, running as far away from you as possible."

Kay turned her attention briefly to Carole, surprised to find the proud woman weeping, her back bent, her shoulders heaving, her bony hands clenched tight at her chest.

"I—I never wanted this," Carole whimpered. She didn't care about her appearance anymore. She didn't pat dry the tears that smudged her makeup, nor did she touch her hair to make sure every strand was in place. Something in what Bill had said must've hit home hard. "But you're wrong," she said, her voice modulated by sobs, "Blanche wasn't here, she was in New York."

Kay looked at Blanche. She stood calmly, pale, drained, silent. Why hadn't she said anything in her defense, if she'd been out of town?

"Is it true?" Bill asked, looking at Blanche.

She lowered her eyes under his intense gaze. When she spoke, her voice was strangled with emotion. "Dylan and I met with the Chinese investors in New York yesterday."

Bill wrung his hands, his brow scrunched, his gaze agonizing. "If it wasn't you, then you hired someone to kill Alyssa," he said, sounding a little unconvinced. When he said the words, Blanche flinched, looking at him for a brief moment, deeply hurt. "Come on, admit it," he continued, "you never liked Alyssa. Even if she was your niece, you hated her as the heiress of the business. She was in your son's path, and you wanted your—"

Blanche stepped forward and reached for him, her fingertips barely brushing against the fabric of his shirt. His shoulders fell and he breathed out, lowering his head. It was as if that ephemeral touch had wiped away all his rage, leaving him tired and drawn, subdued, defeated. Kay watched his transformation with disbelief, as if watching a raging lion submitting to a frail woman's caress, no whips, no chains, just magic. Then Blanche stood on her toes, closing the distance until their foreheads touched.

"Bill, you know that's not true," she whispered. "We both know that really, really well."

He whimpered and put his arms on her shoulders, the beginning of an embrace held back by something Kay couldn't decipher.

What the heck had just happened? Kay thought, wondering what Blanche's secret was. She'd tamed her brother with one touch, with only a few words.

She would've liked to question them until she uncovered all their secrets, but those weren't hers to uncover. By the looks of things, none of those people had killed Alyssa or had any prior knowledge of her death. No one could fake the physiological reactions she'd witnessed, dilated pupils, pallor, hypertension, sweating. Her unsub wasn't in that room. It was time for her to move on, and pick up the trail someplace else.

"Well, Detective," Carole intervened, inserting herself between Kay and her children, forcing Kay to step back. Mercurial as quicksilver, she had returned to her normal self, standing tall, chin thrust forward, only a smudge of eyeliner in evidence of her earlier meltdown. "If we're done here, we have a funeral to organize."

"Yes, we're done," Kay replied. "Mr. Caldwell," she called, and Bill raised his head to look at her, breaking contact with Blanche slowly, regretfully. "We would appreciate it if you could stop by the morgue tomorrow morning, say ten o'clock?"

He nodded, averting his eyes. All the rage supporting him was gone. What was left of him was barely standing, an empty husk ready to disintegrate in the slightest breeze.

"Thank you," Kay replied. "And please accept my deepest sympathies."

A few moments later, Kay breathed the fresh evening air thirstily, welcoming the refreshing chill and the smell of dew-soaked earth beneath fallen leaves. Whatever she'd witnessed in there was both inexplicable and, most likely, irrelevant.

Yet her instinct was telling her otherwise. Why was there a gnawing feeling in her gut, urging her to go back, to turn every stone and question everything, to tear through the carefully arranged appearances the family had displayed for her?

Alyssa's killer might've been closer than it seemed.

CHAPTER NINETEEN
Questions

It was almost dark when Elliot drove through the Caldwell Farms gates, but he still hoped he could find the woman he was looking for, or at least someone who knew her and could give him a name and an address. Running the tags of the truck seen picking up Kirsten off the side of the road had led him to Caldwell Farms, the recognizable truck leaving a trail of sightings along the interstate.

He stopped at a fork in the road, then made his choice quickly, leaving the residence to his right and choosing to approach the industrial-like building complex to the left. It was well-lit and people swarmed around it, loading and unloading equipment, moving trucks around, while work orders were tracked on clipboards carried by supervisors wearing hard hats in bright yellow, adorned with the Caldwell Farms logo. Days were long and busy at the end of the November harvest season.

Some of them slowed their end-of-day routine to give the detective's unmarked vehicle a long, suspicious stare before pretending to go about their business, but instead converging in small groups to observe and comment from a safe distance. The red-and-blue flashers hidden in the vehicle's grille were a dead giveaway, and so was the make and model of the custom, an enhanced Ford Explorer. Perhaps some of them might've even recognized him; there weren't that many Texan cops in Franklin County, California.

Elliot climbed out of the vehicle, before putting on his hat and adjusting his belt buckle. Then he took out his phone and reviewed the stills he'd received from his counterpart in Oregon, all taken from grainy, black-and-white surveillance videos from a gas station. One showed the girl he was looking for eating at a table with a middle-aged, somewhat overweight woman dressed in work blues with the same logo he could see on people's hard hats and on the front gate. Another showed the back of the woman's truck, marked with the same branding colors, pulled over at the pump, refueling. Finally, a third image was a barely intelligible shot of the woman's face as she was exiting the restroom area.

He looked at the image of the truck and memorized its tag, then walked around a little until he spotted it, pulled up at the loading dock, waiting for cargo. He approached a group of four men, clustered together a few yards away, and greeted them with two fingers touching the brim of his hat.

"Howdy," he said, noticing how his presence drove the four people to close ranks, as if defending themselves from the approaching predator. He showed them the image, and asked, "Where can I find this woman?"

They stared at one another, then at their boots. One of them seemed particularly interested in a truck backing away from the loading dock, although it was more than 20 yards away.

A hint of a smile stretched Elliot's lips. Blue-collar workers had a reputation for their solidarity, and he appreciated that. "She's an important witness who can help us find a missing child," he clarified. "I'm sure she'd want to help us find her," he added, flipping through the images until he could show them a good, clear one of Kirsten.

"Um, the gal you're looking for is Hazel Fuentes," one of the men replied. "She's over there, where that green light is. It's our breakroom."

Elliot touched his hat again. "Thanks." He walked quickly toward the green lamp marking a door labeled, EMPLOYEES ONLY, and was about to grab the handle when Hazel stepped out of the building, holding an unlit cigarette in her hand.

"Ms. Fuentes?" Elliot asked. A flicker of fear lit the woman's eyes.

"Yes," she replied. "Who wants to know?"

"Detective Elliot Young, from the Franklin County Sheriff's Office." He flashed his badge, but smiled encouragingly. He didn't want the woman spooked, and the investigating detective knew that smiles worked much better than frowns. "We're looking for Kirsten Humphrey," he showed her the photo.

The woman smiled. "Huh… She gave me her real name," she whispered to herself. Then, turning her attention to Elliot, "Mind if I light this up?" She lit the cigarette with slightly trembling fingers and inhaled wholeheartedly. "Ask away." Despite her hand gesture intended to convey indifference, she was visibly scared.

"You took this girl in your truck five days ago, correct?"

She took another drag from her cigarette, sending a cloud of mint-flavored smoke in the air. "Listen, do I need a lawyer?"

Elliot gave Hazel a long look. He wasn't going to charge a hard-working woman for taking in a hitchhiker in the rain and feeding her a warm meal. The day cops started arresting people for that, all hint of civilized humanity would come to an end.

"If you're concerned with failing to report a minor runaway and taking her across state lines, which would make it a federal offense," he said, watching her grow paler as he spoke, "you're in the clear. Looking at this girl's photo, there's no way you could've known she was underage. She looks very mature."

She was quick to grab the lifesaver and swim with it. "No, I had no idea she was a minor," she said, the look of gratitude in her eyes unmistakable. "Tell me, hon, what do you need to know?"

"What did you two talk about over your meal?" Elliot asked.

"Ahh, you know about that too, huh," she replied. "Funny how the world works these days." She closed her eyes for a moment, as if trying to remember all the details of the conversation. "She didn't tell me what she was running from, but I could tell it wasn't good." She frowned as she opened her eyes and looked briefly in Elliot's direction, yet avoided making eye contact. "She was soaking wet and starving, the poor thing. She wolfed that hamburger down as if she'd never seen food before."

"Did she mention where she was headed?"

"San Francisco," Hazel replied. "I thought she might've been headed to Hollywood, you know, being she's so beautiful. She could be a star someday. But no, her mind was made up, to go to the city and get a job, cleaning rooms or waiting tables or something to get herself on her feet, doing honest work."

Elliot shot her an inquisitive glance.

Picking up on his unspoken question, Hazel clarified, "She had a strange reaction to a suggestion I made, about men, about being careful around them, you know. I would bet an entire paycheck this girl's been abused."

"Where did you drop her off?"

"Right there, by the exit ramp. I told her she had better chances of hitching another ride from the highway." She hesitated for a moment, as if deciding whether to share another bit of information with him. "I gave her my phone number; I put a note in her pocket. Then I went about my business."

"Did you happen to see if anyone else picked her up?"

A sad smile colored Hazel's face. "Not for a long time. I came out at lunch and looked toward the highway. She was still there, leaning against the guardrail, hand in the air." She shook her head with disappointment. "People are afraid to stop these days. You never know what freak you end up with. Some of the people who roam these highways, hon, they could kill you for pocket change and the leftovers in your coffee cup."

Giving Hazel his card, he thanked her for her help. "If you hear from her, please give us a call."

She nodded, a look of concern on her face. "Do you think she's okay? Will you let me know?"

Elliot replied, "Will do," and touched his hat briefly before turning around and leaving.

That girl could be anywhere by now. San Francisco, or anywhere else for that matter. A fourteen-year-old girl, desperate, running away from abuse at home, heading into the big unknown with her heart filled with hope. Countless murder investigations started with those words: teen runaway from a broken family, found stabbed, or shot, or strangled on the side of a road or in a gas station restroom.

Could he find the whisper in the whirlwind? All he knew was he had to try. Only yesterday, Kirsten was just another runaway to him, one who got the benefit of attention because of personal favors being called into Sheriff Logan's office, and he detested that kind of work. Now he knew he had to find the girl no matter what. He could ride the rough string; all it would take was legwork and that he could easily do.

He drove out of there, leaving the loading docks behind and heading for the highway. He reached the fork in the road right after another vehicle, identical to his, had turned onto the road coming from the residence. With a wide smile on his lips, he turned on his flashers and flipped on the siren for a brief moment.

The vehicle ahead pulled over immediately, and Kay hopped out from behind the wheel.

Was it just his imagination, or was she beaming?

He bowed his head, taking his hat off for a moment as he approached her. The fine dust of the dirt road appeared like unsettled fog in the headlights of his car, and she was breathtaking standing there, smiling, waving at him, her hair blown into the wind like whirls of golden smoke.

"Howdy, ma'am," he said, wondering if he should take the opportunity to ask her out. Perhaps today would be a good day to do that, since they'd been working separate cases and he could use that as an excuse in the event she flat out declined, to save face. As if saving face would even matter, if she said no. He'd just stand there, cold as a frozen frog, lower than a gopher hole.

"Hey there, cowboy," she replied with playfulness in her voice. "Was I going over the limit?" she quipped, feigning fearful concern. "I've never been pulled over before. Are you going to arrest me, Detective?"

Her words lit a fire inside him. He lowered his gaze for a moment, hiding the heat in his eyes under the brim of his hat, thankful for the darkness surrounding them, for the thin dust floating in the air and filling his nostrils with the smell of dry earth that reminded him of hoofbeats in the Texas arid plains.

He looked straight at her, playing her game. "Not tonight, ma'am, since it's your first offense. I was thinking we could discuss the details of your crime over dinner instead."

She tilted her head ever so slightly, while her smile touched her eyes. "I could eat."

CHAPTER TWENTY

In the Dark

FIVE DAYS AGO

The cold had taken over the dark, empty house, chilling Kirsten's blood, fueling her fears. She paced the rooms one after another, trying all windows, all doors, looking for exits that weren't there. Her bare feet were frozen from the contact with the cold floorboards, and every now and then she sat on the couch, folding her legs underneath her to keep them warm. The socks she'd come with were hanging out to dry in the bathroom, after she'd rinsed them quickly in the shower.

Feeling the chilly air grip her shoulders, she rummaged through one of the bedroom closets and found an old blanket. She wrapped it around her body and returned to the couch, where she sat, leaning against the backrest and hugging her knees underneath the blanket, staring at the dark window. Everything felt damp and smelled musty, the humidity in the air exacerbated by the cold seeping in without any heating to overcome it. How long had the place been without people living in it? Who would keep a house like that, and why?

The answers to those questions scared her out of her mind, so she pushed her fears aside and looked outside the window.

The coyote was gone, and so was the crescent moon, the only thing that had brought any shred of light inside the house. When would he come back? And would he let her go? She realized he wasn't going to take her to San Francisco; that boat had sailed, even in a naïve mind like hers, that scenario didn't hold any water. But what would he do with her?

Anxiety drilled a hole in her stomach. She remembered how the man had opened the fridge and found deli meats, cheeses, and those delicious bread rolls. They felt fresh at the time. Was the fridge still working? How about the microwave? Her hopes revived by the idea, she quickly felt her way across the room and opened the fridge door.

A dim light made her smile, so dim it didn't even reach the dining room table, but it was far more than she'd had before. There was still plenty of food inside, and she ate, standing in the open door, hastily gulping down slices of ham, salami, and Swiss cheese. Then she reached for the microwave door and opened it.

"Yeah," she whispered when another dim light defeated a patch of darkness in the kitchen. She warmed up a roll, buttered it, and layered it with ham and cheese, then gave it another thirty seconds in the oven, taking it out, a mouthwatering, molten hot Swiss sandwich.

She was just about to start another sandwich, when she realized she should probably conserve resources. What if he wasn't coming back anytime soon? What if he was never coming back? And what would he do if he did return?

Slowly, regretfully, she closed the fridge door and darkness regained some terrain. She left the microwave door open, and then crossed the room back to the couch, where she crouched under the damp blanket, shivering, keeping her eyes on that dim light as if it were the first candle at an all-night vigil.

She must've dozed off when the movement of air around her startled her awake. She saw a shadow moving by the door and she screamed, scared out of her mind.

The man turned on the lights with the remote in his hand, and she blinked a few times, blinded. Then she sprung to her feet and tried to run past him to the door, but he grabbed her and set her down on a chair, ignoring her kicks, screams, and clawing fingernails.

"Be still," he said, and the firmness in his tone had a stronger effect than his actual words. His arms felt strong, and the proximity of his body filled her nostrils with a potpourri of fine scents. His cologne, starched laundry, new leather, the air freshener she'd smelled in his car. She complied, feeling like jelly in his hands, yet unable to stop crying.

"When are we leaving?" she asked, whimpering, shivering.

"Not right now," he replied. "Will you be a good girl?" he asked, taking one hand off her arm.

She nodded, and he released her, standing and stepping away from her. "My goodness, you are so beautiful," he whispered, as in a trance. "You look just like her."

"Please let me go," she pleaded, fidgeting on her seat under his intense gaze. No one had ever looked at her that way. No one had ever spoken to her that way. Only in the movies she'd heard men say those words.

"Hush, hush," he whispered, touching his lips with his raised index finger. He took off his jacket, not minding the cold that was already seeping under the strong jets of heated air coming from the vents. Then he kneeled in front of her and touched her feet. "You're frozen, and it's my fault. I'm so sorry, my dear."

She sniffled and frowned, watching him massage her feet with strong, warm hands. She'd also seen movies where girls like her were kept hostage, only to be killed at the end. She tried to pull away, but his gentle grip turned ironclad and she had no choice but to submit to his will.

He stood and sighed, staring at her as if she were someone he hadn't seen in a while.

"Who do I look like?" she asked, as soon as she gathered the courage.

"Huh?"

"You said I looked just like—"

She choked on her words when he pulled out a knife from a holster at his belt and set it on the table within his reach. The long, serrated blade reflected the lightbulbs in the ceiling, making her squint, then look away.

Her instincts had been right. He wasn't so kind after all. A creep, like all the rest.

He caressed her hair, feeling its texture, then frowned just a little, seemingly unhappy. "I like things a certain way," he said, his voice still gentle and warm, but also inflexible. The size of the blade on the table told her pleading with him made no sense. "When you take a shower, don't dry your hair anymore."

Her jaw dropped slightly, his strange request tightening her stomach in a knot. Fear prickled her skin, sending waves of goosebumps emanating from the places he touched. "Please let me go," she said, looking him in the eyes. "I won't tell anyone, I swear."

He smiled, looking at her with eyes filled with some kind of strange yearning. It wasn't like the sickening urges her stepfather's homies had on their faces whenever they watched porn. It was different, yet the same. Different, because it seemed gentle, patient, loving, almost sweet, even electrifying. The same, because it seemed just as demanding and restless, just as urgent. "Such perfection," he whispered, transported, "and never been touched."

She pulled away and tried to run, but he caught her arm in a strong grip. "Don't ruin that," he said, the threat in his voice obvious. "Don't make me do things I don't want to do."

She nodded, swallowing hard, the thought of his oversized knife at the forefront of her mind. He released her arm, and ran his fingers against her cheek. "Now go take another shower, my dear. Don't dry your hair anymore." He stopped for a moment, thinking. "Don't dry yourself at all; just wrap yourself in a towel and come right out. I'll be here this time, I promise."

She cried under the hot water, cried until her tears ran out, fear strangling her, reminding her she couldn't stay in that shower forever. She'd soon have to come out and face whatever he had planned for her.

She squeezed the excess water out of her hair and did as instructed, wrapping a large bath towel around her body, and opened the door. She thought she'd seen him seated at the dining room table, waiting for her, but she only caught a glimpse of him before darkness returned. Screaming, she stepped back into the bathroom, but soon he was there, folding her in his arms, whispering soothing, loving words in her ear, caressing her wet hair, while she sobbed and trembled, her shoulders heaving and her teeth clattering.

Relenting, she let the embrace happen, knowing she could scream all she wanted but no one would hear; she would only make him angry.

He lifted her off her feet then carried her over to the bed, where he set her down gently. The sheets felt like smooth, scented satin under her skin. Her towel came undone and she tried to cover herself, but he hushed her into silent, frozen obedience. Slowly, he unwrapped the towel off her body and stood there, staring at her in the almost complete darkness that was starting to lift with the earliest crack of dawn. Then he put a silk blindfold on her, again shushing her resistance. "You'll see it's okay," he whispered. "You'll just have to trust me."

When she screamed, the coyote howled.

CHAPTER TWENTY-ONE
A Night Out

Kay filled the coffeemaker pot at the faucet, rapping her fingers against the kitchen counter impatiently. She'd sprung out of bed at first light, a whirlwind of upsetting thoughts swirling in her mind, and couldn't wait to get her day going.

The night before had started well, a relaxing, after-hours dinner with a colleague and work friend.

Yeah… right. Go on, keep telling yourself that.

She couldn't even be honest with herself anymore. Her feelings for Elliot were far from the typical feelings she had or, better said, didn't have, for any other colleague. That's why her heart had swelled when he stopped her by the Caldwell Farms gate, that's why she'd behaved so ridiculously juvenile, playing the old, "Are you going to arrest me, Detective?" game, shamelessly flirting with him.

He took her for a burger at Hilltop Bar and Grill, the usual cop hangout place. It was late when they got there, after nine, and she'd hoped they wouldn't run into any familiar faces, but had no such luck. A gang of beered-up deputies hollered when they walked through the door, and it took all her willpower not to rush out of there. One look at Elliot's face told her he was just as inconvenienced, and just as hesitant to admit it and walk out. They'd never hear the end of it if they did.

They sat at a small table, and she secretly hoped the deputies would find something else better to do, but no. They took turns coming by, bearing drink offerings to celebrate her joining the team, her first collar, and so on, but she knew better. They paraded just to be in their business, gathering tidbits of gossip for days to come. Still, she carefully controlled her every move, expression, and word she said, and a grim, visibly frustrated Elliot did the same, sitting across from her like a gloomy and barely functional speechless person. To anyone who was watching, they were two colleagues having a meal and a drink together at the end of their long day, and who'd apparently welcomed their colleagues at their table for a while.

Even so, she didn't feel she could refuse the deputies' invitations to raise a glass with them, without jeopardizing the team dynamics and her integration as the newest member of the Franklin County Sheriff's Office. People might or might not remember someone's actions for a while, but they never forgot how that someone made them feel. Rejection hurts the most and is the most unforgivable—and unforgettable—of all behaviors.

That one drink had turned into three or four, under the constant barrage of the deputies' offers. Deputy Leach paid for a round of tequila shots, and she had to oblige, understanding it was a rite of passage, common in precincts all over the world, where the newbie had to prove themselves in more ways than one. She downed hers while they all hollered, then Daugherty ordered two more rounds, not giving up until she'd drunk them both, even if she would've preferred not to touch anything that deputy had to offer. He stood by their table, not caring he wasn't invited to join them, and pushed the drinks on Kay as if he were a man with a mission. Maybe he was, or maybe he thought he could drink her under the table and embarrass her into leaving the precinct.

She downed the second glass under his insolent stare and slammed it on the table with a mischievous grin. "If you have money to waste, Daugherty, sure, keep 'em coming. We could do this all night long."

His jaw dropped, then he walked away mumbling something, accompanied by his colleagues' roars of laughter. "That chick can drink you under the table, Daugherty," Deputy Farrell shouted, the only woman in the gang. "She's one of us. Get it in that fat head of yours."

But Kay didn't care about the appreciation she received, her mind fixated on one particular deputy.

It irked her badly seeing Deputy Scott in that group, when she knew exactly who he was: a wife beater, a violent abuser who belonged in jail. Making it worse, he came by and muttered a half-unintelligible, "Hello, Detective," his voice ripe with contempt and lust. He offered her a shot glass filled to the brim, his hand shaking slightly, and watched her down it with a grin that quickly faded under Elliot's glare. None of his coworkers seemed to know anything about who he really was or, if they knew, they didn't seem to mind. Someone must've known he was a violent man; the same someone who had buried his wife's complaints, then ratted her out to him, knowing very well the damage it would do to the woman. And that someone was probably drinking with him, having a good time, not a second thought given to Scott's abused wife.

Shooting the group a side glance, she had ground her teeth, muttering an oath that would've made a veteran sailor proud.

"My mistake," Elliot said quietly. She could barely hear him over the ruckus in the bar.

"What are you talking about?"

"Bringing you here," he replied, staring at the scratched melamine tabletop.

She smiled, then chuckled, seeing how looking in his eyes made her even tipsier than she already was. "Hey, I came with, didn't I?" She tilted her head, continuing to smile, then remembered they were being watched and corrected her appearance, letting her smile wither.

"Let's do this again tomorrow," Elliot said, locking eyes with her. "Someplace else, far, far away." His gaze was loaded with intense, mixed emotions, making her wish she'd declined raising so many shot glasses with the deputies, so she could decipher the mysteries of those Texas blues.

They'd finished their meal and left, waving at the deputies who hollered in a standing circle while Scott was dancing by himself in the middle, his moves mixed generously with obscene gestures that fueled his buddies' whoops and cheers.

She followed Elliot to the parking lot, where both their vehicles were parked side by side, and she took out her keys.

"Please," Elliot said, grabbing her hand and closing her fist around the keys. The contact with his warm skin sent a buzz in her entire body, heating her up despite the November chill. "Let me drive you home."

"Uh-huh," she nodded, swallowing hard, unsure if it was his touch, the drinks, or her imagination running wild to blame for her knees feeling weak, for her heart throbbing in her chest.

She tugged at his hand, stopping him in place. He turned toward her, looking at her with a mix of yearning and concern. Looking in his eyes for a moment, then her gaze lingered on his lips, then on the brim of that cowboy hat. She imagined herself reaching up and bringing his face down to hers, feeling his lips crushing hers in a desperate, demanding kiss. Alcohol buzzed in her ears, boosting her courage, driving her senses insane.

Then she heard a loud holler coming from the bar and looked up. Through the smoke-fogged window, she saw Deputy Scott dancing on the table, his shirt gone, wearing a sweat-stained, sleeveless undershirt. A wifebeater.

How fitting.

Reality yanked her forcefully with the strength of thousands of bad memories. Her father, coming back home drunk and horny, beating on her mother, on her and Jacob, his hands grabbing at Pearl, even at her, the lewd urgency in his eyes revolting.

Yet here she was, drunk, in a parking lot, about to grab Elliot and kiss him, driven by the same urges. The proud daughter of her father.

Bile rose to her throat and she promptly dropped to her knees, unloading her stomach contents by the rear wheel of her SUV. Elliot held her hair gently, keeping his cool palm on her forehead for support as she heaved.

The rest of the evening, the drive home in Elliot's vehicle spent in silent, mortifying embarrassment, and how she'd managed to get into bed was all a blur. She'd never been so humiliated in her life.

This morning, the coffee pot spilled over with water, while she was still lost in her thoughts.

"Crap," she muttered, taking the pot to the coffeemaker and pouring the water into the machine. She spilled at least a third of it on the counter, her hands shaking badly, perhaps from embarrassment that lingered around her, sticking to her soul like an oil stain, or perhaps from unshed tears threatening to overflow. Then she tried to set the pot in its place, under the filter, but it didn't seem to fit anymore. She'd done it many times before, but the darn thing just wouldn't go back in its place.

"Get in there, you miserable, good-for-nothing, piece of pathetic shit," she said, her voice rising with each word that marked yet another attempt to force the pot in its place, each new attempt more forceful than the previous ones.

"Whoa," Jacob said, entering the room barefoot and wearing crumpled, mismatched pajamas.

Startled, she turned to look at him, while her hand shoved the offending pot against the edge of the counter by mistake, smashing it to bits.

She stared at the shards littering the floor, still holding the broken pot's handle. "The heck…" she muttered, squeezing her eyes shut, as if to force the image away. Looking at her brother, she tried to apologize. "I'll get us a new one today, I promise. This thing was old—"

"Are you okay?" he asked, grabbing the broom and dustpan and approaching her.

"No, stop right there," she urged him, taking the broom from his hand and staring at his bare feet. "You'll cut yourself."

She swept the floor carefully, collecting all the shards on the dustpan before emptying it in the trash. Then she moistened a paper towel and swept the floor, collecting all the tiniest, barely visible specks of glass that might've escaped the broom.

"There," she said, putting the broom back in its place. "But, thanks to me, there's no coffee." She attempted to be humorous, but the sadness in her heart was too pervasive.

"What are you talking about, sis?" Jacob said, pushing her gently to the side. "Take a seat, you've done enough," he added, and they both burst into laughter. "I'll make us some coffee, hillbilly style."

"I've done enough, haven't I?" she asked, laughter already gone, replaced by unwelcome tears.

"Who woke you up on the wrong side of the bed today?"

She bit her lip, afraid to share what was bothering her, afraid she might bring misery and unwanted memories to her brother's heart. He didn't deserve it. But tears filled her eyes, and the words blurted out, "I'm just like *he* was," referring to their father, knowing Jacob understood. "I go out, I get a few drinks in me, then I want to—" She stopped, choking on the words. "Just like he was… drunk and horny, looking to get laid."

Her brother's hand found her shoulder and squeezed gently. She leaned against him, hiding her face in the sleeve of his pajamas.

"So, you're human after all, sis, who knew?" Jacob's words were unexpectedly soothing, nonjudgmental. "And you chose well. That Texas Ranger of yours is a good man."

"He's not a Ranger, Jake. He's a detective. And he'll probably never go out with me again."

Jacob's grin lit his eyes. He stepped away from her and found an empty bottle in the cabinet, then proceeded to wash it thoroughly. "This might come to you as a big surprise, Dr. Sharp, but men are quite flattered by female attention, drunk or sober. If only you'd specialized in behavioral psychology, then you'd understand."

Irritated and at the same time amused with his sarcasm, she slapped him jokingly, then watched him fit the bottle with a funnel, setting a coffee filter in, followed by two scoops of coffee. Then he filled a small pot with water and set it on the stove to boil.

"I puked on the man's boots, Jake," she confessed, staring at the floor and feeling her cheeks catch fire.

"And a cup of this strong coffee will wipe all that bad taste from your mouth. Just give your brother a chance, will you?"

He waited for the hot water to drain through the filter, then removed the funnel and poured coffee from the bottle into two cups. Handing one to her, he added, "He'll be back, you'll see."

"No, he won't," she replied with a long sigh. "By the time I get to work, he'll already be transferred back to Texas or somewhere as far away from me as possible."

The first sip burned her lips, but it was just what she needed. She didn't get to take a second one before her phone chimed. A message from SSA Strickland was asking about Nicole Scott's case.

She typed her reply after a quick frown at the clock on the wall, just a simple, *I'll keep you posted.*

The day before, she'd been itching to talk to Nicole, but by the time she got the case assigned, Scott had already finished his shift. Had she known he'd spend all evening at the bar, she wouldn't have put Nicole through the ordeal of having to live through another night with that bastard.

But that morning, Scott was supposed to report for duty at eight. If she hurried, she could talk with Nicole before heading out to the morgue for the ten o'clock appointment with Bill Caldwell.

She set the coffee cup on the table and stood, eager to leave. "Can you give me a ride? I left my car at the bar."

Like a bona fide drunk.

CHAPTER TWENTY-TWO
Offender

About 100 yards south of the Scott residence, a crew of workers were fixing a leak in the water main. Several trucks were parked nearby, and an excavator dug through the nearly frozen ground to get to the pipe responsible, overflowing onto the asphalt in rivulets of brownish mud.

Kay pulled her SUV between two of the trucks, then flashed her badge quickly at a curious worker who was headed her way.

"I'll leave this here for a little while," she said.

He nodded and promptly turned back, minding his business.

Walking on the opposite side of the road, she checked to see if anyone could notice her approaching the Scott residence. She crossed quickly, then trotted on her toes up the driveway and rang the bell.

The door opened a few inches, and a woman looked at her with suspicion.

"Yes?"

Kay showed her badge discreetly. "Nicole Scott? SSA Strickland with the San Francisco FBI sent me to talk with you. I'm Dr. Sharp. May I come in?"

Nodding quickly, she shot a couple of worried looks left and right, then opened the door. "Make it quick," she said, looking away.

Her left eye had almost healed, but a few days ago must've been bruised black and swollen shut. Her lip was cracked and inflamed, that injury more recent. Her right eyebrow had a small hiatus, along the line where her supraorbital had been cracked, the broken skin having required at least three sutures sometime in the past.

Ashamed, she cowered under Kay's inquisitive glance and walked away. "You can sit there." She pointed at the sofa covered with a weathered throw. "Make it fast, please; he could come back any minute."

"He's at work today," Kay replied in a reassuring tone.

"How would you know?"

Kay reached out and grabbed Nicole's hand. "I've been a special agent with the FBI for eight years, and I have been assigned your case. I'm also a detective here, in Mount Chester—"

Nicole whimpered and withdrew, turning her back to Kay. "No... He swore to me."

"And he's keeping his word, Nicole. I promise you that. I have no relationships here; I just started my job a week ago." She waited, but Nicole still sobbed, her back turned to Kay, her face buried in her hands. "I'm on your side, I swear."

She didn't press Nicole; she gave her time to process her emotions and decide whether to trust her or not. While she waited, memories of her mother, crouched to the ground, struggling to escape her father's relentless fists invaded her mind, swelling her chest with an anger like never before, burning her eyes with tears that had been held hostage ever since she was twelve.

They say all happy families are happy the same, but all miserable ones are miserable each in their own unique way. It might've been true, but all abusive men were the same, leaving a trail of pain and suffering behind them that never ended, and getting away with it for much too long.

When Nicole turned around, she sniffled and wiped her eyes with her sleeve, while her other hand landed protectively on her belly. Kay's heart skipped a beat.

"Are you pregnant?" she asked, forcing her worry out of her voice.

Nicole nodded. "Almost four months."

"Does he know?"

A fresh tear rolled down her cheek, but she wiped it away with her fingers. "He doesn't care."

Where could a woman in Nicole's situation go? If she were in San Francisco, she could've sent her to one of the several organizations that helped battered women escape abuse, while building a new life for themselves and their children. But here, in Mount Chester, population 3,824 including herself, where could she go? Any moment spent with her husband could prove to be fatal.

"Tell me, who have you talked to at the sheriff's office?"

Nicole looked out the window from behind the sheers, worried; every sound startling her as it would a deer grazing in a clearing, waiting to be preyed upon.

"At first, I wrote a letter and took it there myself; I left it with reception in a sealed envelope. It was addressed to Sheriff Logan himself." A shudder rattled her and caught her breath. "It was a year ago, I think," she added, wrapping her thin arms around her body as if the room had turned unbearably cold. "That afternoon, when Herb came back, he had the letter with him." She choked with her own tears. "You can't imagine," she whimpered. "At the hospital, he claimed I took a fall down the basement stairs, to explain the broken ribs and this," she added, peeling up the sleeve of her sweater and showing Kay a long scar across her forearm.

Kay listened, carefully collecting all the details that could help her identify who the other person was, the one who'd ratted Nicole out to her husband. There would come a day, not soon enough, when she would gladly slap a pair of handcuffs on that sorry bastard.

"That kept me quiet for a while," she continued, her voice sounding tired, exhausted, each word taking its toll. "Going to the hospital scared him a little, and it got better." She paused for a beat. "He always apologized, always told me he loved me, and I believed him. Sometimes it was my fault." She wiped another tear and looked at Kay briefly. "I screw things up sometimes," she added, sounding guilty, apologetic.

"No one screws up badly enough to deserve this, Nicole," Kay said firmly. "No human being deserves to be treated like that, no matter what they do."

The woman stared into the distance, biting on her index fingernail.

"But then it got bad again, and I sent a letter by mail, also to the sheriff," she continued, her voice fraught with mixed emotions. "He came back wielding that letter a couple of days later, and punished me for destroying his professional reputation. I was, you know... He was right. But I couldn't take it anymore."

Before Kay could answer, a car passed by on the road and Nicole jumped out of her skin, rushing to the window to look outside.

"Will you do something for me?" Kay asked. Nicole nodded, her eyes large, her pupils dilated. "Take a seat with me here, on the sofa, close your eyes, and see yourself on that hospital bed, a year ago." She obeyed, moving slowly, hesitantly. Kay reached for her hand, holding it between hers. "Now, imagine what you would say to the Nicole back then, the one bleeding and hurting, the one who couldn't breathe because her ribs were broken."

Her face scrunched and she wailed, letting out a guttural, deep cry that rattled her entire being, ending in heavy sobs. When she quieted down enough to speak, she whispered, her words carried on a shattered breath, "I'd tell her... Hang in there... You'll survive. You'll be free one day."

Kay gave her frozen fingers a squeeze. "Exactly. Are you ready to take control of your life?"

Nicole stared at her, slack-jawed. "I—I can't... He'll kill me."

"Have you ever spoken to the sheriff in person about this?" Kay asked, holding her breath and hoping her supervisor wasn't among the precinct's scum.

"I never dared… Herb always drinks with everyone, including the sheriff, and he's everyone's best friend. That's why I contacted the FBI. I didn't know who else to call." A wave of sorrow jarred her again. "He'll kill me if he finds out, and he will, won't he?"

Kay stood and wrapped her arm around the woman's thin shoulders. "He'll find out at some point, but when he does, he'll have handcuffs on him and won't be able to do anything about it."

Wiggling free, Nicole stepped back. "I can't testify, please don't make me. He'll get out in a couple of years, and he'll come after me. He'll kill me, I swear he will."

Kay hesitated. What were her options, really? Without Nicole testifying, there was little she could do. "We could subpoena your hospital records, get testimony from other people who have witnessed the abuse or the marks on your body." The more she talked, the more Nicole protested, shaking her head and stepping back until she hit the wall. "Or we'll present him with evidence, and he'll take a plea. Part of that agreement will be to never speak with you again, never look for you or your child, and never come within a hundred feet of you." Kay looked at Nicole, wishing she could convey to the woman how personally committed she was to keep her safe. It felt as if she were protecting her mother from her father, all those years ago. It felt vindictive and righteous at the same time. "He'll take the plea; I promise you that." She smiled, and saw Nicole's shoulders relax a little. "He'll have no choice."

Another car drove by, and she had the same reaction, rushing to the window, hand at her chest, panting, scared out of her mind. A pizza delivery sedan slowed and stopped at the house across the street.

"Come with me today, Nicole. I'll take you someplace safe, somewhere he'll never find you."

"Where?" she asked. "There's no such—"

"At my house," Kay replied. "You can stay there for as long as you need, until we lock him up and you get your life back together again. But we have to leave now."

Nicole stared at her for a long moment, weighing her options. "He'll come after me hard," she whispered, starting to gather a few things. Then she stopped and looked at Kay, her eyes welling up again. "Thank you... No one's done anything like this for me before."

A few moments later, they left the house carrying a duffel bag with a few changes of clothes and toiletries, and walked briskly to Kay's SUV. Then, after a twenty-minute drive, Kay introduced Nicole to Jacob, bringing him up to speed. She swore her brother to secrecy, and assured a frightened and shy Nicole he would die before letting any harm come to her.

CHAPTER TWENTY-THREE

Morning

Four Days Ago

It was light when he finally left.

The sun's rays pierced through the window, filtered through barren tree branches, sending dancing flickers of light and shadow on the wall as the wind stirred up the woods.

She lay on her side, curled up, still whimpering, shaking, her entire body aching. The cold was settling in the house once again, as she'd come to know it did in his absence, as if him being there was the only way she could have light and heat. As if to teach her to eagerly expect him, to regard him as a caregiver, not as the monster he was.

In the dappled sunlight, the satin sheets shimmered, their fabric exquisite, at odds with the house fallen in disarray, with dust-covered furniture and antiquated fixtures. Kirsten's eyes lingered on the blood smudges staining the cream-colored sheets, the memory of that moment sending a shudder through her entire being.

He'd promised he'd soon be back, and to soon set her free. She believed the first part, and only hoped the second would be true.

Please, let it be true.

But she wasn't going to lie there, waiting for him to return. She wasn't just some piece of property he'd shelved somewhere among other time-forgotten objects, ready for the dust to settle on her until he wanted to toy with her body again. That wasn't why she'd run away from home. That wasn't why she hadn't stopped by the hospital, in one more attempt to tell her mom what was happening.

Maybe that time she would've believed her.

If she would've only taken the chance and asked her mother to see the traces of white powder dusting her abdomen. She would've believed her then, and she would've taken her away and moved someplace safe, where her stepfather didn't have the keys to the front door.

She curled up tighter, hugging her knees and burying her face in the pillow. "Oh, Mom, I'm so sorry," she whimpered, while her heavy eyes released their load.

Soon her tears dried; she was a street-smart kid after all, and if there was any way out of that dust-covered, forsaken hell, she'd find it.

First, she wanted to rid herself of his stink. A quick shower took care of that, even if she cringed using the same shower gel and lavender shampoo he demanded. She blow-dried her hair quickly, then tied it into a ponytail and got dressed.

It was time to explore her prison, to know every single detail of it intimately, and if she couldn't escape it, then she had to find a way to make it more bearable.

She remembered the fridge and the microwave still had power. She opened the fridge door, and celebrated its weak light by swiping a couple of slices of ham and devouring them in an instant. Then she pulled the fridge out of its place, grunting with effort, and exposed a patch of floor covered in thick dust, and a power outlet with an empty socket.

She tested the spare socket by moving over the fridge plug. The motor kicked back in. She moved it back to the upper socket like she'd found it, then pushed the fridge back in its place, careful to make sure she didn't leave any traces of disturbed dust or grime. When the night returned, she could unplug one of the table lamps and move it there, by the fridge, and she'd have light.

Then she turned on the stove, happy to see the elements were heating up, turning red. Grinning, she switched them all on, and spent a few moments rubbing her hands above the stove, feeling her blood starting to flow again.

Then she started exploring the rooms, one by one.

Her first stop was the bedroom she'd just left, one of the smallest in the house.

She tried to get the window to open, but it didn't budge. It was a two-pane vertical, and the lower sash should've slid up, but it just didn't move. There wasn't any lock on it either, and running her fingers across the entire length of the frame revealed nothing she could grab at, unlock, or use to get the window to open. Finally, she banged against the glass pane with both fists, and later, with the brushed metal leg of the lamp she'd yanked from the bedside table, only to find nothing could break that window. It didn't even sound like glass, when she pounded or rapped her fingernails against it.

With a long, pained sigh, she gave up on the window and moved on. Opening the closets, she found skirts, tops, shirts, sweaters, and slacks, the majority of them a good fit for her body. Yet they didn't seem to have belonged to the same woman.

Or girl.

The styles were wildly different, and so was the quality of the fabric and the brand names on their tags. From dollar store and thrift to Neiman Marcus, from brand new to threadbare worn, the closet held it all.

The shoes she retrieved from the small closet in the hallway confirmed her findings. In shoes, not only the quality and wear level varied, but also the size. Afraid to draw the only logical conclusion possible, she chose a pair of sneakers that fit her well, and proceeded to find some socks to go with them.

Underwear was in the big dresser drawer in the first bedroom, from silk to lace to cotton, from girly to trashy to classy. With two fingers, she picked a pair of panties out of the pile and smelled them cautiously. They were clean, the only scents she could pick up were detergent and dryer sheets. She shoved them in her pocket, eager to change out of hers and into clean ones, at least until hers dried after she washed them. The bottom drawer revealed a treasure trove of socks, neatly paired up in balls. She put on a pair, grateful to keep the chill at bay just a little and not feel the cold floorboards under her bare feet.

A noise outside made her heart stop for a moment, before thumping wildly against her chest. She rushed to a window and checked, but no one was coming to the house. It must've been a bird landing on the roof or a tree branch scratching against the siding.

He wasn't back yet. She still had time.

Careful, as if she expected to find someone in there, she opened the main bedroom door and peeked inside. The king-size bed was made, with a silk comforter and countless pillows, arranged neatly by size, welcoming and lush. She touched the cover, then rubbed her fingers together, feeling the particles that had clung to her skin.

Dust.

That bed had not been slept in for years.

Above the headboard, a framed photo showed a couple on their wedding day in a professionally taken portrait. The man was tall and proud, his smile bold, reassured. The woman was beautiful, and reminded her a little of her captor. She had the same eyes, the same mouth, and the same stubborn chin marked with a small dimple. She was young in that photo, twenty-something. The house Kirsten was being held prisoner in must've been hers and her husband's. It was her captor's childhood home.

The clothes in the his-and-hers closets matched the figures she'd seen in the portrait, and were neatly organized, as if no one had touched a single garment since the two people who had slept in that bed had moved out. Why had they left behind their entire wardrobe? Who would keep a house like that, frozen in time like an antique, yet let it decay?

Or had he?

The windows were new and unbreakable, and all light fixtures were operated by the remote control he kept in his pocket. The man had means to keep the property a certain way, and all decay he had allowed to happen must've been on purpose.

The third room seemed to have belonged to a boy, based on the clothes she found, on the simple, cotton sheets and the lack of throw pillows on the bed. The boy had enjoyed reading the classics, as evidenced by the countless titles placed on the shelves, had been engaged in college sports, and had been a fan of rock and roll bands of the eighties. But what mattered the most was that the bedroom window was equally unbreakable.

She was trapped.

The thought of it twisted her stomach in a knot and sucked the air out of her lungs, panic rampaging through her body. She couldn't think of what the future held; she pushed the thought out of her mind, the questions that came with it, willing herself to breathe and accept she couldn't run. Not now.

Resigned, she went into the living room and curled up on the sofa, looking outside through the picture window, now basked in sunlight. She'd obsessively tried not to think of what all that meant, to push the horror of her discoveries away, but her racing thoughts wouldn't be silenced anymore.

Where were all those girls who'd left behind their clothes and their shoes?

Then, the stark realization of her circumstances hit her like a fist in the pit of her stomach.

He was never going to let her go.

CHAPTER TWENTY-FOUR
Identification

Time had slipped away, despite Kay's efforts to catch up with it and be at the morgue before Bill Caldwell's arrival. She'd hoped she could catch a minute or two with Doc Whitmore, just the two of them, to figure out what could've happened with Rose Harrelson's DNA. Was there something more going on? A fleeting memory of the Caldwells' unusual behavior the night before brought a frown to her forehead as she was pulling into the morgue parking lot, right by a luxury sedan that must have been Bill Caldwell's.

She sucked in a last breath of fresh air right before opening the door and stepping into the morgue. In the reception area, the lights were dim, and the air didn't reek of formaldehyde and death as badly. A lab assistant fidgeted, pacing back and forth between the autopsy room door and the reception desk, visibly uncomfortable with her assignment, which, by all appearances, was to stall Bill Caldwell until her arrival. The moment she recognized Kay, she let out a loud, relieved sigh.

"Good, you're here," she said, shoving her hands in her lab coat pockets, leaving just her thumbs outside in a gesture quite common among medical personnel.

Bill Caldwell had been sitting on one of the chairs lined up against the wall, leaning against the backrest, with his arms crossed at his chest and his eyes closed. He sprung to his feet and pounded toward her, his eyes dark, menacing. "Finally, you're here," he said, his voice low, threatening. "I would've expected you to be punctual, at least," he added, drilling his angry gaze into her. "Especially since I can't even see my own daughter without having a cop present."

"I apologize for my tardiness, Mr. Caldwell," she said, knowing better than to be riled up by the justifiable frustration of a mourning parent. "This is the procedure we have to follow. Now, if you'll excuse me, I'll check quickly with Dr. Whitmore, and we can proceed with the identification."

She didn't wait for him to reply; rushing through the autopsy room doors and finding the medical examiner propped on a four-legged stool in front of his desk, his tall forehead nested in the palm of his hand.

Her sudden intrusion startled him and, until he grounded himself, he seemed lost for a brief moment, as if he'd been careening downhill without being able to stop.

"I—I can't explain it," he whispered, defeated, skipping the usual greetings. "I looked at the data all night, trying to construct scenarios that could've explained what happened, and there are none."

She nodded, silently, knowing just how much an error like that could weigh on the reputed medical examiner, and how much was hanging in the balance for him, after forty years spent hunched over autopsy tables. If the glitch in Alyssa's identification couldn't be explained, he risked having all his cases reopened, all his work scrutinized, and all the felons he'd helped put in jail using DNA evidence or forensics would have new grounds for appeal.

"Let's do things one at a time," she said, taking his hand and tugging gently. He rose with a weary groan, his head hanging low under the weight of shame. "Let's finish this ID and then I'll stay behind. We'll look at everything together, one more time, and we'll sort this out somehow. There has to be a logical explanation for this mess, and we'll find it." She stopped briefly right before reaching the autopsy room swing doors, and dropped her voice to a whisper. "I believe in you, in your work. I've seen how rigorous you are, how disciplined and organized and thorough. Whatever the heck the explanation is for this mess, you and me, Doc, we'll find it."

He shot her a long gaze filled with questions and doubt. Then that gaze shifted ever so slightly, and she thought she deciphered an unspoken *thank you* and a hint of a smile that creased the corners of his tired eyes.

She gave his hand one more squeeze, then exited the room and stopped in front of Bill Caldwell, whose patience was running thinner than a wisp of smoke. "If you could follow me, sir," she said, then led the way to a wall-mounted screen displaying the county logo. On the other side of the wall, a camera was trained on Alyssa's face, feeding into that screen, ready to be turned on. The ME had rolled the girl's body on a table and set it for family viewing, shrouded in a crisp white sheet pulled all the way up to her chin, covering almost entirely the deep, discolored laceration that had ended her life. It was one thing for a parent to *know* his daughter had been killed, her throat slashed, and entirely another to actually *see* it. The image of that would haunt Bill Caldwell's nightmares for years to come, tainting every memory he had of his daughter, his shocked psyche unable to hold on to the good memories and eradicate the single one that would forever burn in his mind.

She knocked on the door frame and the screen came to life, exposing Alyssa's head for viewing.

Kay watched Caldwell's response, careful to catch any glimpse of a reaction that could tell her something, anything, about the DNA mix-up or about his involvement in her death. But he was just staring at the image, his fists clenched hard, his knuckles crackling, knotted muscles dancing along his jawline.

"I want to see my daughter," he urged, "not like this. I want to touch her, to hold her hand."

Unsure how to proceed, Kay looked up at the monitor, fitted with a camera and microphone that recorded the formal identification. Doc Whitmore had obviously heard Caldwell's request, because he opened the autopsy room door, inviting him in.

Bill Caldwell walked into the room holding his head up high and his fists clenched, close to his body, as if he were getting ready to fight an unseen assailant. He approached the table where his daughter lay and stared at her face, his eyes dry, his mouth a thin, tense line. Then he grabbed the sheet and peeled it off with a quick gesture, exposing her upper body entirely. He didn't flinch when he saw her wound, nor did he touch her skin or caress her face to say goodbye. His expression carved in stone, he turned to Dr. Whitmore and asked, "This is my daughter, Alyssa. Is this what you need me to say?"

Dr. Whitmore nodded, jotting the time of the formal identification on a form, then handed him the clipboard to sign. He took it and signed with a violence that nearly tore the paper under the tip of his pen. "There," he said, holding the clipboard in the air, expecting someone to take it from him.

Kay stepped up and took it with a nod. "Are you positively sure?" She saw the glint of rage in his eyes and quickly offered an explanation. "If you recall, there was an issue with a missing girl's DNA—"

"You people drive me insane! Here," he shouted, snatching a few strands of hair from his head and dropping them on the white sheet that still covered part of the girl's body. "Test these, and you'll have your damn proof. She was my daughter, you clueless, worthless schmucks."

Dr. Whitmore grabbed an evidence pouch and tweezers, quickly collecting the strands from the sheet.

"Could we trouble you for some DNA from your wife?" Kay asked, unperturbed. If he was playing it hard, so could she. DNA from both parents would've helped immensely to clear the shroud of confusion surrounding Rose Harrelson's DNA on record.

Caldwell turned to her and stared her down, his pupils dilated, his face scrunched with rage. "You'll come nowhere near my dying wife. You hear me?"

"But, sir, considering—"

"I don't want to hear it!" he bellowed, cutting Kay off. "I haven't even told her Alyssa is dead; it would kill her on the spot. Your pathetic efforts to clear the aftermath of your incompetence are of no concern to me, and they're not worth my wife's life!"

His face was close to Kay's, his breath burning her skin, but she didn't flinch, didn't step back a single inch. She held his gaze, unyielding, while at the same time she had to admit his reaction was understandable. Anyone in Caldwell's place would've probably reacted the same way, given the circumstances.

He was the first to look away, even if for a brief moment. "Do you honestly think I don't know who my daughter's mother is? Check hospital records, for crying out loud. Do your job, Detective; investigate."

He turned to leave, but Kay got in his way. "I have another question, if I may?"

He grunted, but she nodded and whispered, "Thank you," while she turned and picked up an evidence pouch from the table and showed it to him. "Your daughter was wearing this locket when she died."

"And?" he asked, barely glancing at the necklace.

"It's a simple piece of wood on a silver chain, something a child would wear," she said, giving him a moment, but he remained silent, frowning, seemingly confused. "Something a poor child would wear, not someone like your daughter."

"Ah," he reacted, putting his hands in his pockets. "Her, um, mother made that for her when she was little. That's why she wore it."

There was a hint of hesitation in his voice as he said the words, and Kay wondered why that could be. What could he be hiding?

Was it not her mother who had made the locket? It seemed inconsequential to Kay, but if he'd deemed the lie necessary, maybe there was something worth exploring. Something that would, potentially, turn into a lead.

"If there isn't anything else," he said, turning to leave, but Kay touched his elbow with her fingers. He froze in place and glared at her again. "What now, Detective? I've already told you this is my daughter lying there on that slab. I already told you who did it. What else could you possibly want?"

Jumping at the morsel he'd just thrown her, she said, "Why is it that you suspected your sister or her son of killing your daughter?"

"There's no past tense in my suspicion," he replied coldly, speaking quickly, his words firing rapidly like bullets from an automatic gun. "They killed Alyssa. My sister, Blanche, or her son, Dylan, or both. They had the motive and the means. As for opportunity, that has been bought and sold in this family for generations."

Kay's eyebrows shot up. If she hadn't witnessed the scene the night before herself, she wouldn't've been so surprised. She couldn't believe he'd done a full reversal, accusing his sister again. After he'd turned like putty in her hands, after placing his forehead next to hers in a gesture that had been on Kay's mind ever since. "What motive could they possibly have?" she asked, the word *heiress* resonating in her mind, in the voice of Carole Caldwell.

"The estate," he replied, closing his eyes for a brief moment. "Many years ago, my mother decided to run the family business like a monarchy. There's no equal division of goods or decision-making power between siblings. The eldest heir inherits everything, and endows the rest as he or she sees fit. Her craziness has cost me my daughter," he added, grinding his teeth as he said the words. "Dylan is next in line now, and he will decide the fate of the entire business when he takes over. As his parent, Blanche's authority now exceeds mine." He stopped and looked her straight in the eye, "And that, Detective, is worth killing for."

It makes some sense, in a twisted kind of way, Kay thought, remembering that Carole's two youngest children had chosen to distance themselves from the business. Stripped of their rights, they must've done the only thing they could possibly do; they walked away. But why had Blanche stayed? Was there any truth in Bill Caldwell's suspicions of his sister and her son?

"Mr. Caldwell, I have to ask," Kay said, shooting Doc Whitmore a quick glance, to see if he was paying attention, "what kind of estate are we talking about?"

He filled his lungs with air and then let it out slowly, probably thinking how much to disclose.

"Caldwell Farms holds over forty thousand farmland acres, several wineries, a grain mill, about twenty thousand working-forest acres, a lumber mill, and a farm equipment sales and lease business." He stopped for a moment, as if giving her the time to take it all in. "How's that for motive now, huh?"

He didn't wait for her reply; he just walked out of the autopsy room, without as much as one last look at his daughter.

CHAPTER TWENTY-FIVE
Memories

The thought of Kirsten—she'd finally revealed her name—kept him going through the bleak and endless day.

By now, the sun had started its descent and soon the house would be shrouded in darkness, sharpening her senses, priming her for his arrival. She'd be cold, shivering, vulnerable, and scared. Curled up on the sofa, covered in his old blanket, waiting for him. Anticipating his touch on her body. Fearing him, while at the same time wishing he'd be there already, to take care of her, to make her strong.

And yet, he was still pining for *her*, the first girl his flesh had ever known, the one and only love of his life. His Mira.

He closed his eyes for a brief moment and the memory of her filled his mind, a welcome ghost ephemeral as the evanescent perfection of a snowflake right before it melts, untouchable and distant like the clouds in the sky yet there, present, vivid in his dreams, night after night.

He still saw her eyes, round with innocence, her slender body trembling, cold and anticipating and fearing and wanting at the same time, filled with desires that had no name. There, in pitch darkness, he'd reached for her with both arms and she'd folded, wrapping herself around his body like a flowering vine, growing stronger and more beautiful once she was joined with him. He'd become her inner strength, her support, the essence that put the fragrance in her blooming womanhood. While she, his Mira, as he liked to call her, had become his every reason for being alive. She was his wonder, his boundless ocean forever soothing, his very own miracle.

Recalling their blissful nights, stolen moments of pure happiness and endless joy, he refused to open his eyes, fearing the light of day would come crashing in, disintegrating the frail fabric of the cherished memory. When she used to be in his life, everything made sense. The two of them had the world open in front of them, as if it were a mail-order catalog, with everything they could possibly desire already theirs, within reach, easy to achieve if they were together. The love they shared synergized them both. She'd drawn strength and courage from him, and was becoming a heart-stopping beauty, smart and powerful and kind. He'd taken her love and filled his heart with it, inspired and driven to achieve greatness, a primal yearning to lay an offering at her feet and make her proud.

In the rare moments he didn't think of her, he thanked the gods for his unbelievable fortune to have discovered her, to have her in his life, to be able to whisper her name in the middle of the night while she stirred in her sleep, wrapped in his arms, sending icicles of fire through his blood.

Mira.

His very own, amazing Mira.

Then she'd betrayed him. Twice.

The emptiness she'd left behind was raw and hollow, bloodstained and filled with the odor of death, as heinous as a slaughterhouse, as sad as a sailor lost at sea, never to come back to shore, never to know home again.

Since her, his first love, no one had ever come close to touching his heart.

He'd been searching, trying, desperate to fill the void she'd left behind, fiercely frenzied to make the pain go away and forever wipe her name from his aching memory.

The day fate had put the first girl in his path, lost, wandering aimlessly, a young runaway who no one would ever miss, he thought the gods had sent her in answer to his prayers. He'd taken her home and tried his best. She was young, innocent, scared, a pleasure to possess, but she wasn't *her*. Nothing she would do or say could fix that.

After a few days, he found himself tired of her endless tears, her whining, her fears. He'd grown weary of her, frustrated and bitter. While her body lay tense by his side, afraid to move and desperate to keep the distance as if his skin burned her, he was wide awake, his eyes fixed on the ceiling that had witnessed such incredible love.

That girl didn't deserve to be there… She had to go. Her presence was an insult to Mira's memory. But maybe there was another out there who would fill the void, one who'd embrace the love he had to give, one who would never betray him. But he knew he could never let the girl leave, despite her tear-filled promises; the moment she would be free, she'd run to the first cop and have him locked behind bars like an animal.

He had no choice.

He'd never thought of taking a life before. It didn't make him happy; he didn't find the thought of killing those girls thrilling or in the least bit exciting. It was a chore, something he did quickly, out of necessity, like taking out the trash. He didn't like doing it, but he didn't mind it either; he just didn't think about it. It was something he needed to do to make room for the next girl, who might be the one, who might be able to soothe his unhealing heartbreak and bring him what he so desperately needed.

That first runaway girl had gone, many years ago. Others had since come and gone, leaving him emptier and in more pain than he'd thought possible. Now Kirsten, she seemed like she could be the one. She looked just like Mira, just as he remembered, with her long, blond hair, her wonderful blue eyes, and her thin waist that fit so well in his hands. She was quiet and didn't fight him, even pretended to wrap her arms around him, making the lie seem closer to the truth. She was obedient, resigned to spend her days waiting and her nights in the cold darkness he'd designed to set the stage as close to the reality of back then as possible.

But not even Kirsten was *her,* the one he'd do anything to be able to touch again. His first, never-forgotten, true love. His Mira.

He'd given her that name, short for Miramar, because it meant all the things she was to him. The beauty of the ocean, the endless blue of the waves, their restless motion, captivating him, driving him to spend blissful hours admiring the view, the sight of her. Because he wanted to call her by a name no one else would. He'd chosen that name for her after they'd walked hand in hand on Miramar Beach, their whispers safe under the ocean breeze, her eyes sparkling like the sun's rays broken into a million dazzling shards by endless waves.

He'd never dreamed of vengeance for her double betrayal, even if the pain it left behind was as searing as the lethal bite of a venomous snake. He'd never envisioned himself hurting his Mira in any way or making her pay for what she'd done all those years ago; he loved her too much for that. But, lately, he'd found himself thinking that for as long as she was alive, he could never heal. He could never really forget her, get over her, no matter how many Kirstens would stay at the house with him and keep him company at night, if all he could think of was her, of how he wished to hold her one more time, to taste her, to whisper her name over and over while she rose to meet him.

Perhaps the time had come to put the fire out himself, with his own hands, even if that snuffed the life out of him forever.

CHAPTER TWENTY-SIX

Locket

A quiet whir filled the room, no other sound competing against it in the stillness of the morgue. Under the bright, fluorescent lights, the machine extracting the DNA from the roots of Bill Caldwell's hair cycled through its steps, while a faint, acrid smell of chemicals filled the air.

Kay and Dr. Whitmore watched the centrifuge for a long, silent moment, then the medical examiner approached the table where Alyssa's body lay covered with a fresh white sheet.

"Come on," he whispered to the body, pushing the table on its wheels toward the back wall, where refrigerated storage units were lined up in rows of four. "Don't worry… He loves you very much," he continued, talking about Bill Caldwell as if Alyssa could hear his words. "That's why he reacted that way. He's in shock, I believe."

He opened the door to one of the refrigerated storage units and propped the table against the railed edges, then released the clamps holding the table and rolled the body inside with one firm move. He closed the door with a sigh. "Such a shame, to die so young."

Kay glanced at the doctor for a moment, worried. He looked as if he'd aged ten years in the past two days, his spirit bent under the burden of the DNA blunder—as the local media kept referring to it—digging it up and stirring it endlessly in a distasteful attempt to retain the public's interest. Their small town didn't enjoy such drama too often, and there were many who stood to gain from prolonging the ordeal, with little respect for the lives of everyone involved.

She watched him from a distance as he put Alyssa's body away, his words to the lifeless girl tugging at the strings of Kay's heart. He walked a little slower than usual, his head bowed, his shoulders stiff and raised as if to protect his neck from a fatal blow that was yet to come. His eyes looked haunted, and the long hours of work and restlessness had marked dark circles under them.

Kay checked the device's timer and noted there were a few more minutes left before they'd know the truth about the girl whose body had just been stored in unit six.

"May I use your computer?" Kay asked, remembering she had another mystery to solve while waiting for the centrifuge to stop spinning. Someone had betrayed Nicole Scott, turning her desperate letters over to her husband, and she was planning to find out who.

"Have at it," the doc replied, sifting through the evidence pouches on the table.

She typed something quickly, then printed the page and folded it neatly. "How about an envelope?"

"Top-left drawer," he replied, not taking his eyes off what he was doing.

She extracted one envelope, then smiled, a hint of mischief touching her voice. "How about some fluorescent dye? I need it in powder form, not liquid, and that powder better be white," she clarified.

This time, Doc Whitmore shot her an inquisitive glance. "Should I ask?"

"Nah... Just setting a trap to catch a piece of scum, that's all."

He went into the adjacent storage room and returned after a minute with a small plastic container. "Set up on that table, by the corner. It's sterile. And use gloves with this thing or you'll glow under blacklight like a white T-shirt in a disco."

She chuckled quietly, following his advice and finished preparing her letter quickly, before returning the container. "Thank you." Then she sealed the envelope and looked around, searching for a place to put it so she wouldn't forget it.

"Put it in my out tray, there," he said, pointing at a stack of color-coded plastic trays on his desk. "My receptionist will give it to the mail carrier."

"Thanks," she replied, then dropped the envelope and joined the doc by the evidence table. "You know, I was thinking, what if you weren't wrong?" she asked, the bothersome thought churning in her mind half-formed.

"About what?" he asked, cutting the seal off the evidence pouch that held Alyssa's locket.

"The, um, DNA mix-up," she replied, scratching the back of her head. She hated bringing it up, but she'd promised she would help him find answers.

"How was I not wrong?" he reacted, turning toward her angrily and raising his voice. "How many times in your professional life have you had to withdraw a next-of-kin notification and start over, with another family?"

She knew better than to be offended. He was angry at himself, blaming himself for what had happened, for the stain on the sheriff's office reputation, on his career.

"What if that is really Rose Harrelson in there?" she asked, pointing at the drawer where the girl's body was stored.

He scoffed and propped his gloved hands on his hips. "Haven't we established that's Alyssa Caldwell? I could've sworn we have a formal identification signed, witnessed, and recorded. There are thousands of photos of Alyssa Caldwell on social media, and they're a match to the girl in my drawer." He filled his lungs with the cold, slightly acrid air then exhaled slowly, an effort to calm his fraught nerves. "Listen, I know what you're trying to do, and I appreciate it. But there's no way—" He stopped mid-phrase, his gaze riveted on the locket he had taken out of the sealed evidence pouch. "But then again, there's this," he added, holding the necklace in the air.

"Exactly," Kay said, reaching the table in a few quick steps. "This locket and the original DNA indicate the body is Rose Harrelson. Everything else says it's Alyssa Caldwell, including her father."

"There could be other lockets just like it," Doc Whitmore said, pulling a four-legged stool and taking a seat in front of the table. He flipped on the lights above his head and flooded the examination tray holding the locket in bright white light. "Despite what Caldwell said, they could've been on sale at the time, at the local dollar store," he muttered, examining the locket carefully under the lenses of his magnifying glasses. "There could be hundreds of these out there, who knows. It's not conclusive."

"DNA is," Kay replied. "Have you found any evidence of an error having been made in Rose's case? Is there a paper trail showing how medico-legal had gained access to Alyssa Caldwell's DNA, to have something to misfile as Rose Harrelson's?"

Silence ensued, the whirring of the centrifuge seeming louder after she'd stopped talking. The machine spun quickly, separating the components of the sample.

"Don't bother saying anything," Kay said, touching his elbow briefly, "I already know the answers to these questions."

He looked up at her, his gaze a mix of sadness and gratitude, shame and hope.

"In a few minutes, we'll know for sure," Doc Whitmore replied, shifting his eyes toward the centrifuge. "If Bill Caldwell's DNA is a match to our victim's, then that's Alyssa Caldwell in there." He stopped talking, and Kay let him process, knowing his guilt was still blocking his perception. "Well, to some extent," he corrected himself, frowning as he realized what he'd missed. "It will only prove Bill Caldwell is the girl's father, nothing else. The heck with it."

"Let's do some digging," Kay offered, then circled the table and took a seat behind the desk, in front of his computer. She accessed the FBI systems gateway and entered her credentials, running a search for Alyssa's birth records. "Alyssa Caldwell," she mumbled, speaking to herself. "Born here, in Mount Chester, about, um, four months before Rose Harrelson. Went to school here, got her first credit card at fourteen, her driver's license when she turned sixteen." She logged out of the system with a groan. "Nothing stands out. She's as legit and as real as can be, and so was Rose."

"I managed to open it," Doc Whitmore said, holding the locket close to his glasses. "Take a look."

She pulled her chair closer to the table and watched. He had restored the locket to its original appearance of an extended hexagon, but then he twisted the bottom clockwise, the hexagon turning into a stylized heart. Then he pulled the hook that held the chain attached to it and it exposed a tiny photo, weathered and damaged by the time it had spent submerged.

"Who do you think this is?" Doc Whitmore asked, handing it to her.

She pulled on a fresh pair of gloves and took it from his hands, studying the photo attentively. It reminded her of a picture she'd seen at the Caldwell residence, of Bill Caldwell and his wife, taken on their wedding day. She turned back to the computer and ran a quick search to confirm, then announced, "It's Evangeline Caldwell, Bill's wife."

"Alyssa's mother," he mumbled, his frown returning. He took off his headband and rested it quietly on the table, then switched off the LED lamp. "I'm afraid our guest is Alyssa Caldwell after all."

The centrifuge beeped and the whirring stopped, signaling the DNA extraction had been completed.

Doc Whitmore stood and rushed to the machine. Taking out the sample, he loaded it into another machine, where the extracted DNA was to be scanned and visualized, then compared against the existing sample he'd taken from the victim.

The computer took a few minutes, but eventually announced the result with a chime, and Kay realized she'd been holding her breath.

"It's a match," Doc Whitmore announced, rubbing his bearded chin with his fingers. "Bill Caldwell is Alyssa's father, because that girl in my fridge is Alyssa, and there's no doubt about it." He shrugged and let out a long, pained sigh. "Somewhere, somehow, a mistake has been made, and I will own it. I'm the ME, it's my morgue, and the buck stops here."

She was disappointed, although she couldn't quite figure out why. She'd guessed the result since Bill had volunteered the sample; it was logical. And still, knowing the result gave her a strong sense of loss, as if she was missing something.

Allowing herself the time to gather her thoughts and understand what her instinct was trying to tell her, she continued to study the locket, putting it back together again, then reopening it, always following the same steps: holding the tip of the hexagon with her left hand, then rotating the bottom with her right, clockwise, then pulling at the hook toward the left to see the photo. She admired the intricate, delicate handiwork that made the mechanism work so smoothly, even after being submerged for a while. The lacquer had protected the wood, keeping it from swelling too badly.

An intriguing thought crossed her mind, and she quickly restored the locket to its original hexagonal shape. She proceeded to rotate the bottom in the opposite direction, counterclockwise, trying it gently to see if it worked. It aligned itself again as a stylized heart, but when she pulled the hook to the left nothing happened. A smile twitched at the corner of her mouth when she pulled the hook to the right, and it opened, showing a different photo. It was another woman, about the same age Evangeline had been in that first photo, who also seemed familiar.

"And who's that?" Doc Whitmore asked. He'd been watching her work for a while, not saying a word, seemingly captivated.

Her heart thumped in her chest, a chill dancing on her spine as she recognized the woman in the photo. It was Shelley Harrelson.

"We need maternal DNA, Doc," she said, standing abruptly, ready to rush out the door.

"But haven't you heard Bill Caldwell? He's not going to let us get anywhere near his dying wife. You'll need a warrant—"

"I'll get you an elimination sample," she replied, zipping up her jacket. "I'll go back to the retirement home and get a hair sample for you. We need to know once and for all, could this girl be Rose Harrelson?"

"You mean that's—"

"Shelley Harrelson," she said, pointing at the open locket. "If that's Rose lying there in your unit number six, Doc, then how and why did she become Alyssa?" She frowned, staring at the label on the storage shelf door as if the brushed metal digit held the answer to all the questions swirling in her head. "And where on earth is the real Alyssa Caldwell?"

CHAPTER TWENTY-SEVEN
Afterthoughts

The sun's bright rays did little to defeat the nipping cold rolling off of the Mount Chester snow-covered versants, but Elliot kept his window slightly lowered while driving the meandering road that crossed the mountain. Swirls of thoughts chased one another in his mind. Kay, smiling while looking at him from across the tacky bar table covered with empty shot glasses. The glimmer in her eyes, the unspoken fire in her dilated pupils, her shivering touch when she grazed her fingers against the back of his hand.

He wanted to kick himself for taking her to Hilltop, of all places, where the deputies hung out, and for not sending them packing when they'd started taking turns at making her drink, nothing but a disgusting attempt to get her drunk and embarrass her forever in the eyes of the entire precinct.

But she'd held her own, defiant, tighter than bark on a log, pretending not to see the real reason behind their so-called welcome-to-the-office drinks, while her eyes bore into his, her impatience just as unbearable as his own. She'd downed those shots one after another, not a shred of hesitation in her gesture, a hint of disgust curling her lips just a tad after the first shot. Kay probably hated tequila just as much as he did.

And then she'd touched him, urging him to leave, reaching for his hand.

Was it even real? Or was he imagining things? She'd said nothing, nor had she touched him again after that fleeting moment when her frozen fingers had seeded fire in his blood. Maybe she was starting to feel sick and wanted to be out of there, away from the deputies' scrutiny.

On the drive home she hadn't said a single word, the evening ending in a much different way than he'd imagined. She hadn't lifted her tear-filled eyes to look at him again, seemingly mortified.

And he'd said nothing to lift her spirits. He couldn't speak the words that came to mind, that he'd been there too, that he admired her courage withstanding those bullies and proving herself to them in the only way it mattered. That he'd never admired a woman more, nor had he seen someone so brave, not only for the way she'd knocked back those shots, but for how he'd seen her hold her own with a perp's weapon aimed at her chest, how she relentlessly chased the truth with a completely open mind.

That's what made Kay formidable, drunk or sober, a force to be reckoned with.

That morning, before heading out to Caldwell Farms again, he'd driven by her place to give her a lift, but no one answered the door, and Jacob's truck wasn't parked in its usual spot on the driveway. He then drove to Hilltop, where she'd left her SUV the night before.

It was gone.

One minute late, one dollar short; the story of his life.

He swore under his breath. Now last night's heavy silence would linger on throughout the day, leaving marks, seeding doubt, driving a wedge between them. All because he couldn't say a few words while he'd driven her home.

As if he'd been raised in a barn.

But hot will cool, if greedy will let it.

There would be time to catch up with her and say everything he didn't have a chance to. Or maybe just skip through all that and redo last night, wipe the slate clean and start brand new.

He adjusted the brim on his hat and peeled off, heading to Caldwell. He drove straight to the place where Hazel had dropped Kirsten, and pulled over by the side of the road, his flashers on.

He wasn't sure what he was looking for after all that time, but he wanted to see what she'd seen when she had waited for another ride to stop and give her a lift.

In the bright daylight, he noticed things he'd missed the night before. There was a section of about a foot where the rocks lining the edge of the road had been cleared away, leaving barren ground exposed. A partial shoe print was etched in the dry mud, a sneaker by the pattern of it, and possibly a woman's by its size.

Maybe Kirsten had stood there, leaning against the guardrail, her feet on the ground she'd cleared because it must've been uncomfortable to spend so much time balancing her feet on those rounded rocks that slipped and turned under her weight.

He took a few photos of the print, first from a distance, to document its location and the section of cleared ground. Then, grabbing an L-shaped scale from his field kit, he placed it by the shoe print and took a few close-ups.

He was just about ready to leave, when a car sped by well above the limit. Seconds behind him, a patrol car with flashers and siren on passed by in pursuit, the deputy behind the wheel a familiar face.

A hint of a smile lit Elliot's eyes when he recognized the man, the effervescence of the newly found idea energizing.

It was Deputy Leach.

He might've seen something the day Kirsten went missing.

CHAPTER TWENTY-EIGHT
Secrets

It was a disaster of epic proportions, about to blow up in their faces and engulf her legacy in a cloud of shame and destruction so thick no speck of dirt, no patch of land, and no corn kernel would survive it unblemished.

Carole needed to get in front of this thing, to control it, smother its flames before it turned into a blazing inferno. Why had she been blessed with the mind to build an empire out of a 10-acre farm, only to be cursed with weak, selfish children? Her eldest, Bill, was a ghost living with a ghost, that mousey wife of his who just wouldn't die already, to make room for another alliance, to grow the family assets and give Bill, that lame-stick child of hers, a few sons, to carry the name forward. He didn't seem to care about women, since he'd been living like a monk for the past two decades. What kind of man does that? No matter how hard she tried, she just couldn't understand her eldest son.

As for Blanche, she'd resigned herself to a lonely, loveless life, while that no-good husband of hers trolled the Dominican Republic with his latest whore on his arm, all funded by the monthly stipend he pulled from the business. Blanche could've divorced him years ago and found herself a good, strong, loving man. Stubborn as a mule, her daughter, refusing to divorce that sleazy, cheating bastard and blackmailing her own mother when she'd refused. How could she have threatened her with leaving the business? Why? It wasn't like she still loved her husband, or held any hope for his return. No… She just wanted to live her life peacefully, helping her son Dylan learn the ropes of the business, managing the farms with him by her side, her face lighting up whenever he walked into the room. Carole was a mother too, but Blanche's love for her only son wasn't normal.

And now, Alyssa was gone, the pride of Carole's life, her beloved heiress. Alyssa had possessed a mind like no one else's in the family, and stamina, the drive to win, to achieve, as if her blood was on fire all the time. She'd probably inherited that from her, because her granddaughter reminded Carole of herself at that age, eager to spread her wings and fly, proving what she could do. All that greatness, gone in an instant. All the promise of what that girl could've done for the Caldwell legacy, turned into dust, leaving everything in Dylan's hands.

Dylan was a good man, but she couldn't bring herself to love him, to want him at the reins of the company, not as she'd wanted Alyssa.

Could Bill have been right? Could Alyssa's death have been motivated by greed, by the fight for the legacy she had built? A shudder traveled through her thin body. She gathered the edges of her cashmere shawl closer and rejected the thought without hesitation. That never could've happened. Alyssa's death had been nothing but an unfortunate stroke of bad luck, a crime motivated by reasons that had nothing to do with the family, with her or any of the children.

The disaster she had to prevent had very little to do with Alyssa's death, if anything at all. However, the thin layer of dust that had settled over ancient history and its deeply buried secrets risked being swirled up in the air by that nosy detective and by Carole's own children, who, spineless and weakened by the good life they'd been living, couldn't take any of fate's merciless blows without falling apart, without jeopardizing their heritage and the honor that stood with the Caldwell name.

Shameful and lame.

She stood from her bedroom armchair and put her shoes on, adjusted her hair, and applied a touchup of lipstick. Inspecting her reflection in the mirror, she straightened the hem of her burgundy shawl where it had caught against the button of her black jacket. She applied a short, discreet whiff of perfume on her left wrist, then rubbed her wrists together. With the scent of jasmine surrounding her like a halo, she was ready to fight another battle.

One look out the window confirmed Bill's car was gone, but Blanche's was still here. Every morning, staff pulled their vehicles to the entrance and readied them for the day.

Maybe it was for the best that Bill had already left. Blanche was the weakest link at the moment, her overly sentimental view of life rendering her the most likely to crack under pressure. If that detective showed up one more time, there was no telling what could happen. Like knots on the same string knitted into the fabric of time, Alyssa's murder could pull out in the open new secrets and old ones, equally dangerous, threatening to unravel the texture of their lives.

Carole walked quickly to Blanche's suite, her determined footsteps noiseless, stifled by the lush carpets, and rapped her fingernails against her door. She didn't wait to be invited in; a short moment later, she entered, expecting to find her daughter curled up in bed or still getting dressed. But she wasn't there, not in the living room, not in her bedroom, where the unmade bed with twisted sheets and tear-stained pillowcases stood in testimony to the agitated night she had spent.

With an irritated scoff, Carole left Blanche's suite and started looking for her everywhere, losing her patience with every room. Eventually, after trying her on her mobile phone and getting voicemail, she remembered Blanche liked to hide in the upstairs library when she was upset, the somber, quiet room soothing her fraught nerves.

Carole climbed the flight of stairs with a spring in her step, enviable for her seventy-nine years of age, and walked into the library. Standing by the window and staring outside, Blanche sobbed quietly, unaware her mother had entered the room. Rows of bookcases lined the walls, filled with all the novels that had been owned in the family for generations, Carole a fierce collector of such things. The window, shielded in the finest white sheers, let the filtered sunlight in, but that didn't dissipate the solemnity of the space.

Approaching Blanche, Carole reached over to her daughter, and touched her arm gently. Blanche jumped out of her skin, startled, and turned her red, swollen eyes toward her mother with an unspoken plea.

"Please, Mother," she whispered, "let me tell him what really happened." Her voice shattered, strangled by a sob.

Carole's grasp on her daughter's arm turned firm, forcing her to turn and face her. Blanche veered her gaze away, then closed her eyes, allowing more tears to roll down her cheeks.

"Listen, my dear," Carole said, but when Blanche didn't open her eyes, seemingly withdrawn from reality, she grabbed both her shoulders and squeezed a little harder. "Listen to me."

Visibly reluctant, Blanche opened her eyes and met her mother's steely gaze for a moment, before looking away again.

"This secret has the power to destroy all of us," Carole said, unafraid to let the decisiveness in her voice cut like a blade. "You've done a good job keeping it buried so far." She caressed her daughter's hair, sweeping a loose strand off her face with the tips of her fingers. "Don't ruin everything now," she added, lowering her tone to almost a whisper and willing herself to sound caring, empathic, when in reality she felt like shaking the woman back to her senses and yelling at her to wake the heck up. "Don't worry, sweetie. Bill is just upset. But you know he loves you dearly. He didn't mean it; you know he didn't."

"But if he knew—"

"Shush," she said, at the limit of her patience. "There's nothing to know. You wouldn't do anyone any favors except yourself." She stared her down until she felt her shoulders give in under her firm touch. "Ask yourself, is your selfishness a good enough reason to threaten the well-being of our entire family?"

Blanche sighed, a resigned release of air that had been kept captive in her lungs, signaling her defeat.

"That's my girl," Carole said, smiling. She hugged her daughter and held her tight for a moment, then pushed her away. Blanche had weakened with age, instead of becoming stronger, more independent, more self-assured. It didn't take long for the floodgates to open with that one, and oh, goodness, she could cry.

A wimp.

"Will you be okay?" she asked, searching Blanche's eyes.

The woman nodded, but looked away. The floodgates were still open, but she would get herself together shortly. And she'd keep quiet, and they might survive the storm, but only if that detective didn't come calling again.

She had to watch Blanche like a hawk, make sure she wasn't alone with that cop, not even for a minute.

Kay Sharp... *Dr.* Kay Sharp, no less. Carole had asked her assistant to look into the detective's background, because she seemed way too smart for Mount Chester, California, where most deputies were barely high school graduates. Whereas this woman had gumption, and could keenly read people, as if she could flip through their thoughts like one turns the pages of a book. And she was homing in on their family secrets, carefully guarded for decades, getting much too close for Carole's liking.

Dr. Kay Sharp was dangerous.

If push came to shove, she'd be ready to do what's necessary.

Most people could be bought off, although when it came to money, the cop's smarts seemed to be nonexistent, replaced by utter, blatant stupidity. She could've been a successful psychologist with a booming practice in San Francisco, making a killing at whatever number of hundreds of dollars per hour shrinks these days could charge for therapy, with the anxious business executives and spoiled housewives of Silicon Valley as clients. Instead, she'd chosen to work for the FBI and catch killers for a living. Meh, but still, somewhat dignified. But even that she'd left behind for the measly paycheck she made as a detective in the local police force of a town with a population under four thousand.

Not very smart at all. Or maybe she just couldn't be bought.

Well, she thought, caressing Blanche's cheek one more time before leaving the library, *people have random, freak accidents all the time. And that's something that* can *be bought.*

CHAPTER TWENTY-NINE
Disobedience

Since he'd left, she'd barely got out of bed, her body aching all over, her mind raging and screaming inside. It was late in the afternoon, the sun descending already, soon to reach the barren forest canopy visible through the living room window.

It was cold, and Kirsten dreaded getting out of bed, even if that's what she needed to do to find another blanket or borrow a sweater from a nameless girl who once lay in her place.

Soon it would be dark.

A tear burned her frozen temple as it slid toward the pillow. She remembered the night before in vivid, heart-stopping imagery she couldn't get out of her mind. How she'd waited for him for hours after the cloak of night had fallen, heating the house with the stove and using a table lamp from the bedroom for light, plugged into the empty outlet behind the fridge. How she heard his car pulling onto the driveway and had bolted to cut the light and turn off the stove. How he'd stopped in the doorway, sniffing the air, sensing it was too warm.

Then he'd unleashed his rage on her for her disobedience.

"I told you how I like things done," he'd shouted, so close to her she could feel the air vibrating with his rage. "I warned you, don't make me do things I don't want to do."

She sobbed and pleaded for his mercy, while he stared at her, slowly burning through his anger until it was down to a simmer.

Then he unlocked the door with the same remote he never let out of his hand and opened it wide, allowing the cold, humid air to fill the house. Soon, her teeth were clattering again, and she was shivering under three layers of clothing she'd put on.

He wasn't pleased with that either. He'd stripped her naked and sent her to take a shower, reminding her in a voice that left no room for arguments to not blow-dry her hair, just wrap herself in a towel and come out.

She knew why, and she knew what awaited her when she did.

Under the shower, still shivering despite the hot water that scalded her skin, she remembered how loving and yearning he'd seemed the night before. She also remembered how, when she was back at her stepfather's house fighting Potbelly and his cohorts, her trying to wriggle free of their hands holding her down only made the lusting men more aroused, fueling their hunger.

What if the way out required her to be smart and cunning instead? Sheer strength had done exactly *nada* against the window-panes, and would do zilch against that huge knife of his.

When she'd come out of the bathroom that night, she knew what to expect. The house, cold and shrouded in darkness. Him, still a little angry but predictable for the most part, going through the same motions as the night before, and every night before that, as if rehearsing a part in a play with no audience and no limelight.

She'd played her part well, pretending to want him, to enjoy cuddling against his body, caressing him with frozen, trembling fingers while she wished him gone more than she'd wished for anything in her life.

Then she pretended to doze off, trying to catch him asleep long enough to grab that knife and end his miserable existence. But he kept vigil, as if guarding her from unseen perils.

When the first light of dawn started defeating the night, he rose and got dressed, for a moment the charismatic man she'd once hoped would like her still there, his eyes warm and tender, his smile genuine.

Then that strange, loving gaze shifted, and a frown ridged his brow. "Never fucking disobey me again," he said coldly, then left without another word.

She watched his car pull away from the driveway and breathed with ease when he turned onto the main road, vanishing from sight. She rushed to the stove and turned it on, but the elements stayed cold and dark. Her heart pounding in her chest, she opened the fridge to find it just as dark and almost empty, the air inside already stale smelling.

There was no power anymore. No heat. No light. Nothing.

Panicked, she roamed the closets looking for something to wear, but no matter what she touched, the same question made her shy away, repulsed and fearful. What girl had worn that sweater before, and where was she now? Had she escaped and returned to her family? Or was she buried somewhere in a shallow grave, in the woods behind the house, not that far from there?

Eventually, her street sense won, and she put on some heavy clothing. Whether those girls were dead or alive, it mattered not; they didn't care anymore, and she would soon share their fate anyway.

There was no escape.

Unless she could turn the tables on him somehow.

He seemed obsessed with something, the darkness, the cold, the chilling shower routine that preluded their endless nights together. Perhaps she was there to remind him of someone else, like all the other girls could've been.

Then, maybe, there was a way to trick that man into falling in love with her. If she could only figure out who she needed to become.

Roaming the house in the dimming light of the afternoon with a clear purpose in mind, she noticed the portrait of a young girl dressed in a pink blouse with ruffles and a simple black pencil skirt. It hung on the wall in the bedroom where he'd taken her every night, and while she pretended to be asleep in his arms, he stayed awake, not taking his eyes off that image. She remembered how he looked at that portrait sometimes, right before leaving the room, a long and yearning gaze as if saying goodbye.

Kirsten resembled that girl. She was a tall, thin blond with long hair like hers, and a kind, loving smile, a little shy. She wore pink nail polish and light pink lipstick. Her wavy hair hung loose, brought over her right shoulder, causing her head to tilt just a bit, playfully.

Running her hands through her hair, Kirsten brought it over her shoulder, then imitated the girl's shy smile.

She could do it. She could be that girl.

CHAPTER THIRTY
Thoughts

Kay started her drive toward Redding, but after crossing the valley she reached the top of the hill and pulled into Katse Coffee Shop's parking lot. The sun was shooting side rays, already too weak to fight the chill rolling down from the mountain slopes. Soon it would disappear behind Mount Chester, starting a long twilight that commenced two hours before the actual sunset. A trip to Redding and back would put her into early evening, and she'd already skipped lunch. Deciding to grab a coffee refill and a fresh croissant, she mitigated her guilt by making it a working lunch.

The outdoor patio had been closed for the season and the tables had been piled up one on top of another, chained against the fence. The chairs were gone, probably stored somewhere inside. Out of quiet options for a peaceful working lunch, she decided to go inside after all.

She took her order from the counter and found a table, but the place was crowded, and the loud chatter drowned her own thoughts. Realizing that wasn't going to work as planned, she opted for the SUV instead, and sat behind the wheel with the door open, to let the crisp air of the afternoon fill her lungs while she munched on the warm butter croissant. No one made croissants just like Katse; crisp, flaky, light pastry, perfectly golden and delicately sweet. Through the windshield, the chilly sunshine still managed to warm her up and lift her spirits, giving her confidence she could decipher the entangled mystery of the Blackwater River Falls girl.

Who was she, really?

Was she Rose Harrelson? Then why had she become Alyssa Caldwell, and how? Did someone snatch Rose and replace Alyssa, without anyone in the family—parents, grandparents, siblings—noticing the difference? Why would anyone do that, and what happened to the real Alyssa Caldwell?

Because one thing was absolutely certain: even if, at some point, Rose had become Alyssa, originally, there used to be two little girls, born four months apart from each other. There were full hospital records on file for both of them, with photos and all.

Staring in the distance at the snow-covered peaks of Mount Chester profiled against the blue sky, she let her mind wander, playing with scenarios the way children play with Legos. Putting them together, to see if she liked the configuration, if it fit, then taking it apart and building another with the same pieces.

There used to be two little girls, Alyssa and Rose.

Then there was just one.

She finished the croissant and stretched her legs outside the SUV, brushing off the crumbs that littered her pants and sweater. After wiping her hands on a tissue dipped in hand sanitizer spritzed from the small bottle she kept in the second cup holder between the seats, she waved her hands in the air, to dry them out, then fired up her laptop.

She reviewed the case notes from Rose Harrelson's file, and looked at the aged photo. Then she pulled one of Alyssa's older pictures from the internet, taken at her fourth birthday party. For a place like Mount Chester, the birthday of the Caldwell Farms heiress was newsworthy, and had been so since she was born, making it even less likely for Alyssa to have been replaced with Rose without anyone noticing.

No... The entire scenario was stupid, a contrived fabrication of her mind because she couldn't find out the truth.

Although the girls did sort of look like each other.

The same chestnut brown hair or close enough, cute little chin dimples, and the same brown eyes. Coincidence? Possibly. A large enough percentage of the population had that trait, and the two girls weren't the only ones to have chin dimples in Mount Chester. As for hair and eye color, neither was unique.

Kay sighed. She had nothing.

But maybe Shelley Harrelson's path had crossed the Caldwells' path. She'd asked Carole about that, but, before she could answer, they were distracted by Bill's arrival. If she was to solve the original kidnapping, she needed to map the timeline of all those interactions from fourteen years ago, and for that, she needed a lead she could follow. She needed to go back and revisit the Caldwells, whose unusual behavior was a surefire indication of carefully guarded secrets, one of them potentially being the answer she was looking for.

Going back to her imaginary game of Legos, she collapsed all the theories she'd built and decided to split the facts into two different piles, one for Rose and one for Alyssa, leaving all speculation aside.

What did she know about Rose Harrelson? One thing was for sure: she'd been kidnapped. Neither of her parents were involved; that was another fact. A third fact was the investigation into her disappearance had been a model of incompetence and lack of follow-through. Critical questions were never answered, and key witnesses were never questioned.

She picked up a pen from the glovebox and started jotting notes on Rose's case file. *Who took her? Why? Redo the walkthrough at the crime scene. Interview the father's work friends. Find the detective who'd essentially killed the investigation and ask him a couple of questions. Incompetence or ulterior motive? Get Shelley's DNA and establish the identity of the girl in the morgue, beyond any reasonable doubt.*

By later that night, they would know. Doc Whitmore would gladly stay up all night to run the test.

She downed another mouthful of black coffee and switched tasks, leaving Rose's file on the passenger seat and going back to the computer. Before heading out to Redding, she wanted to find out a little bit more about Alyssa, for her second pile of facts.

Alyssa had been born four months before Rose and both her parents were still alive. She'd been at the center of local media attention growing up, and that meant there was a trail of visual testimony about her growing up. And she'd grown to be a normal teenager, with social media accounts filled with selfies and friends—friends whom Kay could interview and learn more about Alyssa.

She closed the laptop and stared at the mountain peaks again, the colors of the afternoon so vivid they seemed surreal. The dark green of the pines. The sharp reds, oranges, and yellows of fallen foliage. And out there, in the distance, white snow on gray stone against a sky of perfect blue.

Fourteen years ago, Kay was battling her own problems, and any news she might've seen about Rose's kidnapping or about Alyssa at the time was long forgotten. But all those people out there, Alyssa's Facebook friends, the people who kept their eyes on the Caldwells, lacking another pastime should be a good place to start.

But first, the girl's true identity. Shelley's DNA would soon reveal what she needed to know.

With a tense smile playing on her lips, she started the engine and took a left turn onto the highway, heading south.

At least Nicole was safe at Kay's place with Jacob, settling in, going through her first day as a free woman. The tension in her smile eased a little; things were starting to look up.

CHAPTER THIRTY-ONE
Orders

Deputy Herb Scott drove his patrol car past Hilltop Bar and Grill, slowing as he approached the old building, but decided to head straight home instead. His head was still pounding, the hangover clinging to him like mud to a pig. Some hair of the dog would set him straight, but until he could see one of everything again, he couldn't tolerate the hollering at the pub.

Luckily, there was plenty booze in the house, and that good-for-nothing woman would rush to get him a glass filled to the brim with the finest single malt he had, saved especially for days when only the finest single malt would cut it.

He pulled the patrol car onto the driveway and came to a stop, too hungover to notice all lights were off in the house, although the sun had set a good while ago. The porch light was off, and he swore loudly when he tripped on the lowest step and nearly fell. Then he unlocked the door and stepped inside.

No smell of fresh-cooked dinner greeted him, just the dark silence of the house. He flipped the switch on and called out impatiently, "Nicole." He stood in the middle of the hallway, waiting for her to rush out of wherever the heck she was and tend to his needs, but nothing happened.

"Nicole," he shouted again, and the echo of his own voice was the only response he got. "Damn that woman," he muttered, releasing his duty belt and dropping it on a nearby chair. He took off his jacket, then undid the button on his pants with a sigh of relief. The waistline of his uniform had grown tighter and tighter lately, adding to his daily misery.

When he entered the kitchen and flipped on the lights, he didn't find anything on the stove. Out of habit, he checked the oven, but it was empty and turned off. The dishes were piled up in the sink, unwashed, and the table hadn't been cleared since breakfast.

"Lazy woman," he groaned. "Where the heck are you, already?" He swore again, thinking she might've gone to the store. There was a reason why she wasn't allowed to leave the house by herself, and she knew it well. If she'd forgotten, he'd be happy to remind her right after that single malt and some dinner she better have ready for him.

He checked the bedroom next, and found the closet doors open, some of her things missing. The suitcase was gone, and so was her purse. Dumbfounded, he stood in the middle of the room, scratching his head. As in a daze, he remembered she kept some cash in a tin in her night table, probably thinking he didn't know about it. But he knew everything; it was his job, his duty as the head of the family.

He opened the drawer and rummaged through the contents, looking for that tin. It was gone, and so was her mother's wedding ring that she kept although she never wore, because her fingers were too thin, and she didn't want to lose it.

The bitch was gone.

His hangover returned with a punch, and he clenched his fists until his knuckles crackled and let out a rage-filled roar. He rushed to the living room and opened the liquor cabinet, then gulped a couple of swills of single malt straight from the bottle, then slammed it on the table, not caring about the droplets that found their way out and landed on the shiny, lacquered surface.

That's when he saw it.

An envelope, unsealed, propped against the TV remote, with his name in block letters handwritten on it.

He opened and read it, although his vision was blurry, the characters dancing on the sheet of paper in front of him.

You'll never see me again.
Don't come find me.

Although there were only two short phrases, he had to read the letter twice to get its meaning.

His woman had left him.

Him!

Thankless, ignorant, disrespectful bitch! A coward to leave him a note instead of confronting him, of telling him to his face. He would've showed her.

His face grew a dark shade of red, while the veins on his temples pulsated in sync with his thunderous heart, fueling his headache. Rage grew inside him until he couldn't see straight anymore, and he looked for something to hit, but Nicole was gone, cowardly escaping the lesson she had coming. His fists landed on the wall instead, the drywall no match for his well-developed arms. The hole he punched in the wall had bloodstains on the edges, but he didn't feel the hurt, only the fury. He rushed into the bedroom again and yanked her clothes off their hangers, stomping on them, tearing them to shreds. Then he moved on to the bedsheets, and when he was done with those, he returned to the kitchen, the dishes in the sink his next target. He sent them flying across the room, where they met the tiled wall and fell to the floor in pieces and shards.

"Aargh! That fucking whore!" he bellowed, turning on his heel, looking for more things to break. "I'll kill her with my own two hands, that's what I'll do." A crockpot flew across the room and hit the window, cracking it before it landed in the sink. "If it's the last thing I'll do, I'll fucking kill that bitch."

That's when his phone rang, the cheerful ring tone at odds with the concert of roars and crashes.

"For fuck's sake," he shouted, as if the caller could hear him. He panted, out of breath, not sure if he wanted to take the call or not, not sure what to do. He'd never felt so angry in his life.

Then he saw the phone's display, as it peeked from the jacket's pocket. Instead of the caller's name, a triple dollar sign appeared, which only he knew the meaning of. Swallowing his rage, he grabbed the phone and answered.

"Hello," he said, panting hard, out of breath.

"Am I interrupting anything?" The caller's voice was cold and stern, the man unwilling to take any of his bullshit.

Scott knew better than to do anything but get ready to take some orders. "No, sir," he replied, barely catching his breath. "What can I do for you?"

"That new cop, Kay Sharp, I need you on her twenty-four-seven," he said, and paused for a second, but Scott wasn't fast enough to reply, still out of breath. "I want you on her like white on rice, you hear me?"

"Y—yes, sir," Scott managed, "but she's a fed, you know. Tailing a fed is dangerous. I've done it a couple of times, but—"

"Then don't get caught," the man replied with a dismissive scoff. "Get the job done. And if she gets too close, get rid of her."

He wondered whether it was the right time to ask for more money, since he was going to work around the clock, and take a hell of a risk. "About that," he started to say, "since she's a fed and all, I think we should discuss a different arrangement—"

"Do you like being alive? Do you like *that* arrangement?" the man asked calmly, and Scott felt a chill traveling through his veins. "Then leave the thinking to me," he added, just as calmly, with an undertone of resolve in his voice that couldn't be misunderstood.

He ended the call before Scott dared finish his thought.

He definitely needed to ask for more money. Triple-Dollar-Sign had always paid him well.

Tailing a fed is dangerous, but killing one carries the death penalty.

CHAPTER THIRTY-TWO

DNA

The azure of the sky had gradually turned purple, then a star-pierced, pitch black, the colors shifting quickly as they always did that time of year. A waxing crescent still lingered above the barren trees, giving the landscape residual Halloween vibes four days into November.

Kay had made good time to Redding Hospital, willfully ignoring the pain that had nested between her shoulders and was climbing up her neck in knife-like stabs. Every now and then, she ran her hand across her nape, trying to relieve the tension that was sharpening the pain jabs, absentmindedly, while her thoughts circled obsessively around Rose Harrelson and Alyssa Caldwell.

Which one of them was lying in Doc Whitmore's morgue? Soon enough they'd both know, and that knowledge would define the course of her investigation. That knowledge would be the first solid lead she'd landed since she saw the girl's body submerged under the falls.

For a brief moment, she found herself missing the serial killer inquiries of her past as an FBI profiler, the discipline in them, the rigor, the clear and simple procedures. Victimology. Profiling. Geography. Elliot might've believed that those cases felt simple for her, because she was good at doing that work, nothing else, but she liked to believe there was more, like her understanding of the criminal psyche, her ability to put herself in an unsub's shoes and anticipate his next move. And if she could catch a serial killer, she definitely could manage collaring the unsub who'd kidnapped a three-year-old, fourteen years ago, or the one who'd slashed Alyssa's throat beneath Blackwater River Falls.

Were they one and the same? She frowned as the thought crossed her mind. *Could that be possible?*

The problem with Alyssa's murder case was simple: there were too many questions and not nearly enough answers. Rose's kidnapping case suffered from exactly the same issue.

Strange coincidences everywhere she looked.

Kay approached the hospital driving at slow speed, dreading the moment she'd have to step through those revolving doors and inhale the air that reminded her of her mother's final days, its many odors mixed together and recirculated by the building's air conditioning. Disinfectant, iodine, laundry detergent, starch, the stale fabric of waiting room chairs and couches, the cracked faux leather of the armchairs in the main lobby, and the plastic mattress protectors in every room warmed up by body heat.

Only yesterday she'd been there, escorting Shelley Harrelson's ambulance to the hospital, in the hope the doctors could save her life from the latest stroke. She didn't hold much hope; she'd seen cases like Shelley and was well versed in the prognosis. Whether she was conscious or not, whether she remembered it or not, Kay had made the grieving woman a promise she had every intention to keep. And to keep that promise, she needed a sample of her DNA.

She stopped the SUV at the curb, then flashed her badge at the approaching security guard. "I'll only need a minute," she said, and the man's scowl dissolved.

Walking past him and through the revolving doors, she showed her badge again at reception and got a room number. A moment in the elevator, then she found Shelley's room.

The rhythmic beeping of the heart monitor greeted Kay as soon as she pulled the sliding door open and entered. By her side, a tall man wearing hospital garb was checking her vitals.

Shelley's eyes were closed, and she was breathing through a tube connected to a ventilator, her lungs no longer able to draw breath on their own. Her head was wrapped in gauze. They must've operated on her to relieve the intracranial pressure generated by the stroke. A gray pallor had touched her skin as if death had already staked its claim over her weak body.

"Are you family?" the man asked in a kind voice. His name tag read, DR. FIELDMORE. He was young, most likely a resident.

"No," she replied, showing her badge again. "I'm Dr. Sharp, with the sheriff's office. How is she?"

He looked at Shelley for a brief moment, then checked his clipboard before speaking. "We relieved the intracranial pressure and stopped the bleeding, but she slipped into a coma. She'll probably never wake up." He ran his hand through his hair and sighed. "She's a seven on the Glasgow Coma Scale. She's not coming back."

Kay nodded. "I understand. What's your plan?"

"We're pulling the plug tomorrow morning."

For some reason, the thought brought a knot in Kay's throat. "So soon?"

"Standard protocol for wards of the state. There's no family, and no hope."

Kay shoved the evidence pouch she'd been clasping in her sweaty palm back into her pocket. Shelley's hair was gone; she wasn't going to be able to get her DNA by taking a couple of hair fibers with the roots still attached. But she wasn't going to leave empty-handed either; she was sure Shelley wouldn't've liked that.

"May I have a sterile flocked swab in individual wrapping?"

He looked at her inquisitively, but decided not to ask. Hospitals required warrants for collection of DNA from their patients, whether dead or alive or in between. "You can find some in this drawer, over here," he showed her, leaving the respective drawer slightly open. "Need a minute or two?"

"Yes, thank you," she replied, swallowing with difficulty.

He left the room, sliding the door silently shut.

Grabbing the stool vacated by the doctor, Kay pulled it by the bedside. Memories of her mother's passing came crashing in, and, for a long, confusing moment, she felt close to Shelley, drawn to her as if it were her own mom lying on that bed, dying all over again.

She took the woman's cold hand in hers and held it for a while, fighting tears and words that demanded to be spoken.

Then she stopped fighting them, knowing that there was a tiny sliver of a chance Shelley could hear her.

"I promised you I'll find out what happened to Rose," she said, her voice not much more than a whisper. "I think I have an idea, but I need your help. I need to be sure."

She reached into the drawer and extracted the swab, then unsealed the end of it and took the cap off. Gently, she inserted the tip into Shelley's mouth and swabbed her cheek, sealing the swab in its container. Fishing out the evidence pouch from her pocket, she slid the swab in and zipped the pouch, signing it and marking down the time and date.

Then she took Shelley's hand in hers again.

"Thank you," she whispered, her voice loaded with tears. The thought of how a family's destiny had been shattered by a single, fateful event choked her, burning her eyes and swelling her chest. It was inexplicable; she was a hardened criminalist with eight years of seeing the most gruesome of crime scenes and catching the sickest, most violent offenders. But there was something heart-wrenching about seeing Shelley on that hospital bed, dying alone.

"I promised you I'll find whoever did this to you, to all of you. However long it will take me—" she said, then stopped, remembering Shelley's unusual reaction when she'd had her second stroke.

What was it that she'd said?

Kay closed her eyes, trying to remember word for word. "All this time... my baby..." Shelley had said the day before, before blood had rushed to her head so violently it had ruptured vessels inside her brain, driven by a strong emotional reaction to... What, exactly? To the news of Alyssa's death? Why did she care? Who was Alyssa to Shelley Harrelson?

"You were trying to tell me something else, weren't you?" Kay whispered. "I think you were, and I believe I know what that was."

Squeezing the woman's hand, Kay set it down gently on the bed, then said goodbye as Dr. Fieldmore returned. She thanked him and left, but then stopped in the doorway to give the woman another long look.

"I'll find out," she murmured, then left, rushing to her vehicle. While waiting for the elevator, she texted Dr. Whitmore a quick note.

I have the sample. On my way.

CHAPTER THIRTY-THREE
Copy

After a while, they all knew.

Not from the start, hope a thick veil of disbelief and self-deception, keeping them clinging to the thought they would soon regain control over what was happening to them.

But they all knew, sooner or later, and when they finally realized their fate, they lost their appeal so quickly he had to will himself to give them more time. More chances, more nights to keep him company, more attempts to make it work, although he already knew the outcome.

Kirsten was about to have the realization that would change her attitude toward him entirely. He'd sensed that about her, in her misguided disobedience, the stiffness of her body lying in bed by his side, the untamed, hateful glimmer in her eyes. She would probably be changed by the next time he visited, and, just like others before her, armed with some strategy deemed to help her escape.

It never worked out well for any of them.

It only poisoned his nights, having to constantly stay vigilant, ready to defend himself against an attack that could come without warning. Her fear of him would only go so far; beyond that certain point, she, like all the others who had walked in her shoes, would decide she had nothing left to lose.

How sad.

When she could have a life with him others only dreamed of, not a worry in the world, being loved with all his heart. If only her eyes would stop throwing poison-dipped daggers and soften a little, just enough to fuel his dreams of Mira. If only she could learn to slow down, relax in his arms, and run her fingers against his face like *she* used to do. Then he'd be able to close his eyes and relive the love he'd lost, even if only for a fleeting moment, before being forced back into the reality that hollowed his heart, touching it with death's wing.

But after a while, tired and filled with the despair of repeated failure, they settled in their cage, slowly losing their will to live. And the memory of his beloved Mira would fade away again, tainted by the girls' defiance, their rejection, their inability or unwillingness to replace the sacred vision with a living copy of the woman who once had filled his heart with joy.

A copy, never the original, even if the copy sometimes tried to lie to him, to get him drunk on his own fantasy, to entangle him in a web of deceit so thick he'd lose all sense of reality. Regardless of her lame attempts, she'd still be a copy.

Never Mira again, never in his arms, never to touch her flawless skin, never to feel her breath against his cheek while she whispered tender words in his ear. Only copies he used for a while then dealt away with, when their own derisive vileness stained the image he held most sacred, burning through the dream like acid through paper.

Soon Kirsten would be there too, at that point of no return. There was nothing he could do to prevent that from happening.

CHAPTER THIRTY-FOUR

Invitation

Kay wasn't patient enough to drive back to Mount Chester and start searching for the information she wanted while the DNA sample whirled in Doc Whitmore's centrifuge. Despite the cold darkness, she chose to squint in the fading light at the information in Rose Harrelson's case file, until she finally gave in and turned on her flashlight, holding it above the pages while the other hand turned them, one by one, after she'd perused them patiently, reading every word.

The information she was looking for had to be in there somewhere. Had Shelley Harrelson been acquainted with Bill Caldwell or with someone else in the Caldwell family? The two families were worlds apart in terms of everything, from social status to circles of friends and the geographies of their daily routines. But what did she know about Shelley Harrelson's daily routine, to be sure she never crossed the Caldwells' path?

Exactly nothing. Zilch. Big, fat goose egg.

If she were investigating a federal case, she would've had access to data analysts and a support team. She would've been able to run detailed histories of employment, residential addresses, even bank records for all those involved, immediately identifying any point where their lives had intersected. But she wasn't a profiler anymore; she'd chosen to return home, against all odds, and become a detective here, in Mount Chester, where the entire sheriff's office didn't have an analyst. They only had a geek who reset their passwords every now and then, and fixed the printers, someone's kid most likely, because he wasn't permanently on staff. The small-town sheriff's office couldn't afford a full-time techie, and Mount Chester would probably have to pass half a million inhabitants before the sheriff would consider adding an analyst.

Nevertheless, the information should've been in there, in the pages of the worst-handled case in the entire history of kidnapping investigations. *Maybe this has a chance to take the gold in nationals,* she thought bitterly, the memory of Shelley dying alone in that hospital room still haunting her. The man who'd done such a bad job finding her daughter was just as guilty of her death as Rose's kidnapper was, at least in Kay's own system of values.

There should've been a list of persons of interest in the case. Everyone who had come in contact with the parents and the missing girl in the week prior to her disappearance, the parents' employers and any relevant work contacts, anyone who could've carried a grudge against either of the parents, anyone who visited their home on a regular basis or in the week prior to Rose's vanishing, anyone who took care of the little girl. All those people should've been clearly identified on a list, interview notes with each person attached to the file.

Almost none of that existed on record. The detective who'd so-called *worked* the case had jotted down a few names on a page ripped from a notebook. The girl's nanny. The neighbor Elliot and she had met the day before, Martha Duncan. A couple of others she'd never heard of.

No reference to any Caldwell whatsoever, but the case file was far from complete.

Fed up with the way the case had been handled, she decided to stop griping and visit with the detective who'd signed most of the paperwork only with his initials, H.S. For that, she had to identify him.

She flipped the pages backward. Somewhere, on the original missing person report, right below the narrative on the second page, there was the name of the reporting officer, and below that, the approving officer. She recognized both names, belonging to deputies who worked in the same office as she did. But then she saw the name typed in the box for "Internally Route To," indicating which detective had been assigned to the case.

Herbert Scott.

She read the name and couldn't comprehend, at first. The Herbert Scott she knew was a deputy, a wife beater and a drunk, but a deputy, nevertheless. She'd been left with no choice but to offer his poor wife shelter at her own house, to keep her and her baby safe from the violent rages of the man. Yet the report indicated Deputy Scott used to be a detective fourteen years ago, when he investigated Rose's disappearance and did an impressively poor job at it.

Kay closed the case file and leaned back in her seat, willing the thousand thoughts racing through her mind to settle and construct a clear picture of what that meant.

She'd thought of how to deal with Scott on the spousal abuse issue. She'd contrived a plan that could put him in jail without having to drag Nicole to court to testify, but she needed a couple of days before she could execute it. She had to identify the leak first, the man or woman on the sheriff's staff who had intercepted the mailed letter sent by Nicole and put it in her husband's hands instead of its intended recipient. She could bury that person under a slew of charges, from the federal crime of mail theft to obstruction of government administration, because the letter Nicole had sent had been addressed to Sheriff Logan with the intention of reporting and stopping a crime.

And then she'd turn them. She'd offer them a deal. They'd have to serve some time in a federal facility, because the thought of that person walking free made the bile rise in her throat. That deal would come in exchange for their testimony against Scott.

Then Scott would take a deal himself, and that meant Nicole and her baby could be free of him. Forever.

That had been her carefully woven plan, shredded to bits by his name typed on a missing person report from fourteen years ago.

She couldn't delay speaking with him about the Harrelson case, but at the same time, she needed to come clean with the sheriff about what was going on.

Pulling her phone out of her pocket, she scrolled through the names and tapped the sheriff's. He picked up almost immediately.

"Detective," he said, his voice energetic and bold against a backdrop of bullpen chatter and office noise. "How's the Caldwell investigation going?"

She forced some air into her lungs. "About that, sir, would you be available for an off-the-record conversation with me?"

He was silent for a beat. "Um, sure. What did you have in mind?" His tone had dropped to somber, quieter.

"When can you leave the office?" she asked, looking at the time and planning the rest of her day. First off, she had to drive back from Redding, then she had to drop the DNA sample at the morgue, and she wanted to stop by the old Harrelson residence, to take another look at that house. Maybe there was evidence that had gone unnoticed by the then *Detective* Scott that could help with the case. She needed about two hours, if not more.

"Not before seven," the sheriff replied. She could hear the frown in his voice, the unspoken questions.

It was almost five. "That's perfect," she replied. "Say, seven thirty at Katse?" For a moment, only the background noise came across the open connection. "Let's meet on the outdoor patio. It's closed now, and it should be completely dark."

The long silence told Kay that Logan had doubts, questioning her motives and probably her sanity. She'd been officially on his team for less than a week and, most likely, hadn't yet earned his trust.

"And none of this, er, conversation can take place in my office?" he eventually asked.

"I'm afraid it can't," she replied, then allowed him the time to decide.

"Okay, yes, I can make it," he eventually replied, before immediately disconnecting the call.

There was nothing left to say.

CHAPTER THIRTY-FIVE
Ultimatum

Deputy Leach downed his burrito with the appetite of a wild hog after a long winter, barely taking the time to chew the large bites he took every few seconds. He looked as if he could eat anything that didn't eat him first, a budding waistline starting to bubble over his duty belt.

Elliot waited patiently for Leach to finish his lunch; it wasn't going to take much longer anyway. Since seven o'clock that morning, he'd been traveling that section of highway up and down, studying traffic patterns, noticing trucks that drove by the place where Kirsten had last been seen after Hazel Fuentes had dropped her off by the Caldwell Farms entrance.

At about ten, he'd received a call from Hazel, who'd asked all the Caldwell truck drivers if they'd seen the girl and had managed to narrow down the time window of her disappearance. The last of her colleagues to have seen Kirsten when he drove off the farm had left at 3:15 p.m. that day. The first one who was sure no girl had been lingering by the ramp was headed south for a delivery, having left at almost five.

That meant whoever picked up Kirsten had driven by between 3:15 p.m. and 5:00 p.m., on October 28, exactly one week ago. With that time frame in mind, he'd asked Leach for some help. The deputy was working speed enforcement on that stretch of highway every day, except Mondays and Wednesdays when he was off. Since Kirsten was last seen on a Thursday, he hoped the deputy would offer some insight.

"So, Detective, what can I do you for?" Leach asked, wiping his mouth with a paper napkin and letting out a heavy sigh of satisfaction, loaded with heavy scents of hot sauce and guacamole, barely discernible in the stuffy, smelly air of the diner. He leaned forward, pushing the empty plate aside and resting his elbows on the greasy melamine surface of the table. After cleaning his teeth with his tongue and belching a couple of times, he managed a smile.

"I'm trying to locate a young girl," Elliot said, showing him Kirsten's photo on his phone. "She was last seen by the Hilt exit, heading south."

He shook his head, still staring at the girl's photo. "Nope, haven't seen her."

"It was a week ago, today," Elliot specified.

He shook his head again. "I usually stay on the side road right at the bottom of that valley, so they won't see me. The speed limit changes at the state line, and they come rolling down that hill, right to papa." He chuckled, rubbing his hands together. "I made last month's quota by October twenty-third; can you believe it? Great spot, that one."

"What traffic have you noticed?" Elliot asked, hiding an eyeroll under the brim of his hat.

"Traffic?" he asked, while his eyes scanned the diner's posted menu.

"Any marked vehicles that caught your attention? Any traffic stops you pulled that day that I could interview?" Elliot paused for a moment, but Leach was staring at the menu, sucking his stained teeth. "Come on, man, give me something I could use. This girl's been gone a week."

"UPS drives by every day at about four," Leach said, seemingly thinking, but Elliot wasn't sure he wasn't trying to decide between another burrito and some dessert. "I see Amazon Prime trucks too, but those never speed."

"Why don't you pull your notebook and give me the tags for the vehicles you pulled over a week ago between three and five?"

Leach glared at him but kept his mouth shut. He leaned to the side to ease the weight off his right buttock, then extracted a curved, leather-bound notebook and threw it on the table. "There, Lieutenant," he said, marking Elliot's rank with venom in his voice.

Elliot picked up the notebook; it felt warm to the touch and carried a slight odor that he didn't want to identify. He flipped through the pages back to October 28, and found no entries for the entire afternoon. Only one car, late that evening at about seven, had driven 12 miles over the limit and was issued a $238 fine.

"That's it?" Elliot asked frowning.

"No one was speeding that afternoon, sir," Leach replied, his sarcasm heavy, right in Elliot's face. "What's a good cop to do if people won't break the law?"

He'd probably napped the entire time, brought down by a meal such as the one Elliot had just paid for, knowing he'd already made his quota for the month. If one thing was accurate out of everything Leach had said, it was he hadn't seen Kirsten. That tends to happen when people sleep; they don't see much.

Closing the notebook, Elliot set it on the table calmly, then stood. "Thank you, Deputy. I hope you enjoyed your lunch."

He stepped out of the diner, glad to breathe the fresh, chilly air of the evening. Right across the highway, over the hills, the sun was getting ready to set, elongating the shadows of everything and everyone, as if darkness advanced slowly, throwing patches of night here and there, slightly thicker where shadows touched and overlapped.

He reached out for his phone, hoping he'd see a message or a missed call from Kay, but that couldn't be. He would've heard her call or the chime that alerted him of new messages. He'd listened out for them the entire day, and nothing had disturbed the solitude of his fruitless search for the missing teen from Oregon.

He resisted the urge to call Kay and ask her where she would go next to find Kirsten. Instead, he thought about what she'd do if she were in his shoes.

So far, no one had seen the girl, no one had heard a peep from the runaway, and all he knew was she was headed into San Francisco. She might've reached her destination the same day, last Thursday, at the earliest about six or seven in the evening. He didn't have any idea of what vehicle had picked her up or who was driving it.

All he knew was that all vehicles needed gas. The one who'd taken Kirsten might've stopped somewhere along the road to San Francisco, and someone might remember. There might be some video surveillance showing tags if he was lucky enough. Or someone might've seen something, one of the regular drivers who hauled the same route. Those drivers had their favorite fuel stops, and that's where he needed to go.

Unfortunately, Kirsten being a runaway, an AMBER alert could not be issued. But he could do the next best thing: post flyers.

Fifteen minutes and a few dollars spent at UPS bought him the typing and printing of flyers with Kirsten's photo and the sheriff's office tip line number printed in a large, bold font. The flyer stated clearly her last seen location with date and time. Now all he had to do was beat the pavement from one gas station to another and paste those by the restrooms, the one place no driver failed to visit.

It was already dark outside when he'd finished interviewing the first gas station attendee and had pasted the first flyer. At that rate, it was going to take him a while.

"Thank you," he said, nodding at the cashier and offering his card. "In case you hear anything."

The cashier took it and dropped it in the cash drawer without giving it a single look, then beckoned the next person in line and started scanning. The sequence of beeps resounded loudly in the almost-empty store. Elliot touched the brim of his hat in a gesture no one noticed, then headed for his SUV in the biting cold.

When his phone rang, his first thought was of Kay. One look at the screen showed Sheriff Logan's name instead. He took the call and headed to his car.

"Sir," he greeted the sheriff, unlocking his SUV and climbing behind the wheel. He started the engine and turned on the heat. The temperature was dropping rapidly and was forecast to dip below freezing that night. The thought of Kirsten ran through his mind. For a brief moment, he wondered if she was safe and warm for the night or was spending her nights on the street, like countless other runaway kids, shivering, hungry, and scared in some dark alley.

"Where are we with that girl?" the sheriff asked. "Any progress?"

"Some," Elliot replied, careful to hide the disappointment from his voice. "I've managed to track her moves down to the Hilt exit."

"And from there?"

"We, um, I don't know. I'm talking to gas stations and long-haulers now. I'll know more by morning. Some calls might start coming in on our tip line."

"So, essentially, you have nothing," the sheriff said. "Wrap it up and come back to the office tomorrow morning. I'll reassign you."

"I need more time," Elliot said, anger starting to rile him up. The sheriff was giving up way too easily on that kid. "I might be able to—"

"Do you know how many kids went missing last year? Seventy thousand in California, three hundred and seventy in our county only. Most of them come back on their own when they realize it's too cold outside or that mom's cooking wasn't all that bad. And some are never found."

Elliot clenched his fist and slammed it into the steering wheel. Kirsten wasn't some number. She was a scared girl running away from abuse.

"I need more time," he said, keeping his tone low and apparently calm.

"Well, do you have any leads?" Although he knew the answer, Logan asked again as an argument to support his decision to end the investigation.

"Not at this time, but I hope to have something by lunch tomorrow. I need a few days. It's not like we have a bunch of murders piling up unsolved, is it?" he asked, instantly regretting his question. The sheriff had the final say in work assignments, and it wasn't his place to question his decisions. Ticking him off wasn't going to help Kirsten's case.

"Your colleague, Dr. Sharp, might disagree, but I'll give you twenty-four hours. After that, we'll just send your report to Oregon and let them sort it out."

"I need more time," he said, already pulling out of the gas station and heading south to the next one. "Twenty-four hours won't be enough."

"Bring me a lead, and we'll talk about it."

He ended the call before Elliot could acknowledge the order.

The sheriff was right. If the flyers and the gas station interviews didn't generate a lead, he had no option but to give up on Kirsten. Her ride might've not stopped for gas anywhere before reaching San Francisco, and she might be forever gone.

He felt a chill and turned up the heat in the car, wondering about Kirsten again.

Where was she?

CHAPTER THIRTY-SIX

Martha

The Harrelson residence was a ghastly sight in the dark, even after Kay had seen it in the daylight. But she didn't care about the raccoon family who called the shed home, or any number of creatures that could've nested in the abandoned ranch; she was going to process the crime scene like it should've been processed fourteen years ago, hoping she'd find something, anything that was missed.

Ignoring the migraine that was starting to creep up on her, she tested the large flashlight, then climbed out of the SUV and popped the trunk. She had her old forensics kit with her; while she carried a badge, she'd never leave home without it. Dr. Whitmore had taught her how to put one together, during her first week on the job in San Francisco when she was a rookie. "It will save time, legwork, and lives, not necessarily in that order," he'd said, and over the years he'd been proven right several times.

She opened the case and checked the contents. Fingerprint powder, brush, and slides, evidence pouches, luminol, UV light, a pair of yellow glasses to enhance her vision when she checked for bloodstains, and a variety of swabs and sample-collection tools that could come in handy at most crime scenes. Overkill for a compromised crime scene going back fourteen years, but she still wanted to give it a shot.

Closing the case, she carried it to the front door, then put the beam of her flashlight on the fiberboard that had been nailed over the jambs. The nails were rusted badly, and the board panel rattled when she grabbed it by the side and pulled.

Standing in the high beams of her Ford, she took out her keys and inserted the longest key on her chain right next to one of the nails, between the doorjamb and the board, then pulled, forcing the panel away. She repeated the move around the board for each nail, thankful that there weren't that many. The wind had picked up with the promise of snow in the smells it carried over from the peaks of Mount Chester, chilling her to the bone and fueling her throbbing headache.

When the fiberboard panel fell to the ground, a cloud of dust rose, immediately whirling away in the wind. The musty smell of decay coming from the house was lingering, despite the strong gusts.

"Whoa," she heard a woman's voice behind her. Startled, she turned around, her hand on her weapon, squinting against the strong beams to see who that was. "It's Kay, isn't it?" the woman asked in a raspy, tentative voice, approaching slowly.

Still squinting, Kay recognized the fuzzy slippers first, the woman's face still hidden against the powerful glare. She exhaled and took her hand off her Sig. "Martha, what are you doing outside in this cold?" It was the second time the woman had snuck up on her. She had an innate talent for stealth, despite her age and large body.

The woman smiled widely, stepping in front of the beam of light coming from the car. "Not to worry, dearie, I have this shawl, I knitted it myself." She extended a trembling hand and Kay squeezed it. "I couldn't let you leave without saying hello." She stared at the door that barely hung on its hinges, then shot Kay an inquisitive look.

"You shouldn't be out here in the dark," Kay said, knowing her words were falling on deaf ears, wasted on the woman who'd willingly risked her life and health just for the thrill Kay's presence there meant. "And you should never sneak up on a cop. That could be dangerous."

"You're going inside, aren't you?" Martha asked, rubbing her hands together. Kay wasn't sure if her excitement or the biting cold was to blame. "I'm so happy," she said, then touched the corner of her eye to swipe a tear that contradicted her statement. "Someone is actually interested to find out what happened with poor Rose, that sweet little child."

"We won't rest until we find out what happened to Rose," Kay said, her words gentle yet determined, followed by a hint of a sad smile. The best of her efforts could prove too little, too late.

Kay opened the door and entered, glad to see the smell wasn't much worse than she'd sensed outside. Musty, cold, with hints of rotting wood and moist soil, just like fresh-picked mushrooms would smell. She focused her flashlight on the room, checking every corner, looking for animals that could pounce or signs that the structure might collapse, but it seemed to be safe to enter.

Walking through each room, Kay slowly, carefully, noticed every object, every piece of furniture or clothing, every item that had been left behind.

"She didn't take her things, poor Shelley," Martha said, startling Kay again. She thought she'd left the woman outside, by the car, but she was right there, one step behind her, silently watching her work. "She dropped down one day, and that was it. They sealed the place up and didn't care. I emptied the fridge and took the trash out, because I thought she'd be a while and then she'd come back. I never thought she'd—" A stifled sob took the air out of her lungs. "I miss her, you know. Her mother was my best friend. Shelley was like a daughter to me."

Dirty dishes were still piled up in the kitchen sink, and Kay's flashlight caused panic among some insects who disappeared in an instant behind the edges of the counter. Some of the cabinets were still open, as if Shelley had been taken away in the midst of cooking dinner.

Clothes littered the living room sofa, and the dining room table was cluttered with old bills, a set of keys, and a red scarf, too small to be an adult's.

"This was Rose's," Martha offered, seeing the flashlight beam lingering on the item. "Shelley made that for her. She, um, was hoping the cops would bring the police dogs to trace her, but they never came. She was going to give this scarf to the dog to sniff, because she wore it just before she went to bed that night. Rose liked the shiny fabric, and she wore it everywhere, even if it was summer."

"Which room was Rose's bedroom?"

"This one," Martha replied, her voice perking up. Seemingly delighted to be of use, she pointed toward the first bedroom, and Kay opened the door slowly, repeating the earlier routine and checking every corner for possible perils. Then she stepped inside and turned toward Martha. "Let me finish here first, then you can join me."

"Okay," Martha replied. "I know why. I watch crime shows on TV."

The child's room still showed the love Shelley and Elroy had had for their little girl. The bed was dressed in matching sheets and pillowcases with cartoon characters, decayed and fraught by the passing of time. If Kay would've touched them, they would've probably disintegrated. A sketch of Mickey Mouse had been painted on one of the walls, the round ears of the character fuzzy from the cobwebs that extended down from the corners of the room. From the ceiling lamp hung a baby mobile with animal shapes, handcrafted by Shelley most likely.

"She loved that mobile," Martha clarified from the doorway. "Shelley wanted to give it away, but Rose wouldn't let her."

Kay approached the window, where stains left by fingerprint powder had been covered by a thick layer of dust. Detective

Scott—or whoever had run forensics on that crime scene—had only looked on the inside of the windowsill for prints, not outside.

Slipping on a pair of latex gloves, Kay unlocked the window. The sash slid with ease up and down, sending particles of dust swirling in the beam of her flashlight. Behind the glass panel, a mosquito screen was attached, its frame held in place by the fiberboard that covered the window on the outside.

Kay went outside of the house and removed the board from the bedroom window, then shone the light onto that screen frame. It barely stood in place, and she could remove it with two fingers. Then, just as effortlessly, she snapped it back in position.

If she'd had to kidnap the kid sleeping in that bedroom, it would have only been too simple. The screen was easy to remove, the window lifted effortlessly. Shelley remembered she'd left the window open just an inch, and that meant it hadn't been locked. All the kidnapper needed to know was which room Rose slept in.

She studied the exterior of the windowsill, covered in the same thick dust as the rest of the house. She filled her lungs with air, then blew the dust away. It took a few more repetitions until she cleared most of the dust off, exposing clearly where the fingerprint brush had left its swirls of black powder.

On the inside of the sill there had been no fingerprints found. The traces of powder confirmed what was written in the case file. On the outside, no one had bothered to check.

A few spins of her fingerprint brush covered the exterior sill with dark powder, but there were no liftable prints. It wasn't a matter of how much time had passed; forensic history had cases where fingerprints had been successfully lifted after forty years of exposure to air and dust. The fiberboard had shielded the windowsill from the elements, leading to one conclusion. There weren't any prints whatsoever.

Not even Rose's.

"Martha," Kay called, looking at the woman through the open window, "did Rose spend any time by the window, looking outside?"

"She loved to do that!" Martha fidgeted in place, eager to enter the room, but mindful of the line she wasn't supposed to cross. "She stood there, looking at the cars that passed by. Elroy used to tell her the car makes, and she used to squeal with joy and clap her little hands. I don't know if she really knew the difference between a Chevy and a—"

"Did she ever touch the sill?" Kay asked, frowning at the layer of fingerprint powder that had found no greasy marks anywhere on the sill to cling to.

"Huh?" Martha reacted, but then added, "All the time. She grabbed it like this," she demonstrated with her trembling hands. Her shawl fell to the ground. "Oh, dear," she muttered, picking it up quickly and shaking it out vigorously before putting it back on.

There was only one possible explanation for the lack of prints on the windowsill.

Someone had wiped it clean after Rose was taken.

Slamming the lid on her case, Kay headed toward the car. "I'm done here, Martha, thank you very much!"

The woman caught up with her by the time she'd wiped her hands clean and put the case inside the car.

"Have you found anything?" Martha asked, her eyes fixed on Kay's, her hand grabbing her sleeve like she'd done before.

"Nothing yet," Kay replied, then turned to leave. There was no point in sharing her theories with the old woman. Martha let go of her sleeve and took a few shuffled steps to the side. "One question, though."

Martha rushed back to her, stopping a couple of feet in front of her, smiling. "Yes, dearie, what is it?"

"Do you know if Shelley had ever met Bill Caldwell or anyone else from the Caldwell family?"

"Oh, yes," she replied, patting Kay on the forearm as if she was about to share a piece of juicy gossip. "She worked for the Caldwells, for years. She was on their cleaning staff, because a house like theirs, they have more than one woman."

Kay felt a wave of excitement rush through her veins, heating her blood, dissipating her migraine. They *had* met! That was the missing piece of information she'd been trying to find, the one piece of the game critical to solving the puzzle.

"Do you happen to remember when, or how long she worked for them?" Even if Martha couldn't remember, now she knew what she was looking for, and could request the records of Shelley's employment. It would take time, but she finally had a lead.

"Well, let's see," Martha replied, counting on her fingers. "Shelley had dated Elroy for a couple of years right after high school, and they got married the year before she had Rose." A fleeting frown clouded the woman's brow.

"What? What is it?"

"Eh, maybe nothing," Martha replied, turning her eyes away from Kay, preferring to study her own slippers instead.

"Anything you share could prove helpful, you know that, Martha, right?" Kay grabbed her hand and gave it a little squeeze for encouragement.

She nodded, then started talking quickly, as if she'd barely refrained from sharing the long-buried secrets of her best friend's child. "Shelley had been working for the Caldwells for a couple of years when something happened one night. I remember Edna and I spent a few nights worrying. That's Shelley's mother, God rest her soul," Martha clarified, seeing Kay's expression.

"What happened?"

"Shelley came home from work crying one day, and locked herself in her room," Martha said, lowering her voice to a whisper as if there was anyone who could hear them. "She called in sick from work for a few days, and cried, my poor lamb, cried day and night. She wouldn't even see Elroy." She shook her head, emphasizing her statement. "Her mother and I worried so much; you have no idea. No idea unless you're a parent yourself, dearie. Do you have children?"

Kay smiled and shook her head gently. "I still have time." The thought of children hadn't crossed her mind in years, ever since she'd justified her decision to skip maternity thinking her line of work wasn't suited for a mother. But that was a different matter for a different time. "Do you know what was wrong with Shelley at the time? Have you ever found out?"

Martha brought her head closer to Kay. "She came out of that desolation after a while, and started dating Elroy again. A couple of months later, they were married. But," she added, lowering her voice a little more, "exactly nine months after that strange crying spell of hers, Rose was born."

Kay paused for a beat, thinking, allowing the pieces of her Lego game to rearrange with the new information added to the mix. Yes, Shelley had known the Caldwells. But what had caused Shelley's extreme reaction to the news of Alyssa's death? Even if she had been their housekeeper, maybe even Alyssa's caretaker at some point, that didn't justify the response that had caused her second stroke.

Unless…

There was another reason for Shelley's reaction, and Kay didn't know it yet.

"Martha," Kay said, steepling her hands in a pleading gesture, "if you were to venture a guess as to what happened that day with Shelley, what would you say that was?"

Martha looked at Kay for a long, loaded moment. When she spoke, her voice was filled with sorrow. "I'm sure it was something terrible. The poor child never spoke a word of it, and whenever I asked, she'd turn pale and tearful. After a while, I stopped asking, and so did her mother, but…" Her voice trailed off, as if she was still deciding whether to share her thoughts with Kay.

"Please go on," Kay insisted, "you're the only one left who could share details about that day."

Martha sighed, seemingly still undecided. Then, shaking her head a little, she lowered her voice as if afraid someone would overhear her words. "I'd say that someone raped Shelley that day, and that Rose was the child of that rape." She covered her mouth with trembling, knotted fingers. In the car's beams, her eyes glistened.

Reaching inside her jacket pocket, Kay felt the evidence pouch that held Shelley's DNA. Before the light of dawn tomorrow, she'd know.

She'd know if the girl in the morgue was Alyssa or Rose.

If that girl was Rose after all, then she'd been the child of Bill Caldwell, possibly a rape child that he later kidnapped and replaced his own daughter with.

But why?

"Martha, one more question if I may, then I'll drive you home," she said, feeling guilty to keep the old woman in the cold like that.

"Nonsense, dearie, I live right over there," she said, pointing to the left of the property. "Tell me, what do you need to know?"

"What do you remember about Alyssa Caldwell, Bill's daughter?"

"Not that much, really," Martha replied, scratching her forehead. "Shelley had stopped working for the Caldwells right after Rose vanished; it's understandable, poor lamb. But before that, I remember she was saying that tragedy had struck that family. Evangeline was very sick, that's Bill Caldwell's wife. I think she has MS or something, I'm not sure. And then their little girl had fallen ill, seriously ill, you know, like they were afraid for her life."

Huh, Kay thought, her prickling instinct telling her she was headed in the right direction. *Coincidence, you do not exist. Or do you?*

"What was wrong?"

Martha smiled apologetically. "I don't remember... It's been a while, and I'm not that young anymore."

Kay thanked Martha, insisting on dropping her off at her house. Then, as soon as Martha waved at her from her well-lit porch and closed the door behind her, she looked at the time and saw she had less than twelve minutes to get to Katse for her meeting with Sheriff Logan.

She wasn't going to make it on time.

She texted him a message with a quick apology and the time she expected to get there, then turned onto the highway and floored it.

Lego pieces were falling into place, and DNA would soon confirm it.

She felt it in her gut.

If she closed her eyes, she could vividly recall the photos of the two little girls, how she'd thought they look like each other, their wavy chestnut hair, their chin dimples, and she'd dismissed it, writing it off as coincidence, when she should've considered they could be sisters.

And if that was true, that meant one thing.

The girl resting in storage unit number six was Rose Harrelson.

CHAPTER THIRTY-SEVEN
Safe

It's been years since we had people over, Jacob thought, busying himself in the kitchen, clearing the dining table and loading the dishwasher. *I've been living like a monk, before Sis got here, and now we're two monks.*

It would've been so much better if the circumstances were different, and the guest sitting at the table weren't sitting quietly, too ashamed to look him in the eye as if she deserved what had happened to her.

He'd been more than happy to vacuum and spruce up his parents' old room for their guest. It was about time someone scared the cobwebs away from those walls, although Kay had already done her share to refresh the place. His take was more of a symbolic one. He'd lived in an empty house for far too long, and now he just appreciated the company.

Cooking for more than one sure felt better, although he still sucked at it. Being it was so late, and that poor woman was probably hungry and tired and wanted to be alone at last, he didn't risk it. He went for something so simple even he couldn't screw it up. Oven roasted wedge potatoes with a cheese omelet and pickles. Kind of a bachelor dinner, but as far as bachelor dinners went, this was worthy of a Sunday evening, not a Thursday.

The tea kettle whistled, startling the woman. She looked around with the eyes of an injured doe before settling. If that no-good husband of hers were there right now, he would strangle him with his bare hands. Instead, he quickly cut the power to the kettle and the whistling subsided.

"So sorry," he said, with a shy smile. "Kay bought this, it's supposed to be modern, but it still whistles like the old ones we see in British movies." He took two clean mugs from the cabinets, and filled them up with hot water, then opened the drawer where Kay held her herbal teas. "I have chamomile, peppermint, and whatever this is." He flipped one of the teabags and read, "Infinite Serenity." He held it up in the air as if it were a dangerous piece of hazardous material. "Might be good. Wanna try?"

She took it from his hand and tore the wrapper open, dipping the teabag into the water. "Thank you," she whispered, shooting him the quickest of glances before she lowered her eyes again.

She wrapped her cardigan tighter around her thin figure, then put both her hands around the cup and inhaled the scented steam. It had lemon, and some herbal tinge he couldn't place, and the kitchen air was filling with the aroma, clashing with the mouthwatering smell of butter-roasted potatoes. Suddenly curious, he took the wrapper and read the ingredients.

"Lemongrass and linden flowers," he said, then threw the wrapper in the trash. Wondering if it was appropriate, he turned on the radio, thinking it might help her feel better. It always helped him. Maybe the DJ would tell a joke on the air, or maybe the country songs they'd play would not be blue, but funny, like the one about that red SOLO cup he used to hum all day long. Toby Keith played that one.

The potatoes still had twenty minutes or so to go before he could serve dinner, and he struggled with the silence, especially if he was to stand still with nothing to do. He'd finished setting up her room, cleaned the bathroom, loaded the dishwasher, and did everything else he could think of doing to kill time until the food was done. That DJ kept on blabbing something about the weekly countdown, instead of playing some music already.

"My sister will be home soon," he eventually said. She raised her red eyes and looked at him briefly, smiling shyly. "We don't have to wait for her with dinner, you know. I can make us the omelet right now, if you'd like."

She didn't say a word, just shrugged, her thin shoulders poking through that cardigan like meatless bones. If she was going to stay with them for a while, he'd see that she put some meat on those bones and get some rest. She could sleep all day for all he cared; he could take care of her.

"My name's Jacob, by the way," he said, ready to offer his hand if she wanted to shake, but landing it in his pocket awkwardly instead.

Her smile widened, and her gaze lingered a little more. "I know, you told me."

"Oh," he said, then turned toward the sink, suddenly preoccupied with the silverware soaking in there.

"I'm Nicole," she offered, still smiling although her eyes were brimming with tears. "I don't think I said that."

"It's a beautiful name," he replied, starting to get the table set for three. Seeing how she shied away from him when he put plates and napkins on the table triggered memories of his mother, flinching whenever his father walked past her. "You'll be okay," he said, scratching his beard and then wiping the sweat off his palms against the back side of his jeans. He didn't know how to be with people. When he was anxious around them, his palms sweated something fierce. "Kay won't let anything happen to you."

"Thank you," she mumbled, lowering her gaze again.

"And you can stay here as long as you want."

A tear trailed down her cheek and she caught it quickly with a swipe of a finger.

"You'll have your own room and everything. You'll have the main bedroom, so if you need the bathroom, it's right there."

Finally, some music came on that darn radio, ridding him of the need to fill the silence. A song about rediscovering the will to live after a heartbreak.

How fitting.

Finally, the timer on his phone told Jacob the potatoes were done, and he rushed past Nicole to get to the oven, happy the wait was over. In passing, he grazed her shoulder with his arm, a mere accident, nothing more, a fleeting touch most people would've ignored or not even registered.

She yelped and jumped out of her skin, springing to her feet and rushing backward until she ran into the wall, her arm raised to protect her face.

He'd seen the same image before, in the same kitchen, his mother in Nicole's place. Stunned and speechless, he stopped in place and elevated his hands, as if he were surrendering to the cops.

"I'm sorry," he managed to say, after the thumping of his heart released the choke on his throat. "I would never hurt you; I swear I wouldn't."

She still panted, but she lowered her arm and looked ashamed, guilty of some unforgivable sin.

"Look, if you'd prefer, I can wait outside until Kay comes back. Whatever you want, only to make you feel safe." He sidestepped until he reached the side door. "I am sorry," he repeated. "I know you think you can't trust me, but I grew up like this, both of us did. My dad was punching on my mom and I—" He stopped, realizing he was about to say too much. "I could never lay a finger on you. Let me just take the potatoes out of the oven, and I'll go outside and wait in the truck."

He turned and opened the oven, then removed the tray and set it on the stove to cool. When Kay would be home, he'd make the omelet, or maybe he should make Nicole's and feed her now. What's the point in keeping her waiting?

Grabbing a small skillet, he dropped a cube of butter in it, then set it on the stove. He was about to get the eggs from the fridge when he felt her cold, hesitant fingers touch his forearm.

"No one's ever been this good to me," she murmured, her voice strangled, weak. "I'm sorry... I keep seeing him in every corner of the room, about to pounce and hurt me again." Briefly, she raised her tearful eyes and met his, then she rested her cheek against his chest.

"It's okay," he whispered, wrapping his arm around her shoulders. "We'll take care of you."

His words fueled her tears, and soon she was heaving, her face buried at his chest. Where was Kay when he needed her? She'd know the right things to say to make her pain go away.

Unsure of himself and afraid to do or say the wrong thing, he stood as still as possible, comforting her until her sobs weakened.

"I'm so scared," she whispered, clinging on to his shirt, grabbing fistfuls of the fabric and hiding her face in it. "I know he's going to kill me. I can feel it."

CHAPTER THIRTY-EIGHT
Sheriff

The neon sign above Katse was still lit, the neon shape of a coffee cup flickering white against the inky sky, an exact opposite of what the name meant, *black,* in the language of the Native peoples of the Pomo tribe. The chimney let out smoke and vapor right behind the sign, making it appear as if the coffee in the neon cup was steaming, the symbol strong and inviting, a touch of marketing genius.

There were still a few cars in the parking lot, a little surprising at the time, being it was after seven on a weekday in November, when summer tourists were gone, and winter season hadn't started yet.

Kay pulled into the parking lot and came to an abrupt stop, grinding rubber against loose gravel. Sheriff Logan's SUV was parked closer to the dark and empty patio. His back toward her, he was leaning against the hood, his bomber jacket zipped all the way up to his chin, and his hands shoved deep into his pockets.

Either he hadn't heard her pull in or he was pretending to ignore her while she closed the distance between them. Regardless, she did it almost running, eager to get their meeting over and done with.

Out of breath, she stopped by his side. "Thanks for agreeing to meet with me. I understand this is not the usual—"

"Cut the bull, Dr. Sharp, my wife's waiting for me with veal roast in the oven." He'd taken out a cigar and lit it, pedantically slow in his movements, obsessive about his ritual.

"It's about the Rose Harrelson kidnapping case," Kay blurted, still out of breath, although she'd barely sprinted 25 yards. It had been a long day, and she'd been keeping it going on coffee and croissants.

He exhaled, surrounding himself with a cloud of thick smoke that lingered for a moment like a halo before dissipating in the biting wind. "I thought you were working the Caldwell murder. What about the Harrelson case?"

Opening the file to the second page of the missing person report, she tapped her finger on the page. "It was assigned to a Detective Herbert Scott."

"Ah," Logan reacted, a frown quickly furrowing his brow. "I see. And your question is?"

Kay studied his face for a brief moment. His eyes held her gaze unperturbed, his features were relaxed, except for the frown still carving horizontal ridges on his brow. The corners of his mouth were a little stiff when he wasn't sucking smoke from that cigar.

"There's a Deputy Scott on your staff, and no detective with that name. Is he—"

"The same guy," he replied, smoke swirling on his breath as he said the words. "But you knew this already," he added, a hint of a smile in his eyes. "Otherwise, I'd be eating my wife's roast at this time instead of freezing my buns here with you."

She looked away for a moment, then back at him. He was smiling.

"Why am I here, Dr. Sharp?"

She almost invited him to call her Kay, like everyone else did, but decided to do that on some other occasion.

"I hate to do this, but I have to ask you, what happened? How did he end up a deputy, after having been a detective?"

He scoffed, then chuckled lightly, and took another long drag from the cigar before answering. "The right question should be, after you read that file, how come Deputy Scott is still on my force? How come he wasn't fired for the incredibly sloppy work he'd done?"

She nodded, raising the collar of her jacket and zipping it all the way up. The wind wrapped cold fingers around her neck, sending shivers all over her body and fueling the tension that locked her shoulders in a painful cramp.

"Thanks for putting it delicately, Dr. Sharp," he continued, his words carried out on a smoke-loaded sigh. "Just between the two of us, like you intended when you called me out here, it took significant bad performance on the job to present Scott with his choices. Either resign, or be dropped to deputy, but keep his pension if he pulled the whole twenty, without shooting himself in the foot and without killing somebody."

"Anything standing out, performance-wise?" she asked. She was following her gut, thinking there had to be more about Scott's actions than just indifference and indolence.

Exhaling slowly, he switched the cigar from one hand to another, blowing warm smoke into his palms. "To put it mildly, he was derelict in his duties, not motivated to close cases, while at the same time, prone to violent behavior, often times roughing suspects up, threatening witnesses. He cut corners and did a sloppy job with everything." He muttered an oath she didn't catch. "He's a piece of work, that one. Complaints were pouring in from all directions; missing evidence, badly typed forms, wrongly filed records, witnesses bullied and insulted, you name it. Now all he does is traffic stops, and even that he manages to screw up occasionally."

Kay shifted her weight from one foot to the other, dreading the question she had to ask, although she believed she knew the answer.

"Are you friends with him outside of work?"

"What?" he asked, looking at her intently, while a fresh furrow developed on his brow, putting a deep V at the root of his nose.

"You know, drinks with the team, hanging out at the Hilltop, stuff like that."

"Me? With that guy? Hell, no." He arranged the collar of his jacket as if to restore his bruised dignity. "I'm surprised you had to ask, to be honest." He coughed in his elbow, then said in a low voice. "Listen, if it weren't for the unions, the guy would've been long gone. Now, can I go home and warm my bones?"

He turned to leave, but she grabbed his elbow, stopping him. "Not yet, I'm sorry. But I'll make it quick." She filled her lungs with the cold air sprinkled with remnants of cigar smoke. "Currently, I'm also on an assignment from the FBI."

His gaze turned into a bit of a glare. "Why, gee, Dr. Sharp, thanks for sharing." She noticed his shoulders tensing up, his jawline hardening. Out of all things, Sheriff Logan had decided to turn defensive. "Is this about Scott?"

"Yes," she replied quickly, glad he'd asked the right question.

"What's he done now, to gain himself FBI attention?"

"He beat his pregnant wife to within an inch of her life, at least three times in the past year," she said, feeling a knot in her throat as she spoke. "She's been trying to communicate with you, but failed. She's been—"

"Why did she fail? I'm there every day," he reacted, pacing angrily back and forth in front of his SUV.

"It's a long story and your roast will get dry," she said, trying to ease the crackling static in the air between them, but he glared at her, not smiling, not saying a word. "I'll get to the bottom of that before the end of the week. In short, someone on staff has been rerouting your mail as they see fit."

"And turned her in to her husband?" He slapped his hands against the sides of his legs and looked at the starry sky above them. "One of my cops did that?"

"I'll—yes, and I promise you it's in the works to find out who. Just, please give me a few days to wrap this up the right way. There are many risks to consider and manage in domestic abuse cases involving cops."

He nodded.

"How far do you think he'll take things?" Kay asked. "If cornered?"

Turning to face her, he shoved his hands deep into his pockets. "Scott? The man's an unexploded powder keg with an unpredictable fuse."

"Copy that," she replied. Now it was her turn to grimace. All Logan had done was confirm her worst fears, and seed new ones on top. From the little time she'd spent with Scott, she knew the man was intent on something, she didn't know *what*, but he wasn't derelict of duty by accident. He was too controlling for that, too driven, too intense. Maybe if she peeled the layers off that rotted onion, she'd find out what had motivated him to throw away a career as the only detective on staff with the sheriff's office in Mount Chester to be speed-trapping tourists all year long. "I'll keep you posted, sir," she said, then reached for her keys inside her jacket pocket. When she took her hand out, she was holding the keys and the evidence pouch with the DNA sample she'd taken from Shelley.

"Not so fast, Dr. Sharp," Sheriff Logan said, his tone biting as the cold wind. "I'd like to know if you really work for me, or was that just pretend?"

She stared at him wide-eyed.

"Are you here on assignment from the FBI?" he asked again, raising his tone enough to tell her he was furious. "It's a fair question, don't you think?"

She almost smiled, but managed to contain it, knowing the explosive effect her grin might have on the sheriff. "I promise you this FBI thing is temporary, and it will conclude in a couple of days. I work for you, ever since you made me the offer and I took it."

"Then why didn't you tell me about Scott?" His pitch was high, denoting rising frustration. "I figure either you didn't trust me, and you first interrogated me by the book before disclosing your agenda, or you were never one of mine to begin with."

"I just got the case assigned last night, sir," she explained. "And yes, I interrogated you, and I apologize, but I have a battered woman who swears she sent letters directly to you, only to have her husband bring them back home with him the next day and use them as an excuse for another round of beatings." As she talked, emotion filled her voice, seeding a slight tremble in her pitch. She forced a breath of cold air into her lungs, steeling herself.

He clapped his hands slowly, calmly, a hint of a smile coloring his eyes. "I said it before, and I'll say it again. Once your FBI assignment is over, and you rid me of that piece of scum, I'd be happy if you stayed."

"I'm not going anywhere," she replied, still holding her keys and the DNA sample and looking him straight in the eye.

He grinned. "What's that?" he asked.

"A DNA sample from Rose Harrelson's mother," she replied. "I'll drop it off at the morgue on my way home."

"I can drop that for you," he offered, and she accepted with a smile and a nod of gratitude. He scratched his buzz cut hair, as if trying to remember something he had to do. "You should probably know, Scott called in to say he needed a couple of days off, citing family issues."

Staring at him as he climbed into his SUV and drove off, her worried thoughts went to Nicole. Good thing she was safe at her house with Jacob. Scott must be out looking for her and wouldn't settle until he found her and made her pay for running away.

It was time to muzzle that animal.

CHAPTER THIRTY-NINE
Stakeout

You'll never see me again.
Don't come find me.

Scott stared at the handwritten note, rage pulsating though his veins.

"The hell I won't," he muttered, stepping on broken things and torn clothing to put together a small duffel bag with things he needed on long stakeouts. "And trailing that fed twenty-four-seven? Motherfucker."

As if he didn't know what Kay Sharp was up to… nothing good. Why Triple-Dollar-Sign wanted her followed instead of taken out as soon as possible was a question he hadn't had the chance to ask. The man had never been so curt with him before, and he wasn't the type of man Scott wanted for an enemy.

Duffel bag in hand, he stopped in the middle of the hallway, trying to decide. Should he go after Nicole and drag her sorry ass back where she belonged? She had one hell of a mess to clean up while he was gone. Or should he do as he'd been told and hang a tail on that fed before she did who knows what to screw everything up?

One look at his phone told him the time; it was almost seven. Who knew when Nicole had left…? The bitch could be anywhere by now, although she didn't have that many places to go. She could be headed to her mother in Tennessee. If he hustled, he could still make the Greyhound terminal before the last bus left. She wasn't brave enough to hitch a ride with some trucker; no, she'd always been a coward, a scaredy little bitch.

Heading into the kitchen, he flipped on the lights and dropped the duffel bag on the table, atop broken dishes and spilled food. He rummaged through the pantry, collecting a handful of energy bars, a pack of salty crackers, and a few cans of Coke, then stuffed everything into the bag. Satisfied, he zipped it up and headed out, slamming the door behind him so hard it rattled the side windows and cracked the jamb at the joint.

He drove quickly to the bus terminal, flashers and siren on, although he was off duty and didn't have a code. But who would pull over a cop responding to an emergency? Grunting and feeling beads of sweat breaking at the roots of his hair, he swore endlessly, clasping the steering wheel so tight, his knuckles cracked.

A few minutes later, he pulled in front of the bus terminal, chuckling when he saw a couple of people scatter into the woods at the sight of his red-and-blue flashers. Upstanding citizens, he was sure of it. Nicole was nowhere in sight, and a quick question at the ticket counter revealed she hadn't bought a ticket that night, nor was she seen boarding one of the earlier buses that stopped for mere moments in Mount Chester on their way south, to San Francisco and Los Angeles.

Where could the bitch be? Did she have help?

The thought of someone else being involved in his business froze him in place, halfway back to his patrol car. How come he didn't see it before? The more he thought about it, the more it made sense. She couldn't be the organizer of her own escape; she didn't have what it takes. He, on the other hand, knew people; he'd interrogated more perps and collared more thugs than most cops do in their entire careers, just because he knew how to spot their weaknesses, stab a knife in them and twist.

Someone else was involved. Had to be.

Nicole didn't even have a car. Someone else had to have picked her up from the house and driven her somewhere, with luggage and all. Had to have been a man; who else would waste time on the cheating, lying, sprogged slut except some dude who wanted to stick it to her?

The only problem with throwing Nicole's secret lover in jail for the rest of his days was how easily it could be done. A traffic stop, followed by a discreetly placed gram of heroin in his vehicle, then he'd resist arrest. Scott could fake resisting arrest even if his bodycam was on, per Logan's latest, fucked-up directive, and everyone would buy it. Then he could up the ante by finding a weapon in the trunk of his vehicle, one he'd buy off the street beforehand and carry around until the moment presented itself. Even better, a hot weapon, a gun recently used in some San Francisco murder, where the bullets had been recovered by the police. He had connections who'd pay him good money to plant a gun like that on some sorry-ass loser, and he'd gladly do it to Nicole's secret man.

Too. Fucking. Easy.

If fuckboy somehow survived the arrest, one phone call from him, and the asshole would meet a shank behind bars, and Nicole's love story would be over. Would serve him right for screwing his wife, wouldn't it?

He'd wait and see Nicole crawling back to him, begging his forgiveness. It wouldn't take her that long; a day, maybe two.

Then he'd teach her the lesson she had coming all that time.

He let the air out of his lungs slowly, calming his fraught nerves, now that he had a plan, now that he knew what she'd done. It would take some digging to locate the lovebirds, and there was a time for that. Tomorrow, when that fed would be busy doing one thing or another, he'd start asking questions, pulling phone records, and he'd find Nicole and her secret lover.

He climbed behind the wheel and unwrapped an energy bar. All that effort had left him hungry, frustration drilling a hole in his stomach. If he had the time, if he didn't have to chase after the fed, he'd run by the gym and pump some iron until he couldn't feel his arms anymore.

He checked the time again. Almost seven-thirty. Where could that fed bitch be?

A ten-minute drive by the office, but her SUV wasn't there. At that time, she was probably home for the night. A quick search on his laptop revealed her address.

It wasn't far.

He drove over there quickly but without flashers, approaching Kay's residence with his headlights off. Across the street from her house and farther west by 50 yards or so, there was a thick hedge bordering a property shrouded in darkness. He pulled alongside, knowing his car would be hard to spot from the driveway, with a couple of oak trees in the way, and several trash cans pulled at the curb for morning pickup.

Then he walked back to the Sharp ranch, confirming Kay's SUV wasn't there. The light was on in the kitchen, though. He found a good spot to hide, where he could see through the kitchen window without the risk of being seen if the fed picked that moment to pull onto her driveway.

The wind howled angrily, rolling off the side of the mountain and bringing the smell of fresh snow from the peaks. The temperature had dropped below freezing, and every breath he exhaled put a cloud of mist in the air. Trotting in place behind the trunk of a thick oak tree, he kept his eyes fixed on that lit kitchen window, hoping he'd see Kay in there. Then he'd know she was home for the night and would continue his stakeout in his car, with the heater on and some FM station on the radio to keep him awake.

In the yellowish light of the kitchen, a man was setting the table, carrying plates and cutlery from the cabinets and setting them down. He could only see a glimpse of his movements, when he passed in front of the narrow window, but he turned at some point and Scott could see him talking.

He recognized the guy; it was Jacob Sharp, the fed's brother. But who was he talking with?

Approaching the house carefully, after checking to see if there were any headlights approaching, he managed to see a little more from the inside of the kitchen, but not enough to figure out who was in there with the guy.

Was it Kay? Had she put her SUV inside the garage?

Sticking his head out from behind a trash can, he followed every move Jacob made. He kept going back and forth between the sink, the cabinets, and the table, fixing dinner by the looks of it. Then something happened, maybe he was telling a joke or something, because he'd stopped in his tracks and held his hands up, talking quickly, stepping backward. But he wasn't laughing; he seemed serious, worried. Was someone pointing a gun at him?

Scott could see his lips moving from the side, but couldn't hear a sound and couldn't tell what that scene was about. After a while, Jacob lowered his hands and resumed fussing about the food, opening the oven and removing a tray.

Then a woman approached him and cuddled at his chest, crying, while he caressed her hair and wrapped his arms around her.

His heart started racing, blood rushing to his head with dizzying speed.

It wasn't Kay Sharp in that man's arms. It was Nicole.

His Nicole.

Rage invaded his body in an instant, and all his plans were forgotten. He ran to the side door and with one kick, he broke it down and stepped inside.

Nicole's scream fueled his anger, and that twerp, hiding her behind his matchstick body was a joke. That was Nicole's lover boy? The fed's brother?

"Please leave, and there won't be consequences," Jacob had the nerve to tell him, while Nicole cowered behind him like a cornered animal, sobbing hard like she always did when she knew she'd really fucked up.

"This is between me and my wife," he said slowly, his tone low and menacing, his words in a cadence like bullets spewed in slow motion from a machine gun. His nostrils flared, clenching his fists tightly and anticipating the feeling of breaking Jacob's jaw.

"And this is my house, and you're not welcome here," Jacob said, taking a small step forward.

The little fuck had nerve, but he didn't have much time to lose. He brought his fists to his chest and sent a right cross, aiming for the guy's face. Quick on his feet, Jacob sprung to the side and grabbed a skillet off the stove, holding it in the air with both hands, ready to strike.

"Please, Herb, this is not what you think," Nicole pleaded, her words shattered by uncontrollable sobs. "His sister is my friend."

Five simple words, and it felt as if Nicole had poured a bucket of ice water on his head. Since when was Nicole in cahoots with the feds? Who knows what lies Nicole had told that bitch?

His lips a thin, rigid line, he pulled his weapon and squeezed the trigger twice, each bullet hitting its target, lover boy's center mass. Nicole shrieked, and Jacob stared at him in disbelief for a brief moment, then collapsed to the floor, the skillet clattering at his feet.

Calm and feeling satisfied for once that day, he holstered his weapon and reached Nicole in two large steps, smiling, taking in her primal fear, the terror in her eyes. He grabbed a fistful of her hair and dragged her out of the kitchen and into the cold darkness outside, her screams resonating against the silence of the night.

Then she fell silent and still under his hands.

CHAPTER FORTY
Witness

Elliot was almost finished with the cluster of gas stations on the interstate, about 20 miles south of Mount Chester. It had taken him a while, he realized, looking disapprovingly at the digital display above the cashier's desk inside the Chevron. Almost an hour for five gas stations, four of them small, and one of them a truck stop that fueled big rigs and offered drivers complete services, such as hot showers and meals.

In between pasting flyers on bathroom hallways, he'd grabbed a hot dog from one of those spinning grills that kept them warm, lured by the smell like a starving coyote circling a trash can. It had tasted good at the time, his senses deceived by hunger, but the hotdog had left an aftertaste in his mouth worthy to be called gas-station breath.

He paid for the dog and a tin of breath mints, pretending not to notice the loaded smile on the cashier's lips. She was young and athletic, maybe a little too thin, and pale under the fluorescent light. Her straight, blond hair touched her shoulders, and her lipstick glimmered on her thin lips when she spoke. She tilted her head and joked with him, purposefully ignoring the other customers lining behind him one after another, frowning and muttering impatiently. She promised to call him personally if she heard anything about the missing girl, and she regretted she hadn't paid more attention to the people coming through the store, but there were thousands every day.

A tip of his hat widened the girl's smile, for some reason reminding him of Kay, although she was nothing like his partner. Kay was taller, her forehead broader, her lips fuller. Her long, blond hair passed her shoulders, wavy toward the ends. No, that girl was nothing like Kay.

And he was more and more of an idiot.

He touched his hat again and turned to leave, while an older woman commented, tongue in cheek, "Seriously?" as he passed by. Ignoring her, he left the store and welcomed the brisk evening air, even if the chill in it cut to the bone and the wind made him chase his hat all across the gas station, providing entertainment for a couple of rednecks fueling their trucks.

One more exit before he reached San Francisco, where all hope was gone. Four different gas stations, one of them a truck stop also.

He'd been driving for a few minutes when a call came through, the custom ring tone telling him it was the sheriff's office dispatch. He answered on the car's media system.

"Detective Young," he identified himself, knowing all dispatch calls were recorded. "What do you have?"

"A truck driver on the tip line, says he saw your flyers, or something," Deputy Farrell said. The younger deputies on the team took turns in covering dispatch shifts.

"Patch it through," he replied, "I'll take it." In a split second, all tiredness had dissipated, leaving him refreshed, his mind alert, his senses acute.

"Hello?" a man said in a coarse voice.

"Yes, this is Detective Elliot Young. You have information for me?"

"I think I've seen the gal you're looking for," he said, then started coughing, but the sound was muffled, as if he'd covered the phone's mic.

Elliot waited patiently, then asked, "Did you leave your name and contact number with dispatch, in case we get disconnected?"

"Yes, I sure did."

"What do I call you?"

"Ben." He wheezed, then continued, "It's Benjamin, really, but you can call me Ben."

"So tell me, Ben, what did you see?"

"You know the state line between Oregon and California, coming straight down on the highway?"

"Yeah, I know just the place."

"First exit after that, the girl you're looking for, I saw her climb into a fancy sedan." He cleared his throat, then took a gulp of water by the sound of it. "It was a dark gray Lincoln Continental, last year's model."

"That's pretty darn detailed for a casual spotting," Elliot commented, wondering why someone would retain all that information. Could he be trying to set someone up, using the girl's disappearance?

"I drive a big reefer hauling frozen meats from Mexico to Seattle. I've driven this road for seven years now. That's how I pass my time, I look at cars. I know cars, I spend my life surrounded by them. This one really stood out."

"How come?"

"At some point, we were still in Oregon, I was driving my rig right behind it. Then it sped ahead, and I lost sight of it, but then right after the state line I nearly crashed into the darn thing." He paused for a beat, enough for Elliot to hear rustling of cellophane and the flicking of a lighter. "People don't realize we can't stop these rigs on a dime. This guy had stopped his Lincoln on the side of the road, blocking the right lane, and the girl was climbing into the front passenger seat. He didn't even bother to pull onto the shoulder." He exhaled a lungful of smoke that hissed against the phone's mic. "Another car was passing me right then, after the turn, and I had to slam the brakes. I almost jackknifed and killed us all. That's why I remember the dude and his fancy ride."

"Ben, please make my day and tell me you got the tags on that Lincoln," he said, holding his breath.

"Nah, man, sorry. You gotta do some work yourself, ha, ha. But I can tell you they were California tags."

"All right, Ben, thank you, this is very helpful," Elliot said. "Dispatch has your number, if I have any other questions?"

"Yeah, they do. Hey, forgot to say, I don't think they drove that far from the state line."

"Why do you say that?"

"You know trucks have a lower speed limit in California, right? Sure, you do," he added, laughing quietly. "He didn't pass me again. I drove the rig all the way to San Francisco without stopping, but he didn't pass me again, and he should have." He hesitated a little, then added, "I was kinda hoping he'd pass me, so I could honk at him a couple of times and make him soil his pants, if you know what I mean."

Elliot frowned, then thanked Ben and ended the call with the invitation to call him directly if he remembered anything else. It was the first solid lead he'd got, enough to buy him some more time with the sheriff.

What was the distance between the first and second exits on the highway? If Ben's rig had to slow down to 55 per state law, and the Lincoln was going 65 or above, how quickly should the Lincoln have caught up with the rig?

Wishing he'd paid more attention in math class, he wondered if the Lincoln had taken the next exit, and why. Was he a local resident? Could it be that simple? Not a whole lot of rural Californians drove Lincolns. A quick search could point him in the right direction. Or maybe the Lincoln had passed Ben without him noticing or had stopped at a gas station for dinner.

Another phone call disrupted his thoughts, but the name on the display brought a smile to his lips.

"Kay," he said, but didn't get a chance to say anything else.

She was panting hard, barely able to speak. "Elliot, I need you." Her words were barely intelligible, rapid bursts of sounds on loud, erratic breaths. "He shot him," she said, visibly struggling to stay coherent and not cry. "Herbert Scott shot my brother." Then the line went dead.

Elliot slammed the brakes and turned on his flashers and siren, then found a spot where he could cross the median section, a severely graded section of about 40 yards of rough terrain. Once on the northbound interstate, he floored it, the revving of the engine in sync with his churning thoughts.

Why would Herbert Scott shoot Jacob Sharp? What the heck was going on?

CHAPTER FORTY-ONE
Halloween

He'd left a couple of hours ago.

There was little else to do for Kirsten than think. How she got into this mess. What had happened to lead her there, at the house of horrors, reminding her of Dickens and his *Great Expectations*, a place frozen in time, just as it was frozen in the absence of heat. What kind of man keeps a house like that, untouched since whatever screwed him up, only to have a place to imprison girls like her?

She knew the answer to that question, although she was too afraid to say the words, not even in the most private confines of her own mind. In the depths of her unsettled gut, she knew what he was, and how her own Halloween story would end.

It was Halloween, and she'd been captive for four days. No matter how hard she'd tried, what kind of tools she'd used, she hadn't been able to break free from that forsaken place. The windows were indestructible, taking the force of a kitchen chair thrown at them with all her might, without as much as a single scratch. The door, missing a handle on the inside, was locked with several deadbolts. Even the hinges were soldered into place, making sure she couldn't remove the nails that held them together.

And since last night, she'd been without food.

At first, he'd taken an interest in her well-being, feeding her, fixing her sandwiches himself. But then, after he'd caught her disobeying him, he'd cut all the power to the house and stopped replenishing the fridge. The heater worked just for the duration of his stay there, and so did the lights. Once he left, darkness and freezing cold took over, leaving her in a heap, bundled under stale-smelling blankets, wearing clothes that had belonged to others like her, and shivering incessantly. She couldn't tell if it was the cold rattling her body and clattering her teeth, or if it was fear, sheer terror staking its claim as she lay on her side, trying to answer the one question that had kept her awake for the past few days.

How would she die?

There was no doubt how her ordeal would end; the man wasn't one to let girls like her walk and risk having them bring the cops for a visit to the house from hell. No… She'd die at his hands. But how?

There were moments when the prospect of dying sounded almost good, a release, an escape from her prison. Death meant he wouldn't touch her anymore. She'd never have to bear the weight of his body crushing her, the smell of his breath, the feeling of his restless hands against her cold, wet skin.

Death meant she wouldn't be cold anymore.

Closing her eyes, she allowed herself to slip away for a moment, but then snapped back to reality, fully alert, startled by her own thoughts. She stared at the hammered roosters hanging on the kitchen walls, mementos from another era, a time of plaid table-cloths and ruffles and ridiculously cheesy wall art. The roosters held no answers for her, although they might have witnessed many like her meeting their demise.

Would she suffer? Would she scream, like she'd done the nights before when the pain had proven to be unbearable? Silently, she prayed for a bullet to the head, but the image of that big knife he carried with him all the time kept inserting itself into her weary mind.

But she'd be free… And she'd see her mother again.

"Mom," she whimpered, her eyes filling with tears she didn't think she still had in her. "I'm so sorry… I should've stopped at the hospital. You would've believed me this time. I know you would have."

The sound of her own voice filled the cold silence with some shred of proof she was still alive. Maybe her mother could somehow hear her, could feel her words and know she was saying goodbye.

There was no hope left.

The night before she'd tried her last trick: she'd dressed up like the girl in that portrait, even did her nails with the same shade of polish she'd found in a drawer, and had applied lipstick that had probably belonged to her, its label yellowed by time, but its strawberry scent still alive under the cracked surface of the stick. She'd combed her hair just like hers, all brought onto her right shoulder, tilting her head just a little bit.

She'd thought she could maybe make him fall in love with her, with Kirsten, just like he'd been in love with the girl in the portrait. They'd have dinner together, like on her first night. He'd stay a little longer, even if the thought of that sent shivers down her spine, but at least she'd have heat and light. They'd watch TV, and she'd listen to him talk about his day. They'd hold hands, and sometime soon he'd take her for a walk. Then she'd run. Fast, hard, not looking back, until she reached the highway, until she found people who could help her.

Then she'd waited.

When he'd set eyes on her the night before, he was transformed for a while, his jaw slackened, his eyes fixed on her as if she were an apparition from beyond reality. He'd folded her in his arms, whispering senseless words in her ear. "Mira, oh, Mira," he'd said, "how much I missed you." He'd kneeled at her feet and she'd put her hands on his head, gently touching his hair, trying to keep his fantasy alive. He'd taken her hands and kissed them, breathing the scent of her skin, savoring her touch.

Then he'd looked into her eyes. Within a mere moment, the all-consuming love on his face died, the emptiness left behind filled with instant rage. He pushed her away so hard she fell on her back.

"You're not Mira!" he shouted, grabbing her by the shoulder and lifting her back to her feet as if she were a ragdoll. "Who the hell are you?" Then he'd turned away, slammed the door behind him and left, the house engulfed in darkness the moment he departed.

She'd made a terrible mistake trying to be that girl. Now only one question remained unanswered.

How would he kill her?

CHAPTER FORTY-TWO
Blood Money

Kay watched like a hawk as the emergency response team worked to stabilize Jacob. She didn't challenge them or ask unnecessary questions—she wanted them focused on saving his life. Every now and then she wiped tears from her eyes, but she stayed focused, alert, ready to intervene.

Hanging by a thread, Jacob's life depended on a number of factors, and the EMTs were addressing them in perfect order of priority, following their ABCs: airway, breathing, circulation. Jacob was already intubated and hooked up to monitors. They had stopped the bleeding with QuikClot, and his blood pressure had stopped dropping.

He'd been lucky, as far as luck could be mentioned about someone who'd taken two rounds to the upper body. Both bullets had missed the heart and main arteries; he still had a fighting chance, however slim. One had pierced his upper right lung and the other had entered his lower abdomen. Knowing what that meant for Jacob's chances, Kay whimpered, trembling hard, feeling she could barely stand on her shaky legs.

She overheard the driver calling it in on the radio. "Franklin Medical, this is Mobile 5. We're ready to roll with male GSW upper body double tap. Have trauma ready. ETA five minutes."

Rushing to the driver's window, she'd pounded against the glass until he lowered it. The man scowled at her, but eased up when he saw her badge. "Dr. Sharp, sheriff's office. Franklin Medical Center is a Level III trauma center. It can't handle my brother's surgery. Go to Redding."

"Ma'am, um, sorry, but we have procedures. I'm sure you understand. Franklin will transfer after they stabilize, *if* they need to."

How sure was she Jacob should be taken to Redding? What if he didn't survive the commute? Should she throw her weight against the system and its procedures to get an exception? She was a psychologist, not a surgeon; she was a shrink with experience in catching killers.

Her head hung for a moment, while the driver muttered, "Figures," and rolled up his window.

She rushed to the back of the ambulance just as they were ready to close the doors, but didn't climb next to the stretcher. A difficult choice, yet the only one possible, considering the circumstances. Jacob had a team of professionals to take care of him, and, hopefully, a Level III trauma center would be enough to save his life. But Nicole had no one. Other than Kay, no one knew Nicole's life was in jeopardy, and that left Kay with only one possible choice.

She reached inside the ambulance and touched Jacob's leg. "I'm so sorry," she whispered, "but I knew you'd understand." Tears slid down her cheeks, but she didn't even notice. She threw her brother one long look, and squeezed his ankle. "Hang in there, little brother. You can pull this off." Then she slammed the door and tapped against the window twice, telling the driver he could be on his way.

Red flashers and piercing sirens filled the night. Watching the ambulance disappear onto the highway, she heaved, sobs fighting to come out forcefully after having been locked in her chest for so long.

She felt strong arms grasping and holding her, and the heat of Elliot's body weakened her knees. She clung to him, seeking his eyes, and found what she was looking for. His strength, his courage, a partner she could count on. "I did this, Elliot, I got Jacob shot," she cried. "If he dies…" Her words trailed off as her mind grappled with the inconceivable alternative.

"What happened?" Elliot asked, supporting her gently. "Do you want to catch up with them?"

"I can't," she said, afraid her words would stop in her throat. She forced the cold air into her lungs, ignoring the shivers it spread into her body. "He's got Nicole, and he's going to kill her."

He stared at her for a split second, his expression one of utter confusion. He had no idea who Nicole was. Letting go of his arm, she climbed into his SUV. Moments later, he'd started the engine and was headed for the highway as she filled him in with few words.

"He's going to kill her, Elliot, I know he will. We have to find her." She gave him Scott's home address. "It's a long shot, but maybe he took her back home."

He drove fast, lights on and siren blaring, while she put out a BOLO on Scott's personal and work vehicles. Now cops everywhere would be looking for him.

"We spoke last night, and it feels like ages," he said. Although she was trying to figure out where a man like Scott would take his wife to kill her, she sensed the sadness in Elliot's voice. She looked at him, but couldn't read his gaze, her eyes still clouded by tears. "I should've been there for you."

"That's not your job, Elliot," she pushed back, although his statement warmed her heart.

"If it's not your partner's job to have your back, then whose is it?"

She didn't reply. Seconds dragged like hours on the way to Scott's house. When they eventually reached the place, it was completely dark. No trace of the deputy's patrol car anywhere in sight.

"Now what? Where could he possibly be, and how do we find him?" she yelled, desperation strangling her. She'd never felt so powerless, so out of options. Nicole could already be dead by now, or she could be, in a matter of minutes. She'd seen what Scott's rage could do. "We're never going to get to her in time," she said, sounding defeated, as if everything had been already lost.

Without saying a word, Elliot pulled a phone number from the media center's memory and tapped it to dial. "I have an idea," he said, while the phone was ringing.

The name on the display read, DEPUTY HOBBS.

"Yeah," Hobbs said, taking the call with a morose voice. The call had probably interrupted something.

"We need your help," Elliot said, then continued, without waiting for any confirmation. "I know you hang out with Herb Scott. You guys drink together almost every night."

"Well, it's after hours, and I don't think it's anyone's—"

"I don't care what you do or don't do with him," Elliot said coldly. "I need you to think back and tell me if you know of a place where he would go to if he were hiding or in trouble."

Silence filled the car, heavy, only the background noise from Hobbs's end of the line disrupting it, small children playing, a dog barking.

"Think really hard," Elliot said, this time his tone deeper, almost menacing. "Your reply right now will either save your career or guarantee you a stint in jail when Scott kills his wife, and you could've stopped him."

"All right, all right," Hobbs reacted, then muttered an oath. "Jeez, Detective, it's not like we don't work together, for Pete's sake. We're on the same team!" He cleared his throat, then said, "Scott's got a fishing cabin on the lake, right by Blackwater River mouth."

By the time Hobbs had finished giving the directions, they were already rolling, Elliot driving faster than she'd ever seen him, burning rubber at every tight curve on the winding, mountain road that led to Silent Lake.

When they were closer to the cabin, Elliot switched off the flashers and the siren, then killed the headlights. He turned onto a path through the woods, keeping his speed unnervingly slow, his only source of light the setting moon and the stars. Within 100 yards, they saw it.

It was a small dwelling built out of round logs, probably oak, that had been weathered off-black by the passing of seasons. Two small windows flanked the door, cracked and dilapidated, but still serving their purpose. Thick trees surrounded the cabin, their barren crowns touching above. Wind rushed through them with a sinister whistle, while their fallen leaves rustled on the ground, being swept away toward the lake by merciless gusts.

The lights were on in the small cabin, and they could see movement through the windows, Scott mainly, but Kay believed she saw a glimpse of Nicole.

She was still alive.

"You up for this?" Elliot asked, then called for backup and an ambulance using his phone, not sure if Scott was monitoring the police radio.

She checked her weapon, then racked it and climbed out of the SUV. "Let's nail the son of a bitch."

"Backup's eight minutes out," Elliot said. "We should wait—"

At that moment, Nicole's shriek ripped through the silence of the woods.

In perfect sync without a single word spoken among them, they rushed to the door and took position on either side of the entrance, weapons drawn, ready to fire. Elliot kicked the door open, then entered, checking the room. Nicole was on the floor, bleeding, and Scott had just disappeared through the narrow hallway toward the back of the cabin.

Kay followed right behind him, scanning every inch of the room, ready to fire. Elliot signaled her he was going to check the other rooms, while she could stay there with Nicole. Giving him a thumbs up, she crouched near Nicole, urging her to keep quiet.

She'd taken another beating. Her lip was swollen and cracked, smeared blood staining her chin. A new bruise was forming on her right cheekbone, and her clothes were torn and dirty, as if he'd stomped his boots all over her.

Keeping her eyes riveted on the door that led to the back of the cabin, Kay whispered, "How many other rooms?"

"Two," Nicole whimpered, "and a bathroom." She swallowed hard while her eyes glistened. "You came for me."

Kay nodded. "Any other exit?"

She shook her head in a silent no. "Jacob?" she whispered, her voice riddled with pain. "I'm so sorry."

Kay hesitated. "In the hospital." She pressed her lips into a tight line, then raised her index finger to her mouth, willing Nicole quiet. There would be time for that later.

Scott was trapped in the back of the house, and she had no way to warn Elliot there was no other exit. But she could draw Scott to her location, where she was perfectly situated to ambush him, weapon in hand, taking cover behind a small sofa.

"Nicole," she whispered, "I need you to trust me." The poor woman nodded, blinking away tears. "Call Scott. Tell him the cops are gone, looking for him in the woods or something."

She shook her head violently. "No, no, please don't make me," she whimpered. Blood started oozing from her broken lip.

"If you ever want to be free of him, you have to trust me."

Nicole stared at her for what seemed like ages, but Kay held the woman's gaze, reassuring her without words. Then Nicole nodded and drew breath.

"Herb? They're gone," she called out. "I told them there's a back door and they believed me."

Kay held her breath, carefully listening for any sound, a squeaking floorboard, a footfall, anything. Only silence, and Nicole's shallow, rapid breathing.

"Will you forgive me now?" she pleaded, sounding convincing, at least to Kay's ears. "I know it's my fault, but, please, baby, I'm begging you, let's go home."

Someone was approaching, footfalls so stealthy Kay sensed his presence more than heard him coming. Then Scott appeared in the doorway, his shirt stained with sweat and Nicole's blood, his eyes bloodshot, his gun aimed at Kay's chest.

She hesitated a split second, thinking Elliot might've been behind Scott somewhere, and he could catch the bullet intended for Scott. That hesitation was enough for his bullet to be fired before hers. And hers missed.

Kay shrieked and fell to the ground, the pain in her shoulder so fierce it felt as if she'd been shot with red-hot liquid metal. She shifted her weapon to her other hand and turned to find Scott, but he'd vanished, the door to the cabin blown open by the wind, battering against the hinges.

Elliot rushed to the door, but stopped short of following Scott into the woods.

"Go on, I'll be fine," Kay said, her voice shaky, husky, sounding strange as if it weren't hers.

"I'm not leaving you," Elliot said calmly, weapon still in hand. He kicked the door shut, then pulled the curtains to all the windows after securing their locks. "We'll catch him together, both of us."

Kay breathed, adrenaline leaving her body a heap of pain and tired limbs. Backup was only a few minutes away, and she could wait. She looked at the bleeding wound for a moment, the sight of her own blood feeling surreal, as if it belonged to another person. She winced and willed herself though the pain.

Turning to Nicole, she squeezed her hand. "Are you okay?" she asked.

The young woman touched her belly with her hand, caressing it as if to soothe the baby growing inside of her. "He kicked me," she whispered. "He was afraid I took his damn money, but I'd never touch that," she added, shaking her head convincingly as she looked straight at Kay. "It was blood money. I know it was."

Kay frowned, summoning all her willpower to shake off her tiredness and think. "What money?"

Nicole lowered her head and looked at her legs covered in bruises, then curled them underneath her, tugging at the hem of her dress to cover herself up better. "He kept saying only idiots work their asses off for careers and glory. He was the only smart one," she scoffed, "because he only wanted money."

Elliot approached the two women, and extended Kay a hand, but she refused his help, preferring to sit on the floor, by Nicole's side. A concert of sirens grew faintly in the distance, while Elliot rummaged through the drawers until he found a clean towel. "Ambulance is on its way," he said, pressing the folded towel firmly against Kay's wound. "We need to stop the bleeding."

"Keep going, Nicole, this might be important," Kay said, wincing from the pain and closing her eyes for a moment, feeling waves of tiredness and nausea wash over her as she struggled to maintain her focus on her words. "Tell me more."

"It started a long time ago, when some kid went missing," Nicole said. Kay's tiredness vanished in an instant, leaving her brain perked up and ready to work. "He landed that kid's case; he was the only detective. A few days later, he got drunk and told me he scored a bunch of cash. All he had to do was bury that case." She ran her hand over her forehead, a sign of shame, of embarrassment. "That's why I think it's blood money, and I'd never touch it. But I know where he keeps it."

Kay closed her eyes, her Lego pieces swirling up in the air again, refusing to let themselves be assembled in shapes that made sense.

Coincidences were a rare occurrence in her line of work; safe to say they almost didn't exist. When a coincidence presented itself, it usually was a lead waiting to be uncovered. How many other kidnapping cases had been buried by Herbert Scott? Had he been paid off by someone to bury Rose Harrelson's kidnapping case? Seemed that way. Only the kidnapper could've had an interest in doing so. If she followed that money, she could find Rose's abductor.

"Do you know which case he was paid to bury?" Kay asked, hoping to hear the name that had been at the forefront of her mind since Blackwater River Falls.

Nicole shook her head, and shot Kay an apologetic glance. "No, I'm sorry, it was a long time ago." She stared at the smoke-stained ceiling for a while. "It was the week after my birthday, the year my mother died." She mumbled something and moved her fingers slightly, as if counting in her mind. "Um, it was fourteen years ago, last July."

CHAPTER FORTY-THREE
Decision

He was tired of her.

He'd stopped feeling excited to be going back to the house a few days ago, when he'd found her dressed as Mira, trying to look like her, to be her.

How dare she…

Since Mira had left, he'd never been the same, and he never would be, not without her back in his arms. And that was never going to happen, no matter how hard he wished for it, or what he was willing to do to make his dream become reality.

She was beautiful, his first and only love, his Mira. She was shy, and loving, and willing to endure pain only to bring him pleasure. She lived for the nights they spent together in furtive embraces, their secret terrifying and exciting at the same time, the danger of it immense. Yet that never stopped her. When they were apart, she suffered just as much as he did, counting the seconds until they could be together again. When he looked into her eyes, he saw the depths of her love for him, her devotion, her willingness to follow him to the ends of the earth.

Then she was gone, forever taken from him, forever lost. Even if decades had passed since, he'd never forgotten Mira's loving gaze, the look of her beautiful lips when she whispered her love for him, the feel of her body molding around his, a perfect match without equal.

And this girl, this stray, this Kirsten or whatever her name, had dared imitate Mira. She'd put on some clothes that resembled Mira's style, and combed her hair like she used to, but her eyes were cold and filled with contempt, with hatred and fear. There was no love in those irises, no tenderness in her touch. He could feel her body tensing up whenever he drew near, whenever his fingers touched her frozen skin.

She'd done it just to fuck with his mind, to turn him into someone she could push around as she pleased.

No matter how hard he'd pushed himself to imagine Mira in his arms again, the creature he was holding in her stead was dangerous and hateful, a snake waiting for the right moment to sink its teeth into his jugular and kill him on the spot.

She'd been like that from the start, this stray he'd picked up from the side of the road. Like others before her, she'd fought him hard, her eyes shooting daggers of rage at him when he touched her, screaming, kicking, ruining everything for him, even when blindfolded and tied up to the bedposts. He'd held on and hoped she'd learn his routine and try to respect it, she'd learn to love him a little, enough for him to close his eyes and believe Mira was back, even if for a fleeting moment.

Not with her.

Countless days after he'd brought her to the old house, she remained untamed, willing to fight him to the death.

She was not good for him.

But there would be others, soon, and he wouldn't have to endure the loneliness of his nights with only Mira's memory by his side, a ghost, an ethereal fantasy he couldn't hold in his yearning arms.

There would be someone else, someone better, a girl who'd be grateful to share his bed and his life, someone who'd look at him with love-filled eyes. Someone who'd want to spend the rest of her life with him, and maybe then Mira's memory would fade, and he'd be able to stop hurting. Then he'd snuff the life out of

Mira's betraying heart, with his own two hands, knowing he'd be rid of her for good. Knowing she was never coming back to him, no matter how long he waited.

Sitting behind the wheel of his car and looking at the old house, he knew the time to make a choice had come.

Kirsten had to go. He was done trying.

CHAPTER FORTY-FOUR
Discharged

A dissonance of beeps and chimes woke Kay up. The first contact with reality reminded her sharply that she'd been shot. The throbbing pain in her shoulder had her shifting into a different position, just as uncomfortable. Moving woke her up completely, and she realized where she'd spent the night, as foggy memories started coming back, each of them carrying its own brand of pain.

She'd shared an ambulance with Nicole, while Elliot had stayed behind to organize the search for Scott. Once at Franklin Medical Center, she'd demanded to be placed in her brother's room, even if that meant spending the night on a visitor couch sequestered from the waiting room. Eventually, they'd rolled in a second bed, under protest, but the center's relationship with the local law enforcement was valuable enough to be used as a trump card.

They'd patched her up and pumped her full of pain meds, but she still checked in on Nicole. She and the baby were fine. With that single piece of good news, she'd withdrawn to her brother's room, now hers also, and spent an hour speaking to him in a low whisper, telling him how much she loved him, how much she needed him to live, to fight, to come back to her. How brave he'd been, defending Nicole and risking his life for a complete stranger. How proud their mother would've been to see how well she'd raised him.

He was unconscious, intubated, the rhythmic beep on his monitor a grim reminder his life was hanging by a thread. But at least his heart was beating; with that notion telling her there was hope, and finally subdued by exhaustion and pain meds, she'd lain on the second bed and fell asleep before she could cover herself with the blanket.

Elliot had done that later, gently, careful not to wake her, but she'd woken just enough to know he was there, safe, watching over her. She'd mumbled a question about Scott, but he shushed her back to silence and sleep. If he'd been caught, Elliot would've told her so.

She sat on the edge of the bed, holding on with her good hand, fighting a dizzy spell. Then she clumped over to her brother's bedside, checking the notes on his chart and the vitals on the monitors.

The room door slid open and a tall man wearing hospital garb stepped in. His name tag had a Dr. in front of a very long name of Asian origin.

Behind him, she caught a glimpse of Elliot, sleeping on a visitor couch too short for his height, his feet hanging in the air, his hat over his face.

"Good morning, Dr. Sharp," the doctor said, with a quick, professional smile. "I'm your brother's attending, and yours too, for that matter."

"How is he?" she asked, feeling her throat parched dry and her breath scorching. Her empty stomach growled and the weakness she felt in her body spoke of her endless day without sustenance.

"His vitals are stable, and he's recovering nicely. He's not out of the woods yet, but he's been given three units of blood, and the surgeons were able to patch him up quickly. No major damage to any of the key organs. Thankfully, the lower bullet missed his liver by an inch."

Feeling weak, she smiled and sat on the edge of her bed, unsure of her legs. "Thank you," she whispered.

"We'll keep him asleep and intubated for at least twelve more hours." He jotted something on his chart, then placed it on the holder. "That will give you the time to get back on your feet. Your GSW was a flesh wound, but you still need rest, and a good meal."

Kay's phone chimed, the sound stuttering, two text messages being delivered at almost the same time. She turned it off and nodded. "I agree, and my entire body agrees with you. But the man who put my brother in that bed is still at large. I've got to go." The attending stared at her with understanding and a hint of disapproval. "Please call me for any news about my brother, good or bad."

He nodded and stepped aside, making room for her to walk past him. She searched for her shoes and located them under the bed, her feet bare and chilly from the contact with the cold floor. She wondered where her socks had landed. Then she looked up and saw Elliot's blue eyes looking straight at her with concern.

"What's up?" she asked, patting him on the arm. "Thanks for being here for me," she added, before he could answer.

"Anytime," he replied with a quick smile and a nod. "Scott's still in the wind. Logan came by this morning. He's dispatching a K9 unit; they'll bring a dog from Redding."

She groaned, accepting his arm for support while she slipped on her shoes without undoing their laces. "Totally pointless. He won't stay on foot for long. I think, by now, he's long gone. How about the money?"

"It was exactly where Nicole said it would be, at the lockbox in the Greyhound terminal. Almost half a million dollars."

"For one kidnapping?" Kay asked, heading toward the exit. "Nah... That's too much for a single cover-up. Whoever does this once will do it again. Being a dirty cop is a state of mind, not a one-time accident. We should look at all the open cases he worked, and all his collars."

"He's been busy as a hound in flea season, that's for sure," Elliot said, his Texas drawl more noticeable when he used phrases that reminded him of home. In his voice, the disgust for Scott was unmistakable. "I need to run a quick search in the system for a vehicle. A witness saw Kirsten, the missing kid from Oregon, climb into a Lincoln the day she disappeared."

"I have to check these messages," Kay said, remembering the harmony of chimes that had woken her up. One was informing her of the K9 unit dispatch for Scott. Another was an update on Nicole's status, all good news. "Oh," she reacted, after opening up a text message from Dr. Whitmore that sent her pulse racing. "DNA results are back. The girl beneath Blackwater River *was* Shelley Harrelson's daughter… but *also* Bill Caldwell's."

"She was Rose Harrelson after all?"

"Yup. And through some weird twist of fate and criminal wrongdoing, she was also Alyssa Caldwell."

He took off his hat for a moment, long enough to run his fingers through his unruly hair. "I've only been gone a day, for crying out loud. Seems like I missed a truckload of action. How the heck can that happen? And what does it mean? It changes everything."

"It does, doesn't it?" Kay replied, still thinking of all the implications, what that meant for their case. The two cases, the Harrelson kidnapping from fourteen years ago and the Alyssa Caldwell murder had been joined into one multifaceted mystery that was far from being unraveled. There had to be a connection between the two crimes; there always was. "We'll sort it out, partner. I believe I know where to start."

*

One quick glance at Elliot's confused face brought a silent chuckle on her lips as they exited the hospital, and he led the way to his SUV. Her arm was in a sling, worn on top of a disposable hospital gown she'd tucked in her jeans. The bright sunlight, warming her face despite the chilly, northerly wind, made her painfully self-conscious. She cringed, realizing how she must've looked. "It's been a busy day," she admitted, "and I've been in the same clothes for more than one rumba. Could you please drop me off at my house?"

"Sure," he said, leaving the parking lot and turning onto the street. "Then what did you have in mind?"

"I think Bill Caldwell needs to answer two questions," she replied, staring out the window at the peaks of Mount Chester contoured in black rock and white snow against the azure sky. That view never got old. "He should tell us the story behind his relationship with Shelley. A witness—Martha, you remember her, right? She said Shelley might've been raped and that Rose was the child that came from that ordeal."

"Okay, that's a new development," Elliot said, shooting her a quick glance. "You've really been busy."

"Second question is, how did Rose Harrelson become Alyssa? What happened to Alyssa? Does that make Bill Rose's kidnapper?" She asked the questions as they came to her mind with the clarity of a new day and the new evidence brought by the DNA results. The Lego pieces were falling into place again. This time, the structure they built was more solid and led to one conclusion: Bill Caldwell was at the center of the entire case, and he had questions he needed to answer.

"That's more like five questions," Elliot replied, pulling into her driveway and stopping behind her SUV. "Anything else?"

"I'm starving," she said, feeling optimistic for the first time since she'd set foot beneath Blackwater River Falls.

Climbing out of Elliot's car, she headed for the door. He must have watched her struggle to open the door, because he killed the engine, then came to lend her a hand. A few minutes later, they emerged out of the house, Kay's appetite suppressed by having seen the pool of blood dried up on the kitchen floor, stirring up unwanted memories, old and new. The room bore testimony of the struggle it had hosted the night before. Blood smears on the walls and the table, shattered furniture, the side door hanging on one hinge, and scattered dishes were telling a story of a terrifying night she could never forget.

Leaving it behind while she struggled to draw breath and keep her eyes dry, she climbed into Elliot's SUV, trying to wash down the knot in her throat with a few gulps of water from a bottle she found in the cup holder between the seats.

He drove toward Caldwell Farms, while Kay ran the search for the gray Lincoln Continental on the laptop, typing with one hand and feeling shots of pain whenever she moved or twisted her back even a fraction of an inch.

There were no Lincoln Continentals registered in their area. There were plenty in the big cities, in San Francisco over a hundred and fifty, twenty-seven after adding the color filter. None of them were registered in Franklin County, though.

"He could've taken her anywhere," Elliot said, clearly disappointed. "I'll never find this kid. It's a needle in a haystack of needles the size of Dallas."

"Bigger," Kay replied with a quick smile. "Silicon Valley is home to about three million people, while Dallas—"

"Half of that," he mumbled, "yeah, I know. Thanks for making me feel better. If we add the rest of California, we're really screwed."

She turned toward him even though the pain in her shoulder made her wince. "We'll find her, Elliot. You and me. We'll find Kirsten, I promise you that."

He looked at her for a brief moment, the dismay in his blue eyes needing no words. Then he asked, "How?"

CHAPTER FORTY-FIVE
Evangeline

The same housekeeper opened the door as soon as the chime died, recognizing Kay immediately and scowling with suspicion at Elliot's badge. She stood in the doorway, unwilling to let them enter, her lips pressed into a tight line that ran parallel with the creases on her forehead.

Kay shook her head, without taking her eyes off hers. "Do we have to do this all over again?" she asked, gesturing with her phone. "Do I have to remind you—"

"Whom do you wish to see this time, ma'am?" she asked, her politeness a frozen and cracked façade. She still held the door handle tightly with one hand, while the other rested against the jamb, barring their entry.

"Bill Caldwell," Kay replied, almost relieved. The middle-aged woman didn't seem eager to face off with her, or maybe Bill Caldwell had left specific instructions in case cops came calling again.

Her lips parted in a cold smile, a glint of satisfaction flickering in her eyes. "Mr. Caldwell is not in right now. May I take a message?"

Kay studied the woman carefully. Was she lying? No… She seemed happy with the message she was delivering, and that contentment had to come from the fact that she could tell the truth *and* still block them from speaking with her employer.

"Does he normally leave this early?" Elliot asked. "It's not even nine."

She didn't flinch. "He sometimes travels for business or spends the night in the city."

"Which one is it?" Kay asked.

"I'm sorry, ma'am, but Mr. Caldwell is under no obligation to inform me of his whereabouts."

"I bet he isn't," Elliot replied, the sarcasm in his voice searing, but ineffective. The woman remained stony faced.

Unwilling to do an about-face and leave with her questions unanswered, Kay hesitated, her gaze locked with the stern eyes of the woman guarding the door. Maybe there was someone else who could shed some light on what had happened. If the girl in the morgue was Rose, but had lived as Alyssa since she was kidnapped, one of the questions was why. What had driven Bill Caldwell, apparently the only one who knew he was the father of Shelley's daughter, to replace his legitimate daughter? Was it because, like Martha had mentioned, Alyssa had been sick? Had she died that year? Who else would know about it?

"In that case, we'll need to speak with Mrs. Caldwell," Kay said in a tone that left no room for pushback.

"Which one?" the woman asked coldly.

"Bill Caldwell's wife."

"I'm afraid that is not possible," the woman replied. "Mrs. *Evangeline* Caldwell does not see anyone. She is gravely ill." She spoke her name with contempt for Kay's ignorance.

"All right," Kay replied, tapping the passcode to unlock her phone. "I'll ring for a warrant. The officers might pick her up and take her to the precinct for a formal interview, instead of the two of us asking a couple of questions, discreetly, by her bedside. But that's your call."

The woman finally stepped aside, her mouth twitching as if stifled oaths were budding to come out. "Follow me."

She climbed the stairs to the second level without rushing, then led them to the farthest bedroom on the left of a long hallway. She knocked twice, before opening the door and letting them in.

The bedroom was a combination of traditional, lush furnishings and décor, and modern hospital technology. Where it probably used to home a four-poster bed, now a fully adjustable hospital bed took the space, surrounded by monitors and medical equipment on rolling carts. It was as if the world stopped at the door, and, inside that space, the reality of Evangeline's illness changed everything it touched. The curtains were closed within an inch of each other, dimming the light in the room to almost complete darkness, except the far corner of the room, where a sunbeam pierced the darkness and hit the opposite wall. The faint smell of disinfectant and pharmaceuticals clung to Kay's nostrils, reminding her of other hospital rooms she'd visited recently, but here, the scent carried undertones of air fresheners and body wash.

By the bedside, in the light of a small lamp, a nurse in hospital scrubs was reading a novel she promptly put down when they entered. She rushed to meet them. "What can I do for you?" she asked, her voice a low whisper.

Kay showed her badge. "Detectives Sharp and Young. We have a few questions for Mrs. Caldwell."

The nurse clasped her hands together in front of her body. "I'm afraid that's impossible," she replied. "Mrs. Caldwell is resting and cannot be disturbed."

Kay took one step forward, but the nurse held her ground. "I'm afraid I have to insist. This is official police business."

"And I'm afraid I can't allow it," the nurse replied. She was a red-haired woman in her forties with freckles. "My only duty is to my patient's well-being."

"Let them come, Gina," Mrs. Caldwell said, her voice a hoarse whisper. She waved them over with a gesture of her frail hand.

Then she found a remote in the folds of her covers and pressed a button. The bed whirred, elevating her upright.

Evangeline Caldwell was emaciated, her pale skin seeming almost bluish in the pale light of the room. High cheekbones poked through her skin, rendering her gaunt face an almost skeletal appearance, compounded by her thin, dry lips and her expressionless blue eyes. Her arm was like a stick, and her long, trembling fingers seemed too frail to operate the remote.

They approached quickly and stopped by the side of the bed. Evangeline turned her head toward them, but didn't make eye contact. Kay frowned and shot the nurse an inquisitive look. She shook her hand, pressing her lips together.

Evangeline Caldwell was blind.

Elliot shot Kay a quick glance with an unspoken statement, and she nodded, certain she understood where his mind went. Evangeline's blindness could explain why Rose had been living under the same roof as her daughter and she didn't notice. A mother would've noticed the tiniest difference in the color of her hair, the curve of her lips when she smiled, the way her dimples deepened when she laughed.

"Thank you for speaking to us," Kay said, keeping her voice friendly and calm. Careful to not tip her hand and understanding why Bill Caldwell had kept the news of Alyssa's death from his dying wife, she started by offering an explanation for their presence. "We're investigating the kidnapping of a girl of your daughter's age, Rose Harrelson."

The nurse breathed with ease, slowly, and nodded with gratitude toward Kay. The woman evidently knew about Alyssa's death; Evangeline was probably the only member of the household who didn't.

Evangeline raised her hand, but then let it fall back on the covers. "A friend of Alyssa?"

"This kidnapping happened fourteen years ago," Kay clarified, and Evangeline seemed to lose interest. "But, yes, Alyssa and Rose might have been friends at the time."

A flicker of a smile tugged at Evangeline's withered lips. "Fourteen years ago? Alyssa would've been three." A cloud of darkness swept across her face, but she didn't say a word.

"Tell me about Alyssa's childhood," Kay asked. Getting the right answers without being able to ask the right questions and provide context was proving to be a difficult task. "Did she have any friends? Whom did she play with?"

Evangeline turned her head away from them as her eyes filled with tears. "I've been bedridden since she was one year old. I missed my baby's entire childhood. I never played with her, and never met her friends. And I thought that was the worst part, but when she was three, Alyssa nearly died." She stopped talking, struggling to breathe. Gina adjusted her oxygen and Evangeline settled.

"What happened?" Kay asked, seeing that the woman wasn't continuing her story, and knowing she was close to uncovering an important piece of the puzzle.

"Alyssa contracted a bad case of viral meningitis," she explained. "Doctors here tried everything they could, but she was dying. Then darling Bill, he managed the impossible… He chartered a plane and took her to a fancy clinic on the East Coast somewhere. They saved her."

"Amazing," Elliot replied. "Did she have any lasting effects from the disease?"

"No," Evangeline whispered, a faint smile fluttering on her lips. "They were gone a while, but the best experts in the field worked on her case and gave me back my sweet girl." She swallowed with difficulty, and Gina quickly brought a glass of water fitted with a lid and a straw.

A cohesive scenario was starting to form in Kay's mind. Alyssa was dying of viral meningitis, and she eventually died. For some reason, Bill decided to kidnap Rose Harrelson and replace Alyssa with her, but why? For the inheritance? And how did he manage to pull that off? Evangeline's vision might've been declining or gone because of her MS, but how about the rest of the household? Staff, family members, had no one noticed it wasn't the same girl? How long would a child have to be gone for people to forget details such as the curls of her hair, the way she pronounced certain words, the sound of her voice?

"What a heartwarming story," Kay said, smiling widely. "How long were they gone?"

"I don't remember... a few months. Four, maybe six. Time passes by slowly when you're stuck in a bed. I wish—" She stopped talking and squeezed her eyelids shut, sending tears down her cheeks. "I should've died a long time ago. It's not doing anyone any good for me to keep on living, but I do."

"Thank you very much for your time," Kay said. "Seems to me Alyssa didn't know Rose Harrelson after all."

"No. I don't imagine my daughter knew anything about that missing girl; she didn't have any friends at the time. She couldn't have. Even after her return, she spent a lot of time sleeping. Her recovery was long and difficult."

Or the little girl had been sedated, until gradually everyone had grown accustomed to her well enough to stop noticing any slight differences to the girl they once knew as Alyssa.

CHAPTER FORTY-SIX

Daylight

Kirsten had waited for him the entire night, despising herself for wishing him there, because he brought heat and light and sustenance. Because she wanted to live. Yet she dreaded what his arrival meant, the shower ritual that seemed to turn him on, his hands on her wet body, the endless pain brought by his twisted desires.

When the sky had started to turn gray, and he still hadn't turned up, she'd resigned herself to the cold and hunger, and curled up on the couch, wrapped in mold-smelling, raspy blankets that belonged to a different era, wishing she could fall asleep for only one hour. Fear had kept her awake for days now, giving her moments of dozing off when she least expected, only to bounce back from slumber fully awake, ready to fight for her life, exhausted beyond belief.

She knew he would kill her sometime; there was no doubt in her mind. She felt powerless against him, with his large knife and remote control and whatever his devious mind thought of next. She knew she would die. She just wished it would be painless, and soon, to end her suffering.

When the door opened, she sprung to her feet, although she'd slept for only a few short minutes. He'd never visited her during the day before. A chill spread through her veins as she realized the moment of her death might be closer than she'd expected.

"No," she whimpered, looking at him, trying to read his mind. She stood in the middle of the room, a blanket still clinging to her shoulders, while he looked at her with no emotion, as if she were a problem he needed to solve, nothing more. His features were relaxed, the elegance in them that had attracted her at first like a mismatched label, deceiving, treacherous, when instead a warning should've been pasted on that charismatic face. "No, please," she whispered, taking a step closer to him, reaching for his hand.

"Don't," he said, and her hand froze in midair.

The door was open behind him, the sun crashing in, hitting the hammered copper rooster on the wall and sending shards of reflected colors on the walls. If she made a run for it, could she pass by him fast enough to make it outside?

"Don't even think about it," he said, as if reading her mind and grabbing her arm with a steeled grip. "Let's go."

She pulled away from him, but his grip tightened, crushing her flesh, and she screamed. "Please, I don't want to go," she pleaded in a tear-filled voice. "I'll be good, I promise."

He smiled, a weird, lopsided grin that sent shivers down her spine. "You always wanted to go for a walk. You got your wish... Let's go."

He dragged her toward the door while she pulled back, fighting him the best she could, kicking his legs, aiming for his groin and missing every time.

She'd left her shoes by the couch, and she threw them a regretful look. If she caught a chance, she'd run faster in them.

"Please, just let me take my shoes."

He laughed and tugged at her arm again. "Where we're going, you don't need shoes."

She fell silent and finally stopped fighting him. She couldn't win.

He dragged her out of the house, not bothering to close the door behind him. She'd expected to be taken to the car, but he circled the house instead and led her inside the woods.

It was going to be the woods after all, just like she'd imagined night after night. He was going to lug her to some place where he buried the bodies, then shoot her or stab her or strangle her. She almost hoped for a bullet, the prospect of being shot in the head or in the heart the most appealing of the alternatives she envisioned, the most merciful of deaths.

But the man who was pulling her farther and farther into the woods wasn't merciful. He'd proven that time and again tying her up and watching her wet body trembling in the darkness of that icy room, while she writhed against her restraints, trying to break free. If he wanted her dead, he'd probably thought of something excruciatingly painful.

She shrieked when she stepped on a sharp rock, but he kept on going, her thin body an easy burden for his strong build. He didn't stop, and didn't seem fazed by her scream. Her teeth clattered, although the sun had risen above the trees, warming up the air just a little. The barren forest seemed eerily silent, the fallen leaves dampening all sounds. No birds were singing, as if the imminent winter had taken away their voices.

The forest cleared. They emerged on a grassy glade at the edge of a deep ravine, steep and rocky, lined with sharp, moss-covered boulders. A few junipers and twisted cypress trees hung from the rocks, their seeds having found inhospitable ground, but having prevailed, nevertheless. At the bottom of the ravine, about 100 feet down, coyotes circled on the dark ground, the occasional howl seeding sinister echoes against the vertical walls. They must've been the same coyotes she'd seen through the living room window but was never able to hear. Now that she did, their baying cries carried ominous undertones she'd prefer to never have heard.

Fighting a dizzy spell as she looked down, she noticed dozens of white specks at the bottom of the ravine, like bleached matchsticks, scattered throughout the area. Coyotes stopped and sniffed them at times or picked them up and started gnawing, lying down and holding them between their paws.

Bones.

Whitened by the elements and cleaned dry by the coyotes.

A guttural, strangled whimper came out of her chest, as his hand shifted from holding her arm to grabbing her neck, ready to push her into the abyss.

She clutched his arm with both her hands, trying to remove his grip but couldn't. She fought him as hard as she could, opposing his push forward, her feet barely clinging to the edge of the ravine.

"I'll take you with me, you sick son of a bitch," she muttered, her decision satisfying as she stared into his eyes and grasped his throat with her hands. She let herself hang from his throat, while he pushed her, sending her off balance, her feet dangling in the air above the ravine. Then he shook her off, pushing her with the one hand that still clutched her nape, and she fell, screaming.

Flailing, she grabbed the edge of the ravine with her fingers, her feet thrashing, desperately feeling for footing. She felt her hands slide against the moss that covered the rocks, and screamed again when she lost her grip and fell another few feet before grabbing a juniper branch that withstood her weight.

Above her, standing on the edge of the ravine, he stared down, straightening his jacket and running his hands through his hair, with a satisfied grin on his lips.

Her hands were sliding off the juniper branch, inch by inch, closer to where it would break under her weight. She panted hard, trying to find something else to grab on to, yet afraid to let go.

When it gave, she screamed for a split second, before the air got sucked out of her lungs when she landed face down on a large cypress rooted between two boulders, her feet close to the wall, her head above the abyss, the only thing holding her a flexing, knotted branch that was crackling and moaning under her weight.

She wrapped her legs around the branch and held her breath until the cypress settled and stopped moving. She grasped tight with both hands, the only direction she could look being down, at the bottom of the ravine, where the coyotes gnawed on bones, snarled, and yipped, looking up, waiting for her.

Nothing else would break her fall if she lost her grip again. Nothing else lined the wall of the ravine but moss and bird droppings.

Petrified, she cried, "Help me, please!" She waited a moment, her muscles trembling with effort as she held on to the branch. "Please! I'll do whatever you want!"

The man laughed, his voice echoing inside the darkness for a moment after he'd already left, silencing the animals circling below.

Then the coyotes started howling.

CHAPTER FORTY-SEVEN
Odds

Kay and Elliot had almost reached the ground floor, climbing down the stairs quickly, their footfalls muted by the thick, plush, burgundy carpet. The visit with Evangeline Caldwell had brought answers and a new theory, a potential explanation as to how Rose Harrelson had replaced Alyssa Caldwell and grown up taking her name and her role in the family.

It hadn't answered the question why.

If Alyssa had died of her illness at age three, why did Bill resort to such an elaborate scheme to replace his legitimate daughter with the illegitimate child? What could possibly have been the reason for that? A man his age could've easily fathered countless other children, even if he wanted to stay married to Evangeline. Why risk jail by kidnapping a child instead?

Carole Caldwell was waiting for them at the foot of the stairs. She wore a black turtleneck with three strings of pearls, just like she had the day before. Both the pearls and the garment were different, and both gave her an air of austere dignity, of somber propriety.

After she locked steely eyes with Kay, she spoke, her words icy cold, their finality searing. "Please don't speak with anyone else in this family without our attorneys present."

Kay exchanged a brief look with Elliot. They had expected that reaction. If anything, Kay wondered why it had taken so long to be asked to leave.

"Your housekeeper can attest we were invited in," Kay stated. "Where is she?"

"On the unemployment line," Carole replied dryly. "Please leave."

"Do you have something to hide?" Kay asked, knowing well enough there was nothing she could do the moment Carole had mentioned lawyers. Legally, she couldn't ask one more question, yet she had.

Carole's lip curled in a grimace filled with disdain. She gestured them to the door, and crossed her arms at her chest. "Wealthy families have a lot to lose from simple misunderstandings. It's my job to make sure there are none."

Elliot held the door for Kay, then closed it gently behind them. She stopped on the front porch, looking absentmindedly at the house.

"She really fired that woman for letting us talk to Evangeline?" Elliot asked, then whistled.

"Probably," Kay replied. "She has strong reasons why she doesn't want us anywhere near her family." She turned to leave, wondering where they could find Bill. By the time they figured that out, he would be aware of their visit, and of their conversation with Evangeline. He might've already been in the wind. "This family has a lot of secrets to hide."

The sound of an approaching car drew their attention. They turned in time to see a gray Lincoln Continental pull up at the door.

"What are the odds?" Elliot whispered close to Kay's ear.

"Uh-huh," she replied, just as Bill Caldwell climbed out of the vehicle, leaving the door open for a young valet to take the car and park it elsewhere.

Beyond the edge of the driveway, landscapers planted roses in a wavy flower bed they had reclaimed from the perfectly trimmed lawn, moving quickly, digging the holes, and pouring water from a hose, before putting each plant into the ground, before gathering the soil, and patting it around the roots with their bare hands. They watched Kay, Elliot, and Bill like any bored worker would watch any entertainment readily available while doing his work.

Completely ignoring the landscapers, Bill turned to the two detectives. His brow creased, and his eyes darkened when he saw Kay. He seemed to give more than a moment's attention to the sling Kay wore on her arm, the sight of it creasing his brow for some reason. He approached them with a bounce in his step and stopped squarely in front of Kay. "Anything new in my daughter's murder? Did you catch the bastard who did this to her?"

"Not yet," Kay replied calmly, "but we have a few more questions, if you don't mind."

The door opened and Carole stood in the doorway. She held her phone as if she'd just finished summoning her attorneys, her knuckles pale under her withered skin. "You were warned. Not without our legal team present. Not one word, Bill," she commanded, "this ends here."

"Why?" he reacted, turning toward her angrily. "Because you said so?" His raised voice made the landscapers peek curiously from behind the rose bushes. "I don't know about you, Mother, but I'd like to know who killed my daughter. So, let them ask their damn questions."

"William Earnest Caldwell, I am warning you," Carole said, hissing the words at her son.

He didn't blink. Instead, he turned to Kay and said, "Shoot."

Kay drew air and asked the question that had been at the center of her mind for the past day or so, knowing bluntness might work in her favor. "Mr. Caldwell, did you kidnap Rose Harrelson fourteen years ago, to replace your dead daughter?"

Carole gasped, the sound of her strangled voice covered by the clattering of the phone she'd dropped, as it broke into pieces against the marble patio. Perceptive, despite being shocked, she noticed the slacked jaws and curious glances from the group of landscapers, and stepped back into the house.

"Let's take this inside."

CHAPTER FORTY-EIGHT
Flight Plan
FOURTEEN YEARS AGO

The full moon shined above on a perfectly clear sky. The breeze was chilly, bringing fresh air from the mountains and cooling off the rocks after a day of blazing summer sunshine. Pockets of mist lingered here and there, as the night fog was starting to accumulate near the ground, holding the smell of burned jet fuel captive, intoxicating.

The small airport had closed its lobby for the day at seven, hours ago, and most lights had been turned off. Bill nodded in passing at the one staffer who had stayed behind, muttering oaths about the entitled people who couldn't fly during normal business hours and thought the entire world revolved around them. He'd just waved Bill's car and the nanny's car onto the tarmac, glaring at Bill Caldwell from underneath a sweat-stained ballcap bearing the insignia of the San Francisco Giants. The chartered jet responsible for keeping the man after hours on a game night was warming up its engines in front of the big hangars, with the light turned on in its cockpit.

He'd have to pay that frustrated staffer off too; otherwise, the stupid fuck would bitch about him all day long tomorrow, about the late-chartered flight, and why he'd missed whatever pitch or homerun that was going to make history and change his life, if he'd only scratched his balls and got hammered in front of the TV instead of working late. Probably ten grand would cut it, with a side of a clearly stated threat if he opened his mouth to anyone at all.

The jet taxied slowly to their location and stopped, only 10 yards away from Bill's car. The pilot pushed open the airplane door, then climbed down the six steps and approached him.

Bill lowered his window.

"Your plane is ready, sir," the pilot said, gesturing a salute with two fingers raised at his visor.

"We'll board immediately," Bill replied. "Be ready for takeoff in three minutes." He studied his face, his eyes, looking for signs the pilot might've been suspicious of Bill's motives or at risk of pulling a fast one and calling the cops. But the tall man's gaze was honest and direct, his demeanor professional, impeccable. The signature on the five-page NDA he'd been presented with had taken him less than thirty seconds to complete. He hadn't read the document, stating in his line of work, he signed those a lot and relied on referrals for more business; he'd never do anything to upset a client.

Perfect.

"That's it for now, thank you," Bill added, sending him away with a hand gesture.

"Sir," he replied, then walked quickly to the idling plane.

Bill waited until the pilot was back in his seat, then climbed out of his car. He opened the back door and picked up a girl in his arms.

She wasn't moving.

Her long, wavy hair escaped the blanket she'd been wrapped in, waving in the brisk wind. Her tiny body was perfectly still, lifeless, cold.

Carrying her gently and keeping her face covered with the edge of the blanket, he climbed on board the plane and set her down on one of the seats. He strapped her in, then gave the bundled body a long look before returning to the nanny's car.

The woman, a slightly overweight, middle-aged redhead who worked as a nurse at Franklin Medical Center and as occasional nanny for Rose Harrelson, was waiting for him, standing, holding another girl in her arms. This one was sleeping soundly, despite the sound of the idling jet engines spinning only a few yards from her head.

"How did it go?" Bill asked.

"Just like we discussed," the woman replied. "I fixed them dinner, and dosed it with enough phenobarb to keep them in dreamland for ten hours. They won't know what hit them."

"Did you leave any traces?"

The woman seemed offended by the question and scoffed, scowling. "I went in through the window, like you told me, although they were sound asleep, and I have the keys to the front door. But never mind that," she sighed. "I followed all your instructions, to the letter." He encouraged her to continue with an impatient head gesture. "I removed the screen, went in, took the girl, then wiped the sill for prints, lowered back the window, and reattached the screen. Then I drove straight here, and no one followed me." With a satisfied grin, she added, "I checked. Now, do you have my money?"

Bill went back to his car and returned right away with a small duffel bag. He unzipped it and showed her the contents, bundles of cash tied up neatly in color-coded denomination bands, like the banks issued. "Three hundred thousand in small bills, untraceable, like you asked. Are you ready to leave before this blows wide open?" He zipped up the bag and put it on the ground, by the woman's feet.

She placed the girl in Bill's arms, then grabbed the money bag, holding it tight with both her hands. Her face lit up when she clutched the handles like her life depended on it. "Hubby and I have tickets tomorrow morning for Venezuela," she replied, smiling widely. "We'll be long gone by the time they wake up. It's a direct flight from San Francisco. We leave in an hour."

But Bill wasn't listening to the woman anymore, now looking at the girl's face. She was sound asleep, her mouth slightly open, her breathing calm. Her chestnut hair waved in the wind, loose strands touching her face at times, a case of déjà vu. A dimple in her chin and the way her lower lip curved above it reminded Bill of Alyssa and of himself, when he was a young boy. Good.

"And the meds?" he asked, looking around carefully to see if anyone witnessed their conversation. The whole thing was taking too damn long. Someone could stumble upon them any second.

"Ah, yes," the woman replied, smiling sheepishly. "I almost forgot." Dropping the duffel bag on the passenger seat of her car, she returned with a small paper bag that rattled with every move she made. She took out two large pill bottles, one orange, one blue. She picked up the blue bottle. "This one is sleeping pills, temazepam. Give these twice a day when you return. You have six months' worth in here." She put that back, then showed Bill the orange one filled with two-color capsules. "This one's a special concoction, valium with a touch of ketamine. It will keep her sedated, and will wipe her memory if you give it daily. Then give it less often and she won't know who she is unless you tell her. That's when you rebuild who she is. You got six months of this one too, only be careful and don't abuse it. She could die."

The woman spoke to him as if he were some kind of idiot.

Holding Rose with one arm, Bill shoved the pill bottles in his pocket, shooting a quick glance at the pilot, hoping he hadn't witnessed the drugs changing hands. He seemed immersed in reading something off a small clipboard, occasionally jotting notes on it.

As he turned to leave, moonlight reflected something at the girl's neck. "What's this?" he asked. He supported Rose's body with one arm, and probed for the small object with two fingers. It was a strange-looking, lacquered, wood medallion on a silver chain around the girl's neck. "What's this doing here?" he reacted, thinking he'd throw the locket away as soon as they landed on the East Coast.

The nanny shot the small, shiny object a glance. "Her mother made that for her. She screams like a scalded banshee without it. I figured you should have it, maybe let her keep it for a while, until she forgets all about her past. There's a picture of her parents inside, you know. Don't let her see that."

"Yeah, whatever," he replied. He'd have to change that photo with one of Evangeline as soon as he got to the house he'd leased in Florida. The object might prove useful after all.

From the plane's steps, he waited until the woman drove off the tarmac and left the airport. After climbing on board, he strapped Rose into a seat. He rushed back to the tarmac once more, to pay off the frustrated airport employee and make his day, then went into the cockpit.

"We can take off now," Bill told the pilot. The man smiled and acknowledged with a quick nod.

"Any changes in the flight plan?" the pilot asked, flipping switches and revving the engines.

"No. We're going to Jacksonville; I'm taking my daughters to the Mayo Clinic."

"Yes, sir." The pilot started to taxi toward the runway, the moonlit asphalt glimmering in front of the plane. "We should be on the ground in Florida in about six hours."

Bill went back into the cabin and took a seat across from Rose, fastening his seatbelt. He leaned his head against the wall, feeling the welcome chill of the plastic against his heated temple.

Alyssa was dead, and there was nothing he could do about that. He'd done everything humanly possible to save her life over the past few months, and all had been in vain. The gods were angry with him and had taken away his daughter.

But he had another one, and there was no reason why the world should know about what transpired that night, the only thing he could've done to keep the family name going forward and the estate in the right hands. Otherwise, that little bastard, Dylan, would soon stake his claim and he could never settle for that.

He closed his eyes and dozed off just as the plane entered the runway, getting ready to take off.

Outside, hiding in the shadows by the airport building, a woman watched as the plane accelerated and lifted off, disappearing into the night. She followed the moonlit fuselage flanked by flickering strobes until she couldn't see it anymore. Then she wiped a tear and disappeared, unseen, walking calmly, with her head up high, while her long, blond hair blew into the strong breeze.

CHAPTER FORTY-NINE
Mother and Son

Carole closed the door with shaking hands she quickly hid behind her back. The blood had drained from her face, leaving her skin a sickly shade of grayish pale. Standing in the middle of the lobby, she looked at Bill, her gaze merciless and mortally wounded at the same time.

"What are these people talking about?" Carole asked, her voice a trembling whisper.

A lopsided smile stretched Bill's mouth, while a glint of amusement colored his eyes. "The statute of limitations has run its course, Mother. There's nothing they can do." He shifted his eyes from Carole to Kay while his smile widened, full of pride. "So, yeah, I kidnapped Rose Harrelson, and there's nothing you can do about it. There, I said it." He punctuated his words with a hand gesture, then started pacing the large lobby calmly, with a measured, steady gait.

There was no sign of deception on Bill's face, nor of fear. The man was an enigma, his motivations worth exploring. But had he killed his daughter?

Carole reached him in two angry steps and grabbed his sleeve, stopping him in his tracks. "You took the housekeeper's daughter and brought her to my doorstep?" Carole's voice had climbed to a high, screeching pitch, her words shattered by her panting.

Bill stared at her intently, closing the distance between their faces until their eyes were mere inches apart. "She was *my* daughter," he seethed with searing anger. "Mine!"

It was as if Carole had turned to stone. She'd stopped breathing, taking in Bill's words, and choking on them, as if unable to understand their meaning. "How could you?" she whispered, the disgust on her face palpable, raw. "How could I have not seen it?" She turned away from Bill, veering her gaze as if the sight of him made her sick. "That sweet little girl died of meningitis, didn't she?" She drilled her fiery eyes into Bill's, who withstood her scrutiny unfazed. "It was that trip to the Mayo Clinic, wasn't it? That's when you brought back the housekeeper's daughter and had me—us—take her in as our own blood!" Without warning, she slapped Bill across the face, hard, her bony fingers leaving a red mark on his cheek. "You're no son of mine."

Bill's smile turned into a grin. "Oh, but I am, Mother. I am exactly what you made me, your flesh and blood and guts and evil. And Rose was my daughter, whether you like it or not."

Kay watched the interaction, occasionally exchanging glances with Elliot as their questions were answered. She still didn't understand the reason why Bill had replaced Alyssa with Rose; what could possibly have motivated him? It wasn't just the logistics of nabbing a girl and having an entire household accept her as another, although that, in itself, must've been a tremendous feat. But controlling his own grief, all that time?

Unless…

Kay studied the man again, as if she saw him for the first time, her head slightly tilted. Elliot stared at her with unspoken questions, but she didn't take her focus off Bill Caldwell.

Could he be a high-functioning psychopath? That would explain the absence of fear or remorse, of any hint of a conscience when he talked about a kidnapping that had cost Rose's parents their lives. A psychopath's motivations are exactly that… his and only his, so twisted and feral as to be incomprehensible to other minds. Had he done all that to gain control over the business? Carole had set that ridiculous rule in place, heritage passing as royal blood rights. In her own way, she'd been to blame just as much.

But Bill's motives seemed to go beyond financial; there was a component of emotion there, of raw feelings that were stirred up when the right words were thrown around during the heated dialogue. There was intense resentment between mother and son, going both ways and equally lethal, although Kay had noticed that Carole's acrimony seemed tinted with deep-seated disgust, while Bill's anger seemed fueled by grief. The way his eyes darkened when he confronted his mother, the way he tensed up, pressing his lips into a hard line, as if to keep his words locked inside his chest, the mercurial way his sadness shifted into outbursts of fierce rage, only to simmer and turn inward again, colored in shades of endless sorrow.

He'd just lost his daughter to a violent crime; that, in itself, was enough reason to grieve. Even psychopaths love their children, albeit in their own way, possessively instead of empathically. But the sadness exhibited by Bill seemed to predate his daughter's demise, visibly engrained into the fiber of him, almost like a second nature. The way the family responded to his rage was evidence to that; to them, it was old news. Whatever Bill was grieving for, they all knew what that was, and they were all tight-lipped about it, the secret so terrifying that one look from Carole or from Blanche tamed Bill's rage like water drowns a fire.

But had Bill killed Rose? And what reason could he possibly have had to replace one girl with the other? There had to have been different ways to secure his hold on the family business, easier ways, legal ways.

Kay approached Bill and put a firm hand on his forearm. "We'll have to take you in, Mr. Caldwell."

"For what?" he replied, no hint of fear in his eyes, just curiosity, as if wondering where, in his well-conceived plans, he had gone wrong.

"The kidnapping charge might be out of statute, but there's no statute of limitations in the state of California for rape."

His jaw dropped. "What?"

There was no reason to tell Bill about Martha and her statement; he'd only push back, claim it was hearsay. And so on. Better to cut to the chase and bluff her way into a confession.

"Shelley Harrelson testified that you raped her eighteen years ago. Your daughter, Rose, was a child of rape."

Elliot glanced at her quickly, aware she was lying, but she was well within her rights to do so during a suspect's questioning.

Carole, who moments before would've ripped Bill's head off with her well-manicured hands, approached and stood by his side, grabbing his other arm. "Not another word, Bill. Not until the lawyers get here. I'll get you out of this mess. It's nothing but a fishing expedition. Cops do that to rich people all the time," she added, glaring at Kay for a long, loaded moment.

Her son didn't reply. His face was carved in stone, expressionless, devoid of fear or any other emotion except that tinge of grief that engulfed him like a halo.

"Fair enough," Kay replied, letting go of Bill's arm. "We can wait here for your attorney before we take you in."

"Don't care either way," he said, his voice flat, his stare vacant.

"Just out of curiosity," Kay said, "and you can answer that before your lawyer gets here, because it pertains to the kidnapping and that's no longer a chargeable offense... Why? Why did you replace Alyssa with Rose? It must've been hell for you, to hide your grief, to fear you would be caught if anyone noticed the girl was different."

In reaction to her violation of Bill's rights, Kay earned a stunned glance from Elliot. She continued to interrogate him after he'd specifically requested an attorney present. Although, she realized with a hint of a smile, *he* hadn't asked for an attorney; his mother had. And her demands were irrelevant under the law. Regardless, she wasn't going to stop looking for answers just because that old and pretentious harpy didn't want her family secrets uncovered.

Bill lowered his gaze for a brief moment, then looked at Kay openly, as if he had nothing to hide. That brief moment he'd looked away, that was enough for a psychopath to enter into character, to ready his mind and his body for the next manipulation he had planned.

"My wife has been ill for the past sixteen years. Her illness, as I'm sure you're aware, is made worse by stress and hardship. Telling her Alyssa had lost her battle with meningitis would've killed her. She still doesn't know."

As if scalded, Carole let go of Bill's arm and stepped away. "That's the biggest lie I've ever heard, William Earnest Caldwell! Was your concern for that paltry little weakling who can't die fast enough the reason why you saw fit to have me raise a housekeeper's daughter as my heiress?" The venom spilled from her words, washing away her self-control but hitting the mark with Bill, whose rage was bubbling, about to explode. "I don't believe it!" she bellowed. "It was about the money, wasn't it? You wanted it all for yourself." She drew one step closer, then dropped her voice to a conspiratorial whisper. "It would've killed you if the estate went to Blanche's son, wouldn't it, my darling boy?" Her nostrils flared as she locked eyes with Bill. "Well, guess what? It will."

Rage dilated Bill's pupils. He clenched his fists and took a step closer. Intervening, Kay grabbed his arm and pulled him away from Carole. The two were bound to kill each other if she didn't keep them apart.

But Carole wouldn't be silent either, seemingly satisfied to hurt her son as much as she could, when only moments earlier, she'd promised him support. "Having an heir was your only shot to cut Dylan off," she carried on. "You thought you had no other choice than to bring a housekeeper's child to this home." She paused, looking around as if trying to find something to throw at Bill, but the vast lobby was empty, except for the paintings on the walls and a small console table devoid of any objects. Frustrated, she stomped her foot against the marble floor, the clacking of her heel resounding like a gunshot in the electrified silence. "To you, even a housekeeper's child was better than Dylan. You should be ashamed of yourself."

"That's ridiculous," he blurted. "I could've had armies of children. I was only forty at the time. What are you talking about?"

"Well, we all know you couldn't have," Carole whispered, "now, don't we, dear?" She breathed, a long sigh leaving her withered, perfectly rouged lips. Then she straightened her spine and pushed her chin forward. When she spoke, her voice was cold and factual, devoid of all emotion, as if she'd managed to unload all her baggage somehow. "I don't want this scandal to tarnish the family name, and for that, I'll make sure you have the best legal defense money can buy. But it ends here. I'll make the necessary changes to my dispositions, and you will be entirely cut off from the business, effective immediately."

Bill didn't lower his gaze, and didn't react as Kay would've expected. Only that undefined grief washed over his face, through his eyes. He'd been expecting that; his mother's reaction wasn't news to him. When Rose had been killed, probably his entire plan had fallen apart.

And that meant only one thing, but Kay thought she'd ask anyway. "Mr. Caldwell, if that's true, why did you kill Rose?" she asked, watching carefully for microexpressions on his face, although psychopaths displayed significantly fewer than the average person.

He didn't blink, his pupils didn't dilate, his hands were still; the same grief bathed his eyes for another beat, then cleared away.

"I didn't kill my daughter," he said calmly, just as Blanche entered the living room, walking quickly toward them, followed by Dylan. "I swear I didn't."

"And I believe him," Blanche said, stopping by his side and taking hold of his arm with both her hands. "I can vouch for that. Bill didn't kill his daughter."

CHAPTER FIFTY
Crazy

The wind had picked up, rolling in frozen gusts off the Mount Chester versants and rushing along the edge of the ravine. Some were powerful enough to whistle through the cypress needles, moving the branch that still withstood Kirsten's weight. Terrified of each movement, she hung on to the branch as tight as she could, her muscles aching from effort, her heart thumping in her chest.

Every now and then, when she dared inhale a lungful of air and shouted, she called for help. Her quivering voice echoed against the walls of the ravine, silencing beasts and birds alike. No one answered, and, after a few moments, nature resumed its concert of sounds. The coyotes below gnawed at the remains scattered all over the bottom of that abyss, occasionally sparring over a meaty bone.

Whimpering, she cringed when a stronger gust shifted the branch, threatening to shake her off like an unwanted burden. Eventually, the branch settled, now almost horizontal, the tree giving in beneath her gradually, as if eroded by her weight, slowly defeated. Soon it would tilt downward, and she would slip, unable to hold on against gravity.

Shadows were starting to elongate. She'd held on since sunrise, and the soreness in her muscles told her she couldn't hold on for much longer. She knew there would come a moment when she'd let go, either overcome by exhaustion or thrown off by a wind gust. She'd almost dozed off a couple of times but had forced herself to snap out of it and wake up, renewing her grip on the branch even if the bark cut into her skin.

She'd wrapped her thighs around the branch and had pushed herself closer to the trunk, where it was thicker, one painstaking inch at a time, afraid to let go, yet desperate to move away from the vacillating tip. Then she'd settled, weary, panting and whimpering at the same time, dizzy from looking down and scared out of her mind.

"Anybody?" she called, but her voice came out weak, tiredness taking its toll despite the adrenaline that raged through her body. "Help!"

She listened, but no one answered. "Somebody, please help me," she cried again, as loud as she could, but her call ended in a tearful whimper.

Another blast of wind caught the breath in her lungs. She renewed her grip against the branch while her arms and legs trembled from exertion, pushed beyond their limits by her desperate will to survive. She'd do anything to live, to go back to Oregon and hug her mom again. Then, she'd go straight to the cops and tell them about that house and the man who'd killed so many other girls before her.

A buzzard circled above her head, flapping and gliding with powerful wings. She felt the air moving against her face before she saw it approaching, extending its claws and getting ready to grab on to a tree branch.

"No, no," she cried, too afraid to let go and wave her arm to scare the bird away.

It landed on the branch above her head, his added weight making the cypress waver and creak.

"Aah," she cried, holding on to the branch, desperately trying to stay level until it stabilized. Until the tree stopped moving, she didn't breathe, but then the smell of the bird filled her nostrils with the promise of death.

The bird poked through the cypress needles and pierced her shoulder. She yelped, the sharp pain fueling her anger.

"Not yet," she shouted, "I'm not dead yet!" Then she screamed, hoping the sound of her voice would make it fly away and yet fearing the moment when its liftoff would rattle the cypress again. Then her mind veered, losing grip with reality. She imagined herself telling the story of her ordeal to her friends back home, on the streets of Creswell, Oregon. They'd laugh and tell her she'd gone insane, refusing to believe a word of it. They'd say, "Girl, what the heck have you been smokin'? Some bad crack or something? Shit like that don't happen to people!"

She laughed out loud, her voice sending strange echoes against the rocky walls of the ravine.

She was going crazy. And soon, she'd have to let go. She couldn't take it anymore.

In the abyss opening beneath her weary body, two coyotes growled and yelped, fighting fiercely over a bone.

CHAPTER FIFTY-ONE
Hideout

Scott hadn't expected it, but Triple-Dollar-Sign had come through for him.

He'd rung him after he fled the fishing cabin, even though it was almost midnight, and the man had methodically torn him a new one, not hesitating to call him out on his incompetence, on his inability to stop that nosy fed-turned-detective cold in her tracks. Dead cold.

Little did he know, Scott's concerns were nowhere near that fed bitch, although he would've gladly twisted her neck like a twig, taking pleasure in hearing her bones crack while life left her body, watching it writhe, then twitch, then fall still. But no, his mind was on his hard-earned money.

What had possessed him to tell Nicole about his stash all those years ago? A serious amount of alcohol, if he remembered correctly, but he'd always taken pride in his ability to hold his liquor and keep his mouth shut when drunk. Now the woman was probably spilling her guts to the cops, sending them on their way to clear out every dime he'd squirreled away after twenty years of hard work.

One day soon, he'd catch up with her and make her pay for it, for all of it. If he regretted anything, it was he hadn't killed her before leaving that cabin, so that mouth of hers would finally stop yapping.

He'd run out of there cutting through the woods and looking over his shoulder, expecting to see Young and the rest of the precinct catching up with him, but he'd made it away without seeing anyone. He'd found his car and rushed behind the wheel, then peeled off throwing dirt and pebbles in the air, skidding badly on the muddy, leaf-covered ground.

As soon as he hit the highway, he'd called Triple-Dollar-Sign. He had nowhere to go, and didn't want to leave the area while so many loose ends were left hanging in the air like an old woman's oversized underwear on laundry day.

He could've run to the terminal and tried to salvage his money, but he was too afraid he'd be caught. Maybe the cops were already staking out the place. Could he withstand his entire precinct gathered around him, weapons drawn, and make it out alive? No chance, although he would've enjoyed kicking some of their traitorous faces in. Who'd told the fed about his cabin, if not one of them, one of the men he thought of as his brothers and had invited over for a weekend of beers and fishing?

His only hope remained with Nicole, out of all people. Maybe she'd be smart enough to keep her big trap shut, in the hope she could get her paws on that money herself. Maybe she wouldn't think about it; after all, fourteen years had passed since he'd last mentioned it, his drunken indiscretion never again repeated.

But for now, he had to lay low, and Triple-Dollar-Sign had just the place for it.

With a searing voice slathered in contempt, he'd instructed him to head north and take the third to last exit before hitting the Oregon state line, then drive on a side road due west for about 2 miles. Then he'd find an abandoned farmhouse at the end of a long driveway, on the left side of the road.

The man's instructions had landed him there without issues, but he hadn't stopped with the directions, guiding him to access the fuse box in the garage and flip a few switches that had Scott frowning in the weak glow of his flashlight. Someone had improvised some twisted circuitry in that fuse box, bypassing certain fuses but centralizing the rest onto a switch fitted with a remote emitter. Why on earth would anyone do that?

But rich people were different from folks like him, and they got to do whatever they wanted, because they could afford it. Like keep that farmhouse like that, in complete darkness, unheated in the brisk November cold, smelling of musty air and mold, letting it rot in the damp darkness like an old carcass.

He'd instructed Scott to enter the house and turn on the heater. Before ending the call, the man had warned him to stay in the living room and not set foot in any of the bedrooms, and to keep his nose out of any business that did not concern him. Triple-Dollar-Sign had concluded his warning with another threat, this time telling Scott his life was hanging by a thread if he didn't walk the line.

And Scott believed the man. He'd met him a few times, enough to know he could end his life without losing a moment's sleep over it, one killer recognizing another without a hint of a doubt.

But he wasn't there to watch his every move.

Entering the farmhouse, he turned on the lights, then ensured the heater had started pushing hot air through the floor vents. The house was frozen, in time as well as in temperature. It was as if he'd stepped back a few decades, the hammered copper roosters hanging on the kitchen wall making him scoff. His grandmother used to have something like that.

While the walls were cracking back to life under the flow of warm air, he wandered through the house, opening every room, turning on the lights, making sure there were no surprises waiting for him in the dark, cobwebbed corners. There was nothing; only a home frozen in time, the only things that spoke of the present day being the rolls of toilet paper in the bathroom, and the sliced cheese in the fridge he'd munched on, still good although the power had been off for who knows how long.

One of the small bedrooms caught his attention, though. It was just as frozen in time as the rest of the house, its closet filled with outdated clothes and shoes, but the bed was unmade, the wrinkled sheets wet, and a large bath towel, also wet, just as wrinkled, as if someone had gone from the shower straight to bed. The pillow felt soaked under his touch, the filling holding in the moisture that hadn't dried in the absence of heat.

"What the hell?" he mumbled, smelling the pillow from a close distance. It smelled of fresh shampoo infused with lilac, as if someone had just slept on that bed, not minding her wet hair in that cold, creepy house.

Shrugging it off, he left the room, turning off the lights and closing the door, careful to leave everything as he'd found it. Then he fell asleep on the couch, under some blankets he found there, thrown to the side as if someone had risen from their sleep in a hurry.

The last sensation he had before slipping away into deep slumber was the smell of the old blankets, stale, moldy, laced with hints of soapy lavender.

CHAPTER FIFTY-TWO
The Secret

Blanche led her brother into the living room. Carole followed reluctantly, an expression of dismay written on her features since she'd learned that Rose Harrelson had been raised as the heiress to the family business. Two steps behind her, Dylan ended the procession. He was an intriguing man, Blanche's son. Dressed sharply in a charcoal suit and white shirt, he distanced himself from the family drama, keeping quiet, seemingly uninterested, occasionally checking his phone. Kay could sense by the ridges on his brow and the nervousness of his gestures he didn't share his mother's devotion to Bill. It would've been impossible to expect that, given how Bill never missed an opportunity to call the young man a bastard and a slew of other names. Seeing his mother take the side and care that much for the man who constantly insulted him must've been traumatic and infuriating for Dylan, yet he didn't show it.

Kay followed the family into the living room, Elliot by her side. Her partner was following her lead, but she could tell he was aching to ask Bill about the missing girl from Oregon who'd last been seen climbing into a Lincoln just like his. How did that girl play into all this? Or was it a strange coincidence, a game fate played with people throwing them curveballs only to have them chase shadows and waste time? There were almost a thousand such vehicles registered in California.

The living room was large, with a vaulted ceiling and picture windows that welcomed the sunshine in. Decorated tastefully in white with black accents, the room reflected Carole's personality the most, somber yet perfectly arranged, contained, calculated. The portraits on the wall were a family history from what Kay could tell, with the centerpiece above the fireplace a group photo of Carole and her husband when they were young, surrounded by their four children. Bill must've been about twenty years old in that picture, Blanche was a young teenager, and the other two were tweens. Something drew Kay's attention to the image, but she couldn't put her finger on what that was. Her gut was telling her something was off, but what? She kept looking at the photograph from a distance, wishing she could put everything on hold for a minute and approach the portrait, study it, uncover what had triggered her attention.

Overall, there were dozens of things off with the Caldwells. The list was a long and impressive one, starting with the absurd way Carole had decided to manage the estate, and ending with whatever it was that filled the air with electricity whenever Blanche entered the room.

No one sat on the white leather sectional sofa and armchairs set at the center of the living room, the Caldwells choosing to remain standing, clustered together in a tight circle as if intent to keep the two cops out of their family business. Kay approached Bill and placed a hand on his shoulder.

"Mr. Caldwell, I hope your attorney will be joining us soon. We're placing you under arrest."

With his face scrunched in anger, Bill Caldwell gave Kay a long stare. "I didn't kill my daughter, and don't know who did. If I'd known, his body would be somewhere you would never find, rotting away in the sun." His words sounded honest and cold, a statement of fact coming from a man whose family owned tens of thousands of acres of land.

"Oh, dear," Carole said, quick to take a seat on an armchair. Her appearance of staunch composure was starting to crack. She seemed weak at the knees all of a sudden, feeling for the armrest and holding on to it with white knuckles.

Blanche tugged at her brother's arm, pulling him away from Kay in a protective gesture. Her blue eyes searched Kay's with terror in them. Her hands, gripping Bill's arm tightly, trembled a little.

"I'm going to let that pass and write it off as the words of a grieving father," Kay said. "But that doesn't change a thing. We are taking you in. You're being charged with other crimes, the rape of Shelley Harrelson among them."

That phrase chilled the air instantly. Blanche let go of her brother's arm and stepped back. She gazed at him not with disgust or disappointment, but with sadness and pity, with empathy. Bill lowered his eyes, ashamed, then raised them and looked at his sister apologetically.

Kay noticed the interactions in disbelief. The dynamic between the two siblings was completely off, adding to the list of things that raised questions about the Caldwell family. She realized the worst thing she could do was drag Bill out of there and interrogate him at the precinct, where he'd be calm and in control again, hiding behind his overpriced attorney. No... If she wanted to get to the bottom of whatever was happening in that family she needed to stay put, observe, and occasionally ask the right questions to keep stoking the fire to unravel the mysteries.

Blanche reached out for Bill's arm again, as if she'd forgiven him, but her eyes searched Kay's. "I can prove to you my brother had nothing to do with his daughter's death."

Kay frowned. "Prove? How?"

"Alyssa, well, the girl we all knew as Alyssa came to me, when she found the second photo in her locket."

"There was a second photo in the damn thing?" Bill reacted. "Whose?"

"Shelley Harrelson's," Blanche replied, lowering her voice to barely a whisper, keeping her eyes fixed on her brother's face.

"You knew?" Bill asked, turning his entire attention toward her as if the whole world around them had vanished.

Blanche paused for a beat, then wiped a tear from the corner of her eye. "I saw you that night, on the tarmac. I'd come to say goodbye, thinking you'd had enough of this charade, fearing you were going to leave us forever." She shook her head slowly, lowering her gaze. "I didn't know who the second girl was. I heard about the kidnapping later, but, um, I couldn't say anything. Not to you, not to anyone." She looked at Bill a certain way, like she'd done before, and his features settled, as if his sister's gaze had washed away the turmoil inside him.

What was going on between those two? What kind of power did Blanche have over her brother? Everything was off about their interactions, and yet Kay couldn't quite put her finger on it, like she couldn't about what was off about the family portrait. And yet her gut kept prodding her to stare at that photo every chance she got.

Blanche broke eye contact regretfully, and turned to Kay again, shooting Elliot a glance in passing. "She came to me looking for answers, about the woman in the locket, about her past. I discouraged her curiosity as much as I could, but she was determined to find out."

Bill's frown reappeared, digging trenches at the root of his nose. "I don't believe you. She never said anything to me. She was a happy child, no worries in this world."

"She was a smart girl who had a mind of her own," Blanche replied. "Last time she spoke to me, a couple of days before she died, she said she was going to speak with the detective who had investigated Rose's disappearance."

"How did she know about Rose's disappearance?" Kay asked.

"She found out who Shelley was, starting from that photo in her locket. Someone on the staff must've told her. I think she showed the photo to everyone, asking them if they knew who the woman was. Then she looked her up on the internet and found the articles about Rose."

Another wave of rage surged over Bill. "You're lying, to protect your good-for-nothing bastard," he shouted, then pushed her away. She faltered, but managed to regain her balance, although the physical violence seemed to have hurt her more than his words. Elliot approached with one quick step and flanked Bill on the other side, ready to intervene.

Bill's eyes drilled into Dylan, who watched everything from a distance, his expression impenetrable. Was it because he was the new heir, and he didn't care about the static, knowing he'd won the sickening game Carole had devised? Being called all sorts of names in front of everyone else had to have left its mark on the young man, and still, he didn't seem to care. Maybe it had been like that throughout his entire existence. Maybe he'd gotten used to taking whatever Bill was dishing, the reason why the thirty-one-year-old hadn't revolted against Bill's abuse another mystery. He withstood his uncle's fiery gaze with calm and a little contempt fluttering at the corners of his mouth.

Without any warning, Bill pulled out a gun and aimed at his nephew. The young man's expression shifted from calm to stunned shock, his eyes rounded and his mouth agape, yet no words came out. Before Bill could squeeze the trigger, Elliot tackled him, but he still fired. The bullet hit Dylan's neck as Blanche screamed. The young man fell to the ground, his hand pressing spasmodically on his bleeding neck, a look of bewilderment in his eyes.

"You shot me, you sick son of a bitch," Dylan groaned.

Elliot had taken Bill's weapon and had the man on his knees, with his hands cuffed in front of him. Procedure demanded the suspect to be handcuffed behind his back, but Kay had signaled Elliot to make an exception. She wanted Bill's hands to reveal, through gestures and reactions, as many of his secrets as possible.

Bill watched, shocked, how Blanche sobbed at the side of her son, and grieved with her as if someone else had just pulled the trigger. Then Blanche turned toward him, closing the distance between them until she towered over him, lowering her face disfigured by anger until it almost touched his, her small fists clenched at her chest.

"You stupid, arrogant fool. Dylan is your son. Yours and mine!"

CHAPTER FIFTY-THREE

First Night

Thirty-One Years Ago

They were moving.

Bill's mother had decided to build another house, at least three times as big as the old one, and to abandon the home of his childhood. She'd chosen a large piece of land closer to the highway, on a gentle slope, adorned with mature trees that would bring shade to the house in the summer. Like always, if his mother had chosen, so it was. Decided.

In June that year, they'd broken ground. Every day, his parents spent more and more time at the site of their new home, supervising the installation of fixtures and appliances, giving direction, driving people crazy. His mother had invented the notion of control freak, and the wealth of the family was a paradox, because, as he'd learned in business school, companies that were managed by such controlling, mercurial, and incompetent leaders were doomed to fail. Only theirs wasn't, making Bill wonder about the worth of everything he'd learn in class.

He still had a few classes left, and he'd graduate that fall with a bachelor's degree in business administration, ahead of schedule by almost a year. All the time he'd been a student, he lived at home, raising eyebrows left and right, from his parents who would've welcomed the opportunity for their son to socialize and meet wealthy young women at Stanford, to his coeds, who would've loved to hang out with the handsome young man who drove a black Porsche convertible.

Only he chose to drive it home every night.

No one knew the reason why, and Bill wasn't sharing.

Moving day approached, and Carole decided to send the tweens to camp, to get rid of their constant bickering about who would get the biggest room, if they would have their own TV, or how their stuff would be moved. Bill and Blanche were the only ones left behind, both willing to help their parents with the logistics of the move.

It came down to them to supervise the movers as they picked and chose from select items Carole wanted moved. The bulk of the stuff was to stay behind, even the hammered copper rooster hanging on the kitchen walls, a gift from Bill's great-grandparents whose image had found its way into the stylized logo of the company. The furniture, TV set, most of their clothes, everything was to be abandoned, and Carole couldn't care less what was to come of it. "It belongs to a different era," she'd replied when asked, and she was adamant about it. In her new house, everything was going to be new.

That night, their parents were going to stay at the new house, supervising the delivery and installation of the custom furniture. Bill stayed at the old house, wrapping up some homework for his economics project, while Blanche was just happy to be left alone, to read and watch TV on the sofa by the large picture window with a view of the woods.

When he finished his homework, Bill moved to the living room, and found Blanche reading and listening to music. He suggested a movie and some microwave popcorn, and she squealed with joy, but asked him to give her the time to take a shower first. She rushed into the bathroom and soon he could hear the water running and Blanche's melodious voice humming a pop hit they both liked.

Then everything went dark.

When the power went out, Blanche screamed. Bill jumped off the sofa and rushed to the bathroom. He knocked on the door, but Blanche kept screaming, sobs mixing with her wails. Hesitating for a split second, he opened the door and let Blanche's cries guide him to her in the pitch darkness.

She was standing in the bathtub, shaking hard under the flow of hot water. He turned off the faucet and extended his arm, grazing against her breast by accident. She latched onto it with both her hands.

"It's okay, Blanche, it's just a power outage, nothing more."

"I'm so scared," she whimpered. "I can't see. I can't—"

"Shh… It's okay," he said, grabbing a towel off the rack and handing it to her.

"N—no," she quavered, not letting go of his arm. "You do it."

"I'm right here. I'm not going anywhere."

She heaved, crying uncontrollably. "I'm afraid I'm going to fall."

That was Blanche, sensitive, frail, her vivid imagination her worst enemy.

Letting her hold on to his hand, he managed to land the towel on her shoulders, but she still didn't move. She shivered, her teeth clattering, although it wasn't that cold.

"Come on, step over the tub. I won't let you fall."

"Uh-uh," she whimpered. "I'm afraid. I'll just sit down in the tub until you find a flashlight."

"Chicken," he joked, "cluck-cluck-clackity-cluck, my sister's yellow and I'm out of luck," he improvised, then laughed out loud. She joined in his laughter, tears still coloring her voice. "Come on, don't be such a pain."

Unclasping her hand off his arm, she slapped him on the shoulder. "I'm not a pain. I'm afraid of the dark. But don't tell anyone. Maddie will laugh at me and Kendall will start turning off the lights whenever he can." Her teeth rattled. "I'm freezing. Do you think the heat's still working?"

She was going to catch a cold. She was wet, her long hair dripping, and the power outage could take a while. Without warning, he scooped her in his arms and took her out of the bathroom. She squealed and wrapped her arms around his neck.

Unsure where to go, he stopped in the hallway in front of the bathroom, still holding her. Moonlight lay silver in the living room just enough to see the shimmer of her blue irises, the heat in her eyes lighting a fire in his body. He breathed, trying to think, to stay rational, but the shape of her wet breasts against his chest blocked every ounce of reason he had left.

He closed his eyes for a long moment, still holding her shivering body, and startled when her thin fingers touched his lips.

"No," he whispered. "Stop it." Deciding to put her down and go out for a run in the cool mountain breeze, he carried her into her bedroom and set her gently on the covers, moonlight guiding his steps. As he lay her wet body on the silk sheets, her towel came undone, exposing her perfect body.

She clutched his neck and pulled him toward her. "Stay with me," she pleaded, "until the power comes back. Please." She caressed his cheek, then ran her thumb across his lower lip, and he came undone.

He thought he was pulling away, but was pulled into her, yearning to feel her wet body against his, to smell the shampoo in her dripping hair, knowing he could warm her up and keep her safe in his arms. Before he took her, he realized he'd always loved her like that. Not like a sister, but like a lover he'd been waiting for. She was the reason he'd driven home every night after school, and risen at six every morning to drive back. Seeing her, even if only at the dinner table, was the reason he existed.

And still, she was his sister. The thought of what he was about to do made him dizzy and nauseous, but he couldn't stop. He reached for her, touching her lips with the tip of his thumb, wondering if his kiss would be welcome. She trembled under his touch, her body drawing closer to his, folding into his. It was as if their entire existence depended on Blanche and him becoming one.

And they did.

That night burned a blazing memory in his mind, one he'd recall for years to come. She'd slept in his arms, breathing gently, her chest barely moving, while he didn't dare fall asleep, because he didn't want to miss a single moment. When he reached out and touched her, she responded, craving him just like he did her, like an unbreakable and lethal addiction. She was shy and had never before been touched, but her instincts drew her to him mercilessly, her soft body undulating and molding around his, a perfect match.

The power came back moments before their parents returned. He barely made it into his bedroom, and that night he would've gladly skipped dinner if it wasn't for his yearning to see her again, to search her eyes and read in them if she felt any regret or just overpowering joy. But she was her normal self, at times making him wonder if he'd dreamed it all, until she caught the opportunity to smile at him a certain way.

He was hooked, hers for life.

She was the one, the only one for him, and she fell in love with him just as hard. They snuck in each other's bedrooms for a while, careful to not get caught, and never thinking or talking about the future. Their parents, tired from spending their days at the new house, barely noticed them at all.

It was the best summer he'd ever had. They took day trips together. Big Sur, Miramar Beach, Half Moon Bay, Inverness, Drakes Bay, walks on deserted beaches watching the angry waves of the Pacific smashing against the rocky shore. They hid from everyone, because no one would understand.

One day, it all came to an end. Carole came home late to find Bill sleeping on the sofa and Blanche pale, sick, throwing up in the bathroom, crying. Carole locked herself in the bedroom with her daughter and didn't emerge for hours. When she came out, she communicated her decisions in a tone no one dared take lightly.

"Blanche will be going to boarding school on the East Coast," she announced. Carole's words cut him like a knife, gutting him, leaving him breathless. He searched Blanche's eyes, but she avoided looking at him. "She'll finish high school over there, maybe continue to an Ivy League college. She will leave tomorrow morning." Then she turned her attention to him. "It's time to find you a wife, my dear boy, someone who can bring happiness to you and wealth to this family. Count on me for that," she'd added, patting him on the shoulder. His mother's touch burned his skin, and, for a moment, he envisioned himself breaking that arm and wringing her neck. But Blanche wasn't there for him anymore; she was looking away, avoiding his gaze, distancing herself.

That night, hours after he'd closed the door to his bedroom and succumbed to the tears that burned his eyes and choked his every breath, she came to see him one last time. There was fire and pain in their embrace, then, while their tears blended, they made promises to each other. They'd write. They would rent post office boxes under fake names and correspond in secret. They'd stay true, even if Carole forced Bill to marry. As soon as he came into his own money, he'd come find her.

She'd never kept those promises; her first betrayal. She'd simply vanished from his life, leaving his mailbox empty and his heart shattered. The next summer she didn't return, and the one after that, she told everyone she was going to Europe instead.

She was gone.

That same year, he earned his graduate degree, cum laude, and his father had asked him what he wanted as a graduation gift. He must've expected something else, because when Bill had asked to let him keep the old house, the man's jaw dropped. He and Carole exchanged a quick glance, then his mother shrugged.

He'd been living there for a while with his new wife, Evangeline, every day feeling like the gilded prison of a caged bird, endless hours passing slowly one after another while he lived a lie and pretended to care about his future child and the stranger who was carrying her in her womb. Evangeline's pregnancy came as a relief, offering an excuse to keep his distance from her bed. When she miscarried, he was secretly thankful for the extended reprieve, and continued sleeping in the next room.

When Blanche suddenly returned, she'd been gone five years. He'd heard the news from Kendall, and had driven like a madman to the new house to see her. When he rushed into the large living room, there she was, a grown woman now and stunningly beautiful, her long, blond hair wavy and smooth, her blue eyes warm and loving when she looked at him, a glint of the old fire still smoldering in them.

He called her by the name he'd given her, whispered it only for her to hear. "Mira, my beautiful Mira." And she'd smiled.

Then he saw the brat she was holding by the hand, and his heart withered. Her second betrayal.

"This is Dylan," Carole was quick to introduce him. "He's three." She paused and smiled tenderly at Blanche. "Your sister had an adventure with a Frenchman in Europe, and, well, this is Dylan," she ended, laughing. She ruffled the twerp's hair, then added, "Isn't he the sweetest little boy?"

He drove away in a rage that night, not sure where he could go to quench the inferno blazing in his chest. How could she have betrayed him like that? She was his Mira, the only woman he'd ever loved, the only one he ever would. A Frenchman? What did that make Mira, if not a cheating slut? And yet, he would've done anything for another night in her arms.

He couldn't stop driving, not knowing where to go. His aimlessness drove him to Redding, where he saw a young girl in the red-light district, whose blond hair and thin body reminded him of the Mira he once knew. He took her with him, searching for a place where he could recreate his best memory and relive his first night with Blanche.

That night, he decided Evangeline had to move to the new house, and so would he.

The old house belonged to him and Mira.

Forever.

CHAPTER FIFTY-FOUR
Family Portrait

"This is Detective Kay Sharp, FCSO, I need a bus to my location, stat. Thirty-one-year-old male, GSW to the neck. Stat!"

"Where do you need me?" Elliot asked, his hand gripping Bill's arm firmly. Caldwell was kneeling on the floor, reaching for Dylan, but Elliot kept him away.

She'd pushed Blanche away, and Carole, who'd rushed to Dylan's side sobbing, but the time to grieve wasn't there yet. The bullet had grazed his neck, missing the carotid and jugular, but still lacerated enough smaller blood vessels to make exsanguination an imminent risk.

Kay kept pressure on Dylan's neck, fighting him at the same time, her thoughts rushing to Jacob, of how she'd found his body lying on the kitchen floor, the raw memory of his blood bursting between her trembling fingers making her whimper. Yanking her back into the moment, Dylan clawed at her hands trying to reach his wound, flailing, making things worse with each accelerated heartbeat that pushed more blood out of his body.

"Here," she replied, looking briefly in Elliot's direction. "Help me hold him down."

Elliot turned to Bill. "I'm going to let go of your arm now, to help your son. One move, one word, and you're a dead man, you understand?"

Bill nodded, his eyes riveted on Dylan's agonizing face, on the blood oozing between Kay's fingers as she kept pressure on his wound.

"Hold his legs, gently," Kay instructed Elliot. "We have to slow this bleed." Elliot squatted and put some pressure on Dylan's legs, but the gleaming hardwood was slippery, and Dylan's thrashes almost threw him off balance. He set a knee down and grabbed the young man's ankles.

Still keeping pressure on his bleeding wound, Kay looked at Dylan with a reassuring confidence she wasn't feeling. "You need to lower your heart rate," she told him in a firm voice. "You need to breathe in for three seconds, hold it in for four, exhale for five. Can you do that for me?"

He whimpered, his eyes rounded in fear. "I—I'll try."

Kay breathed with him, the vagus nerve stimulation having an immediate effect in lowering his heart rate. "Good," she whispered, shooting a side glance toward Bill.

He'd dropped to his knees in front of Blanche, sobbing hard, his shoulders heaving. "Mira... my son... our son. Why didn't you tell me?"

Blanche wiped a tear from her eyes. "You hated him the moment you laid eyes on him. You never even asked. And then she—"

She looked briefly toward Carole, who stood, pale and dignified, yet shocked, her trembling hand covering her agape mouth. Was it because she was at risk of losing the last heir to her precious estate? Or was the unforgivable secret they'd been keeping for so long, now out in the open, a threat she could not control?

But Carole snapped out of it and looked at her son with cold eyes. "It was the right thing to do, son. The only thing we could've done."

Bill's eyes turned hateful, searing. "Damn you, Mother. You ruined our lives!"

EMTs rushed in, and for six tense minutes while they stabilized Dylan and loaded him on the stretcher, no one spoke, the secret they were guarding so treacherous it kept even the most intense of emotions muzzled, silent.

"Where are you taking him?" Blanche asked, while the EMTs were rolling Dylan to the bus.

"Franklin Medical Center, ma'am."

She squeezed his hand and promised him she'd be there in just a few minutes, then they reconvened in the large living room, where the picture above the fireplace still gnawed at Kay's gut.

Then she suddenly realized what she'd been missing, and it had been right in front of her the entire time. Fascinated, she approached the photo and studied it from up close. Then, she turned to Carole with an empathetic smile.

"I understand why you had to keep these two separated, why you broke up their romance and lied about Dylan. They were siblings, right? Incest is illegal in the state of California, and it's been like that for a while." Carole nodded, a hint of a bitter smile tugging at the corners of her mouth. "Not to mention, the scandal. It would've destroyed everyone."

"Exactly," Carole replied. "I had no other choice."

Kay wiped the fake smile off her lips, dipping her voice in ice. "Only they weren't siblings, were they?"

Her question dropped like a bomb, filling the air with tension, thick as fog on a fall morning.

"What?" Bill asked. He'd been on his knees all that time, but he sprung to his feet and approached Kay. In a split second, his arm landed firmly in Elliot's grip, tightly enough to make him wince.

"Were they, Mrs. Caldwell?" Kay pressed on, ignoring Bill and focusing on Carole. The woman had destroyed their lives. She deserved what she had coming.

Carole turned and walked away, then, probably realizing the issue wasn't going to go away on its own if she ignored it, approached Kay and grabbed her hand between hers. "I have no idea what you're talking about, my dear. But I'm begging you, this family has been through enough. It's time for you to leave, even if that means taking Bill with you without legal representation. Our lawyer was in San Francisco when I called; that's why he's delayed, but he'll meet you at the precinct. Now, please leave or I will have you escorted off my property."

"You knew," Kay replied calmly. "You knew they were not related, and you kept it under wraps to save your own reputation."

"That's it, you're leaving, or else." Carole walked over to the desk phone and picked up the receiver, then quickly dialed a number. Before the call could be answered, Blanche snatched the phone out of her hand and slammed it down hard.

"I want to know," Blanche said, standing by Bill's side and glaring at her mother. Then she turned to Kay, her voice pleading, filled with tears. "It's our right to know."

Kay nodded slowly, thinking there should've been laws against what Carole had done to her children. They'd lived all their lives under the burden of immense guilt and shame for their love, forced to lie to themselves and everyone else, including their son.

She looked at Carole, anticipating the look her words would bring in the woman's eyes. "You see this chin dimple you and your husband both have?" Kay pointed at the picture above the fireplace. Bill touched his chin absentmindedly. "It's called cleft chin, and in the vast majority of cases, it's inherited, unless there's trauma involved. The gene that carries it is dominant." She paused for a moment. Carole had turned pale as a sheet, while Blanche and Bill seemed confused. "That means either parent will pass it on." She turned to Blanche, pointing at her chin. "Blanche isn't your daughter, and was not your husband's either."

"Oh, God," Blanche whispered, starting to cry.

Bill clenched his fists, glaring at his mother, and bellowed, "I'll kill you!" Elliot held him back with difficulty, as he fought to free himself and pounce on Carole. "If it's the last thing I do, I'll end your miserable life. You destroyed us," he sobbed, shaking, heaving, his rage melting into powerlessness and defeat. Then he reached out to Blanche with both his cuffed hands. "Mira… I'm so sorry. I should've known. I felt… We both felt it. Our love was real."

Blood draining from her face, Blanche grabbed Carole by the arm. "Was I adopted? Why did you hide that?"

Carole looked at the two of them with infinite contempt. "I don't owe you any explanation," she said, thrusting her chin forward and grinding her teeth. "I did what I had to do to protect your legacy."

"What legacy?" Bill scoffed. "It's a bloody farm! When the wind blows from the south, your precious legacy smells of manure! You're nothing but a snob, a pretentious farmer full of airs and delusions of grandeur. You're pathetic." He spat on the floor at Carole's feet, but the old woman didn't flinch. "I envy Blanche for not having your blood coursing through her veins."

"Please tell me," Blanche said. "Please. It's my right to know."

Kay looked at the endless arrogance on the woman's face. There was no empathy there, for either of them, no remorse for the damage she'd done. "It will come out at the trial anyway," Kay said. "You'll be under oath and you'll have no choice but to answer. Right now, it's in your best interest to cooperate."

The old woman lowered her head, seemingly defeated, at least for a moment. "My husband had an affair," she rasped. "Typical sordid story, nothing original. His assistant, a gold-digging blond with short skirts and no morals, had him wrapped around her finger. A few months later, she showed up on our doorstep with you," she gestured toward Blanche. "We offered a cash settlement against her sworn silence and she sold you cheap." She shook her head, lost in memories. "But then, as you were starting to grow, I noticed things. We're all dark-haired, you're a blond. Our family, on my husband's side, they all have brown eyes, but yours remained blue. I sent your DNA and William's to be tested, and I knew." She sighed, closing her eyes for a long moment. "I've known since you were two."

"Why did you keep me? You must've hated me so much," Blanche asked, her skin deathly pale and her lips quivering.

Carole shrugged. "It's not about you. It never was. My dear William deserved the pang of guilt he felt whenever you and I were in the same room," she said, her voice dipped in venom. "I'd look at him and he'd lower his gaze like the cheating bastard he was, living the rest of his days in shame for his betrayal. He deserved every minute of it."

A shudder shook Blanche's thin shoulders, and her stare went blank for a moment.

"Then why?" Blanche asked, her voice filled with immense regret. "Why did you destroy us? Just to punish him?"

Carole straightened her back, shaking off whatever guilt had rubbed onto her. "Can you imagine the scandal, if people would've learned that my husband brought a slut's child to my doorstep?"

"Who would've known? And who would've cared?" Kay asked, curious to see how Carole's mind worked. Rarely she had the chance to watch a sociopathic narcissist unravel.

"This is not for people like you to understand," the woman replied, each word dipped in venom. "I believe I'd asked you to leave. *Now*, please."

Kay ignored Carole's request, staring at the family portrait hanging above the fireplace. Her gut kept nudging her about that image. There was something else she needed to see in that photo, something relevant. She stared at it for a moment, seeing how Bill and Blanche were lost in each other, their foreheads together like she'd seen them the day before, her hands on his face, wiping his tears.

Then Kay looked at Carole, who'd started calling for a housekeeper, pacing the room furiously. The help must've been hiding from her, anticipating her rage at the slightest mistake.

The entire situation seemed familiar in a strange kind of way, as if she'd seen it before, only from a vast distance. How? What was her gut trying to tell her?

She closed her eyes for a moment, structuring what she'd seen unravel, what she'd learned about the players. Carole was a narcissist, a malignant one, and a sociopath. She'd abused her children psychologically, but mostly Bill. She'd had them all play her games, but the youngest two had saved themselves and put distance between them and their mother, even if that forfeited their right to inherit. Smart people. Bill and Blanche had stayed, overcome with guilt, yet still in love with each other. Bill's first romance had been stifled by Carole brutally, who had effectively castrated the young man. He grew up resenting her, never recovering from the trauma he'd suffered at her hands, carrying a burden of guilt and shame for decades.

And he'd raped Shelley Harrelson, evolving into criminal behavior from a young age. Then he'd grabbed her daughter when it had served his purpose, with no remorse and no concern for the family he'd destroyed. Like mother, like son.

She'd confirmed what she'd only suspected before. Bill Caldwell was a psychopath, and he had his mother's genes and upbringing to thank for it, his trauma, the life of lies she'd built for him. But the nature of the trauma, his fixation with Blanche, his mercurial moods, and the short temper he'd plentifully demonstrated etched the portrait of a serial killer. One who hadn't discovered himself, one who hadn't killed yet.

When the next thought rushed through her mind, Kay gasped, feeling a chill run through her veins. What if he had?

"Show me her photo again," she told Elliot, unable to take her eyes off the portrait. "Your missing kid from Oregon."

He took out his phone, still holding Bill's arm with one hand, and brought up Kirsten's photo, then showed Kay the screen. She looked at the portrait again, and Elliot followed her gaze. Goosebumps churned her skin.

"I'll be damned, she looks just like Blanche," Elliot whispered.

Did that mean anything? Was it another coincidence, on top of Bill owning a gray Lincoln? Maybe, but the chances of it being coincidental had just dropped dangerously close to zero.

As if reading her mind, Elliot started typing quickly on his phone's screen, and moments later, a chime announced a new text message. He tapped the screen again to open it, then showed it to Kay.

The Lincoln Bill Caldwell was driving earlier that day had been tagged in San Francisco under the company name. That's why it didn't pop up in the first search.

Coincidence seemed less and less likely. She needed to stir things up a little bit more.

"However disheartening the family drama we've witnessed," Kay said, raising her voice a little to command attention from everyone, "the reason for our visit here is to investigate the death of Bill's daughter."

Bill pulled himself away from Blanche and looked at Kay as if he had difficulties remembering he used to have a daughter. He seemed as if he'd been awakened from a trance, his stare vacant and immensely tired, drawn, devastated.

"Where is he?" Kay asked, approaching Bill, inserting herself between him and Blanche, forcing him to focus on her instead. "You paid him then, didn't you? You paid him to bury the kidnapping case."

Bill nodded, then lowered his head, staring at the gleaming hardwood floor.

"Where is he?" Kay asked again, grabbing his other arm and shaking him a little, forcing him back to reality. "When she found the locket, and saw the photo, your daughter must've reached out to him, asking questions. She must've somehow found out who was the detective in the Rose Harrelson kidnapping case, right?" He slowly raised his eyes, looking at her with an unspoken plea to be left alone to grieve. "But Scott couldn't risk it, could he?" Kay pressed on, feeling in her gut she was getting close. His shoulders had dropped, a sign of relaxed muscles that come with abandonment, with the admission of defeat. She lowered her head to catch his eyes and held his gaze imperatively. "It fits," she said, some of her words intended for Elliot although she didn't break eye contact with Bill. "Scott has a military background, and can slice a throat without hesitation. Make no mistake: the cop you paid off fourteen years ago is the killer of your child. And you're protecting him."

He stayed silent, seemingly lost in his thoughts.

Then Elliot showed Bill Kirsten's photo. "How about her?" Elliot asked, the anger in his voice unmitigated by his Texas drawl. "You were seen taking her in your car, and then she vanished. Where is she, Bill?"

Carole and Blanche were stunned. They looked briefly at each other, their previous angst dissipated by Elliot's words.

Kay leaned closer to Bill, whispering close to his ear. "She looks just like Blanche used to, when she was that girl's age, doesn't she?" He stiffened a little, but clenched his jaws and didn't say a single word. "It must've been like you were back in time, holding Mira in your arms again, reliving the best nights of your life."

"Mira," he said, reaching out to Blanche, as if Kay's mentioning her name had reminded him of her.

Still whispering, Kay continued her plea. "Blanche always loved you, Bill. You were the love of her life, just like she was yours. You made a mistake, not trusting in her love, not recognizing yourself in Dylan, but it's understandable, and she's already forgiven you. Look at her… She's right here, by your side, instead of Dylan's." Her words flooded Bill's eyes. He lowered his head, but otherwise made no effort to control or hide his tears. "And now, you're making another terrible mistake. You're letting your daughter's killer go free."

When he looked up at Kay, she shivered. It was as if she were staring into the eyes of a dead man. When he spoke, his words had a finality in them she didn't understand.

"I'll take you to him."

CHAPTER FIFTY-FIVE
Scott

The main door was wide open, Kay impatiently waiting outside, although she couldn't take her eyes off of Bill. The finality of his voice when he'd agreed to take them to his daughter's killer, the expression in his sunken eyes baffled Kay. She watched Bill grab Blanche's hand between his and raise it to his lips. He kissed it gently, while she caressed his face, whispering unintelligible words. Then he pulled away and she let him go, her hand falling limp when he'd stopped holding it, her eyes squeezed shut and brimming with tears.

Then Bill let himself be loaded into Kay's SUV and Elliot took the wheel. A sense of calm, of inner peace had descended upon him, making her wonder how it was possible. No one really understood the psychopathic mind, although she came close. There was some mental process going on, something that helped him deal with everything that was happening. Having no remorse and knowing no fear, he still felt pain and loss like anyone else did, maybe even worse.

"Take the highway, then the next exit," he directed, his voice steady, unfazed. "I believe I know where he is."

Kay searched his eyes, looking for signs he might be toying with them, taking them for a ride in the metaphorical sense, but there was nothing in those barren eyes but immense grief and that sickening calm.

"You had no idea Scott had killed your daughter, did you?" she asked.

"No," he whispered simply.

It made sense. If he was unaware Rose had discovered her true identity or was about to, he would've had no way to figure it out. To him, the death of his daughter had come as a complete surprise.

"Have you seen Scott since fourteen years ago?" she asked, following up on a hunch so thin it seemed invisible.

A beat. "Yes. I've asked him to do things for me at times," he said, shooting her a direct gaze tinted with frustration. "Some he failed to do well." His lip flickered with the beginning of a lopsided grin. "He was supposed to kill you."

Her eyebrows shot up. "Really? Why?"

Elliot glared at him through the rearview mirror with silent menace in his eyes.

"You were getting too close," he sighed. "He just screwed up, I guess. It's hard to get good help these days."

Stunned, she tried to recall if she'd noticed Scott anywhere near her. Then she realized it must've been the way he found Nicole. He'd come there for her, and shot Jacob instead when he found Nicole with him.

Ignoring the pain in her shoulder, Kay turned in her seat to look at Bill. "One thing you didn't share," she said, grinding her teeth in anger, realizing just how close she was to losing her brother because of that man. "Why did you rape Shelley Harrelson? She looks nothing like Blanche, does she?" Kay omitted to use past tense in talking about Shelley, and held back no punches. The bastard deserved everything he had coming to him.

Bill closed his eyes and a grimace of anger washed over his face for a brief moment. When he opened them again, his irises were devoid of any emotion. "My mother and I argued one day," he said, his words slow and relaxed as if telling a long-forgotten story over coffee and cake. "Evangeline was pregnant, and I wasn't—" He swallowed and looked away for a moment. "We weren't having sex anymore. But I don't think it was about sex at all. Mother drove me insane with rage one day with her aberrant plans for my unborn daughter, her precious heiress, whose life she wanted to control minute by minute. When I left that meeting, I downed a couple of glasses of bourbon, then went into my bedroom, where the Harrelson woman was cleaning or something." He stopped briefly, staring at the gloomy fall landscape through the side window. "It just happened... The next thing I remember was zipping up my pants, while she was crying on the floor."

Fuming, Kay struggled for a few seconds to keep her rage bottled in and failed. "Rape doesn't just happen, you sick son of a bitch," she shouted. "What did you do afterward?"

He scoffed and shrugged slightly, not in the least affected by Kay's outburst. If anything, he seemed entertained. "Nothing, really. I sent her home and took a shower. What else could I do?" He breathed calmly, totally indifferent to the facts he was recounting, the complete absence of empathy and conscience a dead giveaway, a confirmation to Kay's initial assessment.

Bill Caldwell was a psychopath.

"You make me sick," Kay muttered, shifting her position in the chair to face forward and ease the strain on her wounded shoulder. She couldn't stand looking at him anymore. Elliot squeezed her hand without a word, and she breathed, the warmth of his touch loosening the iron fist that grasped her heart.

In the corner of her eye, she saw a flicker of a smile tugging at Bill's lip. "Turn here, and drive straight for about two miles. Then you'll see a long driveway on your left."

"Got it," Elliot confirmed.

Struggling with one arm still in a sling, Kay checked her weapon, then holstered it. She thought of removing the sling, but whenever she tried to move her arm, it hurt. She needed to be patient.

"What is this place?" she asked, when Elliot took the left turn and she saw the house in the distance, one window lit with a pale, yellowish light.

"Our old house, Mira's and mine," he replied, a hint of grief in his voice for a moment, then gone in an instant. "He told me you were on to him, and I let him stay until he could finish the job I gave him to do."

"And that was?" she asked, assuming she knew but wanting to be sure.

"Killing you," he replied calmly.

"Wow," she whispered, the universal expression of dismayed shock not nearly enough to convey her feelings. He sat there, handcuffed, in the back of a police car, admitting more crimes than she'd known to charge him with. And he kept on going, seemingly disinterested by the consequences of his confessions. But why? He was smarter than that.

Elliot drove slowly and stopped about 30 feet from the door, then cut the engine. He called for backup, then turned to Kay and said, "Twelve minutes till they get here." But he was determined to go after Scott right then, without delay.

Weapon drawn, she climbed out of the SUV. "Stay here," she ordered.

Bill nodded. "Sure." He closed his eyes and leaned back in his seat, apparently ready to doze off.

He was too damn calm. Something tugged at her gut again, but she disregarded it, focused on the task at hand. They took their positions on either side of the door. She felt uneasy, clumsily holding the gun in her left hand, her balance thrown off by the immobilized arm.

"Ready," she whispered, and Elliot kicked the door open.

"Freeze," he shouted, holding Scott in his sights.

But the man didn't obey. With a roar filled with rage, he forged ahead, lifting Elliot's arm just as he'd squeezed the trigger. The bullet went into the ceiling, then Scott twisted Elliot's arm until he dropped the gun. It fell clattering to the floor, and Scott kicked it to the side with a wide grin.

"Now we're equal, motherfucker," he said, taking two steps back. He reached across a table and drew a large military knife from its holster. "Now we're not." He charged, and Elliot barely had time to avoid the deathly blow.

"Freeze," she shouted, aiming her gun at Scott, trying to slow her breathing to take aim, knowing the risk of missing the target with her nondominant hand. She could hit Elliot instead. The thought of that made her stance weaken and her hand tremble.

As if reading her mind, Scott laughed, right before punching Elliot in the stomach. He buckled, and a second blow followed, straight in his eye.

"Shoot him already," Elliot said, and she took aim again. She drew breath, then exhaled half of it and pulled the trigger. Scott fell on his side, holding his right thigh with both his hands. She took aim again, ready to fire if he so much as breathed the wrong way. The piece of scum didn't deserve to live.

"You okay, partner?" she asked, her voice conveying more concern than she'd wanted Elliot to hear.

Elliot groaned, "I'll live."

"Wait," Scott shouted, "what if I give all of them?" he panted, his wound dripping blood between his fingers. "Carole and Bill? I can give you both."

She laughed. "What could you possibly give me when Bill's the one who brought us here?"

Scott frowned. "Motherfucking bastard," he muttered. "Carole, then," he said, still negotiating.

"Not interested," she replied. "You're going to jail for the rest of your life. No deal."

"She put a contract on you, and I can testify to that." Scott smiled crookedly.

"*She* did?" Kay asked, almost amused. "I thought Bill did."

"They both did," Scott replied. "It's not like I didn't need twice the money, and they didn't need me to tell them what the other was planning, right?" He grinned, showing crooked, yellowish teeth. "Now, do we talk deal? I'm dying here, you stupid bitch."

"Not nearly enough." She'd get Carole to confess a different way. She didn't want the man who'd shot her brother within an inch of his life to see daylight again. But he could still answer some questions.

"Why did you kill Alyssa?"

He groaned, then clenched his jaws. "You can't possibly pin that on me," he shouted. "It was Bill's job to keep the old kidnapping business under wraps. Great job he did at that," he added, spitting some bloody saliva on the floor. "The girl showed up at the precinct, no less, telling everyone she had questions about a kidnapped girl from way back when. She had my name, you know. There was nothing I could do, and it's all on Bill." He stopped briefly, enough to wipe his mouth with his sleeve and wince in pain when he shifted his position on the floor, then he continued, "I just grabbed her and left, took her to Blackwater River Falls. No one's ever there at eight in the morning. No one was supposed to find her; I'm good at what I do."

Appalled, Kay stared at the man, her eyebrows raised. It was as if he were advertising his murder-for-hire skills. Only a twisted, sick mind could think of doing that with other cops present and in the absence of a deal bearing the signature of the district attorney.

"No deal," she said slowly, savoring the words. "You'll die in prison."

Without warning, he pounced on her, his body weight too much for her to withstand. She fell to the floor, screaming from the pain in her wounded shoulder, her breath knocked out of her lungs. She still clutched the handle of her gun, but she couldn't fire it from underneath his body. But his weight started to shift away, as Elliot pulled his arm, twisting it to his back. He squirmed free and turned, hitting Elliot in his side with a strong punch with his right.

Lying on the floor, she fired, the bullet entering the back of his head at an angle and exiting above his ear, missing Elliot by a few good inches. She breathed when she heard the bullet crash into the ceiling lamp, covering them with glass shards and dimming the light by more than half.

Moments later, they returned to the SUV. Elliot walked with a bent gait and kept an icepack over his swelling eye, improvised from ice cubes she'd found in the freezer wrapped in a small towel. She looked inside to check on Bill, and her breath caught.

He was gone.

CHAPTER FIFTY-SIX

Ravine

"He's gone," she shouted, looking around desperately, knowing he couldn't be too far. They were in the middle of an open field, the grasses weighed low by ground frost. If he'd run toward the highway, he'd be visible from afar, nowhere to hide. In the distance, behind the house, the edge of the woods drew a straight line cutting across miles of terrain, running parallel with the road.

In the corner of her eye, she caught a hint of movement. "There—" She pointed at the forest, where she'd seen Bill's tall frame disappearing between the barren trees. He wasn't easy to spot, his dark suit almost the color of wet tree bark in the dimming light of dusk.

They sprinted in pursuit, both running crookedly, faltering at times. Her shoulder hurt every time her legs pounded the ground, but she didn't stop. Her mind raced, twisting and turning hypotheses and theories. That's why he'd been so calm. His plan was already conceived, his exit strategy clear. But going where?

He was gaining a lead, but soon the woods cleared, and they found themselves on a stretch of grassy flatland, Bill's silhouette frozen still some 50 yards ahead of them in a strange pose.

He'd stopped running. He stood calmly, looking straight ahead, not caring about them. That annoying feeling tugged at her gut.

"Is there a ravine or something over there?" she asked, panting, out of breath. Then, without waiting for an answer, she sprung ahead, running as fast as she could. Elliot kept up with her, his footfalls heavy, grunting at times.

She knew where she'd seen that eerie calm before. In people who'd decided to end their lives. In suicidal patients she'd worked with during her hospital rotation.

She was a few yards away when he dove, headfirst, falling to his death in perfect silence. Kay reached the edge just in time to see him splat at the bottom of the deep, rocky ravine.

Then a woman's shriek ripped through the air.

CHAPTER FIFTY-SEVEN
By a Thread

Two fire trucks pulled close to the ravine, silencing their sirens as they entered the grassy stretch of land. Kay directed them with one arm raised high in the air, while Elliot rushed over to speak to the driver of the first truck. The darkness lit by their red flashing lights seemed surreal, altering the colors of the landscape and blinding her whenever she looked that way.

In the silence left behind by the sirens, Kay heard a whimper coming from below.

"Somebody, help me, please," the girl cried, her voice weakened by the prolonged effort to hold on to the cypress branch that had been supporting her weight over the abyss.

Kay rushed to the edge and kneeled in the damp grass. "We're right here, okay?" she shouted, making sure her voice carried over to the girl. "Just a few more minutes, that's all. I swear it won't be longer," she said, while a frown of concern dug trenches on her forehead.

A strangled whimper came from below. She squinted, but couldn't see much in the darkness, the flashing red lights doing more harm than good to her night vision. But those flashers told the girl help had arrived. "Hang in there, okay? You've done so good, surviving this, holding on the way you have," Kay added, forcing herself to sound convincing, but fearing the adrenaline was leaving the exhausted girl's body, weakening her muscles and softening her resolve. "What's your name?"

"I—I can't..." the girl replied, stuttering, then trailing off.

"Yes, you can," Kay demanded, standing up to meet the firefighter who was approaching with Elliot by his side.

"I'm Chief Hopper," the firefighter introduced himself. She shook his hand and nodded, but her question was for the girl below. "What's your name?"

Silence engulfed the scene for a long moment, then her weak voice was barely audible. "Kirsten."

"Good," Kay replied, looking at Elliot. "I'm Kay. My partner and I have been looking all over for a girl named Kirsten. She's from Oregon."

"Oh, God," she cried, then started sobbing. "I can't—I can't hold on."

"One minute, Kirsten," Kay asked imperatively. "Count with me. Count the seconds, every three of them. One," she started, then listened, and heard nothing. "Four," she continued, shouting, her voice demanding.

"Seven," Kirsten's weak voice came through, and she held her thumb up smiling widely.

The fire crews deployed powerful worklights that flooded the scene with brightness. One of them approached with a thermal-imaging camera and showed them the image of the girl's body lying down on the branch, in shades of red, green, and blue on the screen of a tablet.

"Ten," Kay and Kirsten counted together as three more seconds had passed, a little louder this time.

"Yes, that's it," Kay cheered, "keep going. We're almost there."

"We have to secure the tree first," the man holding the thermal-imaging camera said. His name tag read, BOONE. "It might give when we least expect it. I'm surprised it held so long."

One of the trucks had extended the ladder above the ravine. A basket was attached to it with a winch that the driver controlled from inside the cabin. Inside the basket, a young man held on to its edge with both hands, his helmet appearing too big for his slender body. Seen from up close, that basket seemed large enough to hold three people, but dangling in the air, above the abyss, it seemed frail and a very bad idea.

"Thirteen," Kay shouted, just as she heard Kirsten say the word. "Way to go." Then she clenched her jaws and said, "Bring that basket back. I'm going down there."

Chief Hopper took two steps closer. "With all due respect, Detective, you can't go down there. We know what we're doing. And you're not able to take care of yourself," he added, giving her immobilized arm a long look.

"Sixteen," Kirsten said weakly.

"Yes," Kay acknowledged her, then turned to the firefighter. "And I'm telling you I'm going," she replied, her impatient glare drilling into the man's eyes. "She's exhausted, barely holding on, and about to let go. You need a shrink down there. Please."

"Nineteen," Kirsten counted, but this time, Kay didn't acknowledge.

Chief Hopper shook his head, then turned to look at the sheriff, who'd just arrived, as if to ask for his help.

"You heard her," the sheriff said. "Might be worth it to take her advice."

Hopper pressed his lips together for a split second before giving the order in his suit radio. "Bring the basket back."

"Twenty-two," Kirsten said, her voice trembling. "When are you coming?"

"Now, sweetie," Kay replied. "Before you can count to forty, I'll be there."

Kirsten whimpered, then, a moment later, as Elliot helped her climb into the basket, she counted, "Twenty-five."

The basket was solid, welded from thick metallic bars, but seemed dangerously frail. The firefighter next to her attached a belt with a safety cord to one of the edges, using a large carabiner, then wrapped it around her waist and tightened it with a firm tug.

"What's your name? I'm Kay," she asked, wondering if the man could see how scared she was. But the firefighter seemed barely twenty, and he didn't seem to care one bit about the basket dangling at the end of a steel cable and starting to descend.

"Mike," the man replied, smiling awkwardly. He wore a retainer, his teeth still a little crooked but white. "You should've stayed up there, ma'am," he added, still smiling. "Last thing we need in here is a civilian panicking."

"I promise I won't panic," she replied, wondering if she was going to be able to keep that promise. The movement of the basket unsettled her stomach. She fought the urge to heave, gripping the bar with her good hand until her knuckles hurt.

"Bend your knees a little and let yourself sway," said Mike. "It'll be better."

She nodded, thankful and embarrassed at the same time.

The basket descended a few more feet until it reached the cypress. She could see Kirsten's body in the strong lights coming from above. The second fire truck was positioned on the other side, its floodlights on, and that crew was preparing another basket.

"I'm here," Kay said, "see?" She wanted to wave her hand at the girl but didn't dare take her grip off the bar. Realizing the paralyzing effect her own fear had, even if she was securely attached to that basket with a safety strap, gave her a new level of understanding of the girl's ordeal.

"Don't let me fall," Kirsten cried, turning her head to look at her. She was lying flat, her arms wrapped around the branch and clutching it tightly. Her legs were wrapped around it too, closer to the trunk of the tree. Under her weight, the branch had started to give, no longer pointing up, but down.

She could slip at any moment.

Forgetting her own fear, she grabbed Mike's arm, drawing his attention, but he was already reporting his findings by radio.

Much to her surprise as well as Kirsten's, the basket started to ascend.

"Please don't leave me here," the girl cried. "You promised!"

"What the hell?" she asked Mike, still holding on to the stiff fabric of his turnout suit.

"We need to come from above," he clarified. "We're not going anywhere without her, don't worry," he replied, pulling himself free from her clutch and opening a large kit. He pulled a small battery-operated chainsaw and some straps, neatly packed and fitted with carabiners at one end and adjustable buckles at the other.

Kay turned her attention to Kirsten. "We're not leaving you, I swear," she said, doing her best to hide the panic she'd been feeling ever since she'd seen how frail that branch seemed, slowly bending under the girl's weight. The tree's roots were partly visible, snaking between rocks as they'd grown over the years in that unlikely place.

The basket had stopped climbing, now slowly shifting sideways until it was positioned above the cypress. Mike was kneeling on the floor, holding on to the chainsaw with one arm.

"What are you doing?" Kay asked, horrified. "You can't possibly think of cutting that tree with her on it. One mistake—"

"There's no other way," Mike replied. His voice was somber, sounding more mature, as if he'd suddenly aged a few years. "If you can, keep her calm while we remove some of the upper branches. It will ease the load on the root and allow the straps to reach her."

Her heart pounded and waves of nausea alternated with chills rushing up and down her spine as she watched Mike wrap a strap around a branch and secure it to the basket, then slide the small chainsaw between the side bars of the basket and start to cut.

The moment the chainsaw started to buzz, Kirsten screamed, and Mike had to stop.

"Kirsten," she said, keeping her voice steady, calming. "I need you to work with me on this. I need you to stay calm and—"

"*You* stay calm!" she lashed out, then started to sob. "I can't anymore... Please help me."

"We'll get you out of here, and then you and I will have one hell of a dinner," Kay offered. "Your favorite meal, as many fries as we can eat, and ice cream too." Her sobs had quieted a little, and Kay gestured at Mike to continue. "He's just cutting some branches, that's all. We can't reach you otherwise."

"Uh-huh," she whimpered. "I'm afraid," she added, barely audible over the sound of the chainsaw. When Mike finished sawing through the branch it fell against the strap, getting entangled in another one under it. Mike reached and grabbed it, then lifted it and threw it out of the way.

"I know you are, sweetie," Kay replied. "Soon this will all be over, just a bad memory. We'll call your parents—"

"No!" she shouted. "Promise me you won't."

"We won't," Kay said quickly. "If you don't want to, we won't. For now, let's plan that dinner, you and I. Are you hungry?"

She didn't reply. She just lay there, afraid to look up at Kay, afraid to make even the tiniest move. The sound of the chainsaw varied its pitch as branch after branch was removed. Kay listened intently for a while, hoping Kirsten would reply, but couldn't hear anything. Not a whimper, not a word.

"Talk to me, sweetie," Kay pleaded. "Tell me something, anything. You see, I'm a little afraid to be up here, you know."

The girl stayed silent, but Kay could see her tears streaming down her face, glimmering in the powerful lights. "Promise me you won't take me back home," she eventually said. "You don't know—"

"I promise," Kay rushed to answer, knowing she needed to keep Kirsten focused on positive thoughts, on her will to survive.

"We're ready," Mike announced. He pressed a button and spoke into his radio. "Lower it slowly, one inch at a time." The basket started to descend, incredibly slowly, touching some of the remaining branches on its way. Kirsten whimpered, each move threatening to throw her off balance.

Kay's heart thumped in her chest, her blood rushing through her veins in an almost panic-like state as she watched Mike roll out two straps and secure them to the basket. Then he threw both of them over Kirsten's body. After checking they were attached safely, he climbed over the basket's railing, hanging on to it with one hand, while reaching for the loose ends of the straps with the other.

"I'll run these under your body," he said, sliding his hand with the end of one strap between Kirsten's chest and the branch.

"No, no," she shouted, her voice filled with unspeakable fear. "You'll make me fall."

"I won't let you fall," Mike said, slowly pulling the end of the strap under her body.

"No, please," she whimpered. She was starting to move erratically, threatening to lose her balance.

A strong wind gust hit that moment, sending the basket slamming against the tree. Kirsten screamed.

Kay gasped, then quickly dropped to her knees in the basket. She removed the sling that immobilized her left arm and reached between the bars to Kirsten, grabbing her forearm with both her hands and squeezing tightly. "I won't let you fall either," she said. "You hear me? I won't let you fall."

Mike slid the second strap between her thighs and the branch, then pulled it tight until it was secure around her body. "We're good to go," Mike said into his radio. "Wait for my signal." Then he tugged at the straps again, checking to see if they were tight enough, and said, "You need to let go now, ma'am."

Kirsten held on to the branch just the same, petrified. "No, I can't... Please don't make me."

Another wind gust slammed the basket sideways into the wall, sending loose pebbles into the abyss below. Mike shot Kay a worried look, and she nodded.

"On three," she mouthed, still clutching Kirsten's arm tightly, ignoring the throbbing pain in her shoulder. "Kirsten, breathe with me," she asked. "Take a deep breath, and hold it in a little." She watched the girl's chest swell, and signaled Mike.

"Now," he spoke into his radio.

The basket started to lift, taking with it Kirsten's body, hanging like a ragdoll by the two straps wrapped snugly around her. She screamed and writhed, clasping desperately at Kay's arms as soon as she lost the grip on the cypress.

"You're okay," Kay said softly, even as she continued screaming. "I won't let you go. You're going to be okay."

By the time the basket touched down by the fire truck, Kirsten had fainted.

CHAPTER FIFTY-EIGHT
At the Bottom

Elliot's mouth was a little crooked, his swollen cheek detracting from its symmetry. He smiled, nevertheless, and hadn't stopped since they'd loaded Kirsten into an ambulance and the EMTs had said she was going to be okay. She was in shock, dehydrated, and exhausted, but her vitals were strong.

"We were lucky," Elliot said, patting Kay on her good shoulder for the fifth time.

They had descended into the ravine, where the entire team took photos, collected evidence, and helped Doc Whitmore load the remains in body bags or plastic cases. The ground was moist and smelled of coyote urine and feces, and of decomposing flesh. Kay looked up toward the edge of the ravine, feeling almost claustrophobic at the bottom of the pit; it had to be at least 100 feet to the surface. The grassy edge was barely visible against the night sky, an almost half moon pulling duty with them, shedding some light over the glade. About a dozen LED projectors flooded the morbid scene with bright light.

"You know what else you were?" she asked, but Elliot waited, still smiling. "Diligent. Thorough, prepared, determined. You didn't give up, went against a direct order from the sheriff, and that makes you an awesome cop, Elliot. You didn't give up on this one girl, out of the thousands that disappear every year. That makes you amazing."

He shifted his weight from one foot to the other, clearly a little uncomfortable with her compliment. "And we were lucky," he insisted, still grinning. "We saved a life today." He rubbed his hands together, the chill of the night probably getting to him just as much as it got to her.

"We saved many," she whispered, giving the ghastly place another look. Where there used to be scattered bones on the ground, now crime scene markers littered the area, not enough of them available, some used multiple times with Post-it notes affixed on top and scribbled with Sharpies, going well into three hundred. Had no one murdered his daughter, Bill Caldwell could've carried on forever, killing runaways like Kirsten in the house no one ever visited. Girls like her just vanished, never to be seen or heard from again, too many of them having met their fate at the bottom of that ravine.

She walked over to Doc Whitmore, who was closing another case filled with bones.

"How are you holding up, Doc?"

He sighed, a cloud of mist forming around his face. The temperature had dropped below freezing. "At least eighteen bodies, not counting him," he gestured toward a black body bag laid on the ground by the wall of the ravine. "There might be more. There's no telling how far the coyotes and bobcats have scattered the bones throughout these woods. But I found eighteen skulls, all female, all teenagers. It will take me months to reconstruct and identify all these bodies."

He carried the case next to the wall, where the firefighters lowered the rescue basket and lifted body bags and cases from the abyss, before loading them into the medical examiner's van. Then he returned and set another plastic case on the ground, and started filling it with bones. "I think this is the last one," he said, carefully placing tags with numbers that matched the crime scene marker associated with the respective bone. Doc Whitmore was nothing if not thorough, considering the scene had been completely compromised by wildlife scavengers.

Several of the deputies had gathered around the sheriff, trotting in place, their job done, most likely eager to go home. It was as good a time as any. She counted silently, making sure no one was missing. The entire team was there, including the receptionist, who'd been asked to assist with marking and tagging.

She approached the sheriff and said, "Sheriff, may I ask, have you received a letter informing you that one of your employees is an abusive man who is beating his girlfriend routinely?"

He seemed confused for a brief moment, then a hint of recognition glimmered in his eyes. He threw his team a stern look, then replied, "No, I have not."

"But I have," Elliot announced, pulling a folded piece of paper from his pocket. "Imagine my surprise, when I don't even have a girlfriend," he said, immediately blushing. Few noticed in the fluorescent light coming from the numerous work projectors scattered at the bottom of the ravine, throwing shadows everywhere. "I found this in my office inbox."

"Interesting fact about that letter," Kay said, then turned quickly and picked up the UV flashlight from the doc's kit. "May I?" The doctor nodded, inviting her to proceed with a hand gesture. She turned it on and approached the group of deputies. "The letter was treated with a chemical that sticks to your skin and makes it light up under UV light."

She studied the group. Most of them had shoved their hands into their pockets, but that was understandable at below freezing temperatures. One deputy was trying to distance himself from the group, walking slowly toward the back of the ravine.

"Daugherty," Sheriff Logan called, "Get here. Let me see your hands."

The man froze in place, then turned and approached slowly. "I don't know anything about no letter," said Daugherty. "This is such bullshit." He kept his hands in his pockets still.

She knew him, and had thought differently about him; she'd been wrong. He'd bought her drinks that night at Hilltop, seemed to be a fun-loving guy. Bulky and sporting a Duck Dynasty beard, she'd rarely seen him without his sunglasses on. She'd never looked into his eyes.

Kay flipped on the flashlight, and pointed it at Elliot's hands. "My partner touched the letter, and he'll glow under this light for a few days, even if he washed his hands really hard." Elliot's fingers lit up, appearing almost white under the light.

"Show us your hands, Daugherty," the sheriff ordered. He complied, muttering an oath and shooting her a venomous glance. His fingers lit up just like Elliot's had.

She looked at the sheriff and asked, "May I?" Logan nodded, his expression grim, disappointed.

"Deputy Daugherty, I'm placing you under arrest for the federal crime of mail theft, and obstruction of government administration. You have the right to remain silent. Anything you say can and will—"

"Oh, shut up with the rights already. You set me up!" he shouted, while Elliot cuffed him. Then the sheriff ordered him taken away. Two deputies escorted him up the rocky path out of the ravine.

"Now you two," Sheriff Logan called, looking at Kay and Elliot, "go home, get some rest."

"Yes, sir," she replied, suddenly aware of the throbbing pain in her shoulder and the tiredness in her bones. She turned to Elliot and said, "I need a drink. Badly."

"Absolutely, whatever the lady desires," he replied, the crooked smile touching his eyes. There was a heat in those eyes she was still afraid of.

She remembered how she'd wanted to kiss him in the Hilltop parking lot after she'd had a few drinks, and her smile withered. She wasn't going to follow in her father's footsteps, getting drunk, then flirty. Maybe a drink, under the circumstances, was a bad idea.

And there was also Jacob.

"You know what? I think I'll settle for tea instead, and take a raincheck on that drink." He frowned a little, not understanding her change of mind. "Take me to the hospital, please. I'll stay with Jacob tonight. They told me they're still keeping him sedated." She paused for a bit, holding back tears that threatened to break loose. She willed her voice to be strong, steady, but all she could do was whisper shakily. "They say he's stable now, but he's been in surgery for a long time and I…" Her words trailed off until she could force some air into her lungs. "I just want to be with him tonight."

"Sure thing," he replied, walking behind her as she approached the wall of the ravine. "Do you want to take the elevator up?" he quipped, pointing at the basket whirling as it lifted the last case of bones to the surface.

Being how tired she was, Kay considered it for a moment, but then laughed it away. "Can you imagine me dangling in the wind there again? No, thanks, I'll walk."

She started to climb the path to the surface, grunting at times, and leaning onto Elliot's arm whenever she needed.

"You know," he said with a hint of amusement in his voice and a sparkle in his eyes, "I should have this bruise looked at. I think there's a couch in that hospital with my name on it."

She turned to him briefly, a tiny smile fluttering on her lips. "I bet there is."

The path narrowed and she stopped, but he gestured gallantly with his hand. "After you, partner."

When she'd turned her back to him and knew he couldn't see her, she grinned widely. She liked the sound of that.

A LETTER FROM LESLIE

A big, heartfelt *thank you* for choosing to read *Beneath Blackwater River*. If you did enjoy it and want to keep up to date with all my latest releases, just sign up at the following link. Your email address will never be shared, and you can unsubscribe at any time.

www.bookouture.com/leslie-wolfe

When I write a new book, I think of you, the reader; what you'd like to read next, how you'd like to spend your leisure time, and what you most appreciate from the time spent in the company of the characters I create, vicariously experiencing the challenges I lay in front of them. That's why I'd love to hear from you! Did you enjoy *Beneath Blackwater River*? Would you like to see Detective Kay Sharp and her partner, Elliot Young, return in another story? Your feedback is incredibly valuable to me, and I appreciate hearing your thoughts. Please contact me directly through one of the channels listed below. Email works best: LW@WolfeNovels.com. I will never share your email with anyone, and I promise you'll receive an answer from me!

If you enjoyed my book and if it's not too much to ask, please take a moment and leave me a review, and maybe recommend *Beneath Blackwater River* to other readers. Reviews and personal recommendations help readers discover new titles or new authors for the first time; it makes a huge difference, and it means the world to me. Thank you for your support, and I hope to keep you entertained with my next story. See you soon!

Thank you,
Leslie

Connect with me!

LW@WolfeNovels.com
www.WolfeNovels.com
https://www.facebook.com/wolfenovels
Follow Leslie on Amazon: http://bit.ly/WolfeAuthor
Follow Leslie on BookBub: http://bit.ly/wolfebb
Visit Leslie's Amazon store: http://bit.ly/WolfeAll

Printed in Great Britain
by Amazon

19484109R00192